Racing The Dead

BOOK 3 OF THE SHADOW ARCANIST

by

Alexander Dawnrider

Dawnrider
—Press—

Racing the Dead
Copyright © 2025 by Alexander Dawnrider
Dawnrider Press
www.alexanderdawnrider.com

ISBN: 978-1737199977

Cover designed by MiblArt
Chapter header by Miss Vie Book Designs

First Edition: August 2025

For Kevin

Who expanded my fantasy experience with D&D

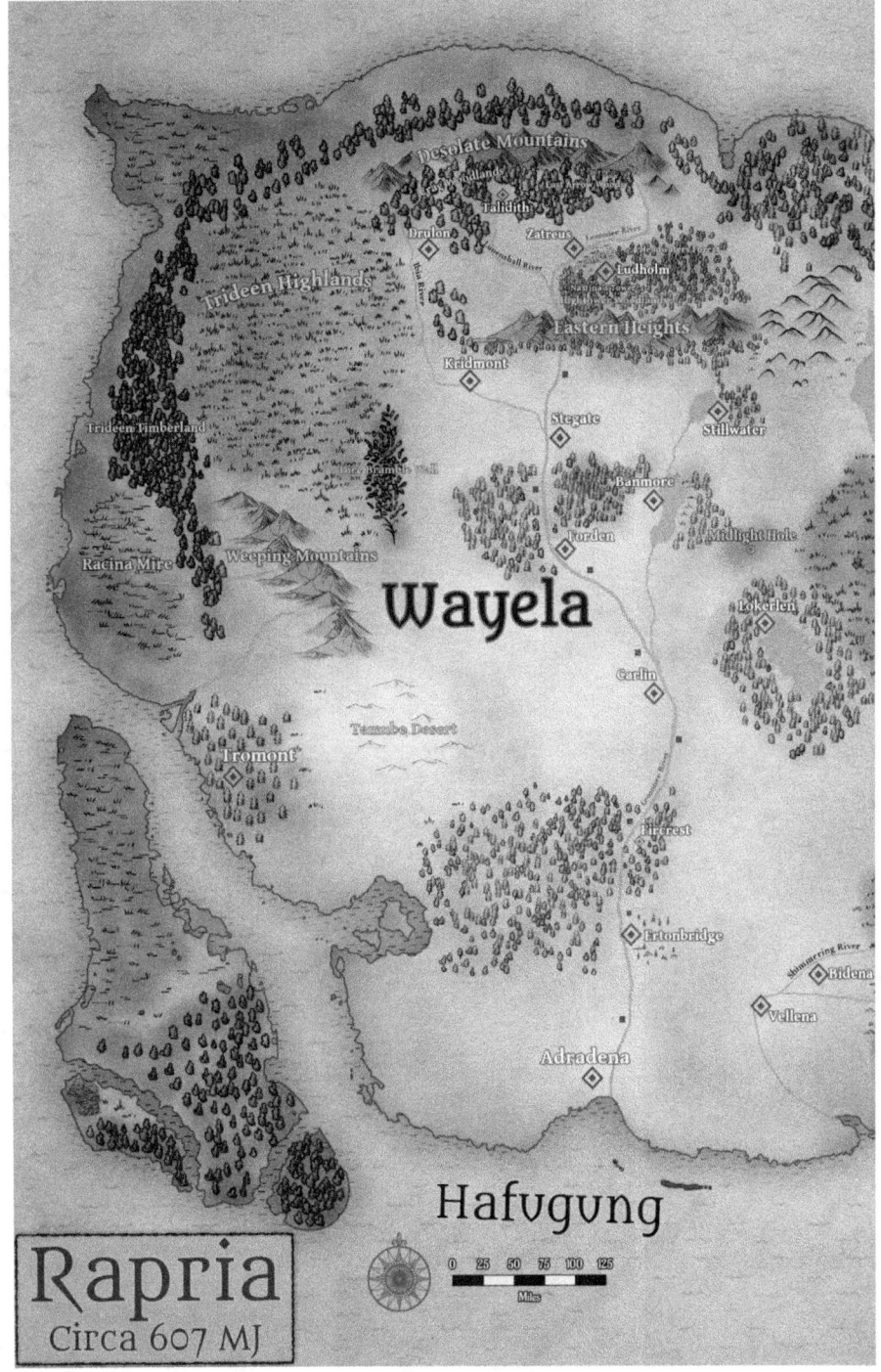

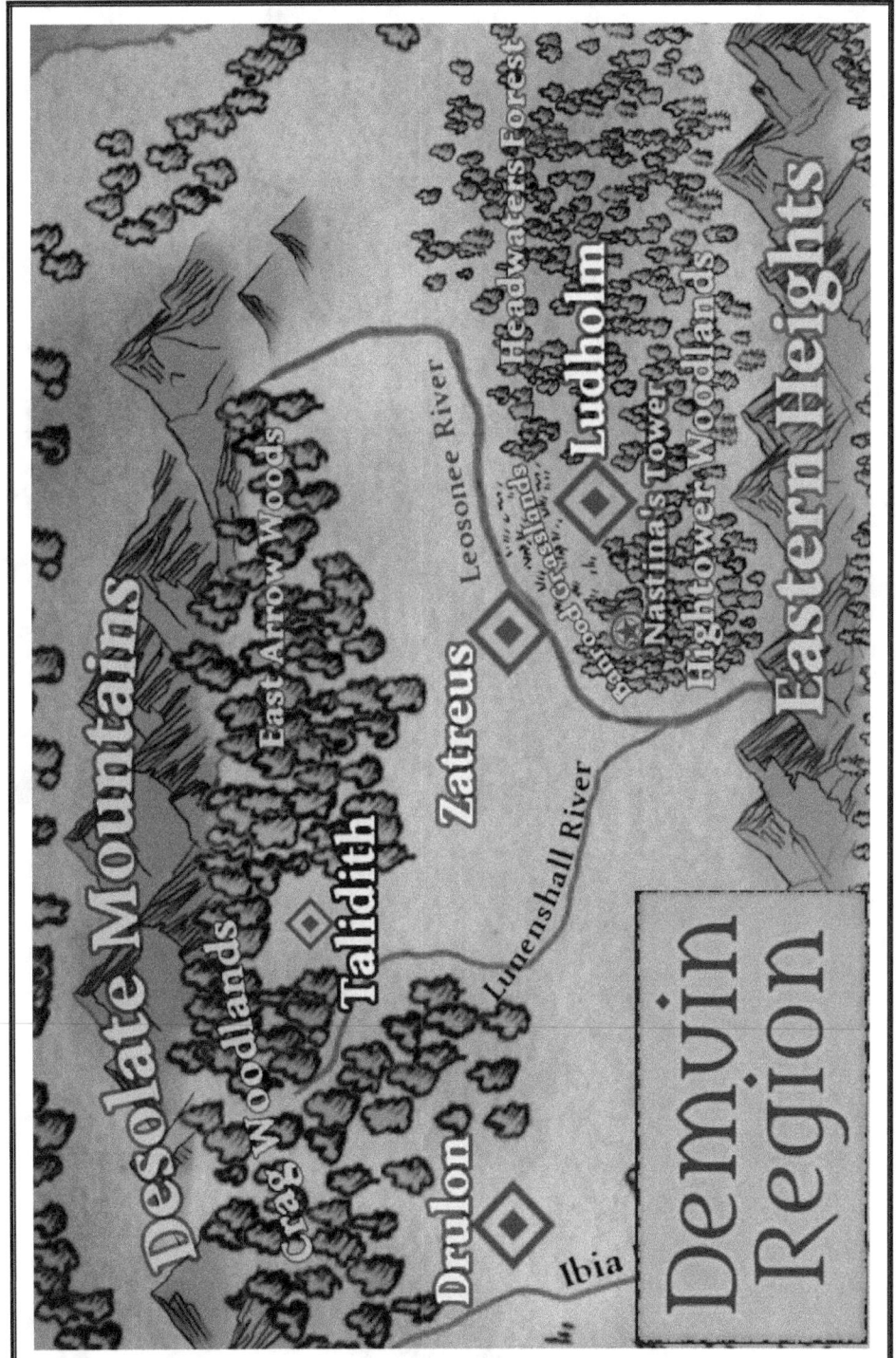

TABLE OF CONTENTS

Prologue
WOUNDED WATERS

"MAN IN THE water!"

The scream cracked through the roar of the river, but no one moved. The air stank of wet earth and desperation, clinging to clothes already soaked with spray. Every hand, every straining limb, fought to cage the raging waterway.

He was the fourth worker to lose their balance and vanish beneath the tumultuous current. The Leosonee River stretched across much of the Wayela continent, serving as a swift trade route for the many cities and towns along its length. At its mouth in Adradena, it emptied into the Hafugung ocean, allowing the passage of goods to the rest of the world.

Tonight, though, it raged, a wild beast in need of taming.

A dozen torches flickered high on stakes, their blue-white flames hissing against the night. The scent of burning pine and damp smoke cut through the din, adding to the midnight moonlight shimmering on the water. In their light, an egyzemor female caught sight of the struggling figure. She hurled herself into the current, massive limbs cleaving waves like oars, hand outstretched.

Her fingers scraped past his sleeve. He vanished again, battered downstream, another conscripted worker swallowed by the waterway's surges.

He shouldn't have been there. None of them should. Not the carpenters, stone movers, or dock workers. What they were attempting went against nature.

The northern port of Zatreus had become wealthy through its control of the river. The Leosonee flowed from the mountains, into the city's harbor, and down the continent.

But that dominance didn't go uncontested. Ludholm, its rival a mere twenty miles southeast, claimed they stole the port from them a thousand years before, and demanded it back.

In reply, a war broke out less than a year ago, with each kingdom sending an army to decide the issue on the battlefield.

"Help!" the man gurgled, spitting up water before being pulled under again. Too deep to touch bottom and too wide to reach shore, the river threatened to drown him, as if issuing a fatal warning to all attempting to restrain it.

A webbed hand grasped his wrist, however, and a fishtailed hafu hauled him from the depths. Native to the sea, these merpeople found their swimming skills critical tonight.

She dragged him ashore, her tail splitting into limbs like human legs long enough to keep him safe, before diving back into the waterway.

The war saw dishonorable tactics from both sides. Zatreus employed the bisegus, the world's changelings, using their morphing fabric for espionage. Ludholm, conversely, sent shapeshifters to infiltrate Zatreus's port with one aim: sabotage the Riverwall, the harbor's flood barrier for the Banrood Grasslands.

Ludholm succeeded. Bisegus intruders used Zatreus's own explosive *robantuz* to destroy the barricade. The breach diverted half the flow onto the plains. Nearly thirty boats, some still loaded, found barely enough water to float. Several moored vessels ended up nearly vertical, damaging both boats and docks.

Lord High Monarch Demzi Lightreaver, the city's leader, ordered a crew to block the river further upstream, allowing for the barricade to be rebuilt. However, even with dozens of humans, egyzemor, hafu, and the four-legged erdi'zal tackling the task, it seemed an impossible assignment.

After several unsuccessful attempts to build a structure in the waterway's rapids, they felled a tree from the local forest and hauled it to shore. Egyzemor and hafu worked together to position it, planning to secure it, and then add more lumber, forming a dam.

It failed to span the river, though, and calls for more trees went up. Hours of chopping lay ahead, meaning a long night for exhausted workers, with fires to ward off chill.

A trio of humans — two men and a woman — waded into the depths, dragging the end of a thick mooring rope to secure the first tree in place. They passed it off to one of the hulking, single-eyed egyzemors bracing it. A frantic toss sent it to the top, where another man scrambled to tie it in place.

A misstep on the treacherously slick bark, however, flung him hurtling over the heads of the others and into the turbulent river.

"Man in the water!"

Chapter One
THROUGH HOLLOW DEPTHS

DESPITE ZATREUS'S EFFORTS to block the river, water continued spilling into the Banrood Grasslands and kept rising. It pooled in crevices, swallowed stones, drowned animal and insect dens, with no sign of stopping. Whatever underground spring fed it didn't slow. Freed from the Riverwall's constraints, it reclaimed the ancient riverbed.

A heavy, damp earth scent rose from the churning water, carrying the chill of the mountains even this far south. The flood chased off most of the plains' life. Everything that could run, fly, or scurry had fled. The dominant group remaining was a horde of nearly a thousand soldiers, though they could no longer count as living. Barely a day ago, they had been two armies, representing the warring cities of Zatreus and Ludholm. For months, they'd maneuvered across the plain, locked in a standoff, each waiting for the right moment to strike.

Olagkoa changed that.

Accidentally freed from its underground prison by the people of Talidith, the creature now moved about Wayela unchecked. Bonded with the fisherman Aedan to access arcana — the world's source of magic — its powers had grown.

The immense mass of mottled grayish-blue flesh loomed over fifteen feet tall — more than double the size it had been when first discovered. Thick tentacles covered most of it, save for a flat protrusion atop its form. A sickly, cloying odor, like rotting meat left in the sun, emanated from its bulk, thickening the night air. Despite a lack of visible eyes or ears, it always seemed unerringly aware of its surroundings.

Part of that awareness stemmed from its telepathic abilities. More than once, it had probed minds and projected the likeness of a loved one — complete with voice and mannerisms. In an attack, it could flood enemies with sensations of fear or pain. If a foe managed to wound it, the creature would rapidly heal, even regenerating lost limbs, making victory short-lived.

With its connection through Aedan to arcana, its newest ability allowed it to reanimate and puppet the corpses it healed. So it set out to build an army, to take revenge on the world that had summoned and imprisoned it.

After invading Zatreus and raiding its cemetery, only to be driven out again, Olagkoa discovered a more convenient source of bodies. With its psychic powers, it forced the two armies into the battle they long prepared for — one that wiped out every soldier, messenger, and aid.

They were reborn, in a sense, to serve a new commander.

The fighters, now merely husks, devoid of emotion, thought, or speech, stood ankle-deep in water, awaiting orders. Olagkoa laid its tentacles on the final three corpses yet to rise. Its body fell unnaturally still, every ounce of will funneled into reanimating the last of its prize. After a full day of such work, its reserves were nearly spent, so each reanimation took longer.

But the army was almost complete. And once they moved, it could feed again.

Far above the creature, five figures watched from a narrow ridge of what once formed the shoreline of a vast lake.

Four rode horses. The fifth, an erdi'zal, crouched with feline patience beside them. They had kept vigil for hours, taking turns dozing in the chilled night air. The bitter scent of damp horsehair mingled with the earthy smell of the surrounding plains. Despite their thick cloaks, the cold seemed to seep into their bones, a constant reminder of the arduous task.

5

Two of them, Eris, a former Talidith soldier, and Tal, a tavern girl, had tracked Olagkoa from the city and tried to prevent the massacre. Neither side had listened, caught in the fever of war and the creature's mental pull. The pair had been forced to watch both sides slaughter each other, then witness their reawakening.

"It appears the thing is nearly done," Eris said, though the others hardly needed the reminder. None had looked away from the undead ranks.

"Buckets," Tal swore from her horse beside him. "I hoped they'd all be drowned."

Eris nodded. The hope had been shared, but they had both seen the creature swim with ease when it crossed the river. The dead were also unlikely to be overwhelmed by water when they no longer required breath. There was a chance the rising waters might sweep them away, but not at the current depth.

Holfast's front eyes locked on the lines of undead. The side-set pair twitched outward, scanning for movement. "They'll be attacking Zatreus next," Holfast said. "Or Ludholm."

"Hey!" Farla leaned forward in her saddle. "We don't know it'll attack, do we?" Her horse stood close to Ranin's, the two women finding quiet comfort in their proximity. Like Eris, both had served in Talidith's Sovereign Guard, though they'd hoped to leave that life behind when they came to Zatreus. The arrival of Olagkoa forced them out of retirement.

The man didn't answer right away. He stared at the thing below. "I can think of no other reason to raise an army," he replied. "Can you?"

"Then we warn whoever it targets. And if it moves beyond those kingdoms, we follow." They had discussed this earlier, agreeing to the task. If any wished to leave, now was their chance.

"The Shell Patrol it is," Tal declared, forcing a thread of cheer into her voice. She coined the name "shells" for the walking corpses days before, much to Eris's annoyance, but no one had suggested anything better, so it stuck. "We follow, try to limit the damage, and see who drops first."

"Let's hope it doesn't come to that," Eris said. "We've got two teams out there looking for a way to stop it, and we might figure something out ourselves."

"You still have me!" Ranin added brightly. "I've stopped it before. I can do it again." During her initial encounter with the creature, when many others died, she resisted its mental projection. That defiance had somehow given her the ability to occasionally disrupt its focus.

Farla's expression grew pained as she reached toward her friend. Though a year older and a few inches shorter, the pony-tailed woman often took on the role of protector to her companion. "Each time, you've collapsed, and I thought I lost you."

Ranin turned at the touch. "I'm getting stronger."

"So is that thing."

"Ranin, you are only to attempt to deter its mind as a last resort," Eris ordered them both. "Farla is right. It is dangerous."

"The creature is done!" The trio jolted at Tal's warning. Below, Olagkoa reared and pulled back its tentacles, the corpses jerking upright like puppets yanked by tangled strings. Water dripping from their weapons and uniforms, they shuffled to rejoin the ranks.

"Perhaps we could draw it away," Holfast suggested, raising a six-fingered hand to indicate the eastern end of the grasslands, far from both cities. "Make it pursue me to keep it from taking further action." Erdi'zal shared a human-like upper body, but their lower halves resembled a mix of feline and equine traits. Most were born and raised on the plains, so racing across this one, though flooded, was not a difficult task.

But Eris gestured his disagreement. "Absolutely not. I've tried that before, even attacked it directly. If it gave you any attention, it would strike you mentally. While you struggled, it would tear you apart or let its army do it. We *cannot* confront it head-on. It's far stronger than when you faced it in the Undercastle."

Holfast's lips thinned, clearly still yearning to act, but he nodded. Of them, Eris possessed the most experience with the creature — and the deepest regrets.

The five returned to silence, settling into their grim role as watchers. After a few minutes, however, the army stirred.

Eris's fingers clenched his reins so tightly his knuckles went white. The last of the corpses rose, dripping and swaying, and a weight settled on his chest. The war machine below was a product of his repeated failures.

Most of the undead were human, though some voladorms, egyzemors, and erdi'zal moved among them. As one, they turned southeast. Olagkoa stretched its tentacles in the same direction, then shoved off with its rear limbs, dragging its bloated bulk into motion. The dead followed in perfect unison.

"It's picked a destination," Holfast said.

"Ludholm," Eris confirmed grimly. "I suppose it decided not to test Zatreus's defenses again."

"Or maybe Ludholm's just closer, and it's lazy," Tal offered.

Farla glanced uneasily toward Ranin, then addressed Eris. "Do we move down into the water and follow, or ride ahead to warn the city?"

"I want you, Ranin, and Holfast to shadow them. With your eyes only! No heroics. Watch from up here. We need to know if it changes course. Tal and I will head to Ludholm and try to alert them. Though judging from how their army responded before, I'm not holding out much hope."

"You're not making me stay behind?" Tal asked. She had forced her way into his company back in Zatreus, refusing to leave even when he tried repeatedly to send her away. Eventually, he'd stopped fighting it, but still sought to keep her out of danger.

"You say that like you wouldn't chase me down if I did," he muttered. The scowl on his face didn't quite hide the warmth in his tone. "You seemed determined to follow me, so I might as well have you close so I can keep an eye on you." He tugged the reins of his horse, turning it toward the city. "Let's get going. We must give Ludholm as much of a warning as we can!"

WYNNA SCREAMED.

Her stomach lurched, her heart pounding as the cry escaped her throat. Blonde hair streaming behind her, she clung to the sides of the sled as it rocketed past stone walls on its downward path. In the fungi-lit gloom, what little she could see blurred by until she clamped her eyes shut.

She hadn't liked the look of the hollowed-out log or the smooth, rounded track in which it sat, but Shimi Zar and Malwin, the egyzemors who'd ridden it before, insisted it was safe. They needed a way to cross several mountains quickly, and this offered the fastest method.

It also terrified her.

Seated just ahead, Leda wasn't faring much better. She'd enjoyed the simulated weightlessness of being carried by the flying voladorms earlier and assumed the egyzemor contraption wouldn't faze her. But she had underestimated the steepness of the descent — and the speed. Now she added her own cries to Wynna's. Cutie, the tiny winged dia-mur, clung to her ear, hiding in the curtain of her thick hair.

Behind them, Erling, the six-limbed erdi'zal, rode in silence. Kneel-ing in the wooden craft, legs folded beneath him, he watched with fasci-nation, even as unease prickled under his skin. He'd spent his youth racing across the Trideen Highlands, his swift limbs carrying him through tall grasses with friends. He had ridden the *ladoskifa* more than once, so speed didn't frighten him. But in those cases, he'd re-tained some control, whether by muscle or by the skiff's sailwheel. This required simply getting in and hanging on.

The only ones clearly enjoying the plunge were the egyzemors and the cat. Graypaw sat between Erling and Wynna, head just clearing the log's edge, intently watching the stone blur past. Shimi Zar perched at the front while Malwin balanced the rear, both wearing gleeful expres-sions and letting out the occasional whoop as the group barreled through the darkness.

The *felgy* — rope-and-wood contraptions that helped them climb to their current elevation — let the mountain dwellers move swiftly be-tween levels of their dark homes. But the entire Eastern Heights range stretched over two hundred miles. Moving supplies through its twisting tunnels could take days or weeks. So, with help from the far more me-chanically minded voladorms above, the egyzemors devised a system of carved chutes and wooden cargo sleds to whisk goods through the rocky peaks in record time.

The good-natured giants quickly found their invention tremen-dously fun to ride.

Shimi Zar had given them a brief explanation while Malwin demon-strated with a quick wave of his hand, complete with whooshing sound effects. She called it a *kocus*, but Malwin grinned and offered the Way-lan translation, "slide." Erling agreed the second name felt more de-scriptive.

Eventually, the women and erdi'zal got over their initial fear and began to enjoy the ride as best they could. The descent lasted nearly half an hour, passing through an ever-changing underground land-scape. They raced through vast caverns with fifty-foot ceilings, and nar-row tunnels so tight the tallest among them needed to duck. Twice, they zipped through chambers bustling with egyzemors on the path below. Once, they passed a cavern similar to the one where Malwin fled earlier, complete with bats, a lake, and lounging bears. A family enjoying the quiet sanctuary gave them a cheer, but the sled sped on too quickly for a reply.

"End," Shimi Zar announced as the log leveled out onto a nearly flat path. It slowed only when a large skin, tethered by ropes, caught the front. A system of counterweights pulled at the rear, gradually reducing their speed until the sled rolled to a complete stop a dozen feet before a wall.

"Fun!" Malwin chortled, lifting himself out of the cramped compartment. He hefted Wynna and set her on the ground, while Shimi Zar did the same for Leda. Graypaw bounded out unassisted and promptly began licking his paws, as if they hadn't just spent thirty minutes hurtling through stone in a hollowed-out log.

"That was exhilarating!" Leda gushed, raking her fingers through wind-tossed hair, trying to calm her blown tresses and the shaken Cutie hiding inside. "Why didn't we use these when we first arrived?"

"No go up," Shimi Zar replied.

"I am guessing they wouldn't do well for going straight down, either," Erling groaned, shoving at the sides of the log but unable to lift his larger back end. "Assistance would be appreciated. I believe my limbs have entered hibernation."

Malwin grunted. He tried to slip his meaty hands between the erdi'zal and the wood, but Erling's body remained too snugly wedged. Shifting one hand to the front instead, he hesitated, casting his friend an awkward look.

"Oh, just do it," Erling huffed, instantly recognizing the cause of his reluctance. "This is already humiliating. But we shall not speak of it again!"

The giant agreed and, with a wince, gripped both ends and lifted. Despite the erdi'zal being nearly twice Wynna's mass, Malwin set him on the stone floor with almost the same ease. As soon as all four of Erling's limbs regained enough strength to bear his weight, he yanked his hands free and flushed a deep, mottled red.

Wynna laughed. "The ride in this thing was worth it just to see your face," she teased, ignoring the others' frowns. "But I am glad it is over. How far now?"

Shimi Zar shook her head. "Not. More up down," she told them, while Malwin pulled their packs from the log. She had left her torch behind before boarding the kocus, but didn't bother to reach for another. The companions had adapted well enough to the dimness, and the glowing fungi, abundant through most of their journey, coated the walls here, too.

"That is unsurprising," Erling remarked. "We are in the easternmost mountain and fortunate to have found access to both the heights above and Grazzlunn in the depths. It would strain credulity, and luck, if the artifact were also located here."

"So, how many mountains do we need to go through?" Leda asked.

Shimi Zar's single brow furrowed as she considered. "Muwsarheg. Arfumaheg. Two. In Crokrusheg."

Wynna's eyes widened at the unfamiliar names. "I am glad I do not speak your language. My tongue would be exhausted!"

With their packs slung back over their shoulders and Erling's legs recovered adequately for him to walk without fear of tripping, the group followed a broad passageway into the next mountain.

There, they used a felgy to begin their ascent to the upper levels. The kocus relied on gravity to move its cargo, requiring each launch point to be at a high enough elevation to carry it the needed distance. Erling again attempted to explain the physics of angles and acceleration, but the others merely nodded and tuned him out. As with the lifts, they didn't much care how it worked, only that it did.

The second trip down the chute proved far less stressful once the initial shock wore off. This time, Erling wedged his pack partly beneath him to ease his exit at the bottom.

It carried them only halfway through the peak, requiring another ride on the felgy. The erdi'zal explained the slope's angle would be too shallow to maintain speed the entire way, launching into a concise lecture on inclines, momentum, and friction, which the others ignored.

The third trip down started the women yelling again, but now in enjoyment. Cutie relaxed, filling Leda's ears with excited chittering. She grinned, her earlier fear replaced by a thrill she hadn't expected. Perhaps she was starting to enjoy this. Even Erling gave up analyzing the experience and simply had fun. Graypaw, already bored with the process, slept curled up near Wynna the entire time.

After three more descents, Shimi Zar announced the remainder of the journey would need to be completed on foot. At Erling's suggestion, they paused to rest and eat. Though only a short while had passed since their last meal, he reminded them that they couldn't predict when it might next be safe to stop.

They had managed a few hours of sleep after their tense meeting with the egyzemor scholar Grazzlunn Khar and their harrowing escape from the Shells. But the revelations the old sage shared about Olagkoa's origins and the mystery surrounding Leda's kind had made for an uneasy rest.

Only a few hours earlier, a half-dozen humans ambushed them. They fled, but when their attackers caught up to them, they had been forced to fight. Only then did they discover the grisly truth.

They remained alert for signs of pursuit. Throughout their travel via chutes and lifts, they'd watched for their undead hunters, and while it seemed they had pulled ahead, there was no guarantee others weren't lurking deeper within the peaks.

As they found a spot, Leda pulled out a selection of her supplies. Cutie crawled down from her shoulder, watching with interest. In her tearful farewell with her parents, she'd forgotten to ask even the basics about caring for a diamur. Hoping he could handle their food, she held each item out in turn, letting him decide.

He turned up his nose at the hardtack, then sniffed the nuts before giving one a cautious lick and grimacing. The jerky appeared more tasty, and he took a few nibbles without protest. But the small assortment of fruit truly lit up his face. Eyes brightening, he eagerly devoured several pieces, each almost half the size of his head.

Wynna watched with a faint frown as she broke off bits of dried meat and fed them to Graypaw. Though the winged figure perched near Leda resembled a tiny, naked man with wings, she doubted its intelligence or worth.

The traffic thickened, with nearly twice as many of the giant, one-eyed egyzemors moving through the broader passageways. "Is it just me, or is this part of the range more populated than where we came in?" Leda asked as they packed away food and waterskins. "I figured *that* was the capital because the *Mocros Venk* was there."

"Is," Malwin grunted.

"And is," Shimi Zar added.

"Well, that's clear," Wynna muttered, though her tone lacked anger. Since deciding to stay with the group, her mood lifted. She still didn't like wandering through the dark with no idea what they might stumble across next, but at least she had a purpose now. And while she would never admit it aloud, she enjoyed the kocus ride.

"The mountain we arrived at, Rafnirheg, is technically the capital of the Eastern Heights, if you can call it that," Erling said, rubbing a bruise his extra padding hadn't saved him from. "My understanding, however, is that word does not have the same connotations as your human cities. For our friends, it is the starting point, but not necessarily the most important point. I believe the reasoning is because in the legend of the Eight Siblings, Rafnirheg, who the peak is named for, was the first child Szemist created, the eldest. Or it may be simply because it is the furthest east. My knowledge doesn't fully extend to their political history."

"That's a lot more than I knew," Leda told him.

"How do you know the artifact is here?" Wynna asked. "I imagine someone would have stumbled upon it by now."

Shimi Zar smirked, an uncommon expression on an egyzemor. "You see." With that mysterious response, she guided them down a dozen more levels with the lifts to a sparsely traveled section. There, she snatched a burning torch off the wall and told them to stay close.

The artifact they sought, according to the elderly Grazzlunn Khar, belonged to a set of six objects infused by arcana. They had been dispatched to different parts of the continent, but their guide, Shimi Zar, claimed to know the location of one. They had traveled for the past few hours through the inside of the mountains toward the destination.

Like before, when she took them to Grazzlunn, the companions felt the weight of the mountain pressing heavily on their minds. The passages she led them through sloped considerably, but didn't narrow. It wasn't the air, though it had grown stale and cooler. Something else pricked at their nerves.

Wynna hugged her chest to fend off the cold and dread. "What is this place? You have another old person living down here?"

"I doubt anyone lives down here," Erling said. "Notice the markings along these walls? They're sharper and deeper than the usual cuts made during excavation. And see how the torchlight bounces off those

13

shiny points? This was an ore mine. Abandoned now, I'm guessing, and for quite some time."

"No." Shimi Zar raised a hand to stop them. She lowered the torch and cocked her head. After a tense pause, she shrugged and resumed walking. "Orifereg."

The word meant nothing to the women, but Erling frowned. "There's one of those ahead?"

"One of *what*?" Wynna asked, hugging herself tighter.

"Worms," Malwin rumbled. "Big."

"And our guide is apparently leading us toward one." Erling jogged forward to catch the female egyzemor's attention. "Why is the artifact down here among these creatures?"

"Guards." Shimi Zar flashed him a smile.

"Are you implying someone put the item down here deliberately, using the worms as a defense against possible thieves?"

"Yes. Me."

"What?"

"Hold on!" Frustrated with another surprise popping up, Wynna stepped forward between the pair. "What are you two talking about?"

Erling stared hard at their guide. "The artifact isn't simply waiting for us to collect it. Our friend here has hidden it among the giant worms down here."

Shimi Zar nodded. "Keep safe."

"When you say 'giant', what exactly do you mean?" Leda asked, staring into the darkness ahead. "The size of a cat or the size of a horse?"

Wynna spun to face her. "You want worms the size of horses?" she demanded.

"Not horses," Malwin assured them both. "Houses."

Both women gasped. "If what I have heard is true," Erling told them, "the orifereg live in the depths of mountains, tunneling through stone and eating anything they encounter." He raised his eyes to the ceiling, which he could just make out in the torchlight. "They are about the same height as this tunnel, and longer than five adult erdi'zal in a line. Is that right?" He directed the last question toward the egyzemors.

Malwin shrugged. "Or bigger."

"Good guards," Shimi Zar added.

"Then why don't you get this thing yourself?" Wynna demanded, fear giving way to anger. She hadn't come on this mission to fight giant *anythings*. That was someone else's job. "You put it there, you retrieve it."

The smile fell from their guide's face. "Long ago," she explained, nodding toward the gloom ahead. "Unknown there."

"But you think we can handle whatever is there and find the artifact?" Leda asked.

Shimi Zar just shrugged.

"Oh, wonderful!" Wynna threw up her hands. "Send in the party of idiots and see if they survive the giant, people-eating monsters in the dark. And if they survive, they get an old relic which is useless without the other five!"

"You have summed up our situation concisely," Erling noted wryly, "If a tad pessimistically."

"There has to be another way to get the artifact without fighting these creatures." Leda turned to Malwin. "Can we maybe lure them out and sneak past them?"

"Lure them where?" Erling prompted. "We don't know the terrain ahead."

"But there have to be multiple tunnels. You said it was a mine."

"A mine we don't have a map to."

"I do." Shimi Zar pointed a thick finger at her head. "In here. Know where."

"That's good, but..."

"Sneak," Malwin encouraged. He then drew the oversized blade from his pack and held it high. "Or stab."

Wynna crossed her arms. "Then you and she can go. We will wait here for you."

Leda frowned at her. "You said you wanted to help Aedan."

"I did. And getting eaten will prevent us from doing that."

"Well, I'm going." She walked to Malwin's bundle and drew her own, much smaller blade, from its loop. "How about it, Erling? Don't you want to see one of these worms for yourself?"

"I am sure they would be a magnificent sight," the erdi'zal said. "And best enjoyed from a distance."

Leda huffed, then turned and crouched in front of Graypaw. "You'll come with us, right?"

15

The black and white feline sat stony-faced, staring at her. It marked one of the rare times he wasn't grooming himself or exploring. He hadn't forgiven her for her earlier accusations.

"Look, I was wrong before. I should have known you wouldn't hurt Cutie. You're not a ... you're not that kind of cat. I was just worried about him. Can you forgive me?"

Graypaw kept his gaze fixed on her for a few moments in silence. Finally, he raised a paw and began licking it, turning away from the woman. Leda sighed, not knowing what that meant, but hoped it signaled a start. "Then you three stay here," she said as she stood up. "But keep an eye out for those dead things. We might have lost them for a while, but I'm betting they know how to find us." When Wynna and Erling grimaced, she added, "Just give us a warning before they overpower you so we can escape."

The two exchanged uncomfortable glances. That particular threat had slipped their memory. "Perhaps you are right," Erling finally told them. "I shouldn't waste this chance to see an orifereg for myself. And you may need my expertise in recovering the artifact."

Wynna nodded. "And I will come too. For Aedan."

Graypaw offered only a single 'meow' as an excuse for his change of mind, and padded toward the front of the group, scanning the darkness for any sign of the threat ahead.

Had he looked back, he would've caught the slight smile on Leda's face as Malwin patted her shoulder with a soft chuckle.

SAVANAH LAY IN her bedroll, utterly miserable.

Her best friend Camille had fled into the night hours ago, and she didn't know if she'd ever see her again.

It started as a simple exercise. Savanah struggled with her feelings for Vyncent Warne, one of the men they traveled with, and his father, Rhashar. Camille, a bisegus with the ability to shapeshift, proposed she take the form of each man so her companion could express her emotions without shame or rejection.

The first part had been easy. Savanah admitted she only viewed Vyncent as a friend and ally, but nothing romantic. It made clear she should quash all the amorous overtones he might pursue for the rest of their journey.

When it came to his father, however, Savanah found herself unable to hold back. She confessed to Camille wearing the form of the man she had affection for, born of years at his side, seeing the commander at his best and worst. It became an impossible love, though, as he perished the year before by the monster their mission sought to stop.

That's when everything fell apart.

She wiped her face, the skin still cool from her shed tears. *How could I have not seen it? She told me why she moved to Talidith. She explained why she copied my appearance. It was always there.*

In their mock confessional, her words had been too much for the bisegus, and they kissed. In Savanah's mind, it had been an impossible moment with her dead beloved, one never experienced while he lived. For Camille, it had been a chance to express her true feelings for her friend.

The action shook both women. Before Savanah fully understood the importance, her friend transformed herself into an owl and took to the night sky.

The men had come running up the tower steps at her cries. Unable to reveal Camille's true nature, Savanah lied, claiming their companion ran off in anger, that her shouts were an attempt to find her.

Vyncent, in his usual dismissive tone, insisted Camille must have been overreacting to an earlier argument. But now Savanah saw it clearly — the tension between the two women had grown because of her. Vyncent's romantic attention pushed Camille into a silent, invisible conflict.

I should have seen it!

Savanah wanted to search for her, to find her and bring her back to their group. Mikel said no, that it was too late in the night, and Camille would return on her own. The tower stood visible from miles around, so she wouldn't lose her way, and they planned to keep the fire going as an extra beacon.

However, the flames had turned to embers, mirroring Savanah's fading hope. The woman hadn't returned, and she wasn't sure she ever would.

And if she did? What would either of them possibly say to ease the pain? Savanah did love Camille, but she viewed her like everyone else saw them, as sisters. But she thought of Vyncent as a brother, too, and that hadn't stopped a kiss. *From now on, I'm keeping my lips to myself!*

Could she love Camille in that way? She didn't know. She loved her mind and her spirit, but save for the red hair, the bisegus's body mirrored her own by choice. Savanah had no idea what her true form looked like. No one understood how the shapeshifters appeared when they weren't mimicking someone. She accepted that truth in friendship, but would that be enough for something more?

Savanah stared across the remains of the fire to where the men lay asleep. They slept while her world unraveled. She hated them for it — and envied them too.

They were still hundreds of miles from Adradena and five artifacts short of what they needed to defeat Olagkoa. If Camille didn't return by the morning, would they be forced to go on without her? Was their mission more important than their relationship, whatever form it might eventually take?

But she knew that answer. Camille might vanish into anyone or anything. If she didn't want to be found, she wouldn't be. Blending in with the other races ensured her kind's survival over the millennia. *She trusted me with her secret, and now I may never see her again!*

A fresh wave of sorrow washed over her, bringing tears to her eyes. Her bedroll protected her against the chilled air, but nothing could ease the icy despair in her heart. Lost in confusion and sorrow, the archer wept softly in the darkness.

Consumed by grief, she remained oblivious to the faint sounds of sniffles and the rustling of dirt emanating from beyond the confines of the small clearing.

Chapter Two
DIRE WARNING

"WHAT NEWS OF the river?"

Demzi Lightreaver, High Monarch of Zatreus, leaned on one elbow, her posture less regal than surrendered. The deep blue of her robe lay rumpled and spotted where her restless fingers picked at the fabric. Somewhere in the night, she'd lost the clasp for her hair. It now fell in a wild, blood-red curtain down her back. The akkum she'd sipped the evening before had long worn off, replaced by exhaustion that pressed heavier than drink ever could. Only the lavish cushions of her silver throne kept her upright, lending her the dignity expected of a ruler.

"Our people have slowed it, but stopping it completely may be impossible." Jarontaldor Berkenshire, her chief advisor, looked worse. His soaked, blue-and-gray military uniform clung to his frame, and his black boots were caked with river mud. Orange streaks brightened the wiry beard at his chin, but the man behind it blinked too often, his verdant eyes dry with sleeplessness.

The pair faced each other in the throne room of the castle, Wolfsight. They could have met in smaller quarters, but after the chaos of the past few days, both agreed their presence belonged somewhere visible. To be present. To be seen *acting*.

Built to flaunt Zatreus's wealth, the chamber stretched grand and cavernous, with high windows on the rear wall and stone arches bracing the balconies flanking each side. A guard stood within each lower arch, part protector, part witness to any discussion between the throne and its petitioners.

Neither sergeant nor monarch had slept since the Riverwall's destruction the previous evening, which explained why they were in the great hall just a few hours past midnight. Both remained busy with the fallout, and this provided their first opportunity to discuss the results of their efforts. Lightreaver's voice tightened. "What about the harbor?"

"Not good," Jarontaldor said. "Most of the boats were hauled ashore, cargo cleared. But all the big ones took damage when the water dropped. Two are gone. The *hovhiza* we kept to pull the *rwizichi* managed to avoid being drawn into the flood, and their hafu trainers moved them further down the river, beyond the breach. No casualties have been reported."

The monarch rested her chin on her hand, her eyes half-lidded. "Let us hope that remains the case. Any sign of the saboteurs?"

"No. We believe they were bisegus, making them impossible to track. They vanished in the chaos. Wolfsight is in an uproar. Steelfang deployed the soldiers we can spare to quiet the streets, but word is spreading of what happened. The common folks may not riot, but the merchants will rage once they understand what this means for trade."

"If any of those quill-pushers from the Council protest, send them to help block the river." Lightreaver raised her head, eyes narrowing as she took in his state. "You look as though you've done it yourself."

"I have," he said simply. "While you were securing the castle, I lent a hand. A man fell in —a couple, truth be told — and I was among those who pulled him out."

She rose swiftly from her throne, concern replacing fatigue. "Why haven't you changed out of those wet clothes? You must not put yourself at risk."

"Of catching a cold?"

She touched a fingertip to his mustache, brushing away a lingering drop. "You're my advisor. I can't have you dying on me. At least not until your duty is done."

He smiled. "I would not dare. I doubt there's a further threat of an assassin striking, though. With the Riverwall destroyed, Daymon has what he wanted."

"Indeed." Remembering they weren't alone, she stepped back. "And an assassin had ample chances to kill me amid the chaos. I'd almost forgotten it myself. But my concern was more personal. You're the only one I can trust."

Jaron nodded, recognizing the reason for her putting distance between them. They were old friends, with him serving her father as a younger man. His death compelled them both to mature far too quickly, forcing a formal barrier between them they must not cross, especially in front of witnesses. The guards in the alcoves might be silent, but they still saw and heard everything the pair said. "I will remain at your side, henceforth."

The High Monarch sank back into her throne. "We have more matters to discuss. Holfast confirmed what that young lad recounted about both armies being destroyed by the creature. Once we have secured the river and harbor again, I intend to bring the fight to Ludholm's walls. We need a new force for that. How long do you think it will take to raise one?"

Jaron's expression darkened. "While I agree with the sentiment, I am not sure re-engaging in warfare is the proper course of action at this time."

"We'll not let that craven cur win! He must be punished for his crimes against Zatreus."

"And he will be, I promise you that. As to the rest" — he hesitated, tugging at his ear — "well, I'm no expert on matters of morale, but our people have been through a lot. First the creature's invasion, then the death of the army — which the soldiers' families will learn about before long — and now the destruction of our harbor. I just think announcing another offensive might not be the best for their spirits."

"My responsibility is to Zatreus, not to each individual's feelings." Irritation crept into the ruler's voice. "We need a new army, regardless. At present, we're nearly defenseless. Considering Steelfang's poor results dealing with monsters and saboteurs, I wouldn't trust him to hold the city if a single vornuk came knocking."

Her assessment of Zatreus's guard commander wasn't entirely fair. No one could've known how to handle the young fisherman, his townfolk followers, or the tentacled monstrosity that appeared at the gates demanding entry. The latter forced its way inside, displaying powers beyond anything the city experienced.

Having encountered Olagkoa before, when coming to the aid of Talidith's people, Jaron knew it was unique, but he didn't argue. "We can handle the task. But recruitment and training aren't our only issues. Our weapons and uniforms supply is already strained by the war. Replacing them will require time, and with trade significantly reduced..."

"Just get it done. We'll collect compensation from Daymon's hide when we seize Ludholm."

The burly man's eyebrows shot up. "You mean to *capture* the city?"

She shrugged. "It might be the only way to stop this from happening again. I want to see that man rotting in our dungeon by summer's end."

Jaron dipped his head. "Speaking of Ludholm... there's more bad news."

She slumped back into the throne, weariness dragging at her spine. "Tell me."

"Last night, you instructed me to locate the prisoners which the Matron had arrested. I have had our cells searched. They are empty, all of them."

Her expression darkened. "They escaped? Are our defenses so weak that criminals can just walk free?"

"Not without help. I reckon that is the case here."

"So someone within the castle, perhaps among our soldiers, is now aiding traitors? I find that idea even more unsettling than the thought of an assassin in our midst."

"Do you want Steelfang to question the ranks?"

The High Monarch shook her head, sending her tresses tumbling over her robe's tall collar. "I am sure they will all declare loyalty. There is no point in disrupting our defenses further. We can find the answer much easier through the source. Find the Matron and bring her here. She danced around the subject before, but I am no longer in an accommodating mood. Go yourself, in case some of our guards have changed their allegiance."

"As you wish, High Monarch." Jaron turned and marched from the chamber, muddy boots leaving a trail behind him.

Although Joice Nilado's office lay only one floor above the throne room, Jaron took nearly half an hour to return. When he did, frustration etched his face, and the short, round woman at his side looked every bit the reluctant prisoner. Her forest green robe hung askew, as if thrown on while still partially asleep, and her silver pendant swung wildly against her chest with each stubborn shuffle of her slippers.

He released her a dozen feet from the throne with a grunt. She hissed, but as she turned to face the High Monarch, her scowl melted into a saccharine smile. Dimples bloomed on her cheeks, but her steel-gray eyes remained cold.

"My dear Lightreaver," she purred, "what a delight to be summoned at such an hour. I would have preferred the comfort of my council chamber — and perhaps a civilized glass of *Raudona* — but I applaud your choice to surround yourself with guards. With an assassin still at large, one can't be too careful."

The woman on the throne straightened, surprised by Nilado's calmness. "What matter do you *think* I've brought you here to discuss?"

"Why, the damage to the Riverwall, of course, and the ruinous effect it has on trade." The Matron twirled her pendant lazily, the aquamarine stones catching the torchlight. "I have met with the Council, and we are moving all current activities to our caravans. Slower, yes, and some goods might spoil, but I believe we can convince our partners to accept more durable alternatives. I've already sent instructions to Ven —"

"I did not summon you to discuss trade. Shifting commodities to the land routes is obvious, and I made that realization hours ago."

Nilado's expression froze for a heartbeat, then morphed into something sterner, almost motherly. "So... you've decided to involve yourself in Zatreus's commerce directly. You really should have consulted me first, so the Council members could be informed that they now answer to you."

"They have *always* answered to me," she replied through clenched teeth. "As do you. I have had Jaron fetch you here so that you have a chance to answer to me fully."

"Of course," Nilado murmured, smoothing her robe with a small smile. "Though you might consider a gentler term than *fetch*. A knock on my door, a whispered word, and I would have presented myself expeditiously."

Jaron opened his mouth to object, but Lightreaver motioned for him to remain quiet. She recognized Nilado's attempts to divert their attention from the real issue, and wouldn't let that happen this time.

23

"Then you will not hesitate to explain what has happened to the individuals you had arrested. The merchant, Sarvendor, and your Council member, Linda."

A practiced smile curled the Matron's lips, but it didn't reach her eyes, which gleamed with a calculated sharpness. "I would not hesitate, indeed, if I had any notion as to their current condition. Are they not currently languishing in your dungeon?"

"They are not. Someone released them, though I gave no such order. Since you orchestrated their arrests without my knowledge, I assume you have similarly arranged their release."

"Not I. You have made it crystal clear on more than one occasion that the city's defenses fall under your jurisdiction." Nilado folded her arms firmly across her chest, shifting her weight to project an air of seriousness. "But since you've chosen to handle trade decisions, perhaps you wish me to assume a more commanding hand in our penal system."

Again, Lightreaver mentally dodged the change of topic, leaning slightly forward herself. "So you claim you had nothing to do with their release?"

"I swear by the ancient pacts of commerce, I released no one from your custody, nor instructed anyone else to do so." She gestured toward the alcoves, steering the conversation away. "This should be taken up with your guards. Considering how they let that creature in, I am puzzled by your lack of discipline in the matter. You really should have reprimanded the entire city militia, as I suggested, not merely that fool Steelfang."

The High Monarch smiled inwardly. Every evasive turn confirmed that Matron had something to hide. "Your suggestions are noted, but I still make the decisions. You claimed those prisoners were spies, but you have never explained precisely how you came to that conclusion. What proof do you have that they worked for Ludholm, or that they intended harm upon our city?"

Nilado shook her head with a disapproving 'tut-tut', as if scolding a child. "My dear, we have already been over this. The voladorm merchant opened the eastern gate to release the creature when your soldiers tried to stop it. He is the leader of a cult who wishes to see the downfall of all those in power. Linda was among his followers and sought to aid the beast on two occasions, claiming to be acting on your authority."

24

"Spies," Lightreaver pressed. "You said they were spies. What you described is a pair of fanatics, not traitors. So I will ask you again, why do you say they are agents of Daymon?"

"I offer my deepest apologies for refuting your words, but you are mistaken. I have never made such a claim."

"Do not try my patience." Lightreaver leaned forward, knuckles whitening against the throne's arm. "Less than a day ago, you stood in this spot and told me the pair were spies for Ludholm."

"Spies, yes. But I never said anything about Ludholm, nor did I intend to imply it. If you drew that inference from my words, then it is incorrect."

"Who else would be spying on us?" Jaron snapped. The High Monarch held her irritation in check, but her sergeant made no such effort.

Nilado met his glare with feigned innocence, her eyes gleaming with calculation. "I thought that would be obvious to a military man. Who brought the creature to our gates? Who moved nearly three hundred strangers into our city during a time of war? Who refused to turn over their weapons, despite our hospitality, and pushed to join our defensive ranks?"

"The trio from Talidith? You're yanking my beard. Those are good folks, and they were in need."

"Were they? From your report, they had shelter in their underground fortress, along with enough food to last months. *Until* they convinced *you* to destroy it."

Jaron's fists curled, his jaw clenched. He remembered the desperation, the bitter cold, the looming disaster when they arrived with wagons just before winter. The woman before him, however, was twisting those events into something more sinister. "That was to trap the creature! We had no choice."

"Yet the creature and Talidith's population came here, once you showed them the power of robantuz." Nilado gestured broadly to the chamber. "A thriving city for them to take over. Settlement with armed soldiers inside and a destructive monstrosity on the outside. Was it not one of their own who demanded entry for it?"

"Their kingdom lay in ruin," Jaron growled. "I saw the devastation of their castle myself."

"Did you? Or perhaps it was the beast making you *see* what *they* wanted you to." She lowered her arms and leaned in, her voice a silken whisper. "That is one of its powers, is it not?"

25

"Enough," the High Monarch snapped, silencing the rising argument. Bickering wouldn't solve anything. "Your suggestion is utterly baseless and absurd on its very face. Talidith's people have done nothing but express gratitude and integrate themselves into our population. They were also instrumental in driving the creature from the city. That is certainly not the action of a group wishing to use it against us."

"Only when they realized our defenses were preparing to dispel it," Nilado countered. "They had Linda order Steelfang not to leave the western entrance, and when that failed, Sarvendor opened the other gate to save the beast."

Lightreaver didn't like how much sense the Matron's claims made. One of Talidith's men *had* followed the creature to the Banrood Plains, and now both armies were dead. If Finn's story held any truth, the thing had gained control over them, and they were likely on their way back to seize the city by force, perhaps with the trio she sent out leading the assault.

But she also knew Nilado's gift for words, able to spin up doubt to get herself out of a disagreement. "All of this is conjecture. You still have not told me how you learned your prisoners were spies. Or why you have not brought any of this information to me before, when it could have been acted upon?"

The Matron shrugged. "I only discovered it recently, myself. I responded as swiftly as I could to apprehend the infiltrators before they could do more damage. You appeared too busy with the threat on your life, saying you had neither the time nor the patience to listen to what I found."

Lightreaver remembered the conversation, and the topic of spies never arose. Instead, the woman before her proposed she go into hiding and let someone else assume the ruling position of Zatreus. Only temporarily, of course, but once removed from sight, it would only take a single act of betrayal to remove her permanently, as had happened to her father. "If you had stated outright you believed there was a plot to overthrow the city, I would have been more receptive."

"Perhaps. Perhaps." Nilado laced her fingers together. "And what course of action will you pursue regarding the Talidith refugees?"

"Nothing, yet. With the alleged spies gone, there is no way to ascertain the truth of what you claim. Since you have not yet provided me with any proof, I have no choice but to investigate the matter myself, starting with the guards who tend the dungeon." She leaned back on her throne, weariness creeping over her once more. "I am sure they can shed some light on the mysterious vanishing prisoners."

"You need not make the effort," the Matron told her. "Give me time, and I shall provide you with all the evidence you require to confirm my story. We are both busy with more pressing matters, you will agree, so grant me three days. That should be enough of an interval for me to gather all my sources."

Lightreaver knew she was probably stalling for time, but if her words proved true, the city lay under a far greater threat than any of them imagined. "Three days. No more. But I warn you now." She straightened, gaze sharp as drawn steel. "If I find that you've fabricated this entire tale, I won't merely replace you as head of the Council — I'll see you stripped of your wealth and escorted to the gates at sword-point. Understood?"

For a heartbeat, Nilado's mask cracked — an eye twitch, a blink too fast. Then she covered it with a grin so broad it bordered on manic.

"No need for threats," she said, voice slightly too high. "I will bring you the proof. You'll see I've only ever done what's best for Zatreus."

BOSO OF THE Broken Tree stared forlornly across the moon-dappled river, leaning on the side of the foyla. The boat's constant bobbing in the current, accompanied by the dull, rhythmic slap of water against wood, made him queasy, but his stomach was too empty to protest.

Lelel, his egyzemor companion, lay uneasily on the deck beside him. The lack of food hit the larger races harder, and the once-strong merchant now looked half-drained, her muscles sagging beneath pale, sluggish skin.

There was nothing aboard for them to eat. The undead Shells who manned the boat had no need for provisions, and the foyla had been taken from Zatreus's harbor already unloaded from its previous journey. Everything Boso and Lelel brought burned up with their cart in Ludholm.

Curse you, Sarvendor, and your wretched god, Nizlan! Boso thought bitterly. He and Lelel followed the leader and his cult, *The Coven of the*

Venerated Gift, thinking it would one day benefit them both. Instead, they lost their jobs and belongings at the voladorm's orders to pursue Savanah's group. *I'd spit on them all, let me tell you!*

His dour gaze shifted to the figure at the bow of the foyla. Aedan, by Boso's estimation, stood barely a man in his early twenties, despite his height suggesting otherwise. He was the reason the merchant pair were now prisoners on the boat, though the erdi'zal suspected the individual possessed even less of a choice in the matter than they did.

Two days ago, Aedan forced the pair to teach him and the Shells how to operate the foyla. A simple craft, it operated by turning a central shaft that spun twin paddle wheels, churning the water with a steady, deep thrum. Teaching the brainless undead to do even that much had been a greater chore, however, and once achieved, they were too far from the shore to turn back.

Not that the odd man would let them. The three made a deal allowing the merchants to travel unharmed with them and advise on any river troubles along the way in exchange for free passage to Adradena. It wasn't an arrangement the erdi'zal ever wanted, but the alternative had been having the life beaten out of them. They chose the course that allowed them to continue breathing.

That might still prove to be the worst option. A quick death would be preferable to the starvation they faced. Boso didn't know how long it would take to reach the southern port, even if Aedan kept his end of the bargain.

Something ahead drew the man's attention, and Boso shifted his gaze to see what it was. Hope surged in his chest at the sight. A city! Walled and set back from the shore by half a mile, but a city nonetheless. Braziers of flames dotted the top of the fortifications, casting a glow over the surrounding terrain. *There will be people there, and they'll have food! I don't have much money left, but surely it would be enough. They might even help us get away from these abominations!*

But Aedan gave no signal to stop. The Shells continued forward without change. Boso's hope twisted into dread. They would have to brave the current.

But he couldn't swim.

He nudged Lelel awake with a paw. "Rise slowly," he hissed when she looked up. "We are approaching a city and will have to make a break for it. Can you swim?"

"Can," the egyzemor confirmed as she rose to stand beside him.

"Good. You'll have to carry me in."

She grimaced but nodded. Porting the horse-sized individual through the cold, relentless pull of the strong current would be a struggle, even for her kind, but she accepted the task stoically, as she always did.

As the boat neared the docks jutting into the river from the city's banks, they jumped. No Shells were posted to guard them, and the foyla's low rail gave them just enough leverage. Momentum flung them past the left paddle wheel and into the dark depths with an icy splash.

Boso flailed, swinging his arms and churning all four legs frantically to stay afloat. The current grabbed him, twisting him around until he could no longer tell which way led to the shore. He got out a single shout before water filled his mouth.

Lelel's powerful grip cinched his waist before he could sink, pulling him through the waves. Still sputtering, Boso tried to calm his panic, but all he saw was the star-littered sky above.

Soon, the pull on his midsection slowed, and cold mud kissed his paw. Lelel eased her hold, and his feet found on the soft embankment. They were at the shore's base, beneath two of the docks. *We did it! We are free!* He took a few deep breaths, coughing to clear the remnants of river water still lodged in his throat.

"Hurry!" his companion urged, pointing up the slope. Her normally scraggly hair hung like seaweed around her face, partially covering her eye, but she didn't take the time to brush it aside as she grabbed a patch of damp, reedy vegetation and pulled herself upward.

Boso heeded her suggestion, though climbing proved more difficult for him. While he clawed at the soil with his hands and dug in with his front legs, the rest of his lower torso stuck out oddly, his back feet touching only air. He muttered a string of curses — a habit he'd picked up since leaving Zatreus — before finally hauling himself onto the flat ground above with Lelel.

As he caught his breath, he spotted the reason for the egyzemor's urgency. Aedan had seen their flight from the boat and already ordered the craft to turn around. While too far away to see the man's expression, Boso sensed his steely glare on the pair. "Run!"

A broad, stone-paved road, weathered but well-maintained, stretched toward the city's entrance. A towering wall encircled the metropolis, its iron gate standing as a formidable barrier against intruders. From other merchants' descriptions, the erdi'zal recognized it as Stegate, but his panicked mind could draw forth no other details. All that mattered was finding refuge within its walls!

A blinding flash and a deafening roar to their left sent them veering in the opposite direction as bricks and earth hurtled wildly. *Rot my wares! What was that?* He grabbed Lelel's arm for guidance when another blast not ten feet ahead of them stopped their advance.

Boso whirled about, looking for the source. He spotted a dozen undead loping stiffly up the docks, hollow eyes glinting with a malevolent, unnatural light. Their tattered clothes hung in shreds, and their guttural growls split the night as they surged forward, intent on reaching them.

Panic shot through the erdi'zal as he urged Lelel to keep running. A third crackling bolt of lightning tore through the air and blasted the earth beside him, sending them tumbling to the ground, stunned.

When Boso's vision stopped swirling, a trio of ghastly faces were staring down at him. Sallow and pitted skin, dry as parchment and cold to the gaze, stretched over gaunt features, the vitality of life long gone, sucked from their forms. He swallowed the rising urge to scream as they reached for him.

They hauled him upright while another half dozen did the same with Lelel. Aedan strolled casually up behind them. "That was most unwise," he said, his eyes moving from one to the other. "Your master instructed you to aid me, so why have you left the boat?"

"Sarvendor is not our master!" Boso snapped, his anger swelling in his chest, pushing back the fear that threatened to consume him. "He can go to the abyss, and so can you!"

The fisherman's lips curled in an unsettling sneer. "You might renounce your fealty to him, but we had an agreement. A deal, you called it. You aid our journey to Adradena, and you are free. I do not believe this to be that city."

"But that will kill us," Boso protested. The trip likely wouldn't take long enough to starve them, but he couldn't face another moment of hunger. Back in his shop, he consumed three meals a day, sometimes more. Those were often shared with his employees, Demitry and Suzan. Now, though, they were gone, the shop destroyed, and not so much as an iceberry pie in sight. "We need to eat to survive. Your servants here seem beyond such requirements, but Lelel and I aren't." He paused to consider the man's emaciated figure. "You must be hungry, too. Let us go to Stegate and have a nice meal. I hear they have a fine boar meat called basura. Doesn't that sound lovely?" The last came out in the most ingratiating tone he could muster under the circumstances.

"Ah, sustenance," Aedan murmured, tilting his head like a curious child observing ants. "I had forgotten your fragile forms must consume vegetation and flesh for your continuance." He gestured toward a trio of Shells, two human women and a younger man, awaiting orders nearby. "You may ingest these. Will that be sufficient?"

Boso's stomach heaved. His throat tightened with nausea so sharp he nearly gagged. "We do *not* eat people. How can you even suggest that?"

"The flesh is clean," Aedan insisted, his tone utterly devoid of emotion. "You do not need to kill them, and they will feel nothing. Is that not better than slaying the animal you mentioned?"

Lelel let out a moan of misery, echoing Boso's revulsion. "We do *not* eat people," the erdi'zal repeated, fighting to keep his voice steady. "But we do eat animals, along with fruits and bread. I beg you, let us purchase some here."

The fisherman seemed to consider the request. "If you have this food, you will continue with us. Understood?"

Boso fought the urge to scream. They were being forced to rededicate themselves for the sake of their survival. It was an unfair arrangement, but that had been the way since Sarvendor assigned the pair to follow the others. "Yes, understood. We agree." He didn't look to Lelel for her consent. They might have had a choice then, at the risk of upsetting the cult leader. Now, though, they had none.

Aedan said not a word, but looked to the walls beyond. The lightning caught the attention of some inside the city, and one of the immense doors to the gate opened to allow a few spectators through. When all they saw were the dozen shadowy figures near the docks, a few ventured further out.

Boso wanted to yell a warning, but the three Shells still holding him might retaliate. Instead, he watched in dread as the trio Aedan had offered up as a sacrifice began a loping trek toward the city. Several more sprinted up from the foyla to join them, and soon, the undead posse approached the citizens.

"There is no need for this," Boso told Aedan, his voice quivering. "Lelel and I are fully capable of securing supplies for ourselves. Call your servants off."

Aedan's lip curled. "And tempt you with another escape? I think a demonstration is warranted for your assured cooperation. Remember, this rests upon *your* head."

The erdi'zal watched tensely as the walking corpses met with the living. A few shouts went up as the citizens questioned the strangers, but the Shells ignored them, instead shoving their way through the crowd and into the city. *If they just retrieve food, no one should get hurt, right?*

Another minute passed before the night erupted in screams. Though only a few hours after midnight, many of the vendor stalls within the walls were still set up. Heeding their telepathic orders, the undead fell upon them, snatching up anything they could hold. When a few locals tried to restrain them, the Shells shoved them aside, often violently.

"I beg you, stop this!" Boso yanked at the skeletal hands gripping his arms. "Forget the supplies. We will go willingly with you."

But Aedan ignored his pleas. From over a hundred miles away, the part of Olagkoa's mind that controlled the fisherman reveled in the chaos and the merchant's distress. Though it puppeted a thousand undead soldiers and planned to unleash devastation on the kingdoms of Rapria, the smaller excursions still brought it satisfaction.

A fresh discord arose from the gates as Shells shoved through the iron doors, their arms laden with a host of goods. Most of the residents darted away, letting them flee stiffly back toward the docks. The few brave enough to stand in their way were kicked aside by the uncaring corpses.

Relief flooded Boso's chest. No one had perished for his hunger. He and Lelel were still unwilling passengers, but at least they wouldn't starve.

However, Stegate was not undefended.

A squad of city guards in deep blue and gold were already closing in on the retreating Shells, swords drawn, shields raised. More were assembling behind them.

And now, the same citizens who stepped aside for the undead were diving for cover from the city's retaliation.

"Halt in the name of the Wardens of Stegate!" an older man, gilded sash crossing his broad chest, called out as he strode to the front. "You have illegally breached our perimeter and stolen from — "

Lightning arched from Aedan's raised hand, striking the stones a dozen feet ahead of the commander, blasting dirt and bricks into the air. For the trained guards, it served as a warning shot. They ignored it, and with a shouted order, the men broke into pursuit of the thieves.

They would have overtaken the Shells in moments, but another blast struck the front line. Their leader fell, his head a blackened ruin, along with the three closest fighters. The explosion compelled the soldiers to break off the chase and consider a different strategy.

They didn't have the time, as a third bolt from Aedan's hand downed five more. Panic broke out, and the remaining Wardens scattered before more strikes could be leveled.

But Aedan didn't stop. A trio of lightning blasts drove the fighters back toward the gate. More assailed the fleeing crowd of civilians. Screams of terror filled the air.

The sight proved unbearable for Boso. He leaped forward with his powerful hindquarters, dragging along one of his captors, as he lashed out at Aedan.

His blow never connected with the man, though. A sharp, burning sensation, as if he'd grabbed a torch, surged through his fingers and palms, then up his arms. He yelled and pulled away, desperately attempting to shake the feeling back into his limbs.

"You dare lay hands on me?" The fisherman's voice remained surprisingly calm, despite the attack. Overwhelmed by pain, Boso couldn't pull free as the two Shells he escaped seized him again, dragging him relentlessly toward the docks. Behind him, twice as many led Lelel in the same direction, the egyzemor not even attempting to fight after seeing the consequences for her companion.

Once on board the foyla, the pair were thrown roughly on the deck while the Shells who plundered the city dumped their haul beside them. Under orders to retrieve provisions, the undead had gathered a random assortment. Along with varying fruit, like moon salal and edar, lay a few loaves of crusty bread, a bound hunk of salted pork, and half a pie. The other half had been smashed against the chest of the corpse who swiped it. Not every item proved edible, however, as they also collected a bottle of scented oil, a woven child's doll, and a slab of raw basura meat.

"You have your supplies," Aedan told them as the boat cast off from the docks. "Now you will do as agreed. Do not disobey again."

Boso nodded glumly, casting a final glance toward Stegate's walls. After the multiple lightning strikes, no one dared follow them, leaving all hope of rescue to fall away. "You didn't have to kill them," he muttered, the feeling finally returning to his arms and hands as a pins-and-needles rush.

"You should not have defied me. Their lives were forfeit because of you." He turned his attention to the river ahead and moved to retake his place at the bow. "They are merely the first. The world must repay me for every hour I slept beneath it."

Chapter Three
DRIVEN

ERIS AND TAL galloped their horses along the edge of the grassland, the rhythmic thud of hooves muffled by the soft earth, riding between the drop to the lowland below and the Hightower Woodlands. As they approached the entrance to Ludholm, they were surprised to see the gates flung wide open and dozens of its citizens outside in what appeared to be a celebration. Braziers on both sides of the walls blazed, illuminating the night. Music drifted to them, accompanied by the smell of roasting meat.

The group quieted as the pair approached. Four soldiers among them drew swords and advanced, forming a protective line before the others. "Halt!" one called out, a man with broad shoulders and ice-white hair. "I am Grekorn Mistoak of Ludholm's Civic Defense. Who are you, and what is your business here?"

"I am Eris Duskmore, formerly of Talidith. We are here to see your leader on a highly urgent matter."

"And what might that be?" the guard demanded.

"I'm Tal, and there's an army marching up your backside!" Tal shouted. "So you better get back inside quick."

The four soldiers laughed, as did several of the revelers behind them. "That will be our forces returning home at last. The war is over, and Ludholm will soon retake its rightful place as the port of the north."

"It is your army," Eris told him. "And Zatreus's. But this is not the homecoming you expected or want. Everyone's been killed."

Though some continued to laugh, his grave tone dulled their enthusiasm. "What do you mean by that? How can they be coming here if they're dead?"

"Because the creature leading them forced both armies into battle, then raised them to walk again." Eris recognized the frowns of disbelief. He'd worn the same himself, once. "I know it sounds crazy, but I swear on my oath as a Sovereign Guard of the Kingdom of Talidith, we are telling you the truth."

Grekorn's expression shifted. He motioned for them to dismount. They did, Tal following Eris's lead. Once on the ground, the four men surrounded them, while another took control of their horses. "Your tale is nonsense, but you are not the first to visit here, claiming to be from Talidith. I'll take you to Lord Daymon, and if he grants you an audience, repeat your story as you have to me. But attempt any treachery, and my soldiers will cut you down."

Eris and Tal nodded in agreement, then allowed the guards to lead them into the city. The roads lacked the cobblestone protection of Zatreus, so they trudged through mud, their boots squelching with each heavy step, and around puddles caused by the spring thaw.

The walls were barely defensive, with large gaps in many places where bricks had crumbled away. The wooden shops and houses were equally dilapidated, with the stench of rot and dampness mixing with smoke from the braziers and bonfires. Several buildings appeared to be on the verge of collapsing, leaning dangerously as if a strong gust of wind could bring them down. At first, Eris believed the kingdom had suffered an attack, then he remembered the two armies had never engaged. *This is Zatreus's great enemy?*

Despite the destitute nature of their city, the people of Ludholm were ecstatic. Children ran through the muck, splashing and giggling with delight, while their mothers scolded them lightly, laughing as well. *By morning, they will all be in tears when they realize their soldiers are never returning. If they survive the rest of the night.*

Grekorn called one of the youths over, a boy barely twelve, and instructed him to find their ruler before turning back to the pair. "We'll wait here for Lord Daymon."

They paused near a rundown animal pen. A handful of hogs offered low, contented grunts inside, wallowing in the mud-covered ground. It hardly seemed the place to meet the head of a kingdom. Even in tiny Talidith, King Valeria maintained a throne room. Eris could see a weathered stone stronghold ahead. "Wouldn't the castle be better?"

"Lord Daymon walks among his people," Grekorn told him. "He is celebrating with them as well."

Tal crinkled her nose in disgust. "Why's your city such a hovel?"

"Blame that on the Skorgan Empire," the guard spat. "Their accursed arcanist tried to force Ludholm under their rule, and when my ancestors resisted, they took the water from our ground and dried up the lake. Then Zatreus was handed the rights to the river."

"That's a load of burral piss," she snapped. "There's no lake. There's never been a lake."

Eris considered the claim, though. The grasslands being so much lower than the surrounding area lent credibility to the story. It also explained the need for the Riverwall. "There will be now," he told her. "We've seen it."

"But that's unnatural!"

Grekorn's eyes flashed with anger. "Zatreus's blocking the river from flowing into the lake was unnatural. We are righting a wrong, restoring the natural order."

His words quieted Tal, and Eris understood why. They couldn't possibly determine the truth here. If the man's recounting proved accurate, it happened many lifetimes ago. That didn't invalidate Ludholm's desire to have a port, but that drive resulted in a conflict that ended in the death of a thousand soldiers. "You started a war for this?"

"That wasn't our doing," came a voice behind them. The trio turned to see the lad returning with a man Eris guessed to be Lord Daymon. "We sent multiple emissaries to the so-called High Monarch seeking a way to share the river. Two were rejected, and the third was killed. Lightreaver then proclaimed war upon our city. We were forced to build an army from the able-bodied men we could spare."

His thin, almost translucent threadbare shirt, ragged waistcoat, and dirty breeches seemed unfit for the ruler of a kingdom. His sunken eyes, unkempt beard, and prematurely graying hair pulled back in a ponytail, though, certainly indicated the weight of leadership rested heavily upon him. Talidith's King Valeria often bore a similar look. Especially near the end, Eris reflected.

"Greetings, my lord," Grekorn said with a stiff nod. "These two appeared at our gates, speaking some nonsense about our army being dead but approaching the city. I would have sent them away, but the man claims to be from Talidith and spoke of a beast."

"Olagkoa," Eris confirmed. "It's leading a legion of living corpses — what's left of both yours and Zatreus's forces — right to your borders. Now!"

To his surprise, Daymon turned to Grekorn. "You and your men will join us at the wall." He then gestured to Eris and Tal. "You two, show me."

The ruler dashed away from the pig pen, his quick, determined strides kicking up loose earth as he hastened toward the city's outer perimeter, forcing the pair to rush to keep up. He made his way around the playing children, wagons, and a handful of buildings to the crumbling stone fortifications. A few large barrels rested against it, filled to the brim with brownish rocks, as if attempts to repair the walls had been abandoned.

A tall flight of wooden stairs, bending and creaking under their weight, took them to a rickety walkway near the top. From there, they could see for leagues, the moonlight illuminating much of the flooding grassland below. While still a few miles away, a large formation of bodies stood in sharp contrast to the rising water everywhere else. Flashes of light bounced off the metal of their armor, while ripples formed with every step of the macabre warriors.

Grekorn and the three soldiers who escorted the strangers followed their leader to the fortifications and saw the approaching force. "As I suspected. It is merely our men returning home. They will be welcomed with open arms and congratulations."

"Where is the creature you spoke of?" Daymon asked, his breathing steady despite their sprint.

Where indeed, Eris wondered. It had been leading the army when they left, but now there was no sign of the tentacled monstrosity. A knot of dread formed in his stomach. *What fresh deception is this?* "I do not know. It must have moved to the rear."

Grekorn snorted. "Your pardon, my lord. I have wasted your time with these strangers' tales. I will deliver them to the dungeon immediately." He motioned, and the other three guards swarmed around Eris and Tal.

"You can't hold us!" the woman protested, placing a hand on the hilt at her hip. "We are trying to help you!"

Daymon bid the men to wait. "Sir Grekorn, there is no need. Our agents have completed their mission, and the war is over. I bear them no ill will for what their ruler has done."

The explanation wasn't lost on Eris. "So you *are* responsible for the destruction of the Riverwall!"

"I do not deny it," the ruler told him calmly. "We seek only to regain what was taken from us."

"You won't have anything if you don't act now. Those soldiers down there are no longer yours. They are coming here to destroy you."

"Come along." Grekorn reached for Eris's arm. "You are not under arrest, but you are clearly wasting our time."

Tal's eyes were wide with panic. All their efforts to save lives were being ignored. "How big is your army?" she challenged. "Look again! You didn't have that many men!"

"That's enough." The knight gestured to the pair as he addressed the other guards. "Take them to the gate."

Daymon did as Tal suggested, though. As the force grew closer, their numbers were easier to determine. "Hold, Sir Grekorn," he said, not taking his gaze off the horde. "Look. Would you say the approaching multitude outnumbers our forces?"

Grekorn gave the woman a scowl, then turned his stare on the land below. The sour expression softened when he recognized what his leader saw. "It does seem rather larger than I recall. What is that following?"

Eris shifted his attention to the rear of the shambling horde. Though partially hidden in the darkness, the form of the tentacled beast, a shifting, darker mass against the gloom, more than twice the size of the soldiers, could be made out. "The creature! That's Olagkoa! Now, do you believe us?"

The ruler's weary eyes sparked to life. "Sir Grekorn," he snapped, "Round up everyone outside and seal the gates. I want anyone capable of wielding a sword at the walls. Something is amiss here, and we had better be prepared."

All signs of Grekorn's disbelief vanished at the orders. "Right away, my lord."

He motioned for the other three to follow him when Eris grabbed his shoulder. "Wait! We have friends coming." He turned a pleading gaze toward Daymon. "Two women on horseback and an erdi'zal. We split so they could keep watch over the creature while we rode ahead to warn you. All are fighters and can aid in the defense."

Ludholm's sovereign nodded to the knight. "Stay alert and send them here when they arrive." Once Grekorn and his men left, Daymon turned to Eris. "Tell me more about this Olagkoa. It seems it no longer besieges Zatreus."

"It drove my people out of Talidith and followed us there," the burly man told him. "It eluded the city's defenses somehow and went on a rampage. Tal and I fought it, along with many others, and finally forced it out. We tracked it to your grasslands before realizing its goal."

Tal nodded. "We warned both armies, but they were too misted to listen."

Daymon frowned. "Misted?"

"She means stupid," Eris said with a sigh. He appreciated Tal's often rather colorful speech, but it sometimes clouded communications. "The creature had already begun influencing them, driving them into battle, forcing the two sides to destroy each other."

"Did you try stopping the beast itself?"

"He did," Tal chimed in. "Almost got himself deaded. Again."

"Olagkoa is incredibly resilient. My people tried many things to kill it. I've had a few personal confrontations with it myself." Eris gestured to the side of his face. The lower part of his left ear was missing, and most of the skin on that section of his head appeared sickly pale. A permanent reminder of his first encounter with the creature.

Daymon eyed the damage. "What does it want?"

"Revenge, I think. Whoever originally found it, trapped it in a cave in the ground. We stumbled upon it when excavation for our underground stronghold, the Undercastle, connected with one of its tunnels." *And I foolishly removed the final barrier holding it in place,* Eris cursed himself internally. *Forgive me, Kehnin!* "If someone had stuffed me in a hole to be forgotten, I'd be pretty angry, too."

The leader scratched his beard in thought. "I see. Ludholm just happens to be the nearest kingdom to take its rage out on."

"Yes."

Daymon stared back down into the grassland. The army couldn't be more than a mile from Ludholm, and at their constant rate of march, they would soon reach the bottom of the slope up to Ludholm's walls. "I have not lost hope that this is some form of trickery on your part. Your compatriots nearly set my city alight when they left. I trust you will not do similarly."

He must mean Savanah and Vyncent! That's why he agreed to see us. He'd already been told about the beast! "No. And for all our sake, I wish this was merely a deception I could dispel."

"Then I pray Diovola is on our side."

A shout from behind drew their attention to the street inside the walls. Farla, Ranin, and Holfast trotted up the muddy route amid the bustling population preparing for the upcoming assault.

Eris took a deep breath, exhaling slowly as he turned to face Daymon. "My companions and I will fight with you. Our knowledge of the creature may help, and most of us are trained soldiers."

"I can fight!" Tal protested, a flash of indignation in her eyes as she realized the 'most' excluded her. "I've rescued you a few times. Remember?"

"I stand corrected." Eris nodded toward the woman. "Four of us are trained soldiers, and Tal knows which end of her sword to hold."

She gave a sharp laugh and reached for her waist. "Don't make me get out Mrs. Bang!"

Daymon watched the interaction with mild amusement. "That is an odd name for a sword."

"It's her hammer," Eris clarified.

A grin split Tal's face as she pulled the stubby, iron-headed construction tool from her belt. Though barely big enough to drive nails into wood, she wielded it with such flair that she seemed prepared to take on an entire army.

Lord Daymon shook his head as he met Eris's gaze. "You keep odd company, but I accept your offer. We will need all the fighters we can, trained or otherwise, if we are ever to see morning again."

"VEN! GET IN here!"

Nilado stormed into her office, not waiting to check if her assistant followed. Rage propelled her through the lavishly decorated room to an immense desk, where she lit a thick candle. *That trumped-up little girl thinks she can order me around? We'll see how well she fares when I'm done.*

Her second-in-command, a human male, sprinted in a few seconds later, head bobbing in constant appeasement. "Yes, Matron. I am here. What do you need?"

She glared at him, then past him, toward the open corridor, where anyone could pass and overhear. "Close the door, you fool!" she snapped.

Ven blinked, as if the idea never occurred to him, and shuffled to obey. When he turned back, Nilado had settled into a wide chair behind the desk, fingers drumming against the polished mahogany surface. He took his place opposite her, awaiting her next command.

"We must move up our timeline," Nilado said once she regained her composure. "That upstart Lightreaver wants me to provide proof that Linda was a spy for Ludholm."

Her assistant ran a nervous hand down his deep pink shirt. His attire always seemed at war with itself, and today proved no different. The bright yellow trousers not only clashed with his top but were far too cheerful for that early in the morning. "Do you have any?"

"Of course not!" Nilado slammed her palm on the desk, making the candle tremble. "That's why we need to move things along. I have three days to produce evidence, or she'll strip me of everything."

Ven looked properly mortified. "But... but that would make you..." His voice trailed off, too horrified to speak the word.

"A peasant," she finished for him, her tone sharp. "A commoner. A nobody. A fate worse than death." Nilado sat, contemplating such an outcome. With a huff, she reached for a quill. "But that will not happen. Not to me."

A few dabs in an inkwell and several scribbles on a bit of parchment later, the Matron had completed a list of instructions. She read them over hastily to herself, waved the paper to dry the ink, then folded it into thirds. "I have plans to placate that spoiled brat, but if they fail, we must move to the next stage faster than we discussed." She held the letter out for her assistant. "Take this to Malrik as soon as it is light."

Ven took it with a rapid nod. "Of course, Matron. It will be done."

She tapped the table in consideration. "You better pack for an extended stay. Take only your most valuable items. Nothing that draws attention. If things go sour on this end, we may need to leave Zatreus permanently."

The man's groveling expression crumbled at the suggestion. "Leave Zatreus? But we are so prosperous here. We have amassed a substantial fortune and hold sway over hundreds of people. Leaving would be worse than peasantry. It would make us fools as well."

"You have always been a fool, Ven. It is my intellect, my shrewdness, which granted me the position here. I hold the power. This is simply the start of a new ledger, one that will recount an even more profitable outcome than here."

He tilted his head at her claim, ignoring the insult. "From cloth?"

"It isn't merely cloth. It's a path to riches beyond anything we could imagine. Once our alchemists discover its secrets and can reproduce it, everyone will want an outfit that conforms to their every whim." She tapped the desk again. "There are a few of them still here in Wolfsight. Take them with you. If we cannot return, they'll be wasted here. And we can't have any of them talking."

"Of course not, Matron."

She stood and turned toward the window. In daylight, she could look out over the harbor and watch the bustle of trade. All that lay obscured by the predawn dark. "I've reconsidered. Leave immediately. The dark will give you cover."

Ven frowned but nodded. "Once I pack."

Nilado spun about, fixing him with a glare. "I said *immediately.*"

The man nearly fumbled the letter as he bowed, retreating toward the door. With a hurried tug, he pulled it open and slipped out, offering a final, breathless, "Yes, Matron."

THE FIRE HAD nearly burned to ash before Vyncent stirred. He cursed softly, crawling from his bedding to rebuild it. Mikel had promised Savanah they would keep it going through the night as a beacon for Camille, but Vyncent saw no point.

If she decides to run off in a tantrum, she can find her way back on her own, he thought, tossing on a few logs. *This trip will be a lot quieter without her.* When the wood didn't catch, he shoved in a few twigs and dry vegetation. Once it sparked, he stepped away.

A sharp crack, like a branch snapping underfoot, snapped his attention up. The fire wasn't burning hot enough for that, and he scanned past it. At first, he noticed nothing unusual, just the long grass waving in the breeze. But the night remained still. Dead still.

Vyncent drew his sword. Though not as untamed as the wildlands of Talidith, the region still harbored hostile creatures. At least two kinds of vornuks would find it a suitable location to live, and the surrounding forest must have its share of wolves and bears.

The swordsman eased forward, never taking his eyes off the shifting vegetation. He reached Savanah, who had finally cried herself to sleep, and nudged her with his boot. "Wake up!" he hissed. "We have company."

She groaned, but her grogginess vanished almost instantly when she saw his drawn weapon. Wordlessly, she slipped from her bedroll and grabbed the bow, her bare feet making no sound on the soft grass. Her gaze followed his to where the ground grew more agitated. Something was digging.

Vyncent stood torn between shouting a warning to the still-sleeping Mikel or leaping forward to stab the troubled terrain. Before he could choose, the soil split open, like a pot of stew boiling over.

A blur of filthy fur and flailing limbs burst out. It landed on four squat legs, each tipped with fingerlike claws that looked disturbingly human. The head appeared anything but human, however, resembling a horse's from a nightmare — too long, with sagging jowls, sunken eyes, and a mane of matted hair. It stood no taller than a wood vornuk, but its appearance was just as alarming.

It spewed forth a guttural cry, sounding somewhere between a growl and a scream, from its teeth-lined mouth as it snapped its head about. Despite its attack, it seemed unsure of its location and shifted its feet to turn.

"Back! Move!" Mikel shouted from behind them. Vyncent and Savanah had already reached the same conclusion and hastily scrambled toward the fire. A second creature sprang from the hole, then a third, each landing with a wet thud not far from the first. The trio spun jerkily from side to side, akin to spiders descending on a web.

"What are they?" Vyncent looked at Mikel. He noticed the black-haired man standing with sword in hand and boots on his feet already, despite appearing asleep only moments ago.

"I'm not sure," he said. "But I have a guess. Stay clear. There is a chance they will return underground."

"And if they don't?" Savanah asked, slipping on her boots.

"Then we'll have to fight or flee. With Camille gone, we are down to three against three. Without knowing for certain what they are, I don't know if that offers decent odds."

"She picked a wonderful time to leave," Vyncent grumbled. As soon as the words exited his mouth, two more of the things jumped out, joining their kin in the bizarre dance. "What do you *think* they are?"

"Carcass beasts. They match the descriptions I've read about. And if they are, we will have to fight."

Vyncent had never heard the name. He already hated it. "Then shouldn't we attack now, when — "

The mad jittering abruptly halted. The first three launched themselves at the companions with alarming speed, jaws wide. Vyncent and Savanah jumped out of their path, but two of the creatures smashed into them, knocking them both to the ground. Only Mikel had moved swiftly enough to dodge the strike. He brought his sword down hard, but it only sliced a shallow groove in the beast's shoulder.

Prone on his back, Vyncent caught the throat of his attacker in his grip, shoving it away to avoid the thing's snapping jaw. Thicker and heavier than it appeared, its fur-coated body moved with the ferocity of a vornuk with nearly the same stench. The swordsman twisted his blade and nicked the creature's neck. It yelped and scrambled off his chest.

He jumped to his feet, gripping the carcass beast by the throat, his fingers sinking into thick, greasy fur. To his right, Mikel sparred with his opponent. To the left, Savanah grappled with the creature that had leapt at her, holding its shoulders at bay to keep its teeth from reaching her. Its rear claws dug into her clothes as it thrashed. She couldn't let go without giving it a clean shot at her neck.

She can't hold it much longer!

With a shout, Vyncent hurled his foe into the others circling the clearing. It struck them with a sickening crunch, scattering fur and limbs. He spun and drove his weapon into the beast pinning Savanah. The blade sank deep into its ribs and punched through the far side, crimson staining the steel. The body collapsed, dead.

He turned to help Mikel while Savanah got to her feet, shoving the corpse off her and picking up her bow. Her sword still lay by her bedroll, and Camille's was stowed on the boat, so the silver artifact was all she had. She drew back on its string and released the magical arrow that materialized there.

Her first shot flew true, but it vanished on impact, dissolving into nothingness with a faint pop. A second. A third. All blinked out the moment they struck, leaving no mark.

While she puzzled over it, the trio charged. They made a direct line for Vyncent and Mikel, their bulky legs propelling them rapidly over the ground, their heavy thuds growing louder with each stride. "Watch out!"

The beasts leaped before Savanah finished her warning. Though Mikel stood nearer — the creature which assaulted him neatly skewered on his sword — all three lashed out at Vyncent.

He shouted, first in shock, then pain, as spiked teeth tore into his left shoulder. The other two battered his legs, driving him backward to the ground.

Blood poured from the wound, the coppery scent instantly filling the air, as the beast wrenched its jaws free and lunged again, this time aiming for the face. Mikel kicked the body off his blade and spun to aid his companion, piercing the animal in the back. It screamed, allowing Vyncent to stun it with a punch to the head.

The two men grappled with the creatures, Mikel searching for an opening to stab without hurting his friend, Vyncent struggling to keep his face and throat intact. The beasts were savage, though, tearing at his limbs and snapping at Mikel's hands.

Dizzy from blood loss and strain, Vyncent knew if either of them stopped, he was as good as dead. With one hand holding the beast on his chest at bay, he tried to bring his sword up with the other. But it lay pinned beneath him, trapped by the weight on his legs.

Then a creature shrieked, and his limb came loose! He brought it up and kicked at the other, landing a solid blow on its head as it bit into his shin. With it stunned, Mikel had the opportunity to gut it, and Vyncent was free.

A second shriek, piercingly close to his ear, made him wince. But the beast that unleashed it released him and sprang away. Dazed, Vyncent looked up to see Savanah standing over him, a thick, burning stick in her hand.

"We have to move!" she barked, grabbing his arm. Her recovered sword hung from her hip, the bow over her torso. Neither proved as efficient as fire against this enemy. "There are more coming!"

Vyncent staggered upright, pain wracking him as he nearly dropped his sword. Multiple bites and scratches bled openly under the tatters of his trousers, and the gash in his shoulder similarly gushed. Savanah threw her arm around him and supported him as best as her shorter frame could. It was enough, and he took a few tentative steps forward.

"Get to the boat!" Mikel shouted. He had sheathed his sword, replacing it with a pair of burning branches, one in each hand. A beast near him howled a high-pitched shriek of agony, having come too close and getting its fur set on fire by the man. "I'll hold them off, but hurry!"

"We can't leave Camille!" Savanah yelled back, but she was already dragging the wounded Vyncent toward the shore.

"We have no choice!" Mikel swung a branch at a creature, and it shied away. A half dozen encircled the soldier, forming a loose semicircle as they searched for a way to bypass the deadly fire he wielded. "Go!"

They stumbled down the embankment, the shifting earth slipping under their boots. Pain ripped through Vyncent's shoulder, and he bit back a cry. Savanah did her best, but he wished Malwin were there instead. The enormous egyzemor would have carried him like a sack of grain down this slope.

Once they reached the valupe, Savanah tossed the branch aside and shoved Vyncent against the boat's side. Its deck sat too high above the shore for him to climb in his condition, so she quickly hauled herself up, then lay flat on her stomach to lift him. After what felt like an eternity of pulling his arms, clothes, and even his belt, she hoisted him over the edge. He collapsed with a groan.

She didn't have that luxury. He protested, but she dragged him farther along the deck, propping him against the cargo hold, then racing to the front and jumping to the ground. They had shored the boat when they landed the prior evening, so she needed to push it back into the river on her own. Her feet dug into the dirt as she shoved against the bow. After a long moment, it broke free from the muddy shore and slid into the water, the rope they had pulled it with dragging after it.

She turned to see Mikel already racing down the embankment, the burning branches tossed aside. A dozen beasts gave chase, howling as they bounded across the spongy ground with gleeful abandon. In seconds, they'd be on him.

For the first time since finding the silver bow in the Undercastle, Savanah wished for an ordinary one instead. She drew it now and released two shots in rapid succession, aimed at the creatures leading the charge.

The magic arrows had done no damage before, but the archer had no other way to help her friend. They struck the sloped ground before the foremost beasts, dislodging the dirt beneath their feet. The pair stumbled, falling into a collection of tumbling legs. Those behind tripped on their kin and fell too, their howls turning to shrieks.

It bought Mikel a few precious seconds. He reached her, and together they sprinted into the water. The current had caught the boat, drawing it further out, forcing the pair to slog through the growing depths until they floundered. They grabbed the drifting rope before the valupe slipped out of reach, letting it pull them along.

Momentum carried a few beasts splashing into the river, but they scrambled back to shore. The others paced the edge, searching for a path to the escaping prey that didn't involve getting wet. When they found nothing, they resumed their howling.

Savanah and Mikel pulled themselves hand over hand up the rope until they lay soaked, their clothes clinging to them with a cold weight, and panting on the deck, their breaths ragged.

When they had recovered a bit, they checked on Vyncent. His breathing remained shallow, and blood loss had left him dazed, but he still managed a weak smile.

"We need to take care of his wounds," Mikel told Savanah. "Do you have any bandages? Spare clothes?"

"I think so. Our supplies from Zatreus were pretty extensive."

While Savanah retrieved them, Mikel stripped Vyncent down, so only Lightreaver's pendant remained around his neck. His trousers hung in tatters and the man needed the shirt off to tackle the shoulder gash. With no balm or medicine, all they could do was rinse the wound with river water and wrap it tight. They similarly cleaned the blood from the dozens of scratches on his legs and arms. Vyncent said little during the ordeal, and by the time they'd finished and bundled him in a galley blanket, he'd slipped into sleep.

With him safe, the pair steadied the tiller, letting the boat drift along in the middle of the river while they changed outfits. Savanah pulled fresh clothes from her pack. Mikel found a simple set stashed in the hold for just this sort of occasion. Finally, they dried their weapons, wiping the swords down, emptying their scabbards of any excess water, and drying the bow with a rag from the boat's galley.

"Tonight was a disaster," Savanah mumbled, staring at the moving shoreline as they sat on the deck, backs against the cargo area. "Vyncent's hurt, Camille's gone, and we lost our bedrolls, cooking gear, utensils..."

"Supplies can be replaced," Mikel told her. "Vyncent needs rest and treatment. We should reach Forden this afternoon. There we'll purchase fresh provisions, as well as some medicine. Maybe some undergarments for our friend here, too."

Savanah blushed. "You noticed. We tried for ages to convince him," she said, blushing. "He just laughed. Camille once told him to wear them in case he needed a doctor to remove his trousers." She paused, gaze fixed on the passing trees. "We'll get her back. Won't we?"

Mikel placed a comforting hand on her arm. "We will. Your friend is quite resourceful. She's probably already in Adradena, locating the next artifact. But if she isn't, we can stop a little further down the river. She has a few hours' head start, but the boat will make up the difference. We'll find her."

"Thank you." A slight smile parted her lips. "I am glad you decided to come with us. We wouldn't have gotten this far without you."

"As I told you, it is my city at stake as well. If the High Monarch believed your mission was the best hope, then how could I refuse?" He stifled a yawn as he looked up into the night sky. "Now, let's try to get a bit more sleep. There are a few hours remaining until dawn. We have a better chance of finding Camille in the light, and if she is still heading south, we'll likely run into her further along."

Savanah sighed. "I dearly hope you are right."

Chapter Four
THE BROKEN ONSLAUGHT

L UDHOLM'S GATES STOOD sealed tight. Every able-bodied fighter lined the wall, breath fogging in the chill night air as they watched the undead army reach the base of the lake basin.

Now Eris saw the truth of it — how did he miss it before? The land closest to the city dipped into an artificial drop, once carved to form a harbor. He had assumed it was meant to repel an attack from Zatreus. Deliberate or not, the steep climb of hard dirt posed a forty-foot natural barrier to the attackers.

Had the Shells retained their former minds, they might have seen the hopelessness of the assault. But these weren't men anymore. They were puppets, dead things moved by Olagkoa's will. And Olagkoa wanted Ludholm.

So they climbed. Hands that no longer felt pain gouged holes into the vertical earth deep enough to grip and dig their booted feet into. They ascended slowly, and many tumbled back into the rising water below before starting again. But neither fatigue nor doubt plagued the mindless corpses, and they continued their advance.

A few volleys of arrows rained down from the battlements, thudding into the lifeless bodies. Holfast gave the order to stop once it became clear the projectiles had no effect on the undead. Even pierced hearts and ruined eyes didn't halt the things.

Daymon stood grimly at Eris's side. He believed the war won, and now faced his own soldiers launching an assault on the city. "This would be an opportune time to impart some of that experience you spoke of," he intoned, glancing at Eris. "How do we kill the already dead?"

"When Tal and I fought them before, we found dismemberment a permanent end to their walking," the man replied. "Removing the head proved the most efficient."

"Which we cannot do until we are in direct combat." Daymon returned his attention to the activity below. They were close enough now for the dull, rhythmic clang of metal against armor to be heard at the ramparts. "Did those whom you battled carry weapons?"

"No. They were mostly peasants from the outer farmlands."

"Then we can assume these will be fiercer opponents. I cannot subject my people to that. Is there another way?"

"Fire!" Eris cursed himself for not remembering that fatal weakness earlier. "We destroyed many by setting them ablaze. If any move close enough, torches may repel them. Or perhaps your archers could send flaming arrows into their ranks. Do you have any pulveld?"

But Daymon shook his head at the suggestion. "Torches would be useless against swords. And if we toss fire down onto them now, it could set the entire grassland ablaze."

Eris considered his words. They had driven Olagkoa from Zatreus's cemetery by filling the confined area with burning items. The creature was petrified of the flames and fled, while the roaring, hungry blaze consumed many of its creations. "That might not be a bad thing. I doubt they could climb a fiery cliff, and it would confine them to the grasslands."

"We would choke on the smoke before the fire reached them," Daymon said flatly. "We will wait to see what they do once they reach the wall."

Both men wore grim expressions as they watched the approaching undead. A few pulled themselves up over the drop-off's edge and struggled to their feet. The walls lay roughly thirty feet ahead of them, with the remains of a gate further along. It served as the entrance to Ludholm's docks a millennium before, but once the lake vanished, they reclaimed the wooden piers and sealed the entry point.

Still, the handful of Shells appeared to believe it was their best chance of breaching the wall. Or rather, Olagkoa held the belief and guided its macabre puppets forward. Eris noticed they walked toward the relief in the stone fortification without the usual shuffling gait he'd witnessed in others. *Are these corpses more mobile because they're fresher, or is the creature becoming more skilled in creating them?*

Even as he observed the smoothness of their gait, the three nearest the wall abruptly turned away, as if disoriented. They wandered briefly, then returned their attention to the stronghold and approached it once more.

Both men stared in confusion as the trio faltered again. Two veered off, but the third stumbled ahead. When it was within ten feet of the battlements, it convulsed and collapsed to the ground.

"What is happening to them?" the leader demanded.

"I don't know," Eris told him. "I've never seen this before."

They continued watching as more Shells tried to reach the wall. A dozen had reached the region before it when two-thirds of them grew disoriented and veered off course. Four pressed on, however, before falling like the others.

Eris searched for Olagkoa in the grassland. *Is there something wrong with the beast affecting its concentration? Does it even need that once the things are active?* He spotted it near the rear of the horde, its massive form churning the dark water as it shoved its way forward, seemingly puzzled by the faltering of its puppets as well.

If its first method of attack failed, then Eris knew what would be next. "Keep watch, but my people must get outside!" Not waiting for a reply from the leader, he raced down the wooden stairs to the bottom of the inner fortifications. "Tal! Ranin! Farla! Holfast! Meet me at the gate now!"

Eris sprinted through the muddy streets, his boots kicking up wet filth as the others rushed to join him. Ranin and Farla clambered down the wall's steps. Holfast, always cautious of the creaking wooden walkways, had been perched atop a slanted roof instead. Now he dropped down tile by tile, shaking shingles loose with each thunderous landing.

Tal was already near the gate. She'd gotten bored waiting for the undead and passed the time rummaging through the barrels of rocks meant for slings and trebuchets. One found its way into her pocket. When she saw Eris, she jogged over with a sly grin. "What's got you razzled?"

"The Shells are faltering. Olagkoa's losing control."

Her eyes lit with something too close to glee. "So we going out to finish them?"

"No. To stop what comes next."

But the gate wasn't unguarded. Two burly men, armed with heavy-looking swords, blocked their path. "You aren't going out there," one said. "The city is under siege."

"We know," Eris answered. "We're trying to prevent something worse."

"Lord Daymon's orders. Gate stays shut."

To his shock, Eris considered fighting their way through. Five against two weren't bad odds. Raising a sword against Ludholm's guards would certainly end any goodwill they had gained, but if he didn't, the city would lose a lot more.

He glanced at Holfast, who gave a tight nod. They were thinking the same thing.

Before either took action, however, Daymon's strong voice rang out behind them. "Let them through. But lock the gate after them." He strode up beside the companions and fixed them with a somber stare. "If you go out there, it is upon your heads. I will not risk any of my men to rescue you."

"We understand," Eris said. The others nodded grimly.

The guards opened the gates just enough for the five to slip through, then metal bolts slammed in place behind them. They ran fast and low along the tree line, hugging the edge of the basin. Once clear of the city's range, Eris motioned for them to drop. He and the women pressed into the wet earth. Holfast ducked behind a thick bush, doing his best to vanish despite his size.

From their position, they gained a clear view of Olagkoa, the army, and the undead scaling the cliff-like bank. More Shells reached the wall but fared no better than the rest. Some collapsed when they got close to the barrier, others began wandering. As they watched, two tumbled over the ledge. They struck the ground with a splash, the water and soft grass below doing little to cushion the blow. One rose shakily again, but the other remained immobile.

Tal was trembling beside him, fists clenched tightly. Her face twisted in rage. "Those ungrateful, blank-brained, sons-of-a-vornuk!" she finally spat out. "We come to their aid, and they let us walk out to our doom."

"We aren't going to die," Eris scolded. "At least, I hope not."

"Why *did* you bring us out here?" Ranin hissed. "We could see all this from safely inside Ludholm."

"Because the assault is failing," the man replied. "I don't know if Olagkoa's powers are waning, or if these new Shells are damaged in some way, but we know it has more than one means of attack. The mental strike."

Farla's eyes flashed in the moonlight. "And you want Ranin to counter that when it does?"

"I believed if we were outside the direct line of that offensive, we would be less affected. But yes, I hoped she might be able to do something about it."

"It's alright, Farla." Ranin gave her friend a soft smile. "This is why we came."

"I know," the pony-tailed woman muttered. "I just don't like it."

As if on cue, the pain erupted, searing into their minds like a swarm of daggers. Eris gritted his teeth, jaw aching, to hold back a shout. Tal whimpered beside him, a small, choked sound. Off to the side, Holfast groaned.

Realizing its planned offensive was ineffective, Olagkoa had unleashed one of its more powerful strikes, sending out a mental blast. The stronghold inhabitants, along with the companions, dropped to the ground, writhing in agony.

Except Ranin.

The woman reached out with her mind, seeking the creature's consciousness. In some other plane or level of awareness, she found it. Twisted and dark, its sole focus was to inflict suffering on others.

At the speed of thought, she took a mental breath and drove her will into it. The beast roared in her skull, and she joined with her own brief scream before her mind fell into darkness.

Back in the physical world, Olagkoa released an ear-splitting shriek that echoed through the night sky. Ranin's strike halted its assault, and the inhabitants of the city, along with the companions outside, began to recover from the mental onslaught.

Eyes wide with tears, Farla scrambled across the ground to Ranin's crumpled body. The woman still breathed, but didn't respond to her friend's frantic shaking.

Eris jumped to his feet, no longer concerned about their location being detected, and moved to the pair. "She'll be alright in a bit," he told Farla, though he wasn't sure of that. Each encounter with Olagkoa's mind left her comatose for a period.

Once Tal and Holfast stirred, groaning but conscious, Eris turned his gaze back toward the army. The undead seemed unaffected by the psychic blast, but its scream from Ranin's counterattack caused them difficulty. Ranks of Shells swayed as if caught in a fierce wind. Those climbing the cliff spasmed and lost their grip, plummeting into the water below with wet thuds and sickening splashes.

So it is having trouble controlling them! It's probably never had this many under its power before. That might be our chance.

"There it is!" a voice rang out from the wall. Grekorn. "Every archer, strike the monstrosity!"

The soldier had taken charge of Ludholm's remaining archers and directed them toward the creature, finally accepting it was the cause of the assault. When it had moved out from the rear of the army, it became an easier target.

A score of arrows rained down on the tentacled beast, nearly half striking true. Their metal tips sunk deep into its flesh, with the long shafts protruding outward. At Olagkoa's current size, however, they looked more like seamstress needles and proved even less effective. A second barrage saw more projectiles hitting the mark, but they still had no effect to the creature.

"They're on the move!" Tal shouted.

Eris shifted his attention back to the army, where the undead had stopped their swaying and straightened, as if awaiting orders. But the biggest shift came from the cliff. The Shells climbing the walls suddenly reversed course, scrambling down like retreating insects. Even the ones at the top started their descent. Only those that collapsed near the barrier remained unmoving.

Not waiting for their comrades, the animated soldiers turned as one to face the forest edge where the companions were hidden. *By the sword, they're coming for us!* Eris struggled to force down his panic when the Shells began marching in their direction, Olagkoa in the lead. A few arrows still struck it from the ramparts, but the archers stopped when they realized they were ineffective.

"Holfast! Help me with Ranin!" He hastily pushed the hovering Farla back as he got his arms under the unconscious woman.

The erdi'zal sprinted over to his aid. "Put her over my hindquarters. I can carry her easily."

It was a rare offer. Despite their resemblance to horses, his kind despised the comparison and rarely let anyone treat them in such a fashion. Still, when Savanah was wounded when confronting Olagkoa in the Undercastle, Holfast carried her to their encampment. He similarly helped Ranin, draping her over his strong back like a blanket.

"Farla, go with him," Eris ordered. "Move as quickly as you can without her falling off. Tal, you go too."

"Oh no! I know that look!" Tal jabbed a finger at his chest. "You've figged some blank-brained idea of throwing yourself at that thing again, haven't you? I'm not letting you!"

He grimaced at her accusation, but she had a point about his previous attempts to defeat the creature himself. He had tried multiple times to prevent her from coming with him, as he didn't want her caught in what he considered his fate. *But there are more I have to protect now, and I can't let them be hurt again!* "This time, you're wrong. I know when the odds against me are too great. I'll be right behind you. Now move!"

The five hurried back to the gate, with Eris and Tal monitoring the activity below. With the water up past their shins, the Shells' march had become a slog. Olagkoa stood too tall for the rising lake to bother it, but it seemed to understand the troubles of its army and matched the pace of the undead. As it shoved itself along, smaller tentacles worked at yanking the arrows from its flesh. Each wound oozed with brownish-orange ichor once the tips were extracted, but the openings didn't last long as the creature's natural regeneration went to work.

Tal reached the gate first, fists pounding. "Open up! Let us in, you cowards!" When no immediate reply came, she grabbed the hammer at her hip and started striking it against the barrier, the clang of metal against metal echoing loudly. "We saved your worthless hides! Open up!"

Eris gritted his teeth. *I shouldn't have led them all out! They followed me blindly, like before.* Daymon had said they would not be allowed to return, and he seemed to be keeping his word.

The soldier scanned the area for any other cover they might use while Tal continued her physical and verbal assault. A wide road flowed west, toward the river, from the gate, with thick forest on each side. They could try losing themselves among the trees, but they would be forced to go slow as long as Ranin remained unconscious on Holfast's back. If Olagkoa was intent on finding them, would that route be enough to discourage it? The alternative was to stick to the outer wall and hope to find another entrance along there, perhaps where the stone had crumbled...

Tal's hammering stopped as the gate abruptly swung open a few feet. "Enter quick or be left out for good," the guard's gruff voice ordered. Daymon had taken pity on them and changed his mind!

The five shoved their way inside, and the iron barrier pulled shut behind them, its crossbar dropping back into place. There they encountered Grekorn, his expression twisted in fury. "You will follow me. Now!"

Eris's face burned with anger. They had come there to help Ludholm, with one of them hurt because of it, and found themselves instead being ordered about. "I will join you, but only after I make sure *my* people are safe." He could feel the knight's eyes boring into his back, but he focused on Farla. "How is she?"

The woman bit her lip. "She's starting to recover. She just needs more rest."

"Then tend to her." He faced the erdi'zal. "I am grateful, Holfast, for your aid. I know the rarity of what you did for her."

Holfast dipped his head in a gesture of approval, his ears twitching faintly at the acknowledgment. Eris then turned to the commander, who seethed as if he might erupt. "I am ready. Lead on."

Grekorn led him and Tal back to the platform at the wall and up the rickety stairs to where Daymon stood watching the grassland below. Both Olagkoa and the Shells continued their slog toward the southwest bank. Before long, they would reach where the companions had been.

Ludholm's leader appeared only slightly less enraged than Grekorn as he addressed the pair. "I approved your reentry only so you might explain your actions," he told them sharply. "What happened out there? Are you in league with this abomination?"

Tal trembled, her expression darkening at his words. "Listen here, you miserable burral-hum — "

Eris swiftly cut her off with his hand over her mouth. Her glare shifted to him, and with it, she delivered a kick to his shin. "What my partner was about to say," he began around clenched teeth, "is we are not working with the creature. Our goal is to find a way to destroy it. We strayed from that task to aid you. We could have let them strike without warning."

"And we could have struck you down as soon as you approached our gate," Grekorn countered. "Or left you to die out there just now."

"You wouldn't have a chance to do either had we not alerted you to the threat," Eris snapped back, then took a deep breath as he released Tal. Fortunately, she had the sense to keep quiet. "The point is, we are on the same side. So kindly refrain from demanding anything from us."

The knight opened his mouth to reply when Daymon lay a hand on his shoulder. "His logic is sound. We owe you our gratitude, but we still need an explanation for these events. My citizens, as well as myself, were subjected to immense agony soon after you left our city. How do you explain that?"

How do you explain anything about this situation without sounding like a madman? "The creature has powerful mental abilities. It can read your mind, make you see things that aren't there, and even project pain and fear into those around it."

"That is absurd," Grekorn snapped. "No one can do that."

"*It* does," Eris responded. He'd had a similar reaction once. "You see it leading an army of corpses. You feel it in your head, but still doubt it?"

"You knew it would attack in this way and fled?" Daymon asked in a calmer voice than his knight.

"I knew it would attack this way and moved to stop it!" Eris retorted. "I thought if we were out of the direct line of the creature, the effects would be less."

"But you didn't stop it," the larger soldier accused.

Eris clenched his jaw, feeling the pressure build as he fought to suppress a biting reply. "If we didn't, do you think you'd be walking upright now? The assault lasted only seconds because we *did* stop it. One of my companions is recovering from the strain, and we hope she hasn't sustained any permanent damage."

"Is this true?" Daymon asked.

Grekorn's expression softened at the question. "They did return with a woman over the back of their erdi'zal."

"Their names are Ranin and Holfast!" Tal snarled at him.

Daymon stroked his beard. "An erdi allowed a human to ride him. That is a rarity. How did you halt the assault?"

"After her first encounter with the creature, Ranin managed to fight against it. Each attempt takes a great toll on her, but she has some ability to stop it temporarily," Eris explained, taking hope in the city leader's willingness to listen.

Grekorn, however, refused to accept his words. "Then why didn't you do that when you first arrived?"

"That's odd," Tal commented dryly. "You look like a soldier, but you talk like a coward. Need a woman to fight your battles?"

The rage instantly returned to the knight's expression. "I'll see you tossed in the dungeon for that!"

"Grekorn! Stand down!" Daymon ordered, apparently as fed up with the man's quarreling as Eris was with Tal's habit of provoking. "You will do no such thing. They have done nothing but help us, even if it isn't as you desire."

A shout from the wall drew their attention back to the activity below. The Shells had arrived at the side of the grasslands and a few had already begun the climb. With it being more of a slope than a sheer face, they made progress rather easily. Soon, a row had ascended to the top, with more following.

"They're coming up for a second attack!"

It certainly appeared to be the case. As more reached the tree line, they were forced to fan out toward the main gate of the city, the way the companions had come. None of them approached Ludholm's entrance, however. Instead, they only moved to make room for more of the undead soldiers.

"Grekorn, get your men to the gate and ensure it's fortified. They are going to push through there or surround us. We are likely in for a siege."

As the man dashed down the stairs to carry out the orders, Eris scanned what little of the wall he could see. The Shells were staying back, but whether by instinct or command, he couldn't tell. Either they retained enough intelligence to recognize that moving too close would bring them the same troubles as the rest, or Olagkoa had conveyed that order to them. *There are too many things we don't understand about all of this.*

After several minutes of watching the Shells creep up the steep slope, Eris, Tal, and Daymon moved to a section of the wall nearer the gate for a better view. Dozens of others watched from other positions, including Farla and Ranin. Still recovering, the dazed woman clung to her friend for support, which the shorter female gladly gave.

Instead of breaching the barrier or surrounding Ludholm, the Shells drifted down the road. Nearly half the army had ascended out of the filling riverbed while the rest waited with the patience of the dead for their opportunity to rise. Throughout all of it, the soldiers made not a sound, their eerie silence more chilling than any battle cry.

They marched near enough now for the city's remaining population to confirm their identities. Even in the moonlight, the deep orange and light brown hues of their Ludholm uniforms were visible, as well as the blue and gray outfits of Zatreus's forces. Many still bore blood stains and rips from their last encounter, which Olagkoa's magic could not repair.

More unsettling were the faces of the Shells. Eris and Tal had seen the two sides race into battle, fueled by the creature's own bloodlust, and their subsequent slaughter and reanimation. It had been easier to think of them as simply objects Olagkoa constructed, not the remains of people. Seeing them now, marching by with no other indication of life except that they were walking, shook the onlookers to the core. Vacant stares. Blank expressions. No spark of memory, no trace of the individuals they'd been.

A hush fell over the observers, and then a few began sobbing. More voices of grief joined in as understanding spread. They had won the war, but lost so much more. Friends, family, loved ones. All victims of the tentacled monstrosity.

Several more tense minutes passed as the city occupants wept for their loss while fearing those they mourned might resume their assault. But while the number of soldiers outside their walls increased, none approached. Instead, they continued pushing their numbers down the dirt road leading away from the gate.

Daymon's voice dropped to a whisper. "Diovola smiles on us tonight. We may yet survive to see morning."

Eris nodded, but said nothing. The Shells had moved on, but Olagkoa remained in the riverbed. At first, he thought it was merely watching the army's rear to ensure its soldiers departed safely. However, the creature had never displayed even a trace of concern for anything but itself. He understood that it might not be able to leave.

A few shouts along the wall suggested others had noticed the same. The evil which had massacred their people and threatened them now sat in the bottom of the valley, trapped.

"We've caught it!" Tal cried out, a grin splitting her face. "The army won't go anywhere without it!"

"And that means we're stuck here, too," he reminded her grimly. "And it might just have them attack the city again for spite."

"Can this beast swim?" Daymon asked, his expression brightening as well.

"I'm afraid so," Eris replied. He and Tal had watched it glide effortlessly across the Leosonee on its way to the grasslands two days before, so it wouldn't drown. "Once the water's high enough, it'll reach the shore easily."

"Then we are as trapped as it is." The ruler gave a harsh laugh. "To finally regain our lake, only to have our kingdom destroyed. Perhaps the gods are not in our favor, after all."

"We'll have to see. It's going to try, at least." Eris pointed to where Olagkoa had begun shoving itself toward the slope. While not nearly as steep as the one by the city, the wall of rocks, dirt, and grass remained formidable.

As the last Shells began their climb, the creature curled its rear tentacles and drove them into the waterlogged ground. This propelled the beast upward a surprising distance, but as the limbs folded to find a new base to dig into, Olagkoa toppled backward into the growing lake with an enormous splash.

The water level had not risen nearly enough to be a threat to the monstrosity, but a cheer went up along the wall all the same. To see an enemy fail, even momentarily, was a reason to celebrate.

Eris half expected a fresh burst of pain to strike down the hecklers, but no such attack came. It was either too focused on the task, still stunned by Ranin's mental shove, or uncaring about the opinions of the defenders. After another minute, the creature twisted upright with a grotesque flex of limbs, then hurled itself forward.

It repeated the attempt, heaving itself upward. Before it readjusted itself for a fresh thrust, however, tentacles from the front lashed out, striking the ground with their single-clawed tips. They drove in like pitons, holding the creature in place long enough for the rear limbs to shove again.

The same citizen who cheered before now groaned, seeing their enemy escaping. "Oh great," Tal muttered. "It's getting away."

"Considering what it can do, I believe that's for the best," he told her. They had similarly driven it out of Zatreus, hoping it would cause less damage outside that city's fortifications. "I'd rather have it fleeing a fight than starting one."

Once it reached the top, Olagkoa resumed its normal means of travel, its heavy bulk squelching over the grass-covered soil. Now level with the city, the towering beast loomed, its full size finally on display. While not yet as tall as the walls, Eris couldn't help but wonder if the monstrosity might knock them over itself. *If it knew the poor condition of them, it might try.*

Fortunately, it seemed to have accepted defeat. It plodded along behind its army as it marched down the road. Those watching inside remained quiet, their former bravado gone. Only once it vanished from view did the tension break. Some collapsed, weeping, a mix of sorrow and terror. Others cursed it and the misfortune that had fallen upon Ludholm. A few raised their heads and voices in thanks to whichever god they believed was responsible for their salvation.

Daymon ordered the bodies outside the walls to be retrieved for examination. Soldiers hauled in corpses, one after another, their limbs limp and uniforms crusted with blood. Whatever Olagkoa had used to give them a semblance of life had vanished, leaving them once again as unmoving cadavers.

"I know what I saw, but I am still struggling to understand it," Daymon admitted as he stared down at the deceased body of a middle-aged man. He had been stabbed through the heart, as evidenced by the clean slice through his shirt and the dried blood stains around it. The flesh beneath it, while pale and clammy, was intact. "What kind of being could do this?"

"That's what some of my people are trying to find out," Eris explained. "You said something earlier that suggests you met a few."

"I have. A trio. Grekorn and his men captured them in the woods. They informed me about this creature and its attempt to breach Zatreus's defenses. I confess I did not truly believe their tale."

"That must have been Vyncent, Savanah, and Camille," Eris confirmed with a nod. Hamund had told him of their mission, along with a similar task Leda, Wynna, Malwin, and Erling had undertaken. *And me as well, it seems.*

"What happened to them?" Tal asked.

"They escaped with some spies Lightreaver had sent to infiltrate my guards, nearly setting the city on fire." He relayed the details without emotion, his voice flat, as if the anger had burned out.

Eris chuckled. He wasn't sure which of the three had done that, but suspected any of them could be the culprit. "I beg your forgiveness for them. Their intention, and mine, is not to cause you trouble, but only to stop what you witnessed tonight."

"I accept that. In truth, I believe they did me a favor. As you have." A smile returned to Lord Daymon's lips as he clapped his hands sharply. "Now, you and your companions must help us in celebration. Not only is the war over, but you have saved us from another disaster this night."

"Your people don't seem in a party mood," Tal muttered, nodding toward the growing crowd in the street as those who had retreated into their homes came out to learn what had happened. Their reactions were as mixed as those who had observed the skirmish, causing many to resume their crying and adulations.

The ruler glanced around, then nodded calmly. "It will take some time to process these events, but despite our losses, this is still a momentous occasion. We have at last righted a wrong perpetrated on our city a thousand years ago. I have a proposal. I want you to be our first ambassadors of the new alliance between Ludholm and Zatreus."

"I doubt peace will come that easily," Eris told him. "I cannot speak for Zatreus, however. Neither can Ranin nor Farla, for we are from Talidith and have only been granted permission to stay as refugees. Tal, on the other hand — "

" — is currently busy aiding him in our quest to stop the beast," she finished for him. "If not for me, he'd have snuffed it already."

"She's not lying," the man admitted. "We must continue on, and soon, to follow the monster and its army. Though Ludholm is safe now, Wayela isn't. If we don't stop it, many more will die."

Daymon's gaze went from Eris to Tal, then back again, as if trying to determine the truth in their words. Finally, he nodded. "I respect your dedication. We are in your debt. I wish you luck on your hunt."

"And I hope for a brighter future for you and your city," Eris replied. He grabbed Tal's arm and led her toward the gate, eager to get away from Ludholm and its ruler as soon as possible. Though they had stopped its destruction by Olagkoa, he doubted the kingdom's troubles were behind it. While he had never met the High Monarch of Zatreus, he was certain she wouldn't let the fall of the Riverwall go unpunished.

"Hunt, eh?" Tal said once they were out of earshot of Daymon. "I like that. Makes it sound as if we have some control over our fate."

Eris waved a hand toward Ranin and Farla to join them. He saw Holfast standing near the gate, as if anticipating their departure. Their horses stood beside him, none the worse for the night's events.

You might still choose your path, Tal. But mine's already written. Either I end Olagkoa, or it ends me.

Chapter Five
THE CRAWLING DARK

T HE TUNNEL SLOPED steadily downward, its damp stone echoing with the faint scrape of their boots. Shimi Zar led at a cautious pace, watchful for any activity in the gloom ahead. Except for the occasional cluster of *siklarag*, their pebble-like bodies scrambling out of the light like tiny avalanches, they appeared to be alone. For the moment.

"How far?" Leda whispered at last.

"Far," Shimi Zar said, without slowing.

"Why not hide it nearer the entrance?" Wynna snapped. Her pulse beat a thunderous rhythm. She hated the dark, hated not knowing what waited in it. She couldn't face their undead attackers again, though. Forced between two disagreeable choices, she had trouble deciding who to be angry at.

"Hiding." The answer was obvious. If you don't want an item to be found, stash it where no people live. Wynna still wasn't happy with it.

"Are these things attracted to light?" Leda whispered, glancing at the torch. "Should we put it out?"

"No!" Wynna hissed. Her whole body tightened like a spring. "It might be the only thing keeping them away."

"Blind," Malwin grunted from behind. He and Erling had moved to the rear to keep an eye on the women, while Graypaw strolled between them.

"There! Now stop making suggestions like that!" Wynna seethed, spinning to glare at Leda.

They continued in relative silence, the only noise being the gentle scraping of their feet on the stone and the constant sound of Cutie jabbering in Leda's ear. His talking was probably too faint for anyone beyond the companions to hear, but it rubbed against Wynna's already raw nerves. "Keep your pet quiet!" she whispered.

"He's scared!" Leda shot back.

"We're all scared." Something caught her eye, a movement on the wall. "I — " A piercing scream choked off the rest of her sentence.

Her friends rushed to her side as she jumped away from the stone. "What is it?" Erling reached for his bow, searching for the cause of her outburst.

"There! It's hideous!" She waved toward the black wall, then quickly drew her hand back. A third of the way up the wall perched a creature composed of wiry hair and spindly legs.

Malwin stepped closer to it, bending over as he examined it. The intruder, a spider, smaller than a handspan, possessed far more limbs than those commonly found in the forest and the corners of people's houses. This looked like someone had stacked several of them together, one atop the next, with each black-hair covered leg ending in a half-inch long barbed spike. Its only indication of front or back came from a pair of pinchers set under one end.

The egyzemor seemed unconcerned by its presence as he casually pulled a knife from his belt and brought it forward. With a swift stroke, he drove the tip through the thing's body. A faint, squelching pop was audible in the sudden quiet, and it shuddered and twitched. Wynna groaned.

With a grin, Malwin held up the blade, the still-spasming creature impaled on its point, for the others to see. "Pokfin," he explained. Wynna hid her face and scurried behind Erling, who, along with Leda, looked disgusted by the monstrosity. Both were animal lovers, but this resembled a creature ripped from a nightmare. Shimi Zar only glanced at it, her attention on the tunnel ahead.

When it stopped trembling and its legs relaxed, Malwin plucked it off the knife and popped it in his mouth. After a few crunches and a loud swallow, he stood up. "Yum." The others shuddered, and Wynna tried not to retch.

"It seems we don't need to worry about any smaller threats," Erling noted wryly. "Our friend will turn them into snacks."

Malwin gave a rumbling laugh, breaking the tension, and they resumed with lighter spirits. There were no more instances of pokfin or other worrisome visitors. Soon they came to a split in the tunnel, with passages sloping down and away on both sides, while the original continued on. They all looked similar, but after a pause, Shimi Zar had them follow her down to the right.

Erling blinked his two sets of eyes as he tried to pierce the darkness. The damp, chilled air pressed down heavier. "I believe we are entering into worm territory. Keep watch for anything moving. Let's hope we can see them before they detect us."

"And if we don't?" Leda prodded.

He pointed toward the blade in her hand. "Then I hope you are skilled with that sword."

Leda grimaced and decided against revealing the sword's rusted and dull condition. She thought of it as a reminder of Aedan, not a weapon, and never gave serious consideration to getting it sharpened. She trained and could handle a blade, but doubted this one would hold up in a fight.

Soon they came to another split, but continued on straight. At the third, Shimi Zar guided them into the left passage. A little further along, passing two more splits, she veered right again. The glowing fungus grew abundantly here, along with a black growth of round spores lining the base of the walls. Erling reached out to touch some, but Malwin quickly blocked him. "Is it dangerous?" the erdi'zal asked, withdrawing his hand.

Malwin nodded. "Ow."

When they arrived at another split, Shimi Zar signaled for them to stop. This time, she shifted her gaze between the two routes, her expression locked in a frown.

The uncertainty made Wynna nervous. "I thought she knew the way!"

"Has changed," Shimi Zar said.

"What? How could tunnels in stone change?"

"The orifereg are diggers," Erling reminded her. "They added their own routes to the existing ones."

Leda's lips pressed tight. "So what Shimi Zar knows might no longer be right?"

"Is right," the female egyzemor gruffed. "Left." She straightened her shoulders and took them into the leftmost passage. It seemed no different from the others, but after they had walked for a minute, she abruptly stopped. "Shhh!"

The rest halted and stared ahead. From the darkness, they could hear a faint rustling, like a heavy mass being slowly dragged over the ground. A moment later, they could make out movement. Something large and sluggish approached. "What now?" Erling asked through clenched teeth, all interest in meeting one of the oversized worms drained away, replaced by a powerful urge to flee.

Graypaw trilled, but it was a warning, not a suggestion, as he turned toward the way they had come. Malwin looked too and recognized the same stilted activity. "Another."

"Quick!" Shimi Zar shouted, then dashed forward a short distance to a side passage. It slanted sharply, and the others stumbled as they followed her in. They sprinted briefly before the tunnel forked, but she only hesitated a second before veering left as one of the orifereg was coming up their way on the right. In a flash of the torchlight, they got a closer look at it, and instantly regretted it.

There was no face, only a huge, gaping mouth, lined with rows of short, thick teeth, worn down by biting through rock but still strong enough to crush anything softer that came along. Behind the jaw was a dark gullet descending into a stone-dissolving stomach.

They rounded the corner at a run, trying to forget the vision, and stumbled into a vast cavern. Pale fungi coated the ceiling, shedding a cold, sickly yellow light over the area below, revealing more of the black spores circling the perimeter and three more of the immense grubs lying still, as if dozing.

The torchlight joined the fungal glow, highlighting every grotesque detail of the beasts sprawled before them. When Malwin compared them to houses, he understated their size, as a single-story cottage would have easily slipped down the throat of one. Their bodies were rust-colored and fat with ridged segments, each topped with a dense, helmet-like dome of gray flesh. Dozens of limp tendrils jutted from their bloated sides, each two feet long and twitching feebly, as if whatever purpose they once served rotted away. Over it all hung the sickly-sweet stench of burned fruit, thick enough to taste.

Four tunnels branched from the chamber's edges, perhaps carved by ancient miners, or by the very monsters that now infested it.

"Wrong turn," Erling whispered as he and the others skidded to a halt.

"Maybe we can go back." Leda took a step toward the entrance, but as she did, her foot slipped and she stumbled into the wall. She wasn't hurt, but as she stood, her boot brushed against a few of the black spores. They squirted a jet of yellow liquid in defense, spraying her boots and part of her hand. Her flesh burned where the secretion touched, and she yelped in pain.

At her cry, Malwin leaped forward to yank her away, but she was already retreating. Others had also heard, though. The worms awoke with a jolt and started moving, slinking toward the source of the sound.

Panic took over. They bolted for the tunnel, only to skid to a halt. The worm they had passed before now blocked their way, dragging its bulk across the stone, filling the passage wall to wall. There was no escape through that route.

"Back!" At Shimi Zar's order, they turned again and tumbled down into the chamber. The worms there were still closing in, but space remained between them, and the female egyzemor took advantage of it, sprinting between the two on the right. Leda followed, but before the others could do the same, the center worm flopped over, blocking their route.

That created a gap on the left side, and the rest of the party rapidly pivoted to it. "This way!" Erling shouted, and the four raced through it and out the first tunnel, with the erdi'zal in the lead. The passage was darker than the cavern, and Wynna was running blind. Only a shout from the others alerted her to the danger when they came to a three-way split. She saw a flash of teeth and screamed, her full-blown panic causing her to swerve.

In total darkness, she kept moving, half sprinting, half stumbling down the sloped corridor, too terrified to realize that Malwin and Erling had gone the other direction.

She had no idea how far she'd run. The surge of terror faded, giving way to breathless dread. The dark encompassed everything. No glowing fungi, no light. Just blackness pressing in from every side.

She froze, straining her eyes and ears in search of her friends. There was no one. "Erling?" Her voice was barely above a whisper. "Malwin?" she asked the darkness again, louder this time. "Leda? Are you there?"

Silence. *Looks like I'm on my own. Figures!* Despite her bravado, she felt panic creeping up her body, threatening to consume her. *It's alright. There is nothing here. I just have to find my way back. Can't be far.*

She took a few steps to the left, her weight shifting hesitantly, extending her arm to locate the wall. The image of the pokfin flashed in her mind, and suddenly she imagined hundreds of them surrounding her in the gloom. She began to retract her hand, but caught herself. *Stop it! There is nothing here!*

When her fingers found only damp, uneven rock, she sighed, and started moving forward again, stepping carefully on the rough stone ground. *There is nothing here. There is nothing here*, she told herself over and over as she crept ahead.

Her fingertips grazed a soft, slick form. She yanked her hand back. *Alright. There is something here. Just don't touch it.* When she reached for the wall again, she found only empty space. There was another corridor, but she had no more idea where it led than the one she was currently following. *Still, it can't hurt to explore it a little. Maybe some of the glowing growths are close enough that I can grab a few for light.*

She stepped toward the opening, straining her eyes to see beyond, but unlike the rest of the tunnels, the floor felt slick. Her foot slipped. Arms flailing, she missed the wall and tumbled, a sharp scream tearing from her throat as she plunged into the dark.

"WE HAVE TO go back for them!"

Shimi Zar and Leda stood in a small chamber, catching their breath as they stared at the giant maw outside. After fleeing the cavern, they'd darted through four more winding passages, each one echoing with the slithering scrape of pursuit, before stumbling into the narrow room. Every turn they made brought them up against another orifereg wriggling after them, drawn to the woman's outcry or the smell of fresh meat. Fortunately, they couldn't squeeze their immense forms through the tight opening of the alcove and had to be satisfied with terrifying their prey from the passageway.

"Will," Shimi Zar answered the demand, "Not now."

Cutie chirped at Leda's shoulder. She had almost forgotten he was there and quickly slipped the sword into her belt so she could take him into her hands. He had learned from his first fall to hold on to her hair, but the running around had still scared him, and he sat trembling in her palm. "Don't worry. We're safe now," she told him, her fingers light on his wings until he relaxed. *If only it were this easy to calm my own fears,* she thought, listening to the oversized monstrosity scraping at the stone outside, like a dog at a door. "You've lived here for a while, haven't you?" she asked Shimi Zar. "How do the egyzemors handle these things?"

"Avoid them." Her voice was back to what Leda assumed was her natural cadence, shedding the stoic, terse manner of the race she was impersonating. Shimi Zar was a bisegus, a shapeshifter, and had been living among the single-eyed giants in the mountain when they met her. Only Leda knew her true nature. "Sometimes, if one reaches an upper level, or one of the more foolish of their kind wants to test his skills, they organize a hunt." She glanced at the rusted blade on the woman's hip. "With weapons much deadlier than your own."

"This is more a keepsake than a weapon." Leda's thoughts went again to Aedan. The young fisherman she fell in love with was currently in the thrall of a monster from another world. What began as a search to save him had already taken her further than she'd ever imagined, and they all had a longer road ahead.

"So it's useless."

Not to me! If they did have any hope of reaching that road, they would have to get past the orifereg at their door. "How did you hide the artifact down here without getting trapped before?"

Shimi Zar shrugged. "There were a lot fewer of them back then."

"But you knew there was a colony down here, and you still led us here," she pressed. "You must have a plan."

"I knew there were a few. But that wouldn't matter once we had the artifact."

"Why? What does it do?"

"Drives them away."

Leda wiped her eyes. The torch Shimi Zar wielded, fueled by pulveld, burned with little smoke, but it wasn't clean, and the soot was building up. A glance at the entrance told her the worm outside blocked their ventilation. *If it was smart, it would block it completely and suffocate us. But then it probably couldn't eat us. Unless...* "This thing tunnels through stone. What if it decides to chew its way through?"

"We'd die." Seeing the woman's discomfort, she moved the torch nearer to the opening to vent it there. "But it doesn't eat raw rock. It has to soften it up first. It makes acid and spits it over what it wants to consume. That starts to dissolve it. After an hour, the orifereg gobbles the mess down."

"I guess that's a relief." Leda looked down at the diamur in her hand. Her attention had calmed him to the point he was nodding off in her palm. "How do you know so much about them?"

"You think I would hide the artifact here without knowing about its protectors? I even thought about taking their form when I brought it in, so they would believe I was one of them. But they are blind, so it wouldn't have mattered."

"That would make you too light, right?"

"You know a bit about our physiology, eh? No, I would be about the same weight, just spread really thin over an enormous body. No match against any of these if they decided I was an enemy." Shimi Zar paused, then added, "Or a really good friend."

Leda missed the joke as she watched the orifereg beyond the opening, running the flesh around its mouth over the stone outside. It conjured to her mind images of a dog whetting its chops, expecting a tasty meal. "How long does it take to make this acid?"

The fake egyzemor blinked and moved her lips, as if making complex computations in her head. "If it didn't have any when we ran into it, we've probably got a few more minutes before it's made enough to destroy that wall."

Minutes! "Can't you do something? You're a bisegus."

Shimi Zar's expression darkened. "You said you wouldn't reveal that to anyone."

"Who's going to care? The worm? You're already speaking very unlike an egyzemor."

"I can't risk revealing myself to the others."

"Even if it means saving the world?"

"Would you toss away your life to save the world?" Shimi Zar asked, turning the question back on the woman.

"I would risk it. And considering our situation, I would say I already am."

"You are a fool! You don't really think you are *that* important, do you?"

Leda's face flushed. "If we can find these items and stop the creature, then yes, I am."

Shimi Zar let out a dry, derisive chuckle. "And if you can't, what do you expect to happen? Rapria falls?"

"I- I guess."

"You still don't know everything. Your little quest is only one possible solution."

Leda felt her frustration rising. This bisegus was very different from Camille. "So why help us?"

"That is my assignment."

"Assignment? From whom?"

Shimi Zar waved a hand toward the entrance. "The one you seek after this. Nastina."

"I still don't see why you can't do something now. The others aren't here, and they could be hurt!"

"Can't you do something?" Shimi Zar used not just the same tone, but an exact mimicking of the woman's voice. "You're a Shiftling."

Leda had been abandoned as a baby and raised by Wynna's family. Earlier that day, she had met her real mother and father, but they were voladorms, the winged race that lived atop the mountains, not humans. And she wasn't alone. Other human children had been born to different races. When one is found, according to Shimi Zar, the child is taken from its parents, told what it is, taught how to handle the changes, and allowed to live its life normally. Or as normal as life could be for someone caught between two races, able to shift form but never belonging to either.

"But I don't know how to change." Tears welled again as she glanced at Shimi Zar's hand. "What about fire? We've got a torch. Can we drive them away with it?"

The suggestion drew a frown. "Didn't you say you liked animals? And now you want to roast one?"

"No! But we don't have much of a choice." She covered Cutie so he wouldn't hear her question. "Do you plan to die in here?"

Shimi Zar stared down at her with a single eye. "I'm not going to die here. And neither are you. Or your friends. But you would be wise not to wave fire in front of an orifereg."

"You have a way out, then?"

"I might. We need to lure the worm away so we can get out. Do you know of anything small enough to sneak past it and make a commotion?" In case her question was too subtle, she nodded at Leda's cupped hands.

"No!" The woman stepped back and brought her protected companion to her chest. He was a gift from her parents that day, and she already felt a strong attachment to him. "We are not using Cutie as bait! He is terrified of those creatures!"

"Of course he is!" Shimi Zar bobbed her head. "No doubt he wants to be as far from them as he can be, right?"

"Absolutely!"

"Then this is his chance! He just flies out past the beast and he's free! He will be the safest of all of us!"

But Leda wasn't fooled. "He won't be safe when it chases him!"

"He won't get caught. You saw how slow they move. I'm sure he could easily outpace it."

"I said no!" The woman moved to the far side of the room, which was only ten feet away, and shielded the diamur from Shimi Zar's sight. "Why don't you do it yourself? You can transform into something that flies."

"And possibly run into our companions? They'd know what I really am."

"No, they wouldn't," Leda encouraged with the same tone she had used to dismiss the risk to Cutie. "Besides, if they were that close to us, the worm would be chasing them already."

"I can't take the chance."

"Then we have to find another solution," Leda concluded. "Maybe the others will — what?" Inside her cupped palms, Cutie chattered and shoved against two of her fingers. She uncovered him, and he immediately leaped into the air to hover in front of her face, his bat-like wings beating hard. He waved his tiny hands at her and began a series of rapid chirps and whistles, a desperate, high-pitched plea. "What's the matter?"

"Sounds as if he wants to try our plan." Shimi Zar took a few steps closer and bent over to look at the diamur. "Is that what you want?"

"Stop it!" Leda snapped. "He doesn't understand us. He — " At the egyzemor's words, the tiny figure zipped over to her face and clapped his hands. His reaction was too exact to be a coincidence. "Cutie, is that right? Do you want to lure the thing out there away?"

For an answer, he flitted back to her, clapping three times. There was no doubt he understood, though Leda didn't know how. "Are you sure?" she asked. He shuddered, then gave a hesitant clap. His meaning was clear. He was afraid, but he would do it.

Shimi Zar and Leda moved near the entrance, letting the diamur approach at his own pace. He fluttered anxiously after them, pausing a few times, then screwing up his courage and continuing forward. As if sensing his apprehension, the orifereg shoved its outer jaw against the opening and exhaled a putrid breath that hit them like a wave of rotten meat and stagnant water, causing the light to flicker and the trio to scowl.

"Now all you have to do is fly out past the worm and down the hall." Leda held up a palm and Cutie plopped into it. "We want it to chase you, so lead it as far away as you can, then come back! Do not let it catch you!"

"And be noisy!" Shimi Zar added. "Chirp or squawk or whatever. They hunt by sound!"

"Don't call it a hunt!" Leda brought her other hand up between the pair. "He's already scared!"

"That's good. It will make him faster. Ready?"

"Give me a moment!" She lifted him close to her face. "You be careful out there. And remember, I love you."

Shimi Zar groaned. "Just do it before he thinks twice about it!"

"I'm doing it!" Leda moved closer to the entrance until the orifereg's teeth were within arm's reach. It was smaller than the others — its head not quite touching the ceiling of the passage — but still big enough to swallow them all in a single gulp.

With one last whisper of encouragement, she held him as high as she could. A foot-tall opening sat at the top, where the worm's hideous lips didn't cover. Just adequate for the petite flyer to zip through. Leda inhaled deeply and shouted, "Go now!"

Cutie dove through, wings tucked tight, then snapped them open on the other side to catch himself. He zipped a dozen feet through the tunnel before turning to face his foe.

Despite their size, diamurs could produce quite a lot of sound when encouraged to. Their normal chattering could be punctuated with chirps, whistles, and brief cries. Cutie brought all of these into play now, releasing a cacophony on the ears of the orifereg.

However, his tiny body lacked the lung capacity to raise his clamor above the level of a loud voice, and the worm showed no interest in pursuit. Even when he anxiously flew up to within ten feet of the creature's mouth and repeated his discordant concert, he got no reaction.

From inside the alcove, the females heard his efforts but saw they had no effect. Shimi Zar scowled, thrusting the torch into Leda's hands. "We need something bigger."

Before the woman could reply, she began to change. Her body contracted, her chest puffed out, and her legs shrank to sticks. Muscular arms flattened and sprouted feathers which spread to the rest of her form. The single eye dominating her face split into two small orbs while her nose straightened into a beak. In a matter of moments, the immense egyzemor had become a diminutive sparrow.

With a curt nod, she launched into the air and glided through the same opening Cutie had used. Once on the other side, she flapped to the far end of the tunnel, the diamur following. There, Shimi Zar landed and began transforming again. Soon she was an egyzemor once more. Facing the monster, she inhaled deeply and bellowed. The outburst startled Cutie, and he zipped away.

The roar got the worm moving. It started lumbering after the sound, eager for easy prey. Once it passed, Leda sprinted out of the room and took off in the opposite direction.

Not waiting to be caught, Shimi Zar turned back to a sparrow just as Cutie returned. She flicked a wing at him and darted toward the orifereg. She aimed for a corner near the top where the worm flesh didn't quite connect with the wall and hurtled through, a terrified but trusting Cutie behind her.

It felt tighter than any tunnel they traversed before, with blurs of deep rust on one side, dark rock on the other, and there was the genuine possibility the orifereg might jiggle the wrong way and crush both fliers into the stone. The tough bisegus could survive it. The diamur wouldn't.

It only lasted seconds, though. They emerged into the open tunnel on the other end and shifted their attention to the bouncing torch light ahead.

The woman carrying it came to an abrupt fork in the corridor, as a worm emerged from the right passage. Not much help in her current sparrow form, Shimi Zar dropped to the floor and changed as Leda stopped a dozen feet before the creature and raised the torch. Realizing what she was about to do, the egyzemor raced forward. "Don't!"

But it was too late. The worm heaved. From deep in its gullet, a stream of saliva shot forth that coated both females and extinguished the flame. Only Cutie escaped from being drenched, swooping away in time.

The enormous creature lurched onward, the threat of fire removed. Shimi Zar scooped Leda up and ran down the other fork, Cutie zooming behind. Fortunately, the split proved too sharp, and the worm's momentum carried it into the tunnel they had come from.

Once safe, they stopped, and Shimi Zar dropped the woman. "Didn't I tell you not to do that?"

Leda held her arms out in disgust, looking at the glistening, ropey slime coating them and the rest of her body, a cold, clammy film against her skin. "What is this?"

"Fire suppressant." She slicked the hair from her face. "What else did you think would happen?"

"It's saliva!" she cried, spitting some off her lip.

"Only fire suppressant they've got. Come on." She grabbed Leda's slimy wrist and tugged.

"Where are we going?"

"After that worm. Be quiet and do what I do!"

Leda nodded as Shimi Zar dragged her back up the passageway. When they neared the orifereg, they slowed. When it paused its forward movement, Shimi Zar halted. When it lunged again, she matched it. She continued this as the creature lurched its way up the tunnel.

Leda finally understood what she was doing and imitated her. If the worms hunted by sound, they would constantly be chasing each other. It made sense that they had learned to ignore the rhythms of their own kind. By matching them now, she and Shimi Zar were hidden from detection.

And it seemed to be working. Their route sloped upward, so they were heading in the right direction. When the worm they shadowed shifted to a side passage, they jumped in behind another and continued the climb. A few more shifts, and they were back to a spot Shimi Zar recognized. It lay higher than where they encountered the first orifereg, suggesting they were safe.

"We made it!" Leda gave her companion a clumsy hug, then turned to her pet. "Come here, Cutie." Thankfully, the diamur remained silent throughout the trip, too terrified to speak. He longed to rejoin his mistress, but swerved away as she raised a hand to offer him a perch. "What's wrong?"

"They have sensitive noses. I'm guessing we stink to him."

Leda sniffed, but couldn't smell anything particularly offensive. "That's silly. Come, Cutie."

He hovered in the air, just beyond her grasp, and covered his nose. Shimi Zar laughed. "Told you."

The woman dropped her arm. "So, how do we get this stuff off?"

Shimi Zar ran a hand over her chest, but the substance clung fast. "No idea. This isn't something I've had the pleasure of being coated in before. I'm guessing lots of water and soap." She accepted the torch from Leda. "The more pressing matter is relighting this thing and finding the others. Please tell me your flint didn't get slimed."

Chapter Six
ECHOES OF DESPAIR

E RLING AND MALWIN fled down the passage to escape the worms, but encountered another immediately coming in from a side tunnel. Without slowing, they veered left at a fork, just ahead of a third orifereg lunging from the right.

Finally, they found a smaller passageway branching away and ducked inside. Between Erling's bow and Malwin's pack, they could barely squeeze through, but the alternative was the worm waiting at the entrance. It wasn't until they paused, breath heaving, with the only sound the ragged gasp in their own throats, that they realized they were alone.

"Where are Wynna and Graypaw?" Erling stared past the egyzemor, hoping the woman and cat had followed and he had only failed to notice. All he saw was the silhouette of an immense jaw.

"Escaped."

Whether Malwin knew for sure or just hoped, Erling couldn't tell. They had no means of helping now, either way. They needed to look to their own survival. Unable to go back with an orifereg stalking the entrance, they continued along the tunnel at a slower pace.

Soon they heard muted clicking sounds, a rhythmic, metallic rustle like a group of gebits hunting. They increased in number and volume as they progressed. Whatever lay ahead, there were a lot of them.

After rounding a slight curve, Erling saw a faint glow in the distance, presumably more of the fungi. Suddenly, something sticky and delicate covered his face and chest. He panicked, grabbing at his torso to pull away strands of webbing, glistening faintly as they stretched and clung, similar to what his pet fire-bellied spider had spun. But those animals were plain dwellers and wouldn't be found underground. "Mal, do those pokfin things manufacture webs?"

Malwin grumbled. "No."

With that enlightening response, Erling pressed on. A few minutes later, their cramped corridor expanded into a medium-sized room. The air hummed with the noisy clicking, and now he saw the source. He moved onto a narrow ledge that seemed to line the chamber, allowing his companion to join him. Below them, the ground teemed with dozens of insect bodies scrambling over each other in a continuous motion, reminiscent of water reaching its boiling point. Each was two feet long, with three legs per side and an extra pair at the front tipped in snapping pincers. Those, along with their segmented exoskeletons, created the sounds they had heard.

In the dim light, their bodies were so pale as to be almost translucent. Between their claws lay a set of organs that Erling couldn't identify. Beneath those sat twin mandibles, whose purpose he did know.

Malwin groaned.

"What are they? More of those spiders?"

"Barlahoms. Nasty."

Erling guessed as much from their appearance. They didn't look like something that would do nice things to a person. "So we will avoid them. I see no need to go down there."

"Do." With a crestfallen expression, he pointed across the sea of bodies to the opposite wall. "Exit."

The erdi'zal stared but couldn't make out any opening. Even with the illumination, his eyes were no match for the egyzemor's. He would have to take his word for it. "Is that the only way out of here?"

"No. Worm."

Erling thought that was meant to be humor, but his friend's expression showed no mirth. "So it's the orifereg or the barlahoms. Well, if we must, we must. How dangerous are these?"

Malwin shrugged. "Medium."

"What kind of answer is that?"

"Dumb question."

Erling nodded. "Perhaps you are right. How can we get across safely?"

"Around."

"That bad." He glanced at the sides of the room. "So we follow the ledge to navigate this hazard?"

Malwin hunched his shoulders again. "Try."

"Your enthusiasm is boundless."

That got a chuckle from the egyzemor, and he took a few steps to the left. The ridge was barely wide enough to hold their forms, but they had no choice. Malwin went sideways to minimize his footprint. Erling had no such option with his elongated backend.

Clicking rose into chirping chaos, the swarm surging like a pot about to boil over. "I think they know we are here." Erling glanced down, decided the sight of the squirming bodies below was too distracting, and promptly returned his gaze ahead.

They continued around the edge, almost reaching the midpoint, when Malwin stopped. "Oh-oh."

Erling froze. "That is not a sound I want to hear. What is the cause?"

"Slimmer."

"The ledge is narrowing? Can we still make it?"

"Maybe." Malwin edged forward a few more feet. "No."

Erling sighed. "Then we will have to try the other way."

Backing up wasn't something an erdi'zal did easily, but the outcropping was too narrow for him to turn around. Twice, Erling stumbled, paws slipping, his rear legs dislodging pebbles that tumbled into the pit. It took them much longer to return to their starting point than their original attempt. Once there, he stepped aside to let Malwin pass. "You can see better than me. Lead the way."

The ridge here was wider, but before long, it too narrowed. At just over halfway to the other side, Malwin stopped again. "No."

Erling saw the exit now, but they had no route to it. "This is not promising. What do you propose we do?" Something struck his stomach with a thump. His hand reached for the spot and pulled back more of the sticky substance. This was stronger, though, and he had to pry it off his fingers. One of the creatures had tried to capture him. "Did you know they could do that?"

Instead of answering, Malwin gripped his pack firmly, then tossed it into the pit. It landed on a few of the barlahoms with a loud crunch and sent several others flying. Once it settled, he drew his sword.

His intent was obvious to Erling. "Oh my. Has it come to that?"

Malwin jumped into the hole, landing on the bundle with a thump. He glanced around. The barlahoms started scrambling toward him, one over the other, eager for the seemingly easy prey. But an armed egyzemor was not a helpless target. He brandished his sword, knocking a dozen away with the side of his blade. He swung again, dislodging more, then continued bashing them aside until he could step into the bottom of the pit.

"What are you doing?" Erling shouted at him to be heard over the deafening clicking and chirping. "Are you mad?"

Malwin slashed a few more times to keep them away. "Jump."

"I will not! I do not have a death wish!"

Malwin slapped the pack, then pointed at the opening that was their escape route. "Jump."

Erling finally caught on. "You crafty fellow! Is it secure?"

He continued swinging. "Jump!"

The erdi'zal had little room to back up, but he leaped over the oversized insects. His front feet reached the sack, and he scrambled the rest of the way up onto it. Now both of them were in the center of the horde, with the barlahoms in a full frenzy.

Erling panicked, watching Malwin constantly sweeping the bugs aside. A few scurried onto him, but he knocked them off with his free hand. Webbing stuck to his arms and head, but he ignored it. "Jump!"

With no other way to help, Erling twisted around, paws gripping the pack tight. He jumped again, scrambling up to the slightest of ledges to reach the exit. After pulling himself forward, he turned to his friend.

Malwin was flagging. He'd been shoving the creatures aside, not slaying them, and they just kept coming. Meanwhile, the webbing was slowing him down, making each swing less effective as the swarm threatened to overwhelm him. One leaped onto his head and prepared to gouge his face.

But an arrow pierced it, carrying its body away into the crowd. Another arrow penetrated one on his arm. Erling had his bow out and was picking off those who Malwin couldn't see or reach. "I'm safe. Get out of there!"

Malwin nodded, performed a large sweep with his sword, then vaulted onto the ledge. Erling shot down the stragglers chasing him, then leaped up beside the erdi'zal. The bugs swarmed, scrambling over the bundle and hopping up after them, shooting webs and chirping wildly.

"Run!" Erling raced down the passageway. Malwin gave a final, sad glance at his pack before running after him.

They exited into a larger tunnel, with barlahoms swarming on their heels. To the right, another worm was bearing down on them. The erdi'zal barked a warning, and they veered hard left. After twenty feet, Malwin whirled about, sword high. Erling saw it and did the same, his bow ready.

The barlahoms were scavengers, usually prowling in deep tunnels for the rock-like siklarag, the spidery pokfin, and anything small enough for them to catch. However, it wasn't unheard of for them to attack something larger, like an egyzemor or even a wounded orifereg. For a healthy orifereg, though, as the one with them now, the huge insects were a delicacy. Their constant clicking made it easy for the blind worms to detect, and these were making sufficient noise to attract every worm in the mine.

Malwin grinned as the massive maw descended on the pale swarm. Erling watched too, grimacing as it sucked them in and crushed them in its powerful jaws. In seconds, it had gobbled down a dozen and showed no signs of slowing.

Worse for the barlahoms, the line of pursuers Malwin had riled up with his blade continued to pour from the passage, oblivious to the fate that awaited them. As they emerged into the larger tunnel, they were pulled into the orifereg's maw, never to return.

The few that escaped scuttled toward Erling and Malwin, but the egyzemor dealt with them easily, sweeping them aside with his sword or kicking them back to the orifereg, where they would join their kin.

Whether the insects sent out some kind of scent, or the rest of them sensed what was happening to the others, there was a surge of them flowing from their nest.

Overwhelmed, the immense worm recoiled, retreating under a frenzy of bites and pincers. But its would-be food kept coming. They swarmed over the orifereg, pinching its lips and flesh, as it continued to retreat slowly.

Soon, Erling couldn't see anything of the orifereg except its mouth, as the frenzied creatures completely engulfed it. With a shudder, he realized that would have been their fate if Malwin hadn't acted.

He turned to thank him, but his companion was already moving again, this time back toward the barlahoms' lair. "What are you doing?" he called out as Malwin sprinted into the opening, as much as anyone his size could sprint. He wasn't gone long. When he reappeared, his sword was at his side, his recovered pack over his shoulder, and three dead barlahoms were clutched in his hand. He flashed a grin and waved the corpses like trophies from a morning hunt, and Erling remembered that for his friend, they might be.

They strode quickly but calmly away from the battle, not sure who would come out the victor, and not wanting to be there when it was decided. Either winner was likely to pursue them again.

When they reached what Malwin thought was a safe distance, he dropped the dead barlahoms to the floor, then his pack. Erling watched as his companion untied the bundle and began sorting through the contents. A couple of pots, a large pan, the giant's massive bedroll and enormous blanket, and two thick cloaks were among the items. There was also something long and solid wrapped in scraps of cloth that the giant held for a moment before setting it gingerly aside. Then he grabbed a pair of ceramic jars with latched lids and set them on the ground, tops open.

If the women had been there, they'd have protested in horror. But Erling, once a hunter, watched in fascination as his friend operated with precision, extracting two tan-colored organs, each over four inches long and an inch in diameter. He examined them briefly, felt them with his beefy fingers, then gingerly placed one in each jar.

Shoving the husk aside, he did the same with the other two bodies, removing a pair of what Erling guessed were glands from each and depositing them into their respective containers. When he was done, he resealed them and replaced them carefully inside the cloak. A moment later, he repacked everything and cleaned his knife on the edge of one of the legs.

Erling couldn't contain his curiosity. "What were those?"

"Glands." Malwin hefted his bundle to his back and continued walking.

"I concluded that." His companion quickly fell in line beside him. "But what kind?"

The giant chuckled. "Pricey."

Clearly, Malwin wasn't offering more, so Erling let it go. "Any idea how to find our way to the others?"

"Look."

The erdi'zal gave up. He guessed Malwin didn't know how to navigate the not-so-empty mine any better than he did. In that case, looking was indeed their best option.

He just hoped their companions were safe. And they had greater luck finding the artifact than them.

WYNNA LANDED HARD on the cavern floor, the unyielding stone jarring her knees and scraping at her hands. The slick chute spat her out quickly, but the plunge remained terrifying, alone, with no hint of light to soften the fall.

She sat there for some time, legs cramped and twisted underneath her, palms pressed against the uneven rock, supporting her gasping torso. Her blonde hair clung to her cheeks, limp as wet string.

When the shock subsided, she eased her legs around and got unsteadily to her feet. Feeling the grit and what she feared was blood smeared on her hands, she brought them near her face, but the blackness kept her from seeing what lay directly in front of her. A sigh escaped her lips as she absentmindedly wiped them against her crimson dress, dirty and frayed from the two-day trip with the burral caravan and the subsequent running about the mountain tunnels. *A little more grime won't matter.*

Wynna looked about, hoping to spot a source of light or something that would tell her where she was. The movement sent a spike of pain through her skull, and she winced. She gripped the back of her neck, figuring she wrenched it in the unplanned descent. *I'm lucky I didn't break it. Ha! None of this feels lucky.*

Unable to see, she resorted to touch, and extended an arm cautiously. Painful fungi, hideous spiders, and giant worms were all possibly hiding in the gloom, but she needed to take some action. The alternative was staying in the darkness, hoping something less deadly found her.

To her relief and disappointment, her fingers met only empty space.

Hesitantly, she stepped forward and probed again. Still nothing. Her knee ached from hitting the floor, but didn't seem damaged. She sighed again and pressed on. She tried not to imagine that the tunnel, if it was indeed a tunnel, went on for miles, with one of the worms at the end, waiting for helpless barmaids to wander into them.

The fall left her disoriented, and she had no idea if she was heading toward the steep passageway that brought her here, or deeper into danger. No breeze stirred, not even a draft, to suggest an exit. The still air smelled damp, and a tinge of something else, like worn leather, tickling her nose.

Besides the sound of her own shallow breathing and thumping heart, the darkness remained silent as a tomb. It was a profound, oppressive silence that seemed to absorb all other noise, a dull ache behind her ears. During all their time in the mountain, there had been sounds of some kind. Footsteps, a murmur of voices punctuated by laughter or angry outbursts, dripping of water, scattering of rocks dislodged by a boot. Even in the abandoned mine, there had been whisperings of wind that found its way to the depths and were searching for an escape, or the occasional clunk or cheep of an unseen animal. Life in the tunnels proved more abundant than she had imagined, but in this lightless room or passage, nothing stirred.

Her foot first met resistance to her probing. Something thick but malleable, like cold porridge, hit the toe of her boots, and she froze. It didn't scuttle or squeak, but that didn't mean it wasn't a threat. It also didn't attack, which was better than most of her encounters recently.

She eased herself into a crouch, wincing at another sting of pain in her knee, until she placed a finger tentatively in the substance. It was cool to the touch, not cold like she expected. When she swung her hand slightly, the stuff parted with little friction.

Curious, she lowered her palm to the surface. The non-liquid soothed her scraped flesh, and she wasted no time dipping her other one in. When she pulled them out, Wynna felt the ooze slip easily off her skin and back to its source, leaving her hands dry.

A wave of exhaustion washed over her, and she rocked backward to rest on the floor. *I'll just stay here for a bit*, she told herself, hugging her knees. *No need to panic.*

With nothing to see or hear, she began going over the events that led her here. Shimi Zar leading them into the mine. Meeting Grazzlunn and being chased by the undead. Leda failing to get the aid of the voladorms and Malwin blowing up at the assembly. Their arrival in the Eastern Heights after a two-day trek through the forest. The wolves. *And for what? Just one more quest after another. And Leda's life getting better.*

So why did she come? Wynna had told her companions it was to help save Aedan, and that was true. She and the fisherman had gotten off to an odd start, but out of all the others, he was the one who came to check on her when her mother was dying. And foolish as it was, he stood to defend her and Tanita against an attacking monster.

But her motives weren't wholly unselfish. Between the rumors on the streets of Zatreus and the creature's followers, she became convinced it could bring the dead back to life. The attack on them a few hours ago all but confirmed that.

She needed that power. If not herself, through the creature by controlling it. *And if the artifacts can stop it, maybe they can force it to do their bidding.*

Her eyes swelled. Her mother! She had failed to save her. No — worse! She left her in the hands of the man who made her sick. *How far back did it go? He must have been doing it in Zatreus, but before that? Was he responsible for her first sickness in the Undercastle?* Kollamar had said she was ill from something she ate. *That had to be it!* Burein had poisoned her and kept feeding it to her until she died. *But why?* she asked herself through flowing tears.

It didn't matter. He would pay! *When this is done, I will find him and kill him!* A year ago, the thought of hurting anyone, at least physically, would have repulsed her. Now she found it cathartic. *Yes, I will avenge my mother. He will suffer like she did.*

And I will bring her back! Despite the events of the past few days, she needed her mother more than she ever knew. Maybe they wouldn't need to conquer the creature. Maybe the artifacts themselves could do it. They allegedly contained arcana, the mystical force that appeared in Rapria almost three thousand years ago. Surely, some of that power could be used to revive Tanita. *And if we gather enough, maybe even bring back my father!*

Wynna touched her forehead as a wave of dizziness passed over her. Her arm moved sluggishly, like she was underwater, and her heartbeat slowed. *But I can't do any of that. I'm trapped in this cave and no one is coming to help.* She slammed her eyes shut as the tears returned. *All of this is useless. We never stood a chance. Now I'm going to die alone in a hole.*

Giving in to the despair, she released her knees and eased her back onto the floor, staring up at a ceiling she couldn't see. Her hands dropped to her sides, her fingers landing in more of the fluid substance. She should have noticed it moving in around her legs, but her mind remained focused on her own misery. More importantly, she failed to realize the ooze had begun flowing up over the toes of her boots.

Why is my life such a disaster? No one has ever loved me, not even my parents. I was destined to be alone. The others will be glad I'm gone. Especially Leda. She's always hated me. And she is right too. I am nothing, nobody. I should have died long ago.

The slime almost completely engulfed her hands, and her boots were now covered up to her ankles. It moved painfully slow, but speed was not how the *vereshka* hunted. Wynna hadn't known it, but she was trapped the moment her fingers brushed the black sludge. The paralytic had passed into her blood through her skin. Exposing the abrasions on her palm to its surface had only sped up the process.

The poison didn't just slow the body. It spread a chill through her veins, a creeping numbness that started in her fingertips and radiated inward. It dulled the mind, unraveling hope and stealing the will to run before the paralysis fully took hold. Once captured, the vereshka would move in and envelop the poor creature. A secreted acid would help in its eventual breakdown and digestion. The prey usually stayed alive for most of the process, ensuring a horrific and painful death.

The vereshka lacked a sense of scale or satisfaction, but if it possessed one, Wynna would've been the most sumptuous meal it had ever eaten. Subsisting mainly on the rodents and insects that wandered into its form, the woman would constitute the finest feast it would ever consume. It already tasted a sample as it began breaking down the flesh of her fingers.

Pain registered in her mind, but the grief the poison produced overwhelmed it. Wynna replayed the memory of the night her father died over and over, letting the sorrow wash over her. She was beyond tears and would have curled into a ball of despair if she still had control of her body.

"Wynna! Must get up. Now!"

As young Wynna watched her mother break down sobbing at the news of her husband's death for the ninth time, a dark figure appeared in the doorway of their castle quarters. He didn't exist there before and didn't belong to the memory. His words were half plea, half order.

"Wynna! If don't move now, will die!"

Then let me die! There is nothing left for me! She couldn't vocalize the words, as her lips were frozen shut, but it didn't matter if the stranger heard her. She was unable to tell if he was a product of her visions or not.

He didn't speak again. Instead, she felt fingers, short and firm, reach under her shoulders and hook into her armpits. A second later, the rough ground moved underneath her as her body was dragged backward, away from the ooze. It barely registered that she was moving, or that there was a very real someone with her. Her mind was numb to everything except her own anguish.

The vereshka, sensing its victim escaping, tried to cling to her shoes and hands, but whatever pulled her proved much stronger, eventually forcing it to withdraw. While it seemingly had the structure of a liquid, it remained a single entity and could not detach itself.

Several minutes passed before her senses began returning to normal. The profound silence in her ears slowly gave way to a dull ringing, and the crushing pressure behind her eyes receded. It was a short time before she could move her body. With it came a burning agony in her fingers. Out of the grips of the vereshka, the poison was wearing off, and with it, the mind-numbing effects that had kept her free of pain. She cried out.

"Know it hurts. Burned fingers. Almost eaten."

The voice was the same one as before. In her drugged state, she had incorporated it into her recalled memories, but apparently it was very real, and the person it belonged to stood here with her. She had been afraid to be alone in the darkness. Now she realized her true fear was *not* being alone. "Who is that?" she demanded. "What do you want?"

"Name Prad. Want help. Did help."

She struggled to recall the past hour, but apart from her crouching and remembering her father's death, she was lost. "What's going on?"

"Caught by vereshka. Trapped. Would be eaten. Saved."

The voice sounded masculine, but soft, with an underlying murmur that she found soothing. The words triggered a recollection of being immobilized. She panicked and shoved her torso off the ground with her elbows. "I couldn't move."

"Yes. Wynna captured. Better now. 'Cept fingers."

"Then thank you," she told him sincerely. More of the events were resurfacing. She had been trapped, physically and emotionally, until the stranger dragged her out of danger. "Wait, how do you know my name?"

"Am friend."

Wynna scowled. "That is not an answer."

"It is," came the simple reply.

"Fine. I have friends somewhere in this place. I hope you know a way out of here, maybe back to them."

"Not yet."

"What do you mean? How did you get here?"

"Same."

Wynna's frown returned. His terse replies suggested he was an egyzemor, but the hands that gripped her earlier were small. "You fell?"

This time, there was a pause. "Yes."

"Any chance we can go climb up again?" When she had slipped into the sloped tunnel, it felt steep, but she had been terrified and blind.

"No."

So no going back that way. "How did you find me? I cannot see a thing."

"Eyes."

"Oh, is that supposed to be funny?"

"Come."

A hand grabbed hers. It was definitely smaller than hers and warm. It also brought pain as supple fingers gripped where hers were burned. She winced and yanked away. "That hurts!"

"Sorry."

She felt the grip again, this time closing around her wrist. Whoever the stranger was, he had to see at least partially in the gloom. "Hold on. What are you?"

"Friend. Come."

She knew she had no choice. If what he said was true, he did rescue her. She had been locked in despair, then the pain in her fingers. If he could see, he might find a way out. Or he might be leading her to a whole den of his kind, where they would kill her and eat her. No. Something about his presence seemed familiar, and she sensed she could trust him.

He tugged, and she followed with hesitant steps. He may be able to see, but she was still walking blind. Fortunately, he understood this, and was considerate enough to only lead, never drag her. Twice he told her to watch a wall as they passed through openings. Thankfully, the ground sloped upward, telling her they were going in the right direction.

The silence bothered her, though. "Do you live down here?"

There was a chuckle from the figure. It reminded her of a rodent chattering, but softer, to match his voice. "No. Traveler."

"And you ended up down here like us? Did Shimi Zar lead you here, too?"

The odd laugh again. "Trust her."

She was about to ask more about the egyzemor when a faint archway appeared ahead. Glowing fungi on the other side shone softly on its edges. Her heart leaped. Light! She doubted she would ever see it again!

They crossed through the entrance and she halted. After a moment, her sight adjusted to the low light, and she got her first look at Prad.

He was human, or seemed to be, but tiny, who only coming up to her chin. His frame was lean, his black-and-white tunic hanging snug across wiry muscles. On his feet were different colored boots, one charcoal, one gray. His face was delicate, with a small, flat nose and keen eyes.

He waited until she finished looking him over. "All right? Anything missing?"

The question confused her. "I just thought —"

"Me monster?" He laughed again. "No. Friend. Come. Found something."

He took her wrist and guided her through two more chambers and a short passageway. She was grateful to see they had plenty of the glowing fungi, but the walls were also spotted with the black spores and she steered away from them. Finally, he brought her to a long, narrow tunnel and directed her to a spot near the wall. Releasing her, he stood straight and looked at her. She shifted under his stare. "What? Why are you staring at me?"

He didn't answer, instead keeping his gaze on her. After a moment, he raised a hand up to his ear and scratched it. Wynna nearly exploded. "Tell me what you want!"

"Found. Look."

"At what?" She made an exaggerated show of looking around the passage. Stone. Fungi. Bits of rubble. "There is nothing here."

"No patience." Rather than explain further, he crouched by the wall and waited.

Wynna questioned his sanity, but huffed and bent beside him. Her knee gave a smaller jolt than before, but she still hissed through her teeth. "You are maddening!" She gazed down at the ground between them and was startled to see a faint glint of metal. She reached for it, trying to brush back the layer of soil over it with her fingers, but they stung. "I see it, but I cannot pick it up. Can you?"

Prad looked surprised at the question, then chuckled. "Hands. Change." His delicate hand brushed aside the pebbles and dirt to reveal a well-crafted, tapered cylinder of solid iron, with elaborate etchings on the sides and flat ends. More digging revealed a two-foot-long thick wood handle with steel bands and a leather-wrapped grip attached to it.

"It's a hammer," Wynna said, recognizing the tool. She had never used one, as that kind of manual labor wasn't required as a cook or barmaid, but she had seen plenty of others swing them. This was larger than those, though. "Some miner lost his tool. So what?"

"No. More." Prad continued removing the surrounding rubble until he was able to lift it out of the recess it was in. Despite obviously being abandoned long ago, the hammer remained in nearly pristine condition. The head showed no signs of use, and the wood was perfectly intact, with no wear or rot. "Magic."

Now Wynna laughed. "I do not know where you come from, but I assure you, this is just a tool for hitting things very hard. Nothing special about it, even if it looks pretty. Leave it." She stood up, being careful not to brush her fingers on the wall. "Come on. We need to find a way out."

Prad looked up at her, his expression one of confusion. "Keep." He raised the hammer toward her, handle first.

"I do not want it!" She showed him her fingers, clearly scarred despite the dim light. "And I cannot carry it, even if I did. Leave the dirty old thing. Even the original owner did not want it."

Prad rubbed his ear, then stood up, gripping the weapon tightly in both hands. "Keep," he repeated, his tone tinged with frustration. "Come." He turned away from her and walked up the passageway, only looking back once to see if she followed.

Wynna didn't notice his irritation as she hiked up her dress and trailed after him. "I do not know why you want the thing. Have your people never seen a hammer before? Do you even have people? You still have not told me who you are or why you are here."

At first, he kept silent, but she continued pushing for answers. "Had people." His words were so soft she barely heard them over his shoulder. "Lost. Found new people."

"And do these new people know you are stuck in these wretched tunnels?"

"They do. Here too."

"You think my friends might meet them?" If there were more of his kind, Erling and the others could have helped in escaping the worms.

For some reason, her query earned another laugh. "Would be interesting."

They passed through a few more passages and two large chambers, following the gentle upward slope of the ground. Only twice did they retrace their route, as Prad changed his mind about the way he had chosen.

The last lingering traces of despair left her, but not her resolve to bring back her parents and have revenge on Burein. Those plans dominated her thoughts.

Still, she found herself intrigued by her rescuer as she watched him scouting ahead of her, the oversized hammer always held before him, upside down in his fists. Why he would bother carrying such a useless burden, she couldn't guess, but he obviously thought it was important.

When he walked, his body swayed, as though each step sent a ripple through him. He seemed both a child and an adult at the same time, comfortable being neither of them permanently.

After nearly an hour, Wynna spotted a flickering light at the far end of the corridor they were walking. As they drew closer, she heard murmurs, and she felt sure whoever lay ahead had a torch.

Not waiting for confirmation, she bolted past Prad, heart pounding, feet scrambling up the last stretch. "Hello! Hey! It's me! Wynna! I'm safe! I'm safe!"

The pair at the top shouted in surprise and turned to greet her. "Wynna! Over here!" Shimi Zar and Leda had gotten the torch relit, but they still had much of the worm mucus clinging to their hair and clothing, glistening in the light.

Wynna ran to them and unhesitatingly wrapped her arms around the shorter woman, hugging her tightly. The burst of affection surprised Leda, especially after their fight and the slime that coated her body, but she gladly returned the embrace.

Then Wynna pulled away and gave Shimi Zar an equally enthusiastic, if slightly more awkward, squeeze before facing both of them. "I thought you would have abandoned me! I was lost for hours!"

"I would never leave you behind!" Leda placed a hand on her shoulder. "We're family, remember?"

Wynna's eyes welled with tears, and she began to wipe them, only to finally notice the layer of mucus her hugs had transferred to her. A quick glance at the others confirmed they were covered head-to-toe in the same sleek saliva. "What is this stuff?"

"Worm spit." Shimi Zar grumbled and picked a glob of it off her sleeve. She flung it against a wall in disgust. "Sebpa!"

"What did you say?"

The egyzemor grimaced. "Worm spit?"

Wynna shook her head. "After that. Did you say 'sebpa'?"

Shimi Zar nodded. "Curse. Means end of goat."

"As in a goat's ass?" Leda asked.

"Yes. Why?"

Wynna's jaw clenched. Her hands balled into fists before the pain made her relax them. "That is what that monster Burein called me. Said it meant 'beautiful baby'. His stupid way of flattering me."

"That 'sepba'."

Leda's hand went to her mouth, but stopped when she saw the shiny palm. "That's terrible. But it was probably just a simple mistake."

Wynna felt the heat rise to her face, but rather than shout, she laughed. "No. He is a fool. And you always make excuses for others. I am sure he knew exactly what he was saying. He never liked me, nor I him." She had already decided his fate, so continuing to react to him was a waste of energy, she realized. As her anger drained away, she added, "When this is over, we will see who is the true sebpa."

Leda kept the surprise at the woman's reaction from her face, but she didn't ask the reason. "What happened to you? Do you know where the others are?"

"I got separated from them and fell down a shaft." She paused, considering if she should tell them about her encounter with the vereshka. *That I felt helpless and on the brink of despair. That my true goal is to find a way to bring my parents back from the dead. No.* "I hurt my fingers and everything was dark, but Prad here helped me to you."

Shimi Zar raised her single eyebrow. "Who?"

"Prad. He is — " Wynna turned toward the passage, expecting him at her heels. But he had vanished. "Where did he go?"

Leda followed her gaze down the tunnel. "There was someone with you?"

"That is what I said!" *Why didn't he come with me?* She started down the slope, figuring he was just out of sight in the shadows, his black-and-white clothing blending in with the dark. But the further she went, the more sure she was that he was gone, possibly back to his own people.

She did find the hammer, leaning against the stone as the miner who lost it long ago might have done. That confounded Wynna even more. *Why did he leave it after insisting on bringing it?*

"I'm guessing your friend isn't that thing." Leda followed her down and approached the wall. "It looks like a big hammer."

"It is. Prad dug it out of some rubble and was determined to bring it along. Why he cared about it, I have no idea."

"Then where is he?"

"Found it!" Shimi Zar stepped between the two women and snatched up the hammer in one hand, lifting it easily to examine it. "Is good."

Wynna blinked. "Why is everyone so excited about it?"

Leda looked similarly confused, then brightened. "Is this the artifact we're supposed to find?"

"Yes." The egyzemor held it out toward her, as if the answer should be obvious just from looking.

"I thought it would glow or something. How can you be sure?"

"I know. I hid." Since the woman had rejoined them, the bisegus-egyzemor had returned to the terse speech pattern.

"You did a poor job of it," Wynna grumbled. "It was lying on the ground near a wall. Anyone could have walked in and picked it up. Then we would have been wandering around here, risking our lives for nothing."

"They wouldn't have known it was special." Even knowing it was enchanted, Leda could see no way of telling. "Probably figure a miner lost it and toss it in some armory."

"That is what I told Prad, but he still wanted to bring it along."

95

"Do you think *he* knew?"

"No! He was a funny little fellow. Talked only slightly more than Shimi here. Liked to laugh. I am sure it was just a coincidence."

"Are you certain he's gone? It would be good to ask him."

Wynna shook her head. "You could ask all you want, but he is not very forthcoming with answers. He may have been scared of you two or the light and returned to his people."

Leda looked at where the tunnel vanished into darkness. "There are more of him down here?"

"I think so. I hoped they would have helped you." She glanced at where the torchlight reflected off the liquid coating them. "What did happen to you two?"

"One of those worms trapped us. We got out, but when I moved too close with the torch, it spewed this junk all over us. Put out the fire. We got it relit, obviously, but we haven't figured out how to wash ourselves off yet."

"Are you serious?" Wynna couldn't suppress a giggle. "So that really is worm spit?"

"Yes. And don't laugh. It could have been acid, according to Shimi Zar."

At hearing her name, their guide stopped examining the artifact and nodded. "Lucky. Come."

I am tired of being ordered around, Wynna thought, but followed her and Leda back up to the top of the tunnel. She was sorry that Prad had vanished before meeting them. She wanted to thank him again for his help. He saved her life, after all. *Good luck, strange little man. I hope you find your people, or whatever it is you are searching for.*

Chapter Seven
Reunion and Revelation

THROUGH A SERIES of questions and gestures, the diamur made it clear to Leda and Shimi Zar that he wanted to search for the others. After discussions and protests, Leda agreed it was their best chance of locating the rest of their party. He was fast, mostly invisible to the oriferegs, and his keen sense of smell could detect the scents of human, egyzemor, erdi'zal, and cat even through stone and worm slime.

He flew off for his mission shortly before Wynna found Leda and Shimi Zar. Since then, the females shared more details of their stories with each other, leaving out the more personal stuff. In Wynna's recount, she claimed to have fallen unconscious and Prad revived her. She left out all mentions of her vows and despair. According to Leda's version of her adventure, the ruse with Cutie worked, but they ran into another worm as they escaped, hence the goo coating them.

An hour passed in the damp hush before faint voices echoed down the stone tunnel, their pitch distorted by the winding paths. Leda snatched up the torch, its flame sputtering in the stale air, and ran to the opening. The light cast long, twitching shadows that danced across the moist rock walls.

A few seconds later, Cutie darted from the darkness. This time, despite the smell, he zoomed in close to her face and planted a tiny kiss on her nose before zipping off into the gloom, chittering.

By the glow of the fungi, Leda spotted three figures climbing toward them: one large, one medium, one small. "Is that you?" she called out.

"I think that depends on which 'you' you are asking about." Erling's firm voice was unmistakable. A low grumble and a loud trill confirmed who his companions were.

"They're back!" Leda shouted, but Shimi Zar and Wynna were already sprinting over. "Are you wounded at all?"

"Malwin has a few cuts from the horde of barlahoms we fought, but other than that, we are unharmed. And you?"

"Some hurt fingers and a coating of worm spit. And we found the artifact!"

Once they reached the top, with Cutie leading the way, flitting from side to side as if he single-handedly saved them all, they exchanged welcomes and hugs, then gave a quick accounting of their adventures. Leda and Wynna shuddered at the description of the barlahom encounter and their eventual demise by an orifereg. Graypaw had rejoined them soon after, then the diamur stumbled upon the trio.

"I wonder what Graypaw's story is." Leda crouched a few feet from the feline. "Is there anything you would like to tell us?"

The cat wrinkled his nose and gave her a sharp meow. He then began grooming himself, making a show of washing his face and sides. It lasted only a few seconds, then he stopped and stared at her again.

His meaning was clear. "Not you too!" she laughed and stood. "He says I need to clean myself."

"I would agree with him." Erling brought a hand to his nose. "I didn't think it was my place to speak of it, but you and our guide do have a certain aroma about you that is disturbing to the senses."

"So I've been told. But unless you have buckets of water and soap in your pack, you'll have to put up with us for a while, duck."

"What about the artifact?" Since learning the hammer was one of the magical items, Wynna had tried guessing its powers. Apart from beating the creature into submission, though, she saw no way for it to help.

"Yes." Erling looked at the object in Shimi Zar's grasp. "While I doubt it would provide a solution to the saliva issue, I am curious as to what role it plays in defeating Olagkoa."

Shimi Zar lifted the hammer high, a sly grin spreading across her face. "Watch."

They did, except for Graypaw, who chose that moment to turn his back on the group and focus on a handful of siklarag scuttling along the base of a wall, their tiny feet seemingly too frail to carry their rock-like shells.

Suddenly, the tunnel lit up, bathing cat and critters in white light. Behind them, the companions gasped, hands snapping up to shield their eyes, as the hammer erupted into a dazzling ball of brilliance. Cutie squealed and dashed away, nearly hitting a wall in his blind flight.

The light only lasted a few seconds before retracting into the artifact. It took another minute for their vision to readjust to the darkness. When they did, the group saw Shimi Zar grinning broadly at the display. "Bright," she explained, as if any of them could have missed that fact.

"It most definitely is." Erling blinked his double set of eyes. "But I fail to see how that will hinder our foe. My understanding is the creature lacks optical receptors."

"It can't!" The demonstration hurt more than Wynna's eyes. It stripped away the hope she held that it could be used to revive her mother. She needed life, not light! "This was a hopeless waste! We've risked everything, for nothing!"

Shimi Zar drew back from the outburst, a confused expression passing over her face. "Will help," she insisted.

"How?" A hot, trembling wave rose up her spine, setting her chest tight and throat raw. Her heart pounded behind her ribs like a hammer against a wall, and her hands clenched, trembling. *I've failed you, mother!* "Tell us how *this* will help control the monster! Right now! You can't!"

"With others."

"The others which will be as useless as this one? How could this possibly be of help to anyone, unless they are idiotic enough to get stuck in a mine full of more monsters?"

It was Leda who stepped forward to calm her. "We don't understand how arcana works. When this is combined with the other items, they may do something different altogether."

"You don't believe that! A hammer that makes light. A bow that shoots fake arrows. A cup that does who-knows-what. This is someone's sick game! And I refuse to play anymore."

"Is not!" Shimi Zar bellowed. The hand with the weapon dropped to her side as she leaned in toward Wynna. "Necessary. Sacred."

The move should have intimidated the woman, but Wynna's heartbreak wouldn't be cowed. "I do not believe you." She moved towards the egyzemor, her jaws tightly clenched. "Unless you can prove it, I'm going home."

"Go!"

"Please!" Leda grabbed Wynna's arm. "You have to trust Shimi Zar. She knows much more about this than any of us. She's a — "

"A what? Liar?" Wynna jabbed a finger toward the female egyzemor. "She said she is the one who hid this hammer down here. Why did she do that? If these items are so important, why hide them?"

"I would wager to keep them safe," Erling offered.

"From who? The creature trapped underground that fears them?"

"Yes!" Shimi Zar grabbed Wynna's shoulder roughly, her face contorted in anger. "You are so arrogant and stupid! Even more than *this one*." She nodded at Leda. "There is so much you don't know, but you whine like a rotten child! Go home!"

She stood that way, Wynna dangling from one hand, the hammer in the other, her chest heaving in exasperation, fire in her single eye, for a long moment. When she calmed enough to glance at the others, they were all staring at her, open-mouthed. It took her a little longer to realize why.

"Uh," she grunted, releasing the woman and taking a step back. She looked away as the anger drained from her. She sighed. "Bastu! I botched it."

The fury had left Wynna, too. "You can speak normally!"

"I believe the difference is more profound than a change in vocabulary," Erling said.

"You mean.... she's like Leda? A half-thing?"

"I am not a half-thing!" Leda protested. "I'm just human from different parents."

"And I am not a Shiftling." Shimi Zar faced them. "I am a member of the *Gupong Talagapa*. I am a custodian, charged with protecting the Arcane Relics. My kind has kept them safe for over a century, waiting for a time when they may be called for again."

"Fascinating!" Erling's eyes lit up. "A secret organization keeping watch over the creature, is that correct? I should have guessed such a critical undertaking had been implemented."

"Hold up!" Wynna crossed her arms, gingerly tucking her hands into the crooks of her elbows, and glared at Shimi Zar. "What has this got to do with your cryptic speech? And why have you not just contacted all these guardians and told them to bring their artifacts to one spot, instead of expecting us to collect them for you?"

"Because we don't know where the others are. To do so would undermine our plan to keep them secret." The egyzemor paused. Her expression said she was weighing her next actions. "And I talk this way because... I'm a bisegus."

"No!"

The cry of anguish came from Malwin. He had been quiet this whole time, listening to the back and forth and attempting to piece Shimi Zar's story together, like the others. This last revelation had been too much for him, however. Eye wide in disbelief, he scrambled away from the group.

Leda sprang after Malwin. "Mal! She's safe! Don't worry!" She reached toward him, her gesture urgent, not unlike trying to keep a child from stepping into danger.

It failed. "Betrayed!" he yelled, still retreating blindly into the darkness, his gaze never leaving the shapeshifter.

"She didn't betray anyone!" Leda sprinted after him. "She's here to help us!"

But her words were lost on him. Shimi Zar had been right about his kind fearing bisegus. This one had appeared in the heart of his home, passing among them, even aiding the group, and he had never suspected a thing. Whether she intended harm or not didn't matter. It was deceitful, and there was nothing to stop her or any others if they did plan to hurt the egyzemors.

But Wynna, the person who had protested every change and surprise so far, giggled. When Erling stared at her, it erupted into a full laugh. "Malwin has no problem with the woman he always protects being of a mysterious race who disguise themselves as human. No! None at all! But when he meets one that looks like him, he goes to pieces. And you thought *I* overreacted!"

Her words, and more importantly, who they came from, impacted everyone there. Malwin stopped fleeing and shifted his gaze to Leda. He consoled Wynna when she learned the woman she had grown up with wasn't who she appeared to be. And he still trusted

Leda, even though she had, in a way, betrayed him as well. Were the situations so different?

They were. He knew Leda for more than a decade, since he first moved to Talidith with Roth. The older man was the one who met her parents. He understood Leda was special, but had never explained exactly how to Malwin. Perhaps because he knew egyzemors distrusted those who hid their true selves.

But Leda hadn't known. Shimi Zar did. One was ignorance, one deceit. So why was Wynna not bothered by the bisegus revelation?

"Malwin's reaction is rooted in centuries of tradition." In the tense environment, Erling had adopted his scholarly tone to defuse it with understanding. "He can't help it."

"And humans aren't?" Wynna countered. "I was taught about the evils of bisegus, how they wanted to eat our souls because they had none of their own. Leda and I should be running away as fast as we can."

Erling blinked at the observation. "That is a fair point. Why aren't you?"

"Because running anywhere down here would lead to death?" Wynna offered, then smiled. *Why am I not upset?* "No. This entire mission has been a disaster. Having it end with a soul eater seems proper."

"That is highly cynical. However, you appear to be handling it well." He looked to Leda. "And you? You were brought up the same, were you not?"

She nodded. "I was told the same stories. But today I learned my parents are a different race, and, like Wynna said, I'm something unknown. Shimi Zar being a bisegus does not seem that strange by comparison." She fixed Erling with her own stare. "Why doesn't this bother you?"

The erdi'zal snorted. "We are an enlightened people. The form changers are an integral part of our world, and a fascinating one at that. We bear no animosity toward them, or any other race."

"Tell that to the erdi'hun!" Shimi Zar called out. "Or worse, the erdi'mus. You loathe them and make their lives miserable, and they're your own kind."

Erling's face reddened. "They are *not* like us. They have a passing similarity only. They earned their punishment from Zaljaka, our creator."

"So much for being 'enlightened'," Wynna sneered.

"Says the human who thinks I'm going to eat her soul." Shimi Zar crossed her arms to match the woman's pose, the hammer jutting out at an angle. "In case you haven't figured out, I won't. Yet."

"I never said I believed you would." Wynna dropped her hands to her side.

"See, Mal. She's not a threat. She's helping us." Leda eased up to the egyzemor and placed a hand on her arm. "Please, come back to the group. We need you. I need you."

He hesitantly lowered his gaze to her, taking his eye off Shimi Zar for the first time since her revelation. The giant looked to be on the brink of tears. This was against everything his people believed for millennia. For one of the few instances in his life, he was afraid.

But the others had accepted the shapeshifter, and his decades among humans had taught him they found it difficult to accept change easily. Besides, he didn't need to tolerate *all* bisegus. Just this one. For the mission.

Malwin held a hand out to Leda. She grabbed it with both of hers. "It will be alright. I promise." He gave her a quick nod, and she guided him back to the others. But when he got closer, he balked.

Shimi Zar shook her head. "Oh, for the love of... would it help if I changed into something besides an egyzemor?"

"That might improve matters," Erling said. "Less of a betrayal."

"You *maldito* are strange. The races of Rapria have been interacting for thousands of years, but you still cling to these primitive ideas. But if it helps..." The others watched as the towering female shrank before them. Bulging muscles became soft, her curves more feminine. Her single eye split into two twinkling orbs, the nose between them grew dainty, and the rough pair of lips turned plump and orange. Her scraggly hair cascaded into thick, glossy locks, matching the hue as her lips. Finally, her simple sack-like shirt and pants, which seemed popular among the mountain population, morphed into a tight brown dress with sleeves down past the wrist, a slit up one side exposing powerful but sleek legs, and a laced bodice revealing a healthy figure.

The transformation complete, Shimi Zar spun slowly in place, the leather, knee-high-heeled boots tapping gently against the stone floor. "Will this do?" If the hammer weren't still gripped in her hand and she wasn't coated in a layer of worm saliva, it would have been easy to believe that the egyzemor had vanished and been replaced by this young human female. Even her voice was different. It had gone up an octave and acquired a gentle lilt.

"Quite impressive!" Erling told her. "And you can take any form you choose?"

"Nearly. Some are easier than others. Like your kind have too many limbs and eyes to play the part convincingly for long."

"Interesting. So there are none of you among my people."

"I didn't say that."

"You are a lot less intimidating this way." Wynna took a step toward the changed Shimi Zar, holding her head high to emphasize the difference in height. Even with the boots, the bisegus stood shorter than her.

"Just because this body is smaller, don't think I can't slam you against a wall and eat your soul anytime I want."

Wynna frowned. "Are you going to keep bringing that up? I said I do not believe in that nonsense."

"Why did you choose to look like this?" Leda asked.

"It's a form I've adopted many times. It can be easier to gain confidence looking like this than looking like that." She waved a dainty hand toward Malwin. To his credit, he didn't flinch. Her change in appearance did seem to have calmed him.

"Oh, you can get more than confidence," Wynna laughed. She spent years using her looks and charms to get men to do things for her. Aedan was tripping over his own feet, literally, minutes after meeting her. With Shimi Zar's current beauty, the two could wreak havoc on a male population. If they weren't trying to save the world.

"I believe the reason for this change was to ease Malwin's concerns. We should ask how feels about it?" Erling turned to the egyzemor. "Will this form be suitable?"

All eyes went to him, except Graypaw, who had taken the opportunity to groom his tail. Their companion looked soothed, but not completely comfortable. "It'll take time," Leda said for him, patting his arm. "I'm proud of you."

"Can we leave now?" Wynna shifted her pack. It rubbed her shoulder raw long ago, and she wanted to be rid of it. "We have what we were looking for, and no others to talk to here. Unless you're keeping someone else down here." The last comment was directed at their guide.

"There's nothing more. We need to get out of the mountains and find Nastina. She'll know what to do next." Shimi Zar grabbed the torch from its wall mount. "I only hope she's home."

SHIMI ZAR, NOW in her transformed guise, led the companions through the winding tunnel to the base of Crokrusheg. They decided they needed food and rest after their adventures in the mine, so she guided them to the Eastern Heights' bustling market caverns, the egyzemor answer to a city street bazaar.

Most of the tunnels had been large enough for three egyzemors to walk through abreast, but the passageway Shimi Zar called the *piacheg* sprawled out as wide as a city street and was similarly lined with sellers showing off their wares. Some had stalls, like the merchants in the city, but most had their items laid out on skin-covered stone slabs that had been carved out of the floor or hauled there. A few had wooden boxes and barrels to hold their offerings. Dozens of torches made all of it clearly viewable.

A haze of mixed aromas hung in the air: earthy fungi, oily smoke, and the sharp odor of something fermenting. The clamor of bargaining voices echoed off the stone walls, punctuated by the rhythmic clang of metal tools and the occasional hiss of a brazier flare.

The tired and broke travelers paid little attention to most of the non-edible articles, many of which had come in with the caravan. All the clothing looked basic and made for the hulking egyzemors, not the smaller humans or the long-limbed erdi'zal.

The choices of food weren't much better. Fruit spoiled fast in the caves, but there were edibles that appeared similar. "These are fungi. It's the staple of their diet," Shimi Zar explained, waving her hand over a collection of dark green toadstools.

"I didn't know they had so many varieties!" Leda picked over the selection of one vendor. She recognized some of the mushrooms, but most were foreign. Along with them were other growths, varying in shape, size, and color. "We know about their finopep, but not all these."

"That's made from drogomba." Shimi Zar scanned the sellers, then pointed to a large basket of dark yellow fungi. "That stuff."

A stone table supported a display of round, gray loaves of bread. Wynna tapped one and found it nearly as hard as the rock beneath it.

"Do they eat this, or use it as a weapon? I am pretty sure it could crush a few skulls."

"*Gomkin*," the middle-aged egyzemor standing over the selection grunted.

"That's the name of it," Shimi Zar confirmed. "Instead of grain, it's made from a fungus. See, they cut one of these open, and pour in stew or finopep. The inside is mostly hollow, so it makes a good bowl. It soaks up the juice and softens enough to eat."

"Someone needs to tell them about bowls."

"They have those too, but they are heavy, and scrubbing them clean is worse than chewing on a gomkin.. This way, it's a self-contained meal, with no wash-up afterward."

Wynna gave a squeal at the next merchant. They had an iron brazier lit, and on the slab beside it was an assortment of insects and grubs, which Shimi Zar gleefully explained to the woman's disgust. "These things with all the legs are pokfin. They look nasty, but they're scrumptious! And these scrawny rodents are *siklarag*. Normally, they have rock-like shells. Too bitter for me. These little worms are *kofalo*. They are juicy, but tart. And I think... yes, that's a *denehag*, with its wings and tail clipped."

The scent rising from the sizzling insects was acrid and nutty, with a hint of scorched shell. Wynna's stomach turned as one popped open on the brazier with a wet snap. "Why don't they eat something normal, like pigs or cows?" Wynna asked, her hand flying to her mouth as she gagged at the description.

Shimi Zar laughed. Before her change, it had been gruff. Now, it was sweet as a stone sparrow's song. "Is this the kind of place you'd raise your livestock? Besides, egyzemors are diggers, not farmers. They've learned to harvest what occurs naturally."

"What's the fire for?" Leda asked.

"To toast them, of course! Nothing better than a toasted pokfin!"

"They have *gyzlets*!" Erling stood with Malwin two vendors away. In front of them, four huge blue-gray reptiles, each three feet long with their tails, were laid out on an enormous slab. A smaller stone beside held several butchering tools. "Please tell me this is what we came for!"

The females turned to see what he was referring to. Leda leaned in toward Shimi Zar. "Does he mean the giant lizards?"

"Gyzlets. Yeah. The eggys do breed them. From what I've seen, it isn't hard. Just give them a cavern with water and fungus, and they multiply like, well, like gyzlets! You skin them, gut them, cut off the legs, tail, head, and..."

"I am *not* eating anything that crawls around in caves!" Wynna announced, scooting away from both vendors.

"Why does this revelation not surprise me?" Erling threw up his hands. "You eat mud-covered animals and slimy fish, yet you turn up the opportunity to experience a truly exquisite sampling of flesh, because of where it lived."

"I'll have some!" Shimi Zar crossed to join the erdi'zal. "So the real question is, how many do we get?"

They selected two of the lizards, then Shimi Zar took Wynna to the far end of the market so she didn't have to see and hear them being prepared. Leda went with them. Both women had spent years working in the kitchens of Shieldarrow, but after the night they'd endured, neither was in the mood to watch a butchering.

When it was over, Malwin added two hunks of meat, wrapped in cloth, to his burden. At Shimi Zar's suggestion, the hammer had been tucked away deep inside his pack. Leda's sword was also once again dangling from its side. The other females weren't armed, and she felt awkward carrying the blade with them.

Once they had included a selection of fungi, which Shimi Zar assured them would taste like the root vegetables they were used to, they discussed where to go for their dinner and sleep. Malwin suggested the egyzemor equivalent of an inn, which was a collection of caves set aside for travelers, but Leda and Wynna were craving the open sky, and Erling admitted the close space of the tunnels was also wearing on him. Even Cutie, once thrilled by every flickering torch, now chirped half-heartedly and drooped like a soggy leaf. Only Graypaw seemed indifferent.

"And those corpses may still be pursuing us," Erling added. "We have temporarily lost them, but they might appear at any time."

"Safe. Surrounded." Malwin waved a hand toward the steady stream of his kin, many of them armed with weapons or tools.

"I appreciate the sentiment, but we shouldn't bring our problems to your people. They've aided us enough. We need to move on."

They made their way to the closest exit, an opening twice the size of the one they used to enter the mountains, with rounded boulders that could be rolled into place to close it. As they stepped outside, the air turned crisp and clean, laced with pine and the faint mineral scent of mountain runoff. The stillness felt vast after the dense, torch-lit market.

Shimi Zar led them a little ways to a grove of trees beside a small lake. There, Malwin and Erling set up two fires while Wynna filled a pot of water.

The sun rose only a few hours before, its warmth still losing the battle against the clinging chill. Light spilled through the jagged cleft between peaks, casting long shadows at the mountain's base. A few *gebits* zipped by, their twin pairs of translucent pinions splitting the dewy air with a hum. A kaleidoscope of *rudzalia* fluttered through a patch of goldenglows, their delicate brownish-red and green wings carrying them from one deep yellow blossom to the next.

Erling eagerly lectured the others on the rarity of the butterflies, explaining they were called *Nesmeaken Zaljaka* in his language, which translated to "Zaljaka's maidens". Only Cutie and Graypaw seemed interested in the insects, however, with the first trying to engage in an aerial chase with one, and the second practicing his stalking skills on the oblivious fliers.

Seeing a chance to finally clean the saliva off themselves, Shimi Zar and Leda bathed in the lake, washing their clothes at the same time. The latter had a single spare dress in her pack to wear while her outfit dried by the fire, but the bisegus carried no supplies or had nothing to change into. She didn't seem bothered by it, as what she wore soon looked as fresh and dry as if newly bought.

"What *is* that made of? How does it transform with you?" Leda asked as she slipped her outfit on, shivering slightly in the early morning air. Her chemise and dress clung to patches where her skin remained damp.

"I'd tell you, but then I'd have to eat your soul." Shimi Zar gave her hair a final shake. Unlike her clothes, it held onto the water stubbornly, but at least the spit was gone.

Leda shrugged the response off. "What happened to not daring to reveal yourself to the others?" She leaned in close to keep the conversation private. "You did that pretty easily, and no one cared."

"Did you miss Malwin's reaction? You two have an obvious bond, but if it wasn't for that, he would have fled into those tunnels and been killed by the orifereg or something worse. You knew, and you aren't that different of a threat to others. Erling is more logic and curiosity driven than most erdi'zal, but I doubt he would be that so calm if it was one of his own who was the bisegus. As for Wynna," she looked at the woman working to dice up fungi with a knife not designed for it. "She is unpredictable. First angry, then suddenly in tears. It is impossible to tell how she will react to any changes. We were fortunate she responded to my revelation with more grace than I expected."

"She's always like that. Quick to change her mood from sweetness to rage. Wynna's been through a lot. Considering her mother was murdered a few days ago, she's doing better than I would have thought."

But Shimi Zar didn't seem convinced. "Loss isn't that easy. You saw Grazzlunn. After his daughter was taken, he devoted his life to discovering what she was. He learned a great deal about the world, and even came close to some of the truths regarding the Shiftlings, but it consumed him. His wife abandoned both him and the mountains because of his obsession. He secluded himself in the depths so he could study uninterrupted. Only in the last few years has he allowed others to visit him, to consult his knowledge. But all that didn't return his daughter to him."

Leda's eyes narrowed. "You could bring her to him. You said you know where she is. Why haven't you reunited them?"

"Not her wishes. She told us long ago she had no desire to ever have any interaction with him. She's never forgiven her parents for giving her up."

The woman considered her own recent reunion. Her mother and father were heartsick that they had to leave her in Talidith, but they were doing what they thought was best for her. She understood that, but it hadn't completely erased the pain. "I can see why. But how is this like Wynna?"

"In a sense, her mother has abandoned her, though through no choice of her own. I'm sure she wishes she could see her again. That grief might push her to do something drastic."

Leda forced a laugh. "This is Wynna. She hates doing anything that takes her out of what she knows." She gestured to where the other female was making faces as the smell of the fungi she was cutting reached her nose, forcing her to toss down the knife and storm away in protest. "Drastic actions are not her strong suit."

"Yet she is here, along with the rest of you. There is a powerful motivation pushing her." Shimi Zar sighed. "Or maybe I'm wrong, and she'll be all flowers and light."

They hiked up the small bank to where the others were working on a meal. Over one low fire, a pot was boiling with the sliced fungi. A spit made of sticks held a slab of the lizard meat over another fire next to it, occasionally dripping fat into the flames, causing them to snap, crackle, and hiss.

The flesh was already turning a pale pink as Malwin flipped it, sending a pungent aroma drifting toward the blue sky. The morning light, softened by shades of orange, lit the countryside better than any torch. Though their time in the mountain had been brief, the brightness now rivaled the midday sun in contrast to the dim tunnels.

"You said this stuff was like our vegetables!" Wynna pointed at the few pieces she hadn't finished cutting lying on a rock. The reddish, spongy growths gave off an acrid odor which caused Leda's eyes to water. "They stink!"

"I didn't mean they were the same as yours." Shimi Zar crossed her arms, mimicking Wynna's favorite arguing stance. "I meant they are like your vegetables to egyzemors. Do not pretend your food doesn't smell! That thing you call broccoli is disgusting, and don't get me started on your carrots!"

"I'm sure it will all be delicious when it's cooked." Leda extended her arms outward, motioning for them to come together. "You've all done a wonderful job."

"Why do you do that? Play diplomat. People can have arguments without needing their feelings soothed."

The words startled Leda. *Do I really do that?* "I- I didn't know I was."

"Thank you! I am glad someone else noticed." Wynna sneered at Leda. "She is always trying to pretend everything is wonderful and we should all get along nicely."

Heat rushed to Leda's face, embarrassment prickling beneath her skin. "It's better than complaining about every little thing that happens! We are all doing the best we can."

"There she goes again! She cannot help herself!"

"Enough!" The bellow came from Malwin. He was slicing off pieces of the cooked meat and setting them in a pan. "Eat!"

They stopped the argument and joined him and Erling around the fire. Shimi Zar hauled over a fallen log with ease, her dainty frame belying the strength she retained from her other form.

Each of them had their own dinnerware in the packs, except for Shimi Zar. She borrowed one of Malwin's knives. Unlike the other women, who daintily cut their meat, Shimi Zar simply chomped off chunks of gyzlet straight from the blade.

Wynna watched her gulp down a sizeable wedge. "How do you ever pass for a human woman with manners like that?" Despite her earlier protests, she was hungry and ate the lizard flesh without protest. Graypaw and Cutie also had their own bits of meat and fungi, respectively.

"What use are manners out here?" Shimi Zar countered. "Don't worry. I can act all lady-like when I need to."

"I guess you lost them living in this place." Wynna nodded toward the mountain behind them.

Malwin grunted, picking apart a hunk of flesh with his thick fingers and jamming it into his mouth. "Wrong?"

"Ignore them, my friend." Erling sliced off a section of his portion and held it between the two thumbs of his hand. The meat was firm, slightly gamey, with a smoky richness that clung to their tongues. "I have found humans have an over-inflated sense of rightness in their ways. It is hard for them to appreciate the customs of others."

"Is that a jab at me?" Wynna demanded. "Because I'm the only human here."

Leda winced at the claim. She was, in every way she understood, a human. Despite meeting her parents and hearing Grazzlunn's explanation, she wasn't convinced she was one of these Shiftlings. "How long have you been living among the egyzemor?" she asked Shimi Zar, steering the topic in a safer direction.

"Since I took over as a guardian." She paused, then added, "So, about twenty-five years this summer."

Both Wynna and Leda's eyes went wide. "How old are you?"

"Now, that's not a question you ask a lady." Shimi Zar took a small bite of meat and made a show of chewing. But she couldn't keep a smile from creeping on her face. "I'm teasing. I am fifty-two."

The pair of females gasped. The seemingly young woman was older than both of them combined! "But that can't be!" Wynna protested.

"Far from it," Erling told her. "Each race has its own life expectancy. For example, egyzemors live a few decades less than humans, on average, while my kind normally lives almost two decades more. I am guessing that span is even greater for bisegus."

Shimi Zar signaled in the affirmative. "It is."

"These guardians." Leda took a slice of boiled fungi onto her fork and brought it to her face. The stench of before had vanished. Now it smelled closer to an apple. "Is there one for each item?"

"There should be."

The woman popped the piece into her mouth to cover her reaction to the answer. The surprise was genuine, though, as it melted on her tongue with a taste of cinnamon. *There wasn't a guardian for the bow. Or was there?*

"Are they all bisegus?" Wynna asked, frowning.

"I don't know. I think they were originally, but that may have changed. The position gets passed along. I was twenty-seven when I took it. Still an immature kid."

"Who are you calling immature? Leda and I are younger than that!"

Shimi Zar sighed. "But you have different aging. At what age are you considered an adult?"

"Seventeen," Leda said. "But some mature early."

"And you are how old now?"

"Twenty-two. Wynna is twenty-four."

Shimi Zar squinted, as if working out calculations. "So technically, I'm only a little older than Wynna."

The blonde woman shook her head. "But you've been a guardian longer than we have been alive!"

Leda stared into the fire. "What's the lifespan of a voladorm?"

"Slightly more than a human." Shimi Zar held up a hand. "And before you ask, no one's figured out how it works with Shiftlings. You should age the same as your true form, but we also don't know how that is affected by you staying human."

"That is an interesting puzzle." Erling swallowed down his last bit of lizard. "Do the forms take on the same qualities as a pure individual, or are they merely cosmetic?"

"That's what we don't know. My kind ages at the same rate, no matter what form we live in." She saw Malwin wince. "We don't do it to deceive you, so much as to survive. We can't help it if the easiest appearances to adopt are of the races who fear us the most. If it helps, my time among your people has been quite enjoyable. They are honest and noble in their ways, and if not for the animosity between our kinds, I would very much like to live with them for the rest of my life."

The egyzemor was unsure how to take this. It was a great compliment, but the thought of her or another bisegus living in the mountains conjured up old fears. Finally, he just nodded.

"I do not see what all the fuss is about." Wynna put aside her plate, her portion of fungi untouched. "You certainly are not scary."

"Fear of bisegus isn't rooted in what they are personally. It is based on the insecurity we all bear that those we are with are not what they appear to be." Erling blinked all four eyes at once, which he did when he was being his most philosophical. "This can happen even among our own races, as everyone has something to hide. They are merely a physical representation of that dread."

"That sounds right," Shimi Zar said. "Doesn't change how people see us."

That's why Wynna was so upset! Leda realized she hadn't considered it from that viewpoint. Wittingly or unwittingly, she had betrayed her friend.

Wynna sat quiet and seemed to be considering the erdi'zal's words, too.

"How far from here to this arcanist?" Erling asked.

"Not far. We should reach her tower by tomorrow night."

Wynna frowned. "A tower? What kind of person lives in a tower?"

"One who likes her privacy," Shimi Zar said sternly. "To this day, she studies the ways of arcana."

"I hope she also likes company, as she will be receiving visitors soon. But we must travel on foot." Erling looked expectantly at Wynna. "We have no caravan this time. Or horses."

But the woman surprised him. "I am sure we can handle it." She let out a wide yawn. "But not before we sleep!"

"Wynna accepted a hardship without protest," Erling teased. "Could our luck be changing?"

Again, to his surprise, she laughed. "Do not count on it. I still have two days to get in plenty of complaints. But for now, just bed."

Chapter Eight
RECOVERY PLANS

S UNLIGHT SLANTED ACROSS the river as the *Swift Salvation* bumped against the shore. Mikel spotted a break in the riverbank just wide enough to land, and the trio wasted no time going ashore.

Vyncent limped after them onto the rough bank. When Savanah told him to stay near the boat, he only nodded and clung to the towline for support.

They hacked through the dense brush until the forest loomed around them. Countless trees, many still not recovered from their winter shedding, stood too close together for a horse and rider to pass. Land travel would've slowed them to a crawl. While the river had its perils, Savanah was grateful they had chosen that route.

All three called out Camille's name for the better part of an hour, with Mikel and Savanah moving deeper into the woods. When they regrouped, despair crept back into the archer's chest. "Did either of you hear or see anything?" she asked.

Mikel shook his head. "I detected nothing."

"I can't see much around here except the river," Vyncent said, leaning against the boat's bow. "And I doubt we will. We don't know if she even came this way. She could be anywhere by now."

"Camille wouldn't abandon the mission, no matter how angry she was." But Savanah wasn't sure of her claim. It hadn't been anger that had driven her away. *I broke her heart. Would I stay on a journey with a person who had done that to me?* "Maybe she returned to the tower. We should go back and look. We could recover our gear."

"We aren't going by land," Mikel said. "Even if we had horses, it would take hours. We might do better with the boat, but I am not experienced enough to sail her upstream."

"We can't stay here, either," Vyncent added. "More of those things could come. Camille made her choice. We can't risk our lives or the mission because she ran off."

Savanah's face flushed with anger. Camille only transformed to help her sort through her feelings. Feelings which *he* had muddled by suddenly playing the romantic. "She would put her life on the line to save you! That's what we signed up for with the Sovereign Guard."

"Not when someone throws themselves into danger!"

Savanah's voice cracked with anger. "Like Aedan?"

Vyncent blinked. "What?"

"Aedan helped me drive Olagkoa back to its cave, risking his life. If he hadn't, he wouldn't be a prisoner of that monster. But we are all risking *our* lives to save him."

"Aedan's not a soldier. He's a fisherman who didn't know any better."

"He knew what he was doing. Him not being trained makes it even braver!"

Vyncent's face reddened, and he edged toward the higher ground where she and Mikel stood, gripping the rope for support. "Are you calling me a coward?"

"Are you planning to run off again because the situation is hard?" she shot back. "Leave the rest of us to finish what you can't be bothered to?"

"If I hadn't left the Undercastle, we would never have gotten help."

Savanah let out a cold, bitter laugh. *He is nothing like his father!* "Is that the lie you tell yourself? Jaron and the others were already on the way. If you hadn't left, we might have contained Olagkoa. Desmund wouldn't be dead, and Aedan would be with Leda now."

"You are blaming me for all that?" Vyncent shouted. "I had nothing to do with it!"

"Exactly! You weren't there when we needed you. When I needed you!" A lump rose in her throat. Did she mean Vyncent, Warne, or Camille? Anger and pain blurred the line. Did it matter?

Vyncent stomped his foot against the sandy ground. "You are never going to let that go, are you?"

"Not while you continue to act like a petulant child!"

"Enough, both of you!" Mikel cut between them, voice sharp as a blade. He blocked the daggers in the glares. "You've obviously got issues to work through, but this isn't the time or place. Whatever happened, it's in the past. We have to get moving."

"That's what I said," Vyncent complained, whining like the child she accused him of being. "But she wants us to stay here forever!"

"Don't put words in my mouth!" Savanah snapped.

"Enough! Vyncent, our duty is to protect each other. I am the one who decided to stop and look for Camille. Savanah, I don't want to leave her either, but we can't stay any longer, and we can't go back. She knew the mission. Do you think she would want us to turn back from it?"

"Of course not. And I didn't say we should." Flustered, Savanah glanced upward. "I just think..." Her words faltered. High above, an owl perched on a branch, still as stone, its pale feathers marred only by a single red dot gleaming like a drop of blood. It stared directly at her. When she met its gaze, it ruffled its wings and turned toward the water.

"Think what? Savanah?"

It's Camille! She hasn't left us. I am so sorry, my dearest friend. I didn't know! "I think we should go. You are right. Camille would want us to continue. She might even catch up with us further along, after all. Come on! What are you waiting for?"

Before they could reply, Savanah strolled down the bank, past a puzzled Vyncent, and began pulling herself onto the boat.

The change surprised Mikel as well, and he stared up at the tree to see what had convinced the woman to leave. He saw nothing.

He heard something, however. The tearing of earth and snapping of branches grew louder, faint but drawing nearer. "Get aboard," he ordered Vyncent as he hastily joined him. "Your discussion has alerted some beast to our presence. I'll give you a boost."

"I don't need your help. And she started it." Despite his refusal, Vyncent's shoulder wound made it difficult to pull himself up to the deck, and he relented, allowing the other man to lend a hand.

"Why do you think she changed her mind?" he asked once they shoved off. Savanah had already taken a seat at the tiller and was guiding the valupe back into the current.

"Because she knows how important this is," Mikel answered. "None of us are backing out of it. We need to find those artifacts."

Vyncent took the rebuff without argument as they watched the retreating shore. Whatever Mikel heard, it never appeared. "You gave those things a name. Carcass beasts. What are they?"

The other man shrugged. "That is a long story and I don't want to get into it here. Suffice it to say, they shouldn't be here, not in Wayela, not at this time. For now, let's focus on the trip ahead. That includes patching you up properly. So no more fighting, at least until we reach Forden."

"I can manage," Vyncent grunted. "But she's the one who wouldn't drop it."

HAMUND ALERON SANK into the wooden chair, a sigh escaping before he could stop it. Kingship never promised ease, but the recent months, especially the last few days, made it feel impossible.

Pirro Bukhid stretched across the cot, a thick blanket swaddling her lithe frame. She usually prided herself on her tidy appearance, particularly now that they lived as civilians, but today, she looked a mess. Her dark skin had paled a few shades, her lips tinged with purple, and her hair clumped in messy tangles. A strand of the charcoal tresses hung down over her cheek, twitching with each exhale.

She breathed — and for that, Hamund thanked the gods. Yesterday, her survival teetered on a thread. One of Talidith's citizens had poisoned the well of the settlement within Zatreus's walls. Nearly twenty people died before Drew, their physician, traced the cause and brewed an antidote. Pirro had been among the sick, collapsing at the moment the man announced he would test the water.

She received the antidote just in time, but the poison had already drained her, and nearly shattered Hamund in the process. He hadn't bothered to wash or shave since the sickness struck. Such activities seemed trivial in light of what others had gone through. What *she* had gone through. *What would I do without you?* he asked himself as he watched her sleeping. *What would I have done if you had died?*

After King Valeria's death and Olagkoa's rise, Hamund took on the role of calm leader, guiding their evacuation from the Undercastle. In return, they made him their new ruler.

Savanah, acting as Commander of the Sovereign Guard, had ordered Pirro to stay with him during the worst of it, and help him with whatever he needed. Now that they'd settled in Zatreus's refugee quarter, the Guard had disbanded, and the crown felt more like a relic than a role.

Despite that, Pirro continued her assistance to the man. Talidith's people still looked to Hamund as their leader, and she seemed to understand that he needed her far more now than when they were fighting for their lives in the dark.

I do need you. Their relationship shifted from simple acquaintances in the Guard to partners in governing, even though she still deferred to his decisions. Now, those lines were blurred.

When she collapsed from the poison, it felt as if he was the one dying. Numb to his very core, his limbs had moved like lead through the hours, his voice steady only by habit while grief gnawed behind his ribs. He'd forced himself to offer guidance and comfort to those around him, even as a silent scream raged within. But when she began to recover, his heart soared, and the world regained its color and meaning.

He added to his prayer the hope that he never had to go through that again.

Pirro stirred, stretching one leg. One hand came up and brushed away the errant hair before opening her eyes. Her lips parted in a weak smile. "You look terrible."

Despite his exhaustion, Hamund dropped to the floor before her and placed a hand on the edge of the cot. "It only matches how I feel. How are you?"

The woman's lids fluttered closed again, as if taking stock. "I ache, my throat's raw, and I'm hungry enough to eat a vornuk. But mostly, I'm tired, like I could sleep all day." Her eyes snapped open, and her voice tightened with tension. "Sorry! What about the sick? I shouldn't be here!"

Hamund chuckled and gripped her shoulder as she struggled to rise. "You *are* one of the sick, so stay put. The others are being tended to and are on the mend, as I hope you are." When she remained tense, he added more gently, "Rest. There is nothing you can do now."

Pirro finally accepted his words and fell back onto the cot. "What happened? I don't remember much after that little blonde woman visited."

"Drew and I figured out that everyone must have been poisoned from the water. He was about to test the well when you collapsed."

"I'm sorry."

"You have nothing to apologize for," he told her, cupping her cheek. The move was instinctive, surprising both, but when she didn't protest, he kept it there. "Once we had a sample, Drew was able to make an antidote. It took a few hours, but soon after we gave it, the sickness began to fade from those affected."

Pirro nodded, causing his fingers to stroke her face. "Then why am I back in our cottage?"

When Talidith's citizens moved into the new quarter, officials assigned houses to families, couples, and individuals. Since they were now considered part of Zatreus, there were no other buildings for official business in the section which suited Hamund. That meant, though, that the cottage he was given became the unofficial seat of power. At the time, sharing the space with Pirro felt like the obvious choice.

He lowered his hand to the cot. "I brought you here. I wanted you to wake up in a more comfortable setting." The gesture had seemed appropriate then, but now Hamund wondered if it might appear too intimate.

His explanation drew a fresh smile from her lips, though. "That is very sweet of you. I appreciate it."

"You have done so much for me, it only seemed right," he told her honestly, his words carrying the weight of everything he'd felt. "I would be lost without you."

Pirro's eyes fell to the floor. "That is kind, but I am only your assistant. I do what I can."

"No!" For reasons he couldn't quite understand, Hamund felt warmth rise to his cheeks at her self-deprecating remark. He placed his fingers under her chin and raised her eyes to his. "You are so much more than that," he said softly. "My constant companion. My confidant. My strength. If not for you — "

A sharp knock shattered the moment. Hamund flinched, then scowled toward the door. *Is peace too much to ask?* When the sound repeated, he released Pirro and rose to open it.

On the other side stood Lukas Dehil and a female erdi'zal, whom the man recognized as Shanna, one of the higher-ranking members of the city guard. "I apologize, Hamund, but she was adamant about seeing you," the former said, his voice tinged with regret.

"It is alright," Hamund told him, then addressed Shanna. "You are always welcome here. What can I do for an official of Zatreus?"

She stood taller than most erdi'zal, clad in the top half of a soldier's uniform on her torso, with a coordinating blanket draped over her hindquarters. Though her kind were typically archers, favoring the longbow, she held an immense sword before her. With her free hand, she extracted a folded parchment from her pocket and shook it open.

"I have come to inform you that for the immediate future, you and the people under your leadership are to remain within the boundaries of your established dwelling region," she read out. "Failure to comply could see the offending party imprisoned indefinitely."

"What have we done to warrant this?" The pronouncement puzzled Hamund. After they led the attack which drove Olagkoa from the city, he thought their standing with the authorities of Zatreus remained good. "Is this because of the sickness? It's been contained."

Shanna fixed him with a glare from her front-facing eyes. "There is an illness among your kind?"

"Someone poisoned our well, making many fall sick and killing twenty of our people. We have been fetching water from other parts of the city, so preventing our movement will hurt us."

"Why was this not reported to the capitol?"

"It happened so fast, and we did not know what it was at first, so we quarantined ourselves. But our physician created an antidote."

"Then you should have little problem maintaining that quarantine. I'll see you have fresh water provided for the duration." Pirro had shoved herself off the cot and staggered up behind Hamund, who quickly wrapped an arm around her for support. The woman's appearance and movements weren't lost on Shanna, who stared at her with disdain. "I thought you said the illness was contained."

"She is recovering," Hamund explained, giving Pirro an encouraging grin before turning back to the erdi'zal. "Will you tell us why you are doing this?"

Shanna raised the parchment again and scanned it until she found the appropriate section. "Accusations have been leveled against Talidith and its population, suggesting collusion with the beast known as Olagkoa in an attempt to overthrow the governing body of Zatreus. Until the veracity of these claims can be obtained, you are restricted from any action that could be perceived as an act against the High Monarch, those operating on her authority, and any citizen not otherwise covered by the prior two clarifications. Raising of arms, even among your own kind, is strictly prohibited."

"That's absurd," Pirro said, trying her best to stand straighter. "Zatreus came to our aid, and we are grateful. We wouldn't do anything against you."

"Be that as it may, it is not my place to question orders. Once the truth is established, if you are found innocent, I am sure you will be able to return to your normal activities."

"And how long will that take?" Hamund asked.

"I cannot say." Shanna flicked the parchment shut, then tucked it back into its pocket. "We are dealing with more pressing matters at the moment."

"She means the Riverwall has been destroyed, probably by Ludholm spies," Lukas clarified, having watched the exchange with a little more understanding than his leader. He had been the messenger to Zatreus when an army of creatures had threatened Talidith. He later befriended members of the city guards, which gave him more access to recent news.

"That information does not affect this action," Shanna said, brushing it aside with a flick of her hand.

"Doesn't it?" Lukas pressed. "Your war revolved around control of the river. Now that you don't have one anymore, that puts an end to it."

"The war isn't over," Shanna countered. "We will take our revenge on Ludholm. And we'll learn what part you and your people played in it. Until then, do not stray far from your homes."

"I want an audience with the High Monarch to discuss this," Hamund told the erdi'zal. "I am sure we can clear up any misunderstanding."

"I will convey your request, but I cannot guarantee a reply." With her message delivered, Shanna turned without a parting word and trotted away from the cottage.

"What have we missed?" Hamund asked once she disappeared from view.

"Plenty," Lukas answered with a weary sigh. "Last night, a series of explosions destroyed the wall holding the river back in the harbor. Now the water is spilling over, filling the Banrood Grasslands. The High

Monarch has been trying to stem the flow further east long enough to rebuild the wall, and trade has been rerouted to the roads." He paused, shaking his head. "But, there is something else far more disturbing. Reports say that the armies of both cities have been killed by that creature and possibly turned into those undead things we fought."

Pirro gasped, but Hamund contained his reaction to a grimace. "That may explain Ranin and Farla's abrupt departure. Once I have helped Pirro back to bed, we will step outside and you can tell me everything you know."

But she grabbed his shirt, her fingers interlacing with the fabric as much to keep herself steady as to draw his attention. "I'm well enough to sit, I think. I'm not missing his explanation. Hold me if you have to."

Hamund's eyes met hers, wondering if her phrasing was accidental or an invitation. He tightened his grip, pulling her closer.

"You heard her, Lukas. Come in and give us the news."

IN THE WAKE of Olagkoa's failed assault, Ludholm teetered between joy and grief, with cheers in the morning shifting to silence by midday.

The water filling the grassland below rose to a depth of several feet, but it would still be a few days before the lake would be restored. Righting a seven-hundred-year wrong felt like ripping a curse from the city's bones. Hope flickered, real, but fragile.

But the toll it had taken on the population couldn't be ignored. Nearly a quarter of its citizens had been brutally slaughtered in the conflict meant to end their hardships. That the victory had come without needing their deaths only made it harder to accept.

Still, many tried to view their situation in a more favorable light. Once the danger seemed to pass, civilians drifted beyond the gates toward the swelling lake. Children who had never seen calm water before shrieked with delight as they splashed through the shallows. The adults keeping watch over them often joined them, unable to resist the opportunity.

The few hafu among them took particular pleasure in the water, some swimming out into the deeper parts to explore. Shallower than the Hafugung and slower than the Leosonee, it proved to be a unique experience.

Other non-humans hesitated to join in, however. The handful of voladorms who spent much of their lives in Ludholm had flown to the Eastern Heights to announce the change in geography to their people. Many egyzemor had done the same. Only the erdi'zal, seeing the loss of a grassland as nothing to celebrate, seemed regretful of the developments.

Most of the city's residents were human. Without the influx of trade, Ludholm had drawn little more than a handful from the other races. With the lake returning, though, that would change as well.

If they could hold on to it.

King Daymon summoned his commander to his side. Grekorn Mistoak obeyed, and together they stepped beyond the perimeter of the assembled citizens. Whether the day would be remembered as a triumph or a tragedy, decisions needed to be made, and actions set into motion.

"I had hoped we would win this war decisively," Daymon explained once they were out of hearing range of the others. "If we had overwhelmed Zatreus's forces, we could have negotiated for a joint trade outlet from a position of strength."

Grekorn furrowed his brow and shrugged — not with confusion, but with disinterest. "What does it matter? Once our boats are ready, they will have no choice but to accept our place alongside them."

"Will they? We achieved our goal with deception, not superior power. Lightreaver must know by now — or will soon — of the destruction of both our armies. Without a deterrent, I am sure she will find a way to thwart us."

"Then we send in our bisegus allies to sabotage them again."

The ruler shook his head as they strolled past a disheveled shop. An older man busied himself with repairing the deteriorating roof, driven by the hope of a rejuvenated Ludholm. "It is not that simple," Daymon explained as he waved to the owner. "The negotiations I planned for would also include the use of their crafts, at least temporarily."

The confusion lingering on Grekorn's face made it clear he still didn't grasp the reason for concern. "Why? Our boats will be completed soon, will they not?"

"Have you not visited our boatyard? Our people haven't needed to build any vessels for centuries. What they produced is barely capable of floating. They won't survive a river voyage, let alone navigate it."

"Then we take what we need from Zatreus!" Grekorn's fist shot into the air, his voice sharp with certainty. "We can't give up now."

Daymon nodded at his knight's enthusiasm. "We will not give up, but we will not descend further into duplicity. That is Lightreaver's way, not ours. We have our win, but we cannot pull our kingdom and our people out of the mud by sinking further into it."

The soldier scowled, his broad shoulders sagging. "What else would you have us do?"

"Restore our knowledge by opening trade," Daymon said calmly. "There must be some boatwrights in Stegate. We can hire them to train our citizens, and in the process, have some made for more immediate use. In return, we offer them some of the new ore we've mined." He pointed toward the city fortifications where a barrel full of the rocks Tal had observed sat.

"Is that wise? We don't yet know the value of it. We might be giving away a fortune."

"Or we might be giving away useless rocks. But we have barrels of the stuff lining the walls, and until we begin sharing it with the other cities, it will have no value at all." Daymon sighed. It did sound like a big gamble, but they were on the brink of regaining everything they had lost long ago. They had to try. "Organize a delegation, perhaps four or five of our people familiar with the ore, to strike a deal. If they fail, we can try Forden, and then Carlin. We'll find someone who can help if we have to send ambassadors all the way to Adradena."

"That'll take time," Grekorn said. "It's a fifty-league ride to Stegate."

"That can't be helped. Another delegation must be formed and sent to Zatreus. The war is over now, but there is a window for diplomacy. Lightreaver might still find it in our mutual best interest to expand its port."

"After she killed our last messenger?" the soldier asked, his voice filled with disbelief. "No man will want that mission."

"Then I will take it myself if necessary. Peace is not made unless one side is willing to open a dialogue." The pair stopped before the barrel, and Daymon picked up a single brownish stone. "But we need not be foolish. Send any men we still have who can wield a sword as protection."

Grekorn's frown deepened. "Even that could prove to be a significant challenge. I'll send some of my armed men. If the war is truly over, there should be no further threat to the city, and they can be spared."

"Good, good," Daymon muttered, his focus on the rock in his hand. "I will draft documents for both groups. They should be dispatched this evening or tomorrow morning at the latest."

"I'll see to it."

"I know." His face brightened. "Along with sending those, I want you to make a third delegation. It only needs to be a few who are familiar with the forest. I want them to deliver some of the ore to Caster Nastina." He held up the bit of raw material, letting the noon sun shine directly on it. A shift in the light made the dull surface briefly shimmer as if it were fluid before it solidified back into stone. "It may sound strange, but something about these stones seems like it might interest the arcanist."

THE SUN DIPPED low, painting the river in streaks of amber and rose as the Swift Salvation nudged ashore at the watchtower near Forden. They had stopped at the city a few hours earlier, as Mikel had promised, and found a physician to treat Vyncent's wounds.

Along with bandages, balm, and a clean set of clothes for him, they also purchased replacement cooking gear and utensils, bedrolls, blankets, and fresh food. Mikel got a change of outfit, too, finally tucking away the bisegus cloth in a new pack.

Savanah bought a bow and quiver of arrows, too. While she loved the silver bow, Nastina had warned her about depleting its supply of arcana, which was critical to stopping Olagkoa. After their encounter with the carcass beasts, who appeared impervious to its magical projectiles, she also wanted the familiar reliability of a normal weapon.

Restocked and revitalized, the trio brought the boat to the next tower. Vyncent kept quiet, and for that, Savanah breathed easier. She had let her frustration with him bubble to the surface, and while she meant what she said, she had no desire to revisit it.

Since spotting Camille's bird form, she watched the shoreline closely and believed she saw her friend a few more times, flying between branches or soaring about the trees. She couldn't be certain, of course. At a distance, the shapeshifter looked like any other owl. If not for the bit of red, Savanah would not have recognized her at all.

She wanted me to see her. To make sure we continue on without her. But why won't she come back? Does she still blame me?

"Are you joining us?" Mikel asked.

She lowered her gaze at the sound of his voice. He and Vyncent had already dropped to the bank and pulled the boat further onto land while she stared at the forest beyond. "Yes. Are you planning for us to spend the night here?"

"This tower is on the opposite shore from where we encountered the beasts. We should be safe here, but I would rather not risk it." He pointed to a grassy area a short distance inland. "We'll have a quick supper, then sleep on the boat."

"I won't argue with that. One encounter with those creatures was enough for me." Vyncent prodded the shoulder where he had been bitten. "But maybe you could find the time to tell us more about them."

Mikel nodded. "It isn't really my story to tell, and I don't know all of it, but I can relate what I've heard. First, let's start dinner. This spot is a bit more visited than the last, so there are multiple fire pits around."

He hiked a short distance up to a worn area and began collecting fallen branches while Savanah handed the fresh food and cooking gear down to Vyncent. Soon, the aroma of frying fish filled the evening air. Slabs of crumbly Dewford cheese, hunks of dark bread, and a few kliku fruits rounded out the meal. They had even splurged on a few bottles of cyser. While the fermented apple and honey mead had an intoxicating effect on humans, they didn't intend to get drunk. Not while they were in the wild.

"You were going to tell us about the creatures," Savanah prodded as they ate. The fire crackled and cast flickering light on their faces, warming their shins while the night air cooled their backs. Dew already crept into the folds of the grass, dampening the hems of their cloaks. Their swords were unsheathed and lying beside them. If anything tried to attack them tonight, they would be ready.

Mikel washed down a bite of fish with a sip of cyser. "What do you know about Viscardi the Mad?"

Vyncent shrugged, but Savanah spoke up. "I've heard the name. He was some prince in Begesh, long ago."

"He likely thought of himself as one. When arcana came to the world, it brought much trouble, as everyone attempted to work out its nature. A hundred years passed before the first arcanist arose, discovering how to channel the power into objects."

He flicked a fish bone into the grass. "In Wayela, it was seen as an oddity. The few who practiced it merely experimented, producing a few useful items, which they sold to the rich. In Samos, the first collection of arcanists was formed to pool their knowledge. They were slow to develop anything, as they were meticulous in testing and recording any results. They viewed it as a scholarly pursuit. In Begesh, the arcanists who arose there were mistrusted and shunned, so few bothered to even experiment."

"We should have done that here," Vyncent grumbled, breaking off a piece of bread. "Then we wouldn't be having to fix what they did now."

"I don't disagree. After a few thousand years, after multiple wars and scares, the three continents forged their own ways of dealing with the growing number of individuals capable of wielding arcana. Samos outlawed its usage entirely, driving those who could into developing hidden groups to study in secret. Wayela founded the Union of Arcany, which in time became twisted into the Skorgan Empire.

"In Begesh, the Order of Wisdom was established. Similar to the Union, it was a place for arcanists to share their knowledge. Viscardi was an apprentice there, working as an assistant. Little is truly known about what happened in their midst, but it is believed he tricked them into teaching him more than they should have. He ultimately betrayed them, wiped their memories, and drove them out to seize control of the Order. He spent several years blackmailing the local towns, threatening to destroy them if they didn't pay him."

Mikel paused and took another sip of mead. "Eventually, he moved to an island, or was exiled there. There, he conducted experiments with arcana, and not only objects. He attempted to merge it with the native wildlife, twisting them into perversions. The carcass beasts were one of his creations."

"That's it?" Vyncent asked. "You could have just said they were the products of a madman. We don't need a lecture on the history of arcana."

"I think we do," Savanah told him. "We are tracking down artifacts imbued with arcana to stop a creature brought here by arcana because of an empire built on arcana."

"Indeed." Mikel cut a piece of fish with his fork and swallowed it before continuing. "It is important to understand that the rest of Rapria didn't handle its arrival the same as us. There are other ways."

"But none of them conjured a monster from another world, right?" Vyncent pressed. "That is our immediate problem."

"No. As I just explained, they created monsters of their own. My concern for them is that they shouldn't exist here. Viscardi eventually died, and his island, along with his work, was abandoned. So why are some of his creations here?"

Vyncent shrugged, unimpressed. "Maybe they took a boat. Does it matter?"

"The island is thousands of miles from here."

"Alright. They took a ship. I don't care."

Savanah frowned at his rudeness but said nothing. "Why are you worried, Mikel?"

"Viscardi was an arcanist," the man explained. "A powerful one. He created many of his own artifacts. Until a few days ago, before we met with Nastina, it didn't matter. Arcana was gone, and with it, the threat. But now we've learned some, like your bow, can be made to hold a supply of arcana."

"And you think if some creatures left the island, the artifacts might have found a way off?"

"Precisely."

Vyncent swallowed a gulp of cyser, then wiped his lips on the sleeves of his new shirt. "I still don't see what the problem is. The beast must've swum to the mainland. I've heard no one claim any of these items could do that."

Mikel pointed with his fork. "They don't swim. You saw how they recoiled at the water's edge."

"I saw nothing from the deck," he sniffed. He pressed a knuckle to the bite, still sore beneath the bandage. "Too busy dying."

Savanah raised an eyebrow at his flippancy. *How did I ever mistake him for his father?* "I saw it. They panicked when they touched it."

Mikel nodded. "Viscardi bred them to fear water, or their altered forms simply don't allow them to swim."

Vyncent scoffed. "That's ridiculous. Why breed them not to swim?"

"To keep them on the island, I imagine," Savanah told him.

"Which means," Mikel interjected, "Someone has to have been there and either brought a few back, or provided a way for them to cross to the Begesh mainland on their own."

"Alright. I understand." Vyncent lowered his plate. "But can we put that aside for now? That is a lot of 'ifs', and our mission is a very tangible 'is'."

"You're the one who specifically asked," Mikel reminded him. "You are right, though. It's not a concern we can deal with at this time." He swallowed the last bit of fish and put down his dish. "And our immediate need is sleep. Even if we spend the night on the boat, I suggest we set up a watch rotation. I'll take the first."

"What happens if something does appear?"

Mikel flashed a grin. "We shove off. Fast."

"Unless it's Camille!" Savanah added in a loud voice, lifting her gaze to the evening sky. "She's welcome back anytime. No questions."

Vyncent frowned. "That's obvious. But not very likely. She would have to be traveling faster than us, not to mention finding a way across the water."

"Don't count her out," Mikel told him, getting to his feet. "She is resourceful. I wouldn't be surprised to see her trot up on a horse in the morning. Or come down the river in her own boat."

Savanah nodded, hoping she was listening to the invitation and praise. "Or even fly into camp."

As they prepared to keep watch for the return of the beasts, a greater threat advanced from upriver. Aedan and the boat of Shells were only sixty miles north and closing the distance fast. When they finally caught up, the Olagkoa-controlled beings had a single objective: seize the bow and any other artifacts in their possession, and leave no one alive.

Chapter Nine
THE FALL OF LONGBRIDGE

"**W**E CAN STOP here for a bit," Eris told the others, reining his horse to a halt. "The army is at least half an hour behind us."

His companions did the same, bringing their animals into a tiny clearing. Holfast continued pacing for a moment, energized by their sprint through the forest.

After leaving Ludholm, they had pursued Olagkoa and its forces. They couldn't risk getting too close, however, lest the creature detect their presence. If it sent its undead soldiers after them on the road, they would be doomed.

Holfast explained that the path emerged at the Old Road, formerly the Northern Passage, a mile north of Longbridge. All these names were only vaguely known by Eris, Ranin, and Farla, having lived most of their lives in Talidith.

They'd agreed Olagkoa wasn't doubling back to Zatreus. It had already bypassed the city once. That left either crossing the river or heading south, and both scenarios involved the small town.

Unable to pass it and the Shells on the road without being detected, they moved into the thick, wooded area to the left. Dense undergrowth lining the path had made it difficult and at times painful to leave it, but they had pressed on into what Holfast called the Hightower Woodlands.

Tight trees and thorny brush slowed the travelers. Brambles clawed at their clothes and skin, snagging reins and ripping at sleeves, while low branches slapped against their faces. But hour by hour, they gained ground on the marching dead. They kept speaking to a minimum due to the fear of being detected by the monster or its creations.

They stopped briefly to raid their supplies, realizing they hadn't eaten anything since midnight. As the afternoon dragged on, they grew more anxious. The ever-present sound of boots against dirt and jangling of armor had faded, and they hadn't heard it for some time when Eris called for the halt.

Holfast assured them the route from Ludholm had no side avenues or junctions, so unless the Olagkoa sent the soldiers into the woods after them, they would have to come out at the Old Road. It gave them a chance to rest.

Farla moved to check on Ranin before turning to him. "How big is this Longbridge?"

"Tiny," came the erdi'zal's response. "It is a village devoted entirely to the handling and maintenance of a bridge which spans the river."

Eris's eyebrows shot up in disbelief. "One bridge? An entire village devoted to that?"

"They're doolally over it." Tal tapped a finger against the side of her head. "Fiercely against Swingbridge. A couple of guys from each were in the Crosseyed Eggy once and got into a brawl. Really going at it. Had to be dragged apart before they deaded each other."

"I'm guessing Swingbridge is another village," the man said.

"Just south of the mountains," Holfast confirmed. "The tale goes that twin brothers, Oliver and Oswin Bridgewater, had come up with different ideas on how to span the Leosonee. Eventually, each had their own built, but still argued over which design was best. Over time, settlements formed around the constructions."

"Bridgewater? Are you serious? What is so complex about a bridge?"

"That is not a question you want to be asking in either place, at least if you don't want to be carried out of town by an angry mob." Holfast's fierce expression hinted that such a punishment had befallen him. "The difficulty, as I understand it, lies in the need for it to be moved to accommodate river traffic. A permanent bridge would be a hindrance to the taller vessels."

Farla held up a hand. "What do we do if it's heading for Longbridge?"

"Same as Ludholm," Eris told her bluntly. "Warn the citizenry and if necessary, stand with them."

Holfast shook his head, though. "As noble as that sounds, even my people don't fight without a hope of success. I doubt all the herriads of the Trideen Highlands could hold their ground against a force of that size, made up of soldiers who cannot die."

"What do you suggest, then?"

"Trap the army on this side of the river. Longbridge has a population of less than fifty. We disable the bridge so the creature cannot cross, then evacuate the villagers. Send them south to the mountains. They can hide there."

"That's hardly trapped!" Tal protested. "Oh, sure, it can't touch your Highlands, but all the rest of Skoim Pral is open. Not just Wayela, but Begesh and Samos!"

All four of the erdi'zal's eyes closed to slits at her insinuation. "I know that. But with the river to the west and mountains to the north, east, and south, we have the best chance of containing it here, at least until a permanent solution is discovered by your people."

Eris nodded. In Talidith, Savanah and the other members of the Sovereign Guard had worked to keep the creature contained within the Undercastle. While that had failed, limiting its movements still seemed their best choice. He only wished he knew more of the surrounding geography to assess the chances of Holfast's advice. "I don't see another option."

"I do," Tal said. "Let it and the Shells into the Trideen Highlands. With all that space, they will have nobody to attack."

Holfast fixed his gaze on her, barely keeping his anger in check. "Even if we could steer them in that direction, the route passes through hundreds of miles of towns and villages. Are you suggesting we displace them all?"

"If we have to," she told him, either not noticing his irritation or not caring.

"No." Eris caught her eye. "If Holfast believes we have a chance of trapping Olagkoa and its army in the terrain here, then his is the best plan."

"So run ahead, scream in panic, and destroy the bridge?" Ranin asked.

Holfast's expression eased. "That is a crude interpretation, but correct."

Eris nudged his horse forward. "Then let's get moving. The bigger head start we can give Longbridge, the better."

With that decided, the four riders and one erdi'zal resumed their travel through the forest. From the sour look Tal gave him, Eris knew she wasn't satisfied with the discussion, but she managed to keep quiet until she and he had fallen behind the others. "What did I do wrong?"

The man glanced at her in confusion. "What?"

"You accepted Holfast's plan over mine."

He nodded. "Because his has fewer unknowns. It isn't anything personal."

"What about in Ludholm?" Tal pushed. "You were ready to send me off to be some dull ambassador."

A laugh escaped his throat. "As if you would accept."

"You sounded serious." The quiver in her voice made it clear that the woman was about to burst into tears.

He heard it and tempered his tone. "I was, partially. The animosity between your two cities won't be over just because one side got what they wanted. Daymon is too optimistic for someone without an advantage."

"You think he's planning something else?" Her voice steadied.

"I do. And if you had stayed behind, you might have discovered what it was."

That quieted the woman for a moment as she considered his words. "So you didn't believe I could do the job!"

One minute she's angry he offered her for it, next she is upset she didn't get it. And she calls me misted! "Nope. I think you would be a brilliant negotiator. You are a bit quick to anger at times, but you speak your mind without fear. The war might have been avoided entirely if there had been more honest dialogue on both sides."

Tal blushed, apparently taking his assessment as a compliment. "So you like it when I argue with you?"

That was her takeaway from what I said? But Eris paused to consider her question. He had opposed Savanah when the creature was discovered, not accepting her claim of it or her plans. That had cost many their lives that day, and countless more since. If he had accepted her leadership, they might not be in this position now.

So was the problem not in the disagreement, but in the acting upon it? Tal had gone against his orders a few times and ended up saving his life at least twice. "No one likes having someone argue with them. I've made poor choices before and will again. You will, too. I guess what I'm saying is it's hard to know what is right or wrong in the moment. So yes, I want your suggestions and insights, but whether those are the correct decisions or not likely won't be known until after action is taken."

"Well," she began, drawing in a huge breath, "that was needlessly confusing."

And I'm not even sure if it's right. How did King Valeria ever manage with rulings that affected hundreds of lives? "Tal, just be yourself," he said with a reassuring smile. "I might need saving again."

That brought a grin to her face, and she nudged her horse to ride ahead, her faith in her value seemingly restored for now. She caught up to Ranin and Farla, and the three fell into a quiet but cheerful conversation.

As they got closer to the forest's edge, the trees thinned out, letting them move much faster. In just over an hour, they emerged on the Old Road, a short distance from the path leading back to Ludholm.

It was late afternoon, with the sun sinking low in the sky. The companions took a few moments to appreciate the open space again after spending most of the day in the woods. The horses appreciated it, too, as they began hungrily tearing up chunks of grass.

Holfast was the first to notice the problem with the waterway, having moved to the other side of the road. "Come see!"

Eris jumped from his saddle and sprinted to join the erdi'zal, with the women following close behind. They halted sharply when they saw the reason for his concern.

"What happened to it?" Tal asked, pointing at the low water. It had sunk to less than half its normal height. Slick rocks jutted from the bank, tangled with pale green weeds. A sour, algae-rich smell clung to the exposed mud.

Holfast glanced up and down the channel. The reduced level stretched endlessly in both directions. "With most of the river pouring into the grassland, little is making it through to its normal route. It will be like this until the lake is full or Zatreus rebuilds the Riverwall."

"This is great!" Tal gushed. "That thing will never get its army across now! It's too low for a boat or bridge!"

Eris didn't share her enthusiasm. "I should have realized this would happen. Ludholm's attack has crippled the entire trade route. How long do you estimate it will take for the Banrood Grasslands to be full?"

"I am no expert on water flow, but I am familiar with that region." Holfast's ears twitched as he calculated. "At the speed in which it was filling, and if there is no breach to its barrier, and if Lightreaver does not find a way to block up the breach, and if — "

"Hey!" Farla interjected. "Just say it, already!"

"Seven to ten days," the erdi'zal told them. "This is really Erling's sort of thing."

"Then trade will be down for at least that long. Traffic will be minimal," Eris said. "That should minimize the number of deaths if we fail to control the situation."

"There is still trade by the road," Holfast said. "That was decreased because of the war, but not ended entirely."

"Maybe one of us should scout ahead and warn anyone along the way of the creature and army," Ranin suggested. "In each direction."

"It may come to that," Eris admitted. "But we haven't been particularly successful in our past attempts to convince others of the threat."

"Then we make the threat!" Farla grabbed the hilt of her sword to emphasize her meaning. "Send them away for their own good!"

Holfast's laugh came out in quick bursts. "I like the way she thinks."

Eris frowned. He'd led a group against Savanah's leadership, making similarly foolish claims. Farla and Ranin had been a part of that. Now he heard how misplaced they sounded. *Let it not come to that!* "Let's deal with Longbridge first. If we can't keep the army on this side, it will no longer be a factor."

After remounting and checking the road back to Ludholm to ensure the Shells weren't about to emerge — between the distance and the fading light, they weren't even visible — the group galloped south. In a short time, they arrived at the village.

If Eris hadn't known the purpose of the settlement before them, he couldn't fail to understand it now. For the most part, it was like most small communities in Wayela's countryside. A few dozen simple houses littered the area, with ample space to provide some farming land and privacy, yet sufficiently close for a semblance of protection. Larger buildings sat on one side for community gatherings and official business. A covered well, complete with rope and pulley, stood near the center, despite the dwellings' proximity to the water-way.

However, two things set it apart from the other villages Eris saw on their flight from Talidith the previous year. The first was the gigantic wooden platform which sat on the opposite side of the road on the river's shore. Twin platforms — one stacked atop the other — over a hundred feet long and twenty wide, dwarfed anything Eris had encountered before. He couldn't explain its workings, but the design clearly functioned.

The other abnormality stood in the center of the settlement. Possibly carved out of a tree or cleverly put together as multiple parts, the towering statue of a man in simple garb and holding an axe stared out across the river to the wilderness beyond. Given Holfast's earlier tale of the brothers, Eris easily recognized the statue as a monument to one of them.

As the companions trotted into the village, they were immediately greeted by a lanky, older man sitting in the doorway of a tiny building. He was dressed in what likely passed for an elegant suit among the locals. A stiff brown jacket, smelling faintly of pipe ash and mildew, clung awkwardly to his bony frame. The ensemble reminded Eris of the straw crop watchers some of the farmers in Talidith erected. His limbs were at least as spindly as the sticks they used. "Welcome, travelers, to Long-bridge," he said, his voice hoarse and raspy from smiling lips. "I am Arti Diragno, Watcher of the Northern Passage. Here we have the finest mechanical apparatus for spanning waterways both diminutive and vast. Constructed from durable, high-quality materials, this — "

"We are not here to use your bridge, as fine as I'm sure it is," Eris interrupted. "There is an army coming that intends to kill anyone they find."

The man's false friendliness dropped away instantly. "If you are not here to cross, then waste not my time. Continue along your way."

"Didn't you hear what he said?" Tal asked, watching him retake his place on a worn chair. "An army is going to wipe out your little town. You need to move. Now."

"I need do no such thing," Arti grumbled, crossing scrawny arms across his shallow chest. "We will not be falling for your tomfoolery this evening. Return to your substandard, ill-conceived walkway and leave us be."

Holfast was the first to recognize the reference. "You have misunderstood our intent. We are not from Swingbridge, and a deadly force is approaching. You need to vacate this area for the duration of their passing."

"Is it indeed? Like when you sent us that woman who claimed to be the long-lost heir to our founder, Oliver Bridgewater, and demanded we turn our hamlet over to her. Or the time you paid that pair of farmers to drive their filthy hogs across our crossway after they had been fed an enormous dinner? We were cleaning pig you-know-what off it for a month!"

"This isn't a trick! We are trying to prevent the destruction of your village!"

A frustrated grunt came from Farla, and she kicked her horse into a trot. "Hey! All of you!" she yelled as she moved in among the houses. "You are in grave danger! An army is coming!"

The man's expression twisted with rage as he leaped to his feet and chased after her. "Halt that at once!"

Tal's face lit up with a smile as she spurred her horse onward to join Farla."Everyone run if you don't want to die!"

Seeing the pair raising the alarm, Eris hastily dismounted and faced the others. "Ranin, keep a watch for the army. Holfast, help me disable the bridge."

The woman nodded and turned her animal as villagers began emerging from their dwellings at the commotion. Eris and Holfast sprinted across the road, gaining a clearer view of the construction as they approached.

Oak beams formed parallel tracks on the slope, supporting two broad wooden platforms. The lower rolled along the ground, while the upper rested on its twin, set to slide forward when deployed. At its rear stood two triangular frames, one on either side, each holding a spoked wheel joined by a solid axis around which thick rope was coiled. A pair of iron spikes kept the wheels locked in place.

Though Eris wasn't experienced with mechanical devices, he thought he grasped the basics of this one. Remove the spikes, the wheels turn, and the platforms roll across the water, the top shifting to the end of the bottom to complete the span. "How do we prevent the creature from using this?"

"A fair question. The only mechanism for keeping it in this state seems to be those pieces of metal. We'd need something stronger, and even then, anything we put in place could be removed."

Eris nodded as he examined the bridge's system further. It was designed for easy deployment, and as the erdi'zal had observed, whatever they could add to hinder that would only be temporary. They needed to disable it more permanently. He placed a hand against the bottom platform and pushed. It didn't move. "Do you think we could dislodge it from these wooden beams?"

Holfast made a similar test of its durability. "Not without a dozen burrals."

"Remove your hands this instant!" Arti, apparently giving up on pursuing Tal and Farla, hobbled across the roadway, his thin limbs jerking with a mix of age and ire. "You are not qualified to operate such a device!"

"Then we'll have to burn it," Eris concluded, barely acknowledging the man. "I'll get the flint from my pack."

"You will *not*!" Arti boldly moved to intercept the soldier. "The sole mission — nay, duty — of this settlement is to provide wanderers with a safe means of reaching the opposite shore. I won't allow a single board of Sir Oliver's bridge to be harmed."

Eris sized him up. Though a few inches taller than himself, the older man couldn't weigh more than a child. "I know it isn't the best way, but we must prevent the army from crossing the river. So, unless you know of another means of disabling it, we — "

"Unthinkable!" Arti howled. "Our causeway stood five centuries without incident! There was the Leosonee flood, of course — "

"Write down today as the next one," Eris snapped, cutting him off. "What's coming down *that* road will wipe out your village, your people, and your precious bridge. You can save yourselves if you act quickly, but that's all. Now move!"

Arti seized the threadbare lapels and puffed out his chest like a rooster about to crow. "As I have asserted before, I do not — unhand me, ruffian!"

Holfast's thick fingers clamped around the man's wiry arm, lifting him as easily as one might hoist a broom. Arti's bony feet kicked at the air as he squawked in outrage.

The intervention allowed Eris to pass. The soldier sprinted back across the road, pausing only to glance down the dirt path for any sign of Ranin, the soldiers, or Olagkoa. Thankfully, it remained empty.

The village, however, was not empty, with the population surrounding Farla and Tal atop their horses, pelting them with questions rather than fleeing. *By the sword! Do these people have no sense?* Against his better judgment, he remounted his horse and directed it toward the gathering. His words likely wouldn't sway them, but letting the towns-folk die wasn't an option. *I won't have more deaths on my conscience!*

"Whatever they've said is true!" he shouted as he came up behind the group. "If you don't leave immediately, your village will be destroyed and all of you killed."

"You can't threaten us!" a male voice cried.

"It isn't a threat!" Farla yelled. "Well, yes, it is a threat, but not from us. We are here to warn you!"

"We aren't falling for it," a woman called out. "Go tell that to your Swingbridge masters."

Tal urged her horse toward the villagers, and the ones in front stepped back. Eris thought she planned to try driving them out, but she kept advancing calmly, giving them time to move aside until she was free of the circle.

"Hey!" Farla yelled. "I told you, we aren't from Swingbridge!"

"That's just what a Swingbridger would say!" someone else shouted. "I bet they broke the river, too!"

Tal wasn't wrong about their rivalry. "We are from Zatreus," Eris called. "The Riverwall there was destroyed, that's why — "

"Swingbridge is the best!"

A chorus of gasps arose from the villagers as they whirled about to see who the blasphemer was. Their eyes fell on Tal, sitting atop her horse and waving her arms. "That's right!" she shouted. "Your bridge is useless! I bet everyone who uses it falls off!"

Eris felt a shared rage roll off the townsfolk, nearly as strong as a mental blast from Olagkoa. They lunged forward like animals, shouts and curses rising out of their ranks as they rushed at Tal. The woman had planned for it, though, and easily guided her horse into a sprint. She didn't go far, however, before turning it back around. "Your bridge was designed by a blank-brained potato herder with hairy legs!" she called out. "I've seen children build better stick toys!"

It wouldn't have worked on most other towns, but those in Long-bridge had a fanatical view of their mission and founder. Eris watched in alarm as they raced after Tal, but she had already sent her steed into a gallop, leading the mob to the road. If she hadn't been on horseback, they would have caught and undoubtedly killed her for her sacrilege.

As they chased her south, Ranin came galloping in from the other side. Behind her, a dull rhythmic pounding rose, like distant war drums, meant the Shells were marching now, instead of shuffling along. "They're coming!"

Eris and Farla whirled about to meet her while Holfast dropped Arti to the ground. "How long?" the erdi'zal asked.

"Maybe ten minutes," came the reply. "No more than that."

"Then we're out of time. Ranin and Farla, follow Tal and the towns-folk. Get them moving faster! I'm not sure they'll have the sense to run even when they see the Shells. Holfast, we've got to burn the bridge!"

"You will not!" Arti shouted. "Help! Help! People of Longbridge! The bridge is in peril! These ruffians are going to set it ablaze! Come back and — "

His cries were abruptly silenced as Holfast seized his shoulder, forcefully clamping a hand over the bony man's mouth.

Eris looked to the villagers, hoping in their fury, they missed the words. Luck wasn't with them today, though, as a half dozen turned to look at them. He swore as one shouted. "They've got Arti!"

Maybe Farla was right about making a threat. "Change of plans. Farla and Ranin, make sure they leave, even if it's at sword point."

"Finally!" The shorter blonde drew her blade as she urged her horse forward. Ranin pulled out her own more reluctantly, but fol-lowed her partner toward the crowd. The rest of the townsfolk realized there was a menace, and it was to their beloved bridge. They redirected their ire to the companions.

Eris kicked his steed into a short gallop across the road, with Hol-fast following close, his feet padding over the dirt. A glance toward the way they came confirmed Ranin's news. A large force was definitely moving their way. Worse, they no longer marched with the slow delib-eration of mindless Shells. They had picked up their pace dramatically, spurred on by the sight of the villagers or Olagkoa's command.

The army would be upon Longbridge in less than two minutes!

Man and erdi'zal sprinted to the bridge. Eris stumbled as he dis-mounted too quickly, then fumbled in his saddlebag for the flint. He snatched up a rock and struck it against the metal, aiming the sparks into the wad of dry grass Holfast had crammed between the bridge's levels. But the kindling refused to catch. "Take my horse and get out of here!" he ordered.

To his surprise, the erdi'zal did as he asked without arguing, calling for Arti to follow. *I've been around Tal too long. She'd still be cursing me out.*

The grass abruptly flamed and began blackening as it burned. Eris's head throbbed as his heart pounded. He caught a fleeting glimpse of the front line of Shells nearly upon the village, their weapons drawn and gripped in lifeless hands, as he grabbed up chunks of vegetation and dried leaves and stuffed them into the flames. The wood blackened, but still refused to catch.

Then the first Shell reached him.

A sword, swung awkwardly by a man who looked forty when he died, clunked against the timber as Eris ducked. The Shell wasted no time in regret over its miss, lunging again. Three more behind it rushed forward to join the attack.

Their limbs lacked the precision of when they were powered by living minds, though, and the four fell over each other, their weapons clashing. One blade drove through another Shell's shoulder, but neither corpse slowed.

I can't let myself be trapped here! Eris backed up and leapt onto the closed bridge. Fingertips dug painfully into the thick wood as his feet struggled to find support, but he held on. After a few seconds' strain, he reached the top.

From there, he glimpsed the village. While only a few Shells had come after him near the river, the rest were pouring into the settlement, weapons drawn but lacking any expressions on their lifeless faces. Most of Longbridge's citizens crowded at the other end, so not in immediate danger.

Not all were so fortunate. Arti, who had been so adamant that their warning was merely a trick, had failed to follow Holfast to safety. The sight of the swiftly approaching undead soldiers had rooted him to the ground.

In his last moments, his panicking mind had fallen back to habit. "I am Arti Diragno," he began, raising his voice to be heard over the thundering of boots. "Watcher of the northern passage. Here we have — "

Then he fell, a Shell's sword piercing his heart.

The half dozen who had left the protection of the crowd to rescue him yelled as a score of the undead veered in their direction. Ranin and Farla urged their horses forward, but there was no way to reach them quickly enough. The women spun their animals back toward the villagers, avoiding the sight of the slaughter. They couldn't escape the dying screams, however, which echoed across the river and sent both trained fighters into a near panic.

Eris witnessed the deaths, though. He barely had time to add them to his mental tally before being forced to consider his own fate. The four he had eluded struggled to follow him to the peak of the bridge, but that wasn't his concern. As the army surged into the village, his avenues of escape were rapidly decreasing. If he hesitated now, he'd be trapped.

He sprinted across the top. In the distance, he saw Holfast running ahead, pulling Eris's horse behind him — the horse he needed to ride to safety. The surviving citizens were in full flight, escaping down the road with Tal in the lead and Ranin and Farla defending their rear. Their speed was the only thing saving them, as the Shells lacked the coordination to keep up with their living prey.

The rest of the army swarmed the simple structures, crashing through doors, stomping on gardens, and sending the few chickens, pigs, and other livestock into frenzied flight. Eris prayed the ransacked homes were empty, and that any babies or children were taken with the other refugees.

Beneath this side of the bridge remained clear of soldiers, giving Eris a chance to reach the ground unhindered. However, a formidable barrier of Shells was swiftly rising between him and his companions, creating an imposing wall that threatened to separate them completely. He was already cut off.

He searched for another route, even turning back toward where the army was coming from. A surge of panic rose in his chest at the sight of Olagkoa, shoving along the road and towering over everything except the trees. In his concern for the Shells, Eris had almost forgotten they weren't the biggest threat.

Times up! One avenue of escape remained. The river! Another sprint took him the length of the bridge. There, he hopped to the dozen feet of ground between it and the former water line. He darted to the side, looking back up at the construction to where he had lit the grass. Elation surged through him as wood finally caught fire. In the evening light, he watched flames licking the oak platform and sending gray billows of smoke into the cooling air. The four Shells who attacked him paid it no attention.

The bridge will burn. I just need to get away, now! He turned to the river. The level had dropped to half its usual depth, revealing a steep, twenty-foot slope of exposed ground between him and the reduced channel. He leaped and landed on the muddy incline, his feet sinking deep into the soft earth. To steady himself, he grabbed a handful of water lilies. Their slimy stalks made them difficult to hold, though, and he almost tumbled further down.

He slogged through the muck. His boots nearly got stuck twice, and a layer of mud coated one arm up to the elbow, marking the spot where he had almost fallen over. *If the Shells come this way, they're sure to be trapped.*

After several minutes, he reached what he hoped was a safe distance and carefully climbed back up to shore. After emerging behind a thicket, he checked his immediate surroundings before raising his head about the thin branches.

Further up from the river sat the road, clear of fleeing citizens. He couldn't see much further from his position, but he took the lack of Shells on it as a sign the others had gotten away cleanly.

He'd emerged on the far side of the village, opposite the path they'd taken in. The settlement lay in ruin, the undead having trampled every inch of ground, broken down every fence, and smashed holes through every building. Since the animated corpses lacked much intelligence themselves, he knew the destruction must have been ordered by Olagkoa.

But why destroy a poor town? Is the creature planning to level all the cities in Rapria? We can't evacuate all of them.

He spotted the tentacled monstrosity shoving itself into the center of chaos, the Shells parting to let its gigantic bulk pass. Seeing the armed soldiers beside the towering horror — barely a third of its size — reminded Eris just how dangerous its sheer mass was. The houses in its way were either smashed by its powerful tentacles or pulverized under it, leaving nothing but a trail of rubble in its wake.

Its path made its immediate target clear. Longbridge's second greatest pride — the enormous statue of Oliver Bridgewater — had drawn Olagkoa's attention. It stood taller than the creature, with the otherworldly monster only reaching its carved chest.

Eris found the comparison both comforting and daunting. Seeing something other than trees dwarfing the beast meant there were still things in the world larger than it. However, it had more than doubled in size since its release, and given time, might even outgrow the statue.

Olagkoa extended a few tentacles to caress the monument, running their barbed tips over the smooth surface. It appeared almost gentle. Then the hooks stabbed into the wood, with more limbs shooting out to embrace the structure.

Whether believing it to be a human its size or simply disliking something taller than it, the creature seemed intent on ripping it down as its appendages grew taut. As it thrust its remaining tentacles into the ground, Eris could hear the statue groan and crack under the strain. To his amazement, he saw it tremble as Olagkoa applied its immense strength to dislodging it.

The Shells around the village resumed the aimless wandering patterns he had witnessed back in Zatreus. Eris recognized this as the beast having eased its mental control over them in its battle with the monument.

With a thunderous crack, Oliver Bridgewater's giant likeness split from its stone base and slammed into the creature. Olagkoa didn't cry out, but the tentacles wrapped around the statue shoved it forcefully aside, then retracted. The broken sculpture tumbled briefly before slamming into the ground, crushing a few houses and a dozen Shells beneath its mass.

The beast seemed not to notice how it had casually destroyed its servants as it rotated, churning up the earth and smashing more buildings in the process. Though it had no face, Eris had seen it favored one side to be its front, and usually oriented that toward its target. Olagkoa brought that section around toward the river, or more specifically, the bridge.

Eris shifted his position behind the thicket as he watched it push and pull itself out of the village and over the road. He could see smoke rising from the far side of the oak crossway, but the construction remained intact. *By the sword! I left it too soon!*

Indeed, the patch of flames didn't even bother the fire-fearful Olagkoa as it passed by. It ran its appendages over the top of the bridge, easily reaching the height Eris had to climb up to. Despite the distance, the man could see its grotesque form over the construction moving with deliberation toward the river.

That's it! Eris bit back a cry of excitement. *The bridge can't span the Leosonee at its current level! There isn't enough water to support it!*

The creature reached the edge of the bank and paused. Tentative tentacles traced the end of the walkway down to where the ground sloped away. They extended further down, probing the mud Eris had recently escaped through. A chill ran down his spine at the sight. Olagkoa had followed the same route as him without hesitation. *Is it hunting me, now?*

After a moment, the beast seemed to give up its investigation, bringing its hefty appendages back to the twin layers of oak. As with the statue, tentacles crawled over it, digging their barbed tips into the wood and gripping the sides of the top platform.

Then it pulled.

The carved monument had been built as a solid, unmoving entity. The bridge, however, was constructed to move easily. Had Olagkoa investigated the mechanism at the opposite end, it could have found and removed the iron spikes keeping it secure, making the forced extension unnecessary. As it were, they might as well not have been there at all, as the wood holding them snapped like kindling.

With a crack, the tentacles yanked the twin platforms, snapping the restraining beams. It took a few seconds for the hundred-foot-long bottom level to extend half its length over the span. As Eris had thought, without the current to buoy it, the entire construction tipped forward. The shift in gravity sent the top rolling ahead, but it landed far from the opposite shore. With a loud splash, it struck the water, shifted another twenty feet, then lodged in the river bed.

Eris clenched a fist in triumph. *It failed! The army is trapped here!* Experience tempered his enthusiasm, though. Olagkoa had proven too resourceful in the past to believe it would give up now.

A sudden shift in the movements of the Shells told him his doubt was right. Their aimless shuffling stopped as they pivoted toward the river. A moment later, they started marching in perfect unison, the synchronized thud of their boots reverberating through the ground and sending tremors beneath their feet.

What are they doing? They can't cross like that. They'll end up in the water. When Eris turned his attention back to Olagkoa, he saw the monstrosity descending the mucky slope. He knew the thing could swim, but did it intend to ferry the undead army over itself?

When it arrived at the edge of the channel, the beast's intent became clear. Tentacles stretched upward, latched onto the underside of the bridge, and pushed. Wood creaked as the platform rose, water sluicing from its far end. When Oliver Bridgewater's greatest invention leveled out, Olagkoa began shoving it further across the span. To Eris's great disappointment, the top extended to the opposite shore and rested on the ground there.

By now, the soldiers had reached the shoreline. Without hesitation, five stepped onto the oak beams, which groaned under the weight but held. Another five moved onto it as the first ones continued their march, then more behind them. Eris stared in disbelief, horror twisting his gut as the Shells advanced. The bridge trembled with each step the ever-growing procession took over its construction. It hadn't been built for this heavy a load, but Olagkoa's powerful limbs somehow kept it intact.

Realizing they had failed, Eris backed away from the thicket. His companions were waiting somewhere further up the road. The survivors of Longbridge would be there, too, unable to return to their village, but he and the others could do nothing more for them now.

Olagkoa and its army would soon be on the far side of the Leosonee, free to wage war on larger kingdoms than Ludholm. They could ravage every village and town along the way, driving them into the ground, and displacing their population. There wasn't a force in Wayela capable of stopping their reign of terror and destruction.

But we have to try! he told himself as he sprinted down the road. *We have to try!*

Chapter Ten
PURSUIT, POWER, AND PERIL

MIKEL NUDGED SAVANAH and Vyncent awake while the forest still crouched in shadow, the air damp and tinged with the earthy scent of moss and wet bark. He took the last watch of the night, and despite no sign of the carcass beasts, he wanted to press on early.

"I'm not opposed to getting up before the sun," Vyncent said with a yawn as he tugged on his boots. "I only want to know why. Whatever artifact the hafu possess isn't about to run away."

"It's not that," Mikel countered as he collected his bedding. "We've taken longer than I intended on this trip, and I doubt we will finish it unhindered."

"Why?" Vyncent stood and folded up his blankets as well. "No one knows where we're going, except the High Monarch and Jaron. And we are trying to defeat an evil monster. Who would want to stop us?"

"Not everyone has the same view of good and evil." Mikel moved on to the newly bought cooking gear, the clink and clatter of pans briefly breaking the morning hush as he tied them together. "Remember Nastina's explanation? The creature was dragged here from its world, attacked, then imprisoned. Who are the malevolent ones in that?"

Savanah donned her own boots and collected her bedding while she listened to the men argue, not offering a word. She remembered Nastina's warning, and worse, the agony she saw when they tried sending Olagkoa back. That ritual had torn the creature apart. Would she be able to repeat it? The Displacement Orb had allowed her to travel over six hundred years in the past to observe the ritual being performed — the same ritual they would have to do once they found all the artifacts. It was brutal, causing the beast great pain. Since then, she'd wondered if she would have the strength to put it through that again when the time came.

"The Skorgan Empire," Vyncent said, answering Mikel's question. "They did all that. Doesn't mean the creature isn't evil."

"I didn't say it did. But do you say it's evil for seeking revenge? If you were treated that way, can you honestly claim you wouldn't want to punish those who hurt you?"

"Our people didn't do anything to it, so why were they made to suffer? Or your city? We lost our entire kingdom." Irritation crept into Vyncent's voice at his companion's line of conversation. "I can't believe you are siding with that monstrosity. It killed my father!"

Mikel lifted his hand slowly, palm open in a calming gesture, recognizing he had pressed too far. "I am sorry. I didn't mean to suggest that. My point is that there could be those who want to aid Olagkoa, and that means stopping us."

"Like Aedan did in the harbor," Savanah added. The fisherman hadn't wanted to help the monster, but whether willingly or unwillingly, they had to consider him Olagkoa's ally.

Vyncent's anger eased. "Alright. I accept that. But it isn't like he is going to get a boat and come after us. Aedan was a fisherman, not a sailor." He paused, then corrected himself. "Is. He is a fisherman."

Savanah nodded. "Vyncent's right. Almost no one knows what we are doing."

"Which also means there is no one coming to our aid. Or to continue on if we fail." Mikel flinched at his own harsh tone. He drew in a steadying breath as he set the cooking ware down beside his bedroll. "Still, I feel the press of time, as if someone were pursuing us already. Carlin is only a few hours away. If we leave now and push on after sundown, I believe we can make it there by midnight."

"Midnight? That's more than a few hours away," Vyncent grumbled, the previous flash of anger gone. "What's so special in Carlin?"

148

"A night in a proper bed and a hearty breakfast," Mikel answered with a broad grin. "After that, it's just two more cities before Adradena."

"So, a hop, skip, and a jump away? I guess if there is bed and breakfast included, we can get started." Vyncent looked at the archer. "Savanah?"

She had been scanning the trees, expecting to glimpse the silent flutter of wings or the telltale red feather, but her eyes dropped at his words. "I'm just hoping Camille might catch up at some point."

Vyncent started to voice a retort, but Mikel met his gaze and gave a subtle shake of his head. "I am certain she will," the older soldier told her. "Maybe that is who I feel behind us."

"If it is, she can join us for breakfast," Vyncent added, despite the warning. "If it isn't, we should get moving even faster. Let's go!"

THE RISING SUN bathed the Eastern Heights in gold, the peaks looming majestically before Eris's group. A cool breeze swept down from the snowcapped peaks, sharp with the scent of frost and stone, drawing a shiver from each companion as they rode onward.

The night left them ragged, with shadows like bruises under their eyes and tension in every movement. After leaving the survivors of Longbridge with firm instructions to seek the nearest town instead of returning home, they doubled back to check if the bridge could still be crossed. Without the extra support of the water or Olagkoa's powerful limbs, however, they decided it wasn't worth the risk. They needed to find another way to reach the other shore.

So they resumed tracking the monster and its army from this side. It was simple to follow their quarry. The steady thud of countless feet drummed through the air, a hollow, rhythmic echo that traveled across the river.

Olagkoa didn't rest, and neither did the dead. Their hunters did, however — and they required food and water. They ate and drank what they could while they rode, but getting sleep was a greater problem. The humans had set up a rotation, where two slept in their saddles, their mounts being led by the others who stayed awake. A pair was already dozing in this fashion. Farla's head lolled against her horse's neck, while Ranin swayed gently with each step, reins looped slack around his gloved hands.

Eris could see it wasn't sustainable. The horses plodded forward, heads low and hooves dragging more than lifting, their flanks slick with cold sweat. Holfast's eyes were half-closed, and his paws dragged as he walked. Neither beast nor erdi'zal could rest. Both were already taxed from their trek through the grasslands. They would have to find another method of pursuit.

He looked to his left at Tal. Her slumped shoulders and drooping head indicated she was near exhaustion. He and the others were soldiers, trained for endurance. She was a tavern server who had forced her way into their fight against Olagkoa and, despite his efforts to discourage her, seemed determined to see it through to the end with them.

At least she doesn't appear angry at me anymore, he thought. She'd been livid when he caught up to them after the destruction of Longbridge. The events had pushed her into the lead of the villagers, leaving him behind with the army of undead, and she accused him of having a death wish. *For whatever reason, she thinks she has to protect me.*

He let a smile turn his lips. For all her stubbornness, it warmed him to have someone who cared what happened to him. He felt the same toward her, but his feelings were steeped more in guilt. Eris counted every casualty as blood on his hands since he helped release the creature. If he couldn't keep her away, he would at least make sure she wasn't added to that ever-growing burden.

Since Longbridge, Olagkoa and its servants hadn't claimed another life. They had kept to the Western Road on the opposite shore and encountered no travelers along the way. Eris hoped anyone catching sight of the tentacled monstrosity would have enough sense to get off the route as quickly as they could.

Cold mist pooled in the narrowing trail as they entered the mountain pass, which would take them and the river through the Heights. Holfast warned them the space would be restricted, so unless Olagkoa planned to take on the inhabitants of the peaks, they would have to come out near Swingbridge. From there, it could choose among dozens of towns and multiple cities to attack. Forden, Stillwater, Banmore, Kridmont, Stegate. All just names Eris had heard before, that would soon become very real.

Does it have a specific goal, or is it making these decisions randomly? Maybe the other groups have learned more about it. I hope they found something. Anything!

One of the erdi'zal's front legs faltered, causing him to stumble. He led the companions, but now Eris wondered how much longer he could continue. "Holfast," the man called, keeping his voice low to avoid disturbing the others. "Come here!"

The normally swift-footed warrior nodded wearily and dropped back beside him. "My apologies. I have not slept, and — "

"I know. We can't continue like this." He pulled his horse to a halt and signaled for Tal to do the same. She did so with a grateful nod, then the pair moved their animals to the other steeds and woke the women gently.

Farla blinked rapidly, rubbing one eye as she sat upright with a grimace. "What's happening?" she demanded, her voice thick with sleep. "Why did we stop?"

"Nothing's happened," Eris reassured her. "But we can't keep on this way. Holfast can barely stand, and our horses aren't much better."

Ranin looked anxious. "We can't stop now!"

"We *must*! At least some of us. Look, the army isn't moving quickly. We can easily outpace it without wearing ourselves out. I suggest we travel in shifts. One group sleeps now, here, while the other keeps up with the Shells. Then, after a few hours, the first one catches up and follows while the second rests."

"What if something happens to the group ahead while the others rest?" Tal asked.

Eris shrugged. "Then they'll deal with it the best they can. I know this isn't perfect, but unless the creature finally decides it needs to sleep, we'll work in shifts."

Holfast yawned and nodded. "My people do the same when we must track a beast for days. I should have thought of it."

"Who takes first rest, then?"

At Tal's question, Eris nodded toward the erdi'zal. "Holfast first. Ranin and Farla can stay with him and finish their sleep. You and I will continue on. After four hours, they catch up with us, then we rest for four hours. I don't know how long before we reach the other side of the mountains..."

"At the pace of the army, about half a day," Holfast interjected.

Eris nodded. "Once there, we'll find a way to cross the river. We might also learn where the creature is heading."

"There's just one place I want that thing to go," Farla said, aiming her glare at the marching figures across the water. "The abyss!"

"Hear, hear!" Ranin chimed in.

Tal's mischievous grin returned. "How about instead, we send it there ourselves?"

"I agree," Eris told them, bolstered by their unwavering resolve. "But for now, get some rest!"

JADA DASIA PICKED up the last of her scattered reports and added it to the pile on her desk. Like the others, it was wrinkled and torn, but mostly intact. Two days earlier, she had been reviewing the handwritten accounts, each detailing the expenditures and profits of a shop under the protection of the Baker's Guild, which she led. She aimed to identify which shops were thriving and which needed extra scrutiny. *With our trade in peril, do they matter anymore?*

She idly ran a hand through her bushy blue curls as she surveyed the rest of the room. With help from a few guards, she cleared away the larger remnants of shattered furniture, but splinters of wood and ribbons of torn fabric still blanketed the area beneath her feet and crunched with each step. Her new desk and chair stood in place, pale imitations of what they replaced. But the smaller, cherished pieces she had gathered over the years were lost forever, along with delicate trinkets now reduced to shards strewn across the cold stone floor.

Near the wall, a dark stain marked where brown tea and black ink had mingled in a sticky pool, the vessels that once held them crushed and broken beyond repair. A few scraps of finger sandwiches lay scattered, the rest claimed by rats who had already come and gone. The tray that had borne them rested nearby, its surface unbroken save for a hoof-shaped dent — a stark reminder of the chaos that had unfolded.

Only her towering wooden cupboard survived intact. It lacked adornment, but its value resided not in decoration but in craftsmanship. Carved from *vasfa* wood, a dense and rare material nourished by the iron-rich depths of mountain soil, it stood a marvel of strength and rarity. Its unyielding structure had weathered the destruction, standing firm as though defying the surrounding devastation.

Dasia could only look at it for a moment before shifting her gaze elsewhere. Mamatay, an infamous assassin among her kind, visited her two nights ago as she worked at her desk. He arrived in the form of Gar, the hafu servant who normally brought her refreshments, and announced his intent to take her before the *matasnakon* to answer for her crimes. The fight between them left her study in ruins. She emerged victorious, but at a terrible price.

She had killed one of her own.

His remains lay tucked away in the back of the cupboard, a compressed ball of flesh smaller than a blood ceriman. It still made her queasy to think about it, but she had no other place to dispose of it that wouldn't be discovered.

Though rare among her kind, killing another bisegus was a deeply shameful act. They retained their shape in death, ensuring their secret remained safe even if witnessed by outsiders. Dasia was forced to trap and suffocate the assassin, reducing him to a final form that left her disgusted. Having spent her life clawing her way toward significance, to see one ending in such an ignominious manner filled her with dread. *If the tribunal discovers what I've done, the punishment will be far worse than surrendering would have been.*

She spun around at the sound of the latch clicking as Joice Nilado shuffled into the room. The woman's boldness irritated her. "I would appreciate it if you knocked before you barge into my study."

"Whatever for? You have no secrets from me." The Matron closed the door behind her, then slipped the bolt into place. "That cannot be said for the rest of Wolfsight. We must take swift action."

"Wasn't that what we did at the Council meeting this morning and yesterday?" Dasia asked as the human woman approached. "I will draft letters to all my shops about the change in transportation and the emphasis on longer-lasting goods when I've finished going over the reports."

"I meant a more pressing matter." The ingratiating smile she relied upon to placate others was gone, replaced by a dour manner. "Lightreaver has been asking questions about the pair I had arrested. She demands proof that they are spies for Ludholm."

But Dasia was in no mood to deal with her now. "So have some documents made that appear to come from Daymon and say you found it on them. It's not like you haven't done it before."

Nilado leaned her considerable bulk against the desk, causing it to scrape across the stone with a slow, grating sound. "No, she thinks she's caught wind of something nefarious and won't let it go that easily. Especially not after our own informants returned with news of an assassin loose in the city. I believe she is looking to connect me to that, then to the murder of her father."

Dasia recovered the dented silver tray and began piling the scraps of sandwiches onto it, hoping the woman would notice her indifference to the information. The Matron and the High Monarch were perpetually locked in a battle for dominance, a conflict that rarely yielded benefits and almost always led to further complications. "Aren't you? If not for the war, Daymon would never have employed an assassin. And if you hadn't had her father killed, she wouldn't be looking for his killer."

"Yes, yes!" Nilado snapped. "And if Zachery Treus hadn't been visited by auger wolves who gave him his vision, the city would never have been built, and we wouldn't be in this bind. However, I didn't achieve success by dwelling on past grievances. I need a solution now, something unquestionable."

"Why not just tell her the truth, that Linda was spying on the Council and reporting it to her cult? You had her and the leader arrested."

"I have informed her of all that. But as I stated, Lightreaver will want more than my word or some papers of their guilt. She has already sought to interrogate them herself, but they appear to have escaped."

Dasia picked up a scrap of cryllan meat, turning it over in her hand with a tinge of regret. Two days ago, it would have been a rare indulgence. Now, its graying texture marked it as spoiled, and the rat bites along the edge showed even scavengers had lost interest. With trade routes disrupted, the chance to enjoy such a delicacy might not come again for a long time. "You are in a bind," she told her flatly, tossing the piece onto the pile with the rest. "Without direct testimony, you doubt the High Monarch will accept your claims."

"Precisely," Nilado said, thumb brushing over her pendant's jewels. "If I do not provide her with proof, she plans to strip me of title and possessions, then turn me out into the wilderness."

A laugh escaped Dasia's lips before she could suppress it, and she turned to face the woman. "If she knew the extent of your treason, you would be lucky to keep your skin."

"And yours. Don't forget, your hands are nearly as dirty as mine. As are Linda's. If Lightreaver has the opportunity to question her, the filthy erdi'zal might blab about some of our other dealings."

"Then shouldn't you be looking for her to ensure her silence?" Dasia watched a smug smile creep onto the Matron's face. "You already have her tucked away in one of the older cells."

Nilado looked down at the desk. "She is no longer a problem. With her removed, I merely need you to speak for her. Confess all your dirty sins to Lightreaver, and she will look no further."

"Then be thrown in prison, too? No, I must pass. Find someone else to be your scapegoat."

The Matron raised her face, the sycophantic smile returning. "I would never leave you in the dungeons. You are far too valuable. Once the High Monarch became distracted with another issue, you would make a miraculous escape."

Leaving her fate up to the duplicitous female didn't sound appealing to Dasia, though. "Why not convince Linda to do this instead? Only provide her with enough of an incentive not to expose us. Perhaps a new position."

Nilado's expression turned dark. "I will *not* reward her betrayal. After what I've done to her, such an option is off the table. I require your assistance."

Dasia shrugged, a human trait she had learned to simulate. "Even with your assurance, I am unable to impersonate an erdi'zal. They possess too many moving parts for one of my kind to handle convincingly. Six limbs and four eyes need to all function independently, along with the ears and tail."

The Matron looked at her, a single slick brow raised. "Is that truly necessary?"

"You think Lightreaver won't notice a few limbs hanging limp, or eyes not blinking?" Dasia countered. "It would be far easier to take the form of the Sarvendor, as long as there is no need to fly. I believe I've heard his voice enough to fake it."

"That is too risky. I don't know where he is, and if he has friends among the guards who helped him escape, one of them might recognize

155

you as an imposter. If that happens, it's only a matter of time before I'm exposed."

The bisegus female noticed the blatant indifference directed toward her. Nilado's selfishness wasn't a surprise, but considering their discussion, she found it disturbing. "As would I. Then you would have to account for why you are using my kind for deception."

The Matron dismissed her concern with a wave. "I could explain it as one of the spies sent by Ludholm. Then, when you are put in the dungeon, I would employ my resources to have you released."

"You don't think they would take extra precautions that even you couldn't get around?"

"So you turn into a puddle or whatever you do and ooze your way out." Nilado straightened, then looked about the room, as if noticing the wreckage remains for the first time. "I thought you had more furniture. What in the name of the Zaljaka's Golden Scales happened to your office?"

At the word 'puddle,' Dasia's expression darkened, a sharp edge creeping into her demeanor. "The assassin came here. I was his target, not the High Monarch."

Nilado shuffled to the new chair, its tall, intricately carved backrest, elegantly shaped silver-inlaid arms, and generously padded velvet cushion was an inviting alternative to standing. The frame groaned softly as she sat. "I hardly think that is a likely scenario. Why would anyone wish you dead? I mean, of the reasons I don't already know about."

"Because of *nagdami*." With her seat taken, Dasia moved to the desk and perched on its edge. "The cloth I provided you with that allowed Zatreus spies to infiltrate Ludholm. It is against our laws to share that with *malditano*. I only provided it to you because you threatened to expose our colony here."

"Let us not delude ourselves," Nilado said, waving a finger. "I have granted you far more than that. And the offer to take Linda's place as head of the Munitions Guild is still available. If you do as I request."

"Everything I do for you only gets me in deeper to your foul little world. Don't you see? I killed another bisegus. For what? A war *you* started!"

"You did what you had to do, as did I."

Dasia slammed her hand on the desk. "Magtot! I want the nagdami back. Return the cloth and suits to me. The war is over. You no longer need them."

The Matron shook her head, her blonde locks swaying with the movement. "The war is far from over. Ludholm has won the first battle, but Lightreaver is undoubtedly planning retribution. Your trick uniforms will be even more useful."

"I don't care. I lived up to my end, now give them back or — "

"Threats?" The woman cocked her eyebrow again. "Or what?"

Dasia momentarily froze. What could she do? All she had was information on the various activities the pair had engaged in over the last decade, legal and illegal. Would that be enough? "Or I'll go to the High Monarch with everything. How you blackmailed me and my people. How you tricked her into declaring war on Ludholm. How you had her father killed, and — "

"You are forgetting your role in all this." Nilado spoke with an icy calm, though her eyes burned with barely contained fury. "*You* impersonated the Ludholm emissary. *You* arranged for Hamza Lightreaver's untimely demise. Any attempts to oust me would only lead to your downfall."

But Dasia wasn't backing down. The remains of her bisegus foe lay hidden less than twenty feet from her. "My life was already threatened, and in return, I betrayed my people for a second time. I no longer care what happens to my position here."

"You speak of your people. Do you wish those in Zatreus to suffer? A word in the right ear, and I'll expose you and your entire colony here. The Purge would come to the city." A sneer curled the Matron's lips as she observed the other female's shocked expression. "Yes, I know what your kind call the Bisegus War. Personally, I don't see why anyone would be scared of you."

Uncertainty chipped away at the shapeshifter's resolve. "You wouldn't."

"You doubt for a moment I would? I am Joice Nilado, Matron and head of the Council of Influence and Affluence, the most powerful woman in Wayela's second biggest port city. I removed Linda and had her punished. Do you think I wouldn't do the same for anyone else who threatened my position?"

Dasia swallowed an urge to correct the woman's boast. Lightreaver was the High Monarch, and no matter what the High Merchant before her thought, that was the true authority in Zatreus.

At the moment, however, both held enough power to ruin her life, and she had been given a chance to delay that fate. It wouldn't hurt to mislead Lightreaver a little longer. "I will look among the others, see if any of them might be sufficiently skilled to pull off the deception you desire."

"I thought you would." A smug grin spread across Nilado's face as the female conceded. "I have two more days before Lightreaver expects my evidence. If you are unable to locate someone with the appropriate skills, then look for ones with a different kind."

Dasia had a sense of what she meant but hesitated before reluctantly seeking confirmation. "What kind?"

"Murder. If it comes down to me or the High Monarch, I will see her dead."

BOSO AND LELEL were just finishing off a late lunch of fruit and bread aboard the foyla when the boat crashed.

As if going over a waterfall backward, the craft's bow lurched upward, sending its occupants tumbling as the wooden planks beneath them groaned. A second later, the rest of the vessel fell. The drop forced it briefly under the surface. A deafening crack split the air as the paddle wheels slammed into the riverbed, shearing blades and wrenching the axle sideways, jolting through the deck in a bone-rattling shudder.

When the boat bobbed up again, it tossed its passengers a third time. Aedan, standing at the front, gripped the railing to keep himself from tumbling overboard. The egyzemor and erdi'zal, already sitting on the deck, were only knocked about. Four of the Shells, however, went over the side, splashing into the rapid depths.

The water had fallen by half, the Riverwall's destruction diverting its source upstream. It had taken this long for the current to catch up with the travelers.

Boso didn't know the cause, nor did he care. Another opportunity had come. As the boat lurched sideways, one wheel no longer turning, he saw their chance. "Lelel! Jump!"

For the second time in two days, the pair vaulted over the railing and plunged into the frigid water below, the cold hitting like a slap to the chest and stealing the breath from their lungs. But in this instance, with the river's volume diminished, they recovered faster. The egyze-mor quickly gripped his companion and propelled them toward the shore.

Even with Lelel's strength, the pair barely made it to the embank-ment without being swept away. Once there, they struggled to climb the steep, newly revealed slope, with the erdi'zal forced to climb in an awk-ward scramble with his backside jutting out.

A white-hot bolt cracked the earth inches from them, blinding Boso with the flash and filling the air with the reek of scorched dirt as they crested the bank. Boso surged forward, seizing her arm and yanking her along just as another crackling strike erupted nearby. The second blast landed farther off, and a third split the sky on the far side of the ridge, too distant to be an immediate danger.

"The lad is shooting wild!" Boso shouted. "We need to get cover!"

Fortunately, this stretch of riverbank had grown dense with vegeta-tion, and a quick sprint brought them to the concealment of the tree line. They dove behind a massive shrub just as another bolt struck the ground nearby, erupting in a shower of dirt.

Lelel sprawled on her stomach, meaty hands shielding her head. Boso's legs lay under his rear torso while he bent over, the best the erdi'zal could do to crouch. Their positions wouldn't do anything to stop a blast of energy, but they hoped it might make them less obvious targets.

When no further strikes occurred, Boso dared to peek out from be-hind the bush. From their distance inland and the dropped waterline, they couldn't see Aedan or the boat. "We should be safe, but move slowly," he hissed to Lelel. She nodded in return, then fell to her knees and began crawling backward. The erdi'zal, unable to perform the same maneuver, was forced to shove himself to a standing position. He braced for a fresh attack as he rose, but the fisherman and vessel were still out of range.

Only when the pair had retreated further into the forest did Boso dare to speak again. "We made it! We're free!" Despite his words, he kept his tone low, in case his optimism betrayed them.

Lelel nodded, her expression brightening with relief, then tugged at her outfit. "Wet." Though little more than a few dozen potato and grain sacks poorly sewn together with frayed twine, she didn't like having it soaked all the same.

"I know." The erdi'zal's leather waistcoat hadn't fared any better. Their last plunge had left it discolored and stiff. Had its many pockets still contained the honey drops he loved to snack on, they would have been ruined beyond use by now. "Once we have put more distance between us and that madman, we can dry them out. Maybe even start a fire. We may have to spend the night out here, but it has to be more desirable than that boat of corpses, let me tell you."

Lelel nodded again. "Where?"

Boso looked around, though there were no landmarks he recognized. This far from the waterway, he could barely determine which direction was north. "I'm not sure. We left Stegate yesterday, and I'm fairly certain the city we passed this morning was Forden, but I've never traveled here on foot. Let's try to head back that way, then return to the river to guide us. That lad with the lightning said they were heading to Adradena, so as long as we don't go downriver, we'll be safe. May the tide swell and wash away their passage! Thank Zaljaka that it dropped for us to escape!"

His companion blinked at his invocation. Their following of a god was what got them into their current mess. Nizlan promised all those who considered themselves above others would one day be punished, and the meek would rise up. Olagkoa was to be the agent who brought down the eternal retribution. But despite their lowly positions, all their devotion had earned them was more suffering.

The erdi'zal understood her look. "If the god of chance isn't on our side, what hope do we have? Let's get going, though, in case he's not, and the lad sends his friends after us."

As they headed further into the forest, they didn't need to worry about their former captors. The foyla tilted awkwardly, its hull listing, dragging a wounded trail in the water as it gurgled and slapped against the bent paddlewheel before finally wedging against the steep western bank.

Aedan, still clinging to the railing, had managed to stay aboard, along with most of the Shells, save for the few that had been flung overboard during the initial chaos. For the nearly twenty stranded individuals, however, reaching dry land became the pressing concern. Another grueling hour crawled by before they finally made their way ashore.

Through it all, not a word was spoken, not a complaint uttered, not a grunt of strain issued. Quiet as the dead, the corpses did as ordered, with jerking, too-smooth motions as they regrouped on the grassy ground. The fisherman leading them, as much a puppet as they were, took a moment to survey the region before deciding on a direction. Their quarry, Savanah and her companions, along with the bow and other artifacts, lay to the south.

Boso had spoken of Adradena, and without further information, that remained as the undead's objective. With the boat destroyed, pursuit would be much slower, and neither Aedan's knowledge nor the creature controlling him could determine how far their destination was.

For the unfeeling Shells, none of that mattered. Whether a day or a year, they would complete their mission.

Only Aedan, trapped in his body by the force of Olagkoa's will, would know the passage of time. Only he would feel remorse over those slain in Stegate by his hand. Only he would know the hopelessness of his captivity.

And he could not even weep.

Chapter Eleven
BORN OF ARCANA

"THIS IS IT!"

Shimi Zar gazed at the ancient building from the clearing's edge. Leda, Wynna, Erling, Malwin, and their smaller companions, Graypaw and Cutie, emerged from the forest behind her. Before them stood Nastina's tower.

The group had spent the last two days hiking from the Eastern Heights. They camped at night and took several breaks during the day, allowing Wynna and Leda, who weren't used to extensive walking, to get some rest. Leda decided to keep wearing the outfit she'd changed into. Wynna finally relented and replaced her own frayed and dirty attire with a light yellow dress with black trim and a green belt.

The journey had been without incident. They camped too far from Longbridge to hear the cries of its citizens or the sounds of the army. Their only concern was wolves, with Wynna expressing her gratitude that there were none on their route, to which Erling responded that they were too close to civilization for them.

Leda doubted the tiny bridge over the stream and stone remnants were what he meant by 'civilization'. When Shimi Zar said 'tower,'

Leda pictured turrets and pennants. The edifice here, along with its destroyed twin, barely passed for ruins. "Nastina lives here?"

"She does!" The bisegus turned to see their reactions.

"In this hovel?" Wynna scoffed. "The poorest farms in Talidith looked better than this!"

Malwin shrugged. Even Erling seemed disappointed by the sight. "I am positive it is more structurally sound than it appears. And it does have a certain charm about it."

"It's strong enough!" An erdi'hun, with hindquarters and horns similar to a goat, appeared in the doorway of a run-down cottage near the tower, a small axe clenched in his fist. "Now, who are you, and what d'ya want here?"

Erling's face darkened at the sight. "It just lost its charm." His gaze went to Wynna. "You are correct. This is a hovel, home to vermin."

"That's so very enlightened of you," Shimi Zar snapped at him. She stepped forward and waved. "Greetings Niggle! We are here to see your mistress."

"And who are you?" The individual moved out from the doorway. "Ah, Lisell. You are welcome." He almost smiled, but it disappeared as he looked past her. "Not the rest of you. Especially not *that*." He thrust his axe toward Erling.

"I would not accept your hospitality even if you offered it." The erdi'zal brought a hand to his face. "I thought I perceived a foul odor as we approached."

"That would be your own ass, you arrogant bastard. Both of them."

Erling grabbed his bow and reached for an arrow. "I'm going to fill your filthy carcass full of holes to air it out."

"You couldn't hit the side of a burral!"

"Stop it!" Shimi Zar threw up her hands as she stepped between them. "I didn't bring you here so you can revert to your petty bigotry." She glared at Erling until he returned the arrow to his quiver. "Niggle, we came to see Nastina. Please tell her we are here."

"Can't. She ain't."

Shimi Zar clenched a fist. "Do you know when she'll be back?"

"I wish I did." Niggle thrust a thumb toward the buildings. "We've had trouble here, and could've used the help."

"What trouble?"

He stuck his arms down stiffly at his side, letting the axe brush the grass in an imitation of the Shells. "Dead people still walking. Not like you'd expect. We took care of them."

The group grew tense. "You had them here, too?" Leda asked.

Niggle relaxed and squinted at her. "What d'ya mean?"

"A bunch of living corpses attacked us in the Eastern Heights," Shimi Zar explained. "We outran them."

"Who is 'we'?" Leda looked at Niggle.

He turned his head toward the tower. "Yop! Zip! Git out here!"

On cue, the two diamurs came streaking out of a window in the base. They zoomed at Niggle, then split off, coming at the party from both sides. Their loud chittering filled the air.

At Leda's ear, Cutie chirped and dove off her shoulder, hurtling at the others. "Cutie, don't!"

But his surge wasn't in defense. The other two squealed when they saw him, and the trio fell into a wide spiral, flying around in an ever-decreasing circle. It reminded Leda of the game the voladorms played with the tiny fliers.

Niggle scowled at the antics. "So you're cursed, too. Not just with the jackass."

Erling snatched an arrow and nocked it. "Keep talking, and I'll ventilate you."

The three diamurs spiraled inward, spinning faster until Cutie shot up at the last second, leaving the other two to crash into each other, which sent them into another brawl.

Shimi Zar shook her head. "They still fight, I see."

"Never stop," Niggle grumbled.

The display delighted Leda, however. "You have diamurs, too! What are their names? Mine is called Cutie!"

His scowl deepened. "Don't care. Her Cleverness isn't here. So you can go. Bye!" He waved his free hand in a shooing motion.

It was slapped aside by Shimi Zar. "Niggle! This is serious business!"

"I am aware! Those brutes tried to kill me!"

Her face contorted in a way a female human's couldn't as her fingers came up as if to strangle the erdi'hun. "I'm talking about the Abomination. It's loose, and we need to bring together the Arcane Relics to destroy it."

"Bah, I know all that. We just had a bunch of fools come through here three days ago." He made a dismissive gesture. "It's being handled."

Shimi Zar dropped her arms. "What do you mean?"

Leda stepped forward to join her. "A second group? Two women who look like twins and a man?"

Niggle's eyebrows shot up. "That's them. They had another with them."

"Who are you talking about?" Shimi Zar demanded.

"When the creature was first freed, our soldiers, of Talidith, tried to reseal it underground." Leda glanced at Wynna, remembering again the fight in the sleeping hall to defend her mother. "Two of them were Savanah, an archer using the silver bow artifact, and her friend, Camille. They were sent by the High Monarch, along with another soldier, Vyncent, to locate something to stop it."

Niggle was nodding. "And her Cleverness told them how to find the lot and booted them. Then she left too, leaving me, Jai, and these two alone." He pointed at the diamurs who had stopped their fighting and were picking at pebbles on the ground while Cutie watched.

Shimi Zar's head snapped back to Niggle. "Jai is here?"

"I just said that, didn't I?"

Her face twisted. "Then why am I wasting my time talking to you? Is she in the tower?"

"I didn't force you to speak to me. I told you to go away."

The hands went up again. "Niggle, where is she?"

A smirk crossed his lips. "Now you wanna talk?"

"In Hugiyo's name!" Shimi Zar moved her hands to cup her mouth. "Jai! Where are you? It's Lisell!"

"How many names do you have?" Wynna asked.

The bisegus grinned back at her. "Same as you, one for every persona."

Will I get a voladorm name too? Maharelago... that's what Father called me. Was that it?

"I am here!" a soft voice rang out. Its owner stepped into the doorway of the tower base.

Jai wore a simple green dress with laced sleeves and a wide collar. Its snug fit echoed the curves of her round face, framed by black hair tucked behind her ears. She studied the party with inquisitive eyes nearly the same color as her hair. "You should know by now not to get flustered by Niggle. Who have you brought?"

"She brought trouble!" Niggle turned his back to the travelers and headed toward the cottage. "I liked the dead things better."

"I'd be happy to make you one of them," Erling called after him. "You've already got the smell." The Shells didn't have any odor, their bodies having been restored to what they were in life while lacking the bodily fluids to produce a scent, but it still counted as an insult.

Niggle flicked his tail in an obscene gesture in return.

"Niggle! Behave!" Jai waited until the erdi'hun had returned to the small house before addressing the others. "I'm sorry. He's just... well, honestly, I haven't figured it out yet. Come on, bring your companions closer. You're welcome here."

Erling replaced the arrow and slung the bow back over his shoulder before joining the others in crossing the clearing. As they approached the tower, the poor conditions of the dwellings became more evident. The cottage, square barn, and tiny shed all slouched in varying stages of collapse, their sagging walls and patched holes evidence of their great age. A covered well, its roof nearly gone and a few of its stone bricks absent, was in even worse shape.

The tower itself looked more like a failed garden, with moss covering its side and sickly plants sticking out from numerous cracks. Its twin had collapsed long ago, and this one appeared likely to join it shortly.

The diamurs, oblivious to the group, began chasing each other through the air, darting around the buildings, even swooping into the cottage windows a few times, drawing a yelled curse from Niggle inside. Cutie joined in, delighting in the mischief. Leda tried to keep a close eye on him, but the trio moved too swiftly, and soon she accepted that he would be safe for now.

Jai folded her hands across her deep blue dress. "Mistress Nastina is away on business, but I will do what I can to help. What brings you to her tower?"

"We came seeking advice." Shimi Zar waved a hand toward Leda and the others. "They are looking for a way to stop the Abomination. They know about it now, and the artifacts. And what I am. We've already retrieved the hammer. It seems their friends are also doing this, and were here a few days ago."

Jai's face brightened. "Of course! I remember them. What advice do you want?"

"For starters, how to find the other relics. Niggle said something about Nastina showing the other group how to locate them. Is that true?"

"She did. If you have the hammer, I think I can show you, too."

Shimi Zar turned to Malwin, who lowered his pack and began sorting through its contents on the grass. "Why didn't you tell me you had friends searching, and they already had one?" she asked Leda.

The woman shrugged. "I didn't know they were, only that they were seeking weapons. We only just learned about the artifacts ourselves a few days ago. And I didn't realize what theirs had to be until now."

Malwin pulled the hammer out of his gear and handed it to Shimi Zar, who then held it up before Jai.

Like Wynna, Leda couldn't see anything special about it, though she knew it had power. "Are there really six of these?"

"Yes. You have the hammer. Your friends have the bow. There's also a sword, a spear, a cup, and a crown." Jai ticked each off on her fingers, her voice dropping just slightly on the last one.

Erling raised a hand. "I believe I have knowledge of the cup's whereabouts. It is with my people on the Trideen Plains."

Jai nodded. "That is where Mistress Nastina believed it was."

"Did the others say where they were going?" Leda asked. It was the first time they had heard anything about the progress of Savanah and Vyncent's mission.

"To the Hafugung. It might be among the hafu living there."

"So that's four of them!" Leda smiled at Wynna. "Not so impossible."

"And I will show you how to find the rest."

Wynna didn't look convinced. "Do you know how these things will stop Olagkoa? A bunch of weapons against that thing's power?"

"The only way to truly stop it is to send it back to its world. The artifacts will do this."

Wynna frowned. "How?"

"The mechanics don't matter now. Your friends have that information, as does Mistress Nastina, and they understand how to perform it." Jai paused, her expression darkening. "There's something else she told your friends, a warning. She believes Olagkoa has tapped into our world's arcana and is using it to fuel its powers. We encountered the dead it animated." A shudder passed through her short frame. "If they were following you and came here, they may be hunting for the artifacts."

"To prevent us from banishing their master," Erling finished for her.

"To capture them for their master," she corrected. "Mistress Nastina thinks Olagkoa wants to use their power to bring more beings from its world into ours. That is the real threat to Rapria."

Shock rolled over the companions. "That's horrible!" Leda gasped. "Rapria wouldn't survive!"

"Certainly not in its current state," Erling added, "which is one I have an affinity for. It is up to our two parties to prevent this disaster."

Malwin grunted in agreement, and Wynna nodded. "Those things that chased us. You said it used its power to bring them back to life. Is it using arcana to do that?"

"Mistress Nastina believes so, but she doesn't yet understand how. And to clarify, they aren't alive." Jai shuddered again. "The energy is only making them seem like that."

"But if they are tracking us, they must have intelligence," Wynna pressed. "That means they have some life."

Jai held her hands out, signaling she didn't possess the answer. "I am a student still. That is a discussion for Mistress Nastina when she is here again."

"Do you know when that will be?" Shimi Zar asked.

"I do not. Her trip was unexpected."

Leda gazed up at the tower. She had hoped the arcanist might be able to tell her more about who she was. What she was. "Where'd she go?"

"I cannot tell you that."

Wynna frowned. "Can not or will not?"

"Will not. She has many duties that take her away from here."

"Like what?"

"Wynna, stop," Leda hissed.

"Why? Are you not curious as to what use a powerless arcanist is to anyone else, besides telling them how to summon evil monsters from other worlds?"

"I said stop!"

But Wynna was working herself up into a full rant. "Think! They have all these relics, they knew where the creature was, and could have destroyed it long ago. Instead, they wait until it gets free, then expect us to clean up their mess."

"Who caused this is immaterial," Erling said. "The need exists, and we are in a position to meet it."

Jai sighed. "No action was taken because, at the time, it was contained."

"Then why hide all the weapons?"

"Do you not know your own history?" Jai snapped at Wynna. "Your people built a stronghold next to Olagkoa's prison. One of your kings found it and released the beast. He wanted the weapons for himself. Olagkoa was trapped again, and the king had the place sealed, but Mistress Nastina ordered all but the bow removed so as not to tempt anyone else."

"What temptation? All that hammer does is make light."

"I assure you, it does much more than that."

Seeing Wynna wouldn't back down, Leda raised a hand to cut her off. "There was something more we wanted to ask Nastina. Well, I did. I want to learn more about what I am."

"It didn't take you long to make it about you again," Wynna chided, but seemed to relax her stance.

Jai looked to Shimi Zar for clarification. "She's a Shiftling," the bisegus explained. "She met her voladorm parents in the Eastern Heights, and Grazzlunn Khar told her what he knew."

"And what *does* he know?"

"That human-looking children have been born for centuries to other races. Her parents surrendered her to be raised among humans before she was collected."

Jai paused. "It's really not my place to speak on it, but I will answer what I can."

"What am I?" Leda hadn't meant the question to be that blunt, but it was the one that had been plaguing her for days.

Jai glanced at Shimi Zar again. "I thought you said she knows."

"I understand I'm a voladorm, but look human. And that I should be able to change."

It was the first Erling had heard of it. "That is fascinating! I did not know you possessed such an ability."

"That's just it," she said, looking up at her friend. "I don't. I've never been anything other than me."

"You are still you if your appearance changes. Lisell is the same person she was as..." Jai addressed the bisegus. "Did you appear to them as something else before?"

"An egyzemor named Shimi Zar."

"There. She is still Shimi Zar."

"Just a lot shorter," Wynna muttered, bristling.

In response, the false woman stuck her tongue out. "That's it. I am eating your soul tonight. And..." She began growing. In seconds, she stood the same height as Erling. "I like being taller."

"That's not fair!" Wynna protested, but her lips were curled in a smile.

Leda ignored all of it, her focus on what she could learn. "Then why can't I look like a voladorm?"

Jai pushed back a lock of deep black hair, securing it behind her ear. "I think Mistress Nastina would say because you still don't believe you are one. You think of yourself as human."

"I am human."

"That's what I'm saying. Until you embrace who you are, you will remain as you are."

Wynna snickered. "That is silly."

"I cannot describe it any other way."

"Why are some of us like this?" Leda pushed, remembering Erling's suggestion in the mountain. "Are we sick?"

Jai shook her head. "It is not an ailment. But how it happened is a long story, involving the Skorgan Empire and an arcanist."

At this point, Leda was desperate for anything that might help her understand who and what she was. "Can you tell us?"

"If you wish. But not here. The sun is beginning to set, and I am sure you are hungry. I'll have Niggle make us something to eat while we move this inside. I'm afraid you will find the interior a bit crowded, as it wasn't designed with egyzemors and erdi'zal in mind."

She stood aside to allow them entry into the lower level of the tower, a large yet cramped kitchen, while she went to see Niggle. When it was just him and Jai, the erdi'hun kept the cooking to the cottage, so the chamber was relatively clean, having not been used since Nastina's departure.

Against the far wall sat an enormous fireplace with a three-legged iron pot resting on its cold stones. Strips of meat and herbs hung from a drying rack chained to the ceiling, while pitchers, bowls, and plates cluttered a ledge on the left. Jugs and canisters perched on shelves above it, with larger barrels and crates of varying sizes set against the opposite wall. A pair of wooden tables filled the middle.

The three women grabbed nearby stools and gathered around one of the tables, leaving the head for Jai. Erling squeezed in beside the second, his backside resting on the uneven stone floor. Malwin did the same, plopping down at the end of the table. Graypaw hopped onto a ledge against the wall and curled up to sleep.

Jai returned a few moments later. "This story takes place in the Third Age, when there was still arcana in the world," she began, lighting two candles and setting them on the table. Their soft illumination gave the room a comforting glow. "Near the end of the Skorgan Empire was the rule of Stevon Redshard, known historically as Emperor Redshard the First. By then, the dream of a united continent blessed by arcana had long been abandoned. Redshard used that power to enslave. The failed Eastern Invasion was half a century behind, when the Pikes were at their peak, and their mission was to subjugate the neighboring homelands of the other races."

Malwin grumbled and Erling frowned. Though hundreds of years had passed, the atrocities perpetrated by the Empire on the non-human people of Rapria were still a painful bit of history that most tried to avoid discussing.

"Redshard, understanding that bisegus were able to move among them undetected, decided he wanted that power for himself. If the Pikes looked like erdi'zal or egyzemors, they could send a large force into those populations and crush them from inside."

"To do this, he sought out an arcanist known to be familiar with bisegus and ordered him to experiment on them. He found one named Vasi Taksil who agreed to the task."

Shimi Zar scowled, but, like the others, kept silent. "Taksil had grown weary of war," Jai continued, "and decided to do the opposite, and he set out to give the other races the ability to look human, and so hide from the Pikes."

"So... I was born of arcana?" It sounded unlikely to Leda, but at the same time, it seemed the logical cause. There was so much they didn't know about the force.

"I'll get to it." Jai offered the words with quiet sympathy. "It took him a long time, but he managed to learn enough about bisegus to craft an infusion. All he needed was a way to create an artifact for it, maybe several, and distribute them to the edges of the Empire."

"Redshard had similar plans. He wanted it infused in a stone pillar so that his soldiers need only touch it to receive the power. They traveled to a small hill that held such a column, and with a troop of Pikes close by, Taksil had no choice but to carry it out."

"The whole idea is monstrous," Erling said, slapping his hand on the table. "If Redshard's men had gained that ability, no race would be safe again. It would be the Bisegus War a hundred times over."

"It was, but Taksil made sure it didn't happen. And to both their surprise, the arcana didn't remain in the stone. It flowed through it and into the earth, diffusing throughout the land. Months of study ended in failure. Redshard was furious and ordered Taksil's death. Before the Pikes could rejoin their emperor, Taksil fled into the countryside. The historical records have no entries of what happened to him after that."

"Your knowledge of the event is far greater than mine," Erling conceded. "All I've ever discovered was that Redshard planned it, but his soldiers betrayed and killed him before he could carry it out."

Jai nodded. "Much of what occurred during the Skorgan Empire has been deliberately destroyed, but Mistress Nastina has spent her life recovering what information she could."

"I thought she spent that studying arcana."

Jai ignored Wynna's snide tone. "In some ways, they are the same. Many advances were made during that period, not all of them bad."

"I'm a mistake." Leda's voice was hollow, her mind still absorbing the meaning. "I'm the result of a failed experiment."

"Not failed. Taksil succeeded. Just not in the way he imagined."

"So this infusion thing affected all of Rapria?" Wynna asked.

"We don't think so. There have been Shiftlings born throughout Skoim Pral, so all three continents have been affected. There have also been some stories out of Duchari. We haven't heard about anything like this in Martica and Noricon, but ships do not travel there often, and it's a touchy subject to ask about."

"That suggests the infusion was landbound and didn't spread beyond," Erling said.

"Except that there are hafu Shiftlings. Sadly, many of those don't survive. The human form is so complete that those babies are born without gills. If the parents don't realize this soon enough to rush the baby to the surface, it drowns."

Wynna's eyes grew wide, her voice cracking. "That's horrid!"

"I'm afraid it gets worse. Especially among the hafu and voladorms, a human is considered inferior, so rather than bear the shame of having one as a baby, the parents will kill it before others find out. Among all races, there exists a hatred for the Shiftlings, as they are seen as failures of the parents."

While the others reacted in shock, Leda's mind went to her parents. Her mother blamed herself for the missing wings. But they let her live. Gave her to humans. Not out of shame — out of love. *They loved me more than I knew!* Tears filled her eyes, and she buried her face in her arms.

Shimi Zar rounded the table and laid an arm across her shoulder. "It's alright. That didn't happen to you. Your parents loved you."

Leda raised her head slightly. "And I've spent my whole life thinking they didn't. I didn't know!"

"It is a tragic part of the story." Jai's own eyes watered. "But like Lisell said, you were fortunate."

"Food's ready!" The erdi'hun's call interrupted their reflection. "If y'all want it!"

Jai turned to Shimi Zar. "Could you and your egyzemor friend fetch dinner? Niggle is a decent cook but a terrible waiter."

"I don't think Malwin is my friend yet." She leaned forward and lowered her voice. "He sort of freaked out when I revealed who I was."

"That's a shame. Malwin, could you perhaps handle helping Lisell with the food?"

The giant shifted an uneasy gaze from one female to the other. "Go on, Mal," Leda prompted. "I trust her, and you trust me, right?"

He stared at her for a moment, then rose wordlessly and clomped out of the room. "That will have to do." Shimi Zar stood and met Jai's eyes. "And please call me Shimi Zar with them. This is my 'Lisell' form, but they know me by that name."

"Of course." Once she had gone, Jai addressed the remaining companions. "Thank you for undertaking this task. I am certain if Mistress Nastina were here, she would say the same."

"There is a puzzle that has been troubling me for a few days regarding your mistress," Erling said.

"Yes?"

"Well, to put it delicately, The Parting was several centuries ago. If Nastina was an arcanist, and I am not doubting her abilities, merely her longevity, how is she still alive today?"

"Good question!" Wynna looked at their host. "Does she have some artifact that prolongs her life?"

Jai smiled. "She does not. And you should never ask a woman how she keeps herself youthful looking."

"My apologies." Erling dipped his head. "But there is a difference between appearance and, well, existing."

"Maybe she does not exist," Wynna suggested. "Maybe she is always 'away'."

"Stop it, both of you." Leda glared at them. "This is rude. Jai has shown us only kindness, and you two are returning it by asking personal questions that she has already said you shouldn't."

Jai placed a hand on her arm. "It's alright. It's a common question, and I understand the curiosity. Mistress Nastina exists and lives here. Your friends who were here could attest to that. For now, you will have to take my word for it. As to the mystery of her... durability, that must remain a mystery. Think of it as part of her arcanist mystique. And here's dinner."

Shimi Zar entered the tower kitchen bearing a tray of assorted fruit and a platter of a large roasted bird, while Malwin ported a bowl of steaming stew. They set these down on the tables. While the giant resumed his seat on the floor, the shapeshifter began rummaging in a cabinet.

"Niggle has done well!" Jai praised as they admired the food before them. "Won't he be joining us?"

"Nope." Shimi Zar pulled out half a dozen bowls and several more plates. "Said something about staying in the cottage where the air wasn't so foul." She tossed Erling a smirk. "Guess that one was for you."

"Then I thank him for his sacrifice," Erling chortled, "So that his presence doesn't rob us of our appetites."

Once they'd distributed the dinnerware and scrounged enough cutlery from the drawers, the party dug in. The stew resembled what Savanah's group had been served, but the roast was identified by Jai as forest drab. Thick chunks of it were sliced off and passed around to everyone.

During the meal, the diamurs swept in. Zip and Yop swiped a few berries from the tray, for once being content with their own, as they perched on a drying rack to feast. Cutie reunited with Leda, chittering excitedly like a child as he took a piece of fruit from her and plopped down beside her hand to eat. On his ledge, Graypaw caught scraps of meat from Malwin, who chuckled each time he tossed him one.

"It's too late for you to continue on tonight." Jai looked around the table. "We don't have accommodations for guests, but you are welcome to sleep in the clearing. We do have firewood, if you wish to build a fire."

Leda smiled. "Thank you. That's quite generous."

"Will you be traveling to the Trideen Highlands next?"

Erling put down his bowl of stew. "That is the plan. There is a herriad who has been too efficient in battle, and is rumored to be benefiting from an item fitting the cup's description."

"And Lisell?" Jai turned to the female. "With the hammer delivered to them, you are freed from your duty as a *talagapa*. Where shall you go now?"

Shimi Zar looked startled by the question. "I was thinking I would continue with them. I've been protecting the hammer so long, I kinda want to see this through to the end." She glanced at Leda and Wynna, then continued her gaze to Erling and Malwin. "If they will have me."

"Of course!" Leda extended a hand across the table. "You can't leave us now!"

"We would be most grateful for your assistance and companionship," Erling added.

Malwin swallowed a mouthful of stew. "You come."

All eyes looked at Wynna as she chewed a piece of drab. "You do not need my approval. Bring the soul eater."

Shimi Zar beamed. "Thank you. All of you."

From his perch on the ledge, Graypaw gave a loud meow. "I think he approves, too," Leda said.

"Well, I should think so!"

The companions laughed, and Malwin tossed the cat another scrap of drab.

"I have a request." Wynna's tone was uncommonly soft as she held up a hand. Deep red pockmarks tinged by gray flesh marred her burned fingers. "Can you do something for them?"

"Wynna!" Leda grabbed her wrist, shock in her voice. "Why didn't you tell us you were hurt? How did this happen?"

"Back in the mine." Wynna yanked her arm out of her grasp. "Can you help?"

Jai took her hand, fingers grazing the edges of the burns without touching the raw skin. "I will try. Come to Mistress Nastina's study with me."

Wynna flashed Leda a glare as the pair rose from their chairs, and Jai led her up the stairs to another chamber. Wynna's mouth dropped open at the sight. Books crammed every shelf and surface. They filled the four bookcases, except for a single shelf devoted to a collection of jars, bottles, and vials. The volumes that couldn't fit were stacked neatly on the floor and stools which littered the room. More covered a large desk set against the far wall and a handful of smaller ones. From a dozen nooks of a lattice sitting at the rear of the desk, loosely coiled scrolls jutted out.

"How did this happen?" Jai approached the line of vessels and began sorting through them, carefully examining the handwritten labels on each.

Wynna eased onto a worn cot against the wall — one of the few spots in the room not covered in parchment — cradling her burned hands in her lap. "I found something on the floor. It was like watery oatmeal. I touched it, and it was soothing."

"Was it black?"

Wynna shrugged. "Everything was black. I lost the others. No light, nothing."

"I see. Found it!" Jai snatched up a clay jar. "Continue."

"I got sleepy and lay down. When I woke, the stuff was burning my hands."

"You encountered a vereshka." Jai moved to stand before her, then knelt, as if not trusting the cot to support their joint weight. "They normally hunt small prey. You were lucky it didn't kill you." She removed the lid. A sweet, jam-like scent of berries filled the air. Placing the container beside Wynna, she dipped her fingers in and pulled out a large dollop of bluish cream. With her other hand, she gestured for the woman to hold out the burned skin. "Remain still."

Wynna winced as she applied the balm. The pain had eased since she was first injured, but it still stung to the touch. In seconds, even that began to fade. "I was rescued by a little man," she explained. "At least, I think it was a man. Called himself Prad."

Jai continued to work the balm into the fingers. "Why didn't you tell the others you were hurt?"

Wynna shrugged. "I didn't think it was important."

"Of course it's important! They don't want you dead."

"If I was, they could always get the creature to bring me back."

Jai's head snapped up. "That isn't funny."

Wynna shrugged again and let her eyes survey the room. "All this in here — the books and papers — is it really about arcana?"

"Most of it. There is a great deal of history, too, but like I said, they are related."

The woman paused. When she spoke, her voice came softer. "Is there anything in here related to bringing people back to life?"

"Some. None of it successful." Jai smeared the excess cream against the jar's edge, and then resealed it with care. "Most of the work focused on infusing objects with arcana to perform specific tasks."

"Could you do the same with a person?"

"Infuse them? No. Not everything can be enchanted." She stood and carried the jar back to the shelf. "Arcana goes most easily into non-living materials, such as metal and stone." Her tone gave the impression that she was reciting a lesson. "Things that were alive, like wood, cloth, and food, are harder. It cannot be infused into living objects, like trees, animals, or people, or flowing objects, such as water or wind."

Wynna tapped one bandaged finger against her leg. "But is that not what the creature is doing?"

Jai replaced the balm in the collection and glanced around the room for something to wipe her hands with. "That's Mistress Nastina's theory. We don't understand Olagkoa's power, so it's impossible to tell exactly what it is doing."

Wynna dropped her gaze to the floor, contemplating her next query. "What do you know about Augur Wolves?"

"You've got a lot of questions." Not seeing anything appropriate, Jai rubbed her hands together, then smeared them down the side of her dress, the residual cream soaking into the fabric. "They are a wolf variety that seems to have prophetic abilities, but there is little evidence to prove that. The most popular example is the story of Zachary Treus, who foresaw the city of Zatreus."

"You don't believe the story?"

"It's a legend, and legends tend to be exaggerated. And it's hard to say that what he saw was prophetic, since he acted to make it happen." Jai pulled one of the vacant stools to the cot and climbed onto it. "Like if you think about having dinner, then make your dinner, was your thought a view of the future or just your plan?"

Wynna brought her hands together slowly. They no longer hurt, but she could still see the burns. "So, if you were to encounter a pack of them, and thought you saw something in your head, it would not come true."

"I didn't say that. I said it might depend on if the person actively works to ensure it comes true. If you do nothing to carry it out, I wouldn't worry about it."

Wynna met her eyes. "I did not say I had a vision."

"I know you didn't. Let me see your hands." She rechecked the burns, gently prodding the damaged parts. "How do they feel?"

"Better, thank you."

Jai gave her a slight smile. "Good. I'm afraid this is all I can do. The pain should fade, but the scarring will remain. Vereshka acid is quite strong."

"But my hands are repulsive now!" Wynna protested. "I cannot go through life like this!"

"Of course you can. No one is going to notice."

"How could they not?" She thrust them into Jai's face.

The woman took them gently by the wrists and pulled them away. "Your friends did not."

Wynna yanked her hands back. "Because they are too self-absorbed. Everything is about them. All I have heard on this journey is Leda moaning about her problems. Her parents. What she is. Where she came from." Her voice cracked. "My parents are dead! I'll never see them again, unless..." She bent forward, sobbing.

Jai lay a hand on her head in comfort. "You are exhausted. When you are ready, we'll rejoin your friends, and I will find a place for you to sleep. Alright?"

Wynna tried to nod, but the tears overtook her.

Chapter Twelve
SUNDERED SALVATION

ERIS, TAL, AND the others cleared the Eastern Heights just past midnight. Though still beneath the mountain's shadow, the road ahead finally opened before them.

They didn't have time to admire the view, however. Moonlight, hidden for most of their passage, now spilled across the path, leaving them exposed. Even if Olagkoa lacked visible eyes and the Shells possessed little awareness of their surroundings, the group hastened to hide themselves among a nearby grove of trees. They dismounted to stretch their legs and let their horses graze.

The pass slowed them far more than expected. After Longbridge's destruction, the creature leading the army faltered, with its pace dragging, its energy ebbing.

Eris wondered again if the strain of manipulating so many bodies was taking a toll. They had never seen it sleep or eat, so how it survived remained a mystery.

The slowdown benefited the Shell Patrol, though. They traveled in shifts, with half the group sleeping while the others continued on. While risky during the day, once night fell, the arrangement became safer. In the lower light, it had been easy to avoid the attention of the army on the opposite side of the river, and the slower pace allowed them to rest up.

That, however, was about to change. "Where do you think they are going?" Farla asked as they watched Olagkoa shoving itself along the road. Despite the brightness of the moon, the creature and soldiers were only visible as silhouettes and shadows from the distance.

They turned to Holfast, the only one among them who had ever traveled this far south. He blinked his eyes in consideration. "Depends. If they continue on the road, they will reach Swingbridge, then Stegate. If they veer west, they will be heading for Kridmont. Either way, they will encounter many towns and villages along the way."

"How far is Swingbridge from here?" Eris asked.

"Around ten miles, I believe. We could reach the village in two hours."

The man nodded. "We should head there. Wherever the creature is going, we need to cross to the opposite shore to track it."

Ranin leaned against a tree. "Won't they have the same problem as Longbridge?"

"Most likely," Holfast told her. "The bridge rests on a massive swivel point. When opened, they float the far end out with ropes. Without the river's usual depth, it's useless."

"But they might have boats," Eris added. Since leaving Longbridge, he had been berating himself for not thinking to check. "We can get across that way."

Farla raised a skeptical eyebrow as she dropped to the base of the tree beside Ranin. "With horses?"

"I don't know. If you have any better ideas, I'd like to hear them."

The group grew quiet. There really were no other options to them. They had taken on the responsibility of tracking Olagkoa, whatever that entailed. None of them could have foreseen the drop in the river and the problems that would present, but that couldn't deter them now. "Maybe the water will be normal by the time we get there," Tal suggested hopefully.

"I like that idea," Ranin chimed in, and Farla nodded.

Holfast, however, did not share the optimism. "Unlikely. Even if the Riverwall were rebuilt today, I think a few days would pass before the regular flow returned. Again, this is more Erling's sort of thing."

Another heavy silence settled over them. Tal wandered over to her horse, stroking its neck as it grazed. Holfast began a survey of the grove for any fruits or berries they could use to supplement their supplies. Farla rested her head on her bent knees. Eris and Ranin continued watching the dark shapes as they marched on the opposite shore. "How does it know where it's going?" the woman mused.

Eris had turned that question over more than once while tracking it. The creature always seemed to know what was around it, despite being blind. "I guess it can feel the road. Maybe sense the wind."

Ranin looked at him. "I mean, we are wondering where the beast might be heading, but how does it know where things are? It went directly to Ludholm, then it found its way to Longbridge."

He didn't have an answer for that. Olagkoa did seem to possess an uncanny knowledge of the landscape. "Maybe it traveled around before being trapped." He paused as a better explanation came to mind. "If it can read minds, it must have learned something of our world from those it encountered."

"Before killing them, you mean?" Tal asked, coming up behind them.

Tal's words struck hard. Guilt twisted in Eris's gut. "Then we need to stop chattering here and get moving so that more don't fall beneath its wrath."

Holfast padded up, holding a half dozen deep red fruits. "I believe now it is going to Kridmont."

"Why?" Eris took one of the proffered blood ceriman.

"If the creature has gleaned knowledge of Wayela, then it crossed the river deliberately." The erdi'zal handed a crimson orb to each of the others. "Stegate rests on this side of the Leosonee. So does Forden after. So whatever the beast's target is, it lies on the other side. The closest major city is Kridmont."

"And how far is that?" Ranin asked.

"I'm not sure," he admitted. "I've only been there once. Probably around a hundred miles southwest."

"So we've got a way to go," Tal said around a mouthful of fruit.

"That's putting it mildly," Eris noted. "Let's rest a bit more and eat. Then we will move on to Swingbridge and figure out how to get across."

WITH AEDAN AND the Shells no longer chasing them, the crew of the Swift Salvation spent an uneventful day on the river.

Carlin sat midway between Zatreus and Adradena, a quiet haven thriving off trade from both bustling ports. They pulled into the city docks near midnight, tethered the boat, and checked into a nearby inn, where they got dinner and a few hours of sleep.

They were up the next morning before sunrise with a hearty breakfast of crispy toast, peppery eggs, thick porridge laced with honey, and bitter ale. The inn's cook was quite skilled, and Savanah rated it as one of the best meals she'd eaten in a week. Considering most of those were dry rations or something tossed together over a fire in the wild, it wasn't a high bar to reach.

Vyncent enjoyed it too. The empty bowl beside him had been refilled twice with hot oatmeal and he shoveled the second helping of scrambled eggs into his mouth.

"Proper food and a roof! I can't remember the last time I slept in a real bed — one that didn't rock with the river." He took a swig of ale and looked at Mikel. "Why do we have to leave so soon?"

The man swallowed a bit of toast. "When we left Zatreus, I said we would reach Adradena in a week if we didn't stop along the way. But we've made several stops since. You may not remember how long it's been, but I do. We've been on the water nearly four days since leaving the harbor, and we are only halfway there. At this rate, it will take another four days to reach Adradena. We need to pick up our pace."

Vyncent shrugged. "What's the hurry? You said yourself the city has probably already found a way to keep the creature out. That Steelfang could deal with it."

"Our people are in there, too, and we still have an oath to protect them," Savanah reminded him as she forked some eggs onto a piece of toast. "Zatreus isn't the only one in danger, either. Even if they repelled it, that thing is stubborn and will move on to another city. It may have already, and that population might not be so resourceful."

Mikel nodded in agreement. "We also have more than one artifact to find. There are six of these abominations we must locate. Even with

Savanah's bow and whatever we recover from the hafu, that still leaves four more. And if each of those takes this long, we will be searching for another month. How much havoc could Olagkoa cause in that time?"

"Alright. I get it. Don't need to team up against me again." Vyncent jabbed his utensil at the remaining eggs on his plate. "But can we at least finish breakfast first?"

"You and Savanah go ahead and finish." Mikel stood up from the small table. "I want to pick up a few more supplies before we leave. Meet me at the boat in half an hour." Before the others had a chance to argue, he strolled toward the door and exited.

Savanah stared after him. Since they had left the clearing by the tower yesterday morning, she'd noticed their companion growing more irritable. Mikel rarely seemed rattled by anything, and she had assumed it was merely concern over the presence of the carcass beasts this far east. Now, she wasn't sure that was the problem. *He's right about us needing to move faster, but he's the one making us stop. Why the change?*

She turned to Vyncent, who was finishing off another bit of bread. "Does Mikel seem upset to you?"

"Nah," he said with a mouthful, then swallowed. "*You* seem upset. I swear you enjoy telling me how wrong I am every day."

I never enjoy the reminder of what I've lost in your father. "You didn't like it when I joked around in the Sovereign Guard. Now you don't like it when I'm serious."

"Be as serious as you want. Just not in my direction." He glanced toward the door. "Maybe Mikel misses Camille. He seemed sweet on her."

"Maybe." *And why did he refer to the artifacts as abominations? He's never used that word before. Something is wrong here.* She patted the table. "Hurry up. I want to return to the boat."

After a bit more grumbling, Vyncent was finally convinced he'd eaten enough, and the two made their way back to the docks. Savanah boarded quickly and cast her eye about the deck. When nothing appeared out of place, she moved to the cabin.

Vyncent watched her from the dock. "What are you looking for?"

What *was* she looking for? Some hint to explain Mikel's shift in mood? "Nothing!" she called back. A sudden fear gripped her, and she rushed to her bunk. From beneath it, she pulled out the silver bow and sheath wrapped in one of the thicker blankets. Mikel had suggested she leave it on the boat, assuring her it would be safer there than the attention she would draw from carrying two bows around Carlin. She grudgingly accepted his logic, but hated leaving it. Did he want it left behind for a reason she hadn't seen? Was she starting to doubt him?

She replaced it carefully. *Mikel has been an unexpected friend on this journey, and his aid has been invaluable. Maybe some of his anxiety is rubbing off on me. I wish Camille were here!*

Savanah did her best to shake the paranoia, and when Mikel returned, she felt a wave of relief wash over her. He carried a small bag of goods from which he pulled a kliku fruit. Gratefully, she accepted it, offering her thanks. *How could I have doubted him?*

Soon they were underway again as the sun broke over the horizon, Savanah at the tiller. The sails puffed boldly under a steady morning breeze, putting Carlin firmly behind them.

As she'd done regularly since Camille took flight, the archer scanned the sky for her friend. Though there was no sign of the bird, Savanah felt sure she was nearby. *She would have enjoyed the breakfast. What is she eating now? Mice, like a real owl?*

The boat had progressed down the Leosonee for a little more than an hour when it began violently shaking. Shocked, Savanah shouted for the others. Before anyone could react, the vessel lurched violently downward, knocking the wind out of Savanah as her stomach churned and her ears popped from the sudden, dramatic drop of over a dozen feet. The once sturdy structure groaned in protest as it collided with the riverbed, the sound of splintering wood echoing loudly, drowning out any other noise.

Savanah held on for her life as the boat's sail continued driving the vessel forward, tearing away more of the hull. She nearly fell into the water as the Swift Salvation tipped sideways, sending the mast into the current.

The others weren't as fortunate. Mikel, who had been standing in the cabin doorway moments before the crash, now clung to the sturdy frame as his feet dangled perilously over the churning, racing current below. Vyncent gripped desperately to the boat's low railing, his torso submerged beneath the water's surface, his fingers gripping the damp wood with a white-knuckled intensity.

"What happened?" Savanah yelled as she scrambled up the now-vertical steering platform. She could see nothing but the gray sky above them and the river below. "What did we hit?"

"Does it matter?" Vyncent shouted. He had fallen near the bow of the boat, leaving him on the other side of the mast from the others. "Get me out! The water is freezing!"

"Hold on!" Mikel began climbing up toward the cabin, his feet pressed against the deck floor. "I'll try to get around to the front."

The boat lurched suddenly, twisting to the left as the partially inflated sail tugged them again. While the water level had dropped to less than half of what it had been, the current still had enough force to move them a further fifty feet forward before the valupe shored up on another part of the river's bed.

Fortunately, flooding in the cargo hold brought the vessel to less of a slant, easing Mikel's attempts and lifting Vyncent mostly out of the water. The latter managed to pull himself back onto the deck, where he collapsed, shivering.

"We need to secure the boat before it gets swept further down the river!" Mikel shouted. "I'm going to climb to the mainsail and release it. Savanah, see if you can remove the tiller. We might be able to jam it into the bottom and use it as an anchor."

Savanah nodded, then climbed carefully to where the long handle attached to the rear of the craft and the rudder beneath it. After a brief struggle, she pulled the entire mechanism loose, leaving her with a curving shaft of wood nearly six feet in length. It was a quick slide down the planks to the railing from there.

Meanwhile, Mikel had reached the sail and released the rigging lines, letting the canvas flap randomly in the breeze. Seeing Vyncent still safe, if miserable, pressed against the taffrail, he turned to see how Savanah was getting on.

The boat pitched sharply, the deck tipping near-vertical. Mikel tumbled into the river — and vanished beneath the waves.

"Mikel!" Savanah shouted as he toppled overboard, and she nearly followed him. She thrust the rudder through the railing to anchor the craft, but the water was too deep for it to touch the bottom.

Fighting back tears, she cursed and let it go. *Forget the boat! I have to rescue Mikel and Vyncent!* She scrambled over the slippery railing, the boat's angle turning every handhold into a treacherous walkway.

One snapped. Savanah's leg plunged into the water. Those rails were meant to stop a fall, not carry someone's full weight. When she hoisted herself up and attempted to advance, they collapsed completely under her.

Her cry was drowned by the rush of water. It poured into her mouth, stealing her breath. Panic surged through her as the relentless current seized hold of her. Kicking hard, she fought her way to the surface, only to glimpse the looming mast hurtling towards her before being pulled under once more. Something brushed her cheek. She lunged for it, heart pounding. Her fingers grazed the drenched canvas, but it slipped from her grasp before she could secure it, and the current swept her along.

As she struggled to bring herself into a swimming position, she felt a rope circle her waist. It tightened and pulled her sideways. No longer caught in the current, she managed to push her head above the surface. Disoriented but grateful to be moving toward shore, she gasped in a lungful of air. When she wasn't immediately tugged under again, she drew in another. Regaining some control over her panicked body, she began treading water, letting the line carry her along.

The river had receded, leaving behind a wide, muddy embankment that curved away and up. She turned her head, trying to see the boat. Instead, her eyes fell upon a sight that ignited a rush of uncontainable joy in her heart. "Camille!"

A face mirroring her own, split into a grin, stared back. "You didn't think I'd let you drown, did you? But save your breath. I still have to get Vyncent. Mikel's already on land."

The archer wanted to cheer, but only nodded. They weren't safe yet, but they would be. *Even with the boat crashing, my day just improved tenfold!*

It took several minutes to bring Vyncent to shore, then another half hour to salvage what they could from the Swift Salvation. Using the mast as a barrier against being swept away, the four of them were able to cross back and forth between the exposed riverbed and the cabin to retrieve their packs, cooking gear, the food Mikel had picked up in Carlin, and the silver bow.

The broken hull had flooded the cargo hold, pinning the boat in place like a fish gasping on land. The valupe had run out of water.

Once on shore, they caught their breath and welcomed Camille back into the group with hugs, smiles, and questions. Despite his words, even Vyncent seemed glad to see her. It was hard not to appreciate someone's arrival when they come just as you needed saving.

For her part, Camille soaked up the adoration without hesitation, beaming the entire time. When it came to inquiries about how she traveled so quickly, her answers remained vague. "I arrived when you needed me most," she stated, and the men finally stopped pressing the issue.

Savanah knew the truth, of course, but couldn't tell them. Camille had told her never to reveal a bisegus to anyone, even another bisegus, and she had promised she wouldn't.

Though early in the day, they collected scraps of wood and started a small fire. From their packs, they withdrew fresh outfits, stripping out of their wet clothes and laying them on the grass to dry. Once comfortable again, the four discussed what to do from the bank.

"She's still got most of her body intact," Savanah said. "Couldn't we patch her up and continue?"

Mikel rubbed his chin, stubble rasping beneath his fingers. "Maybe, if the river weren't so swift. We move her, the current takes her."

"And the hull?" Vyncent asked.

"Split. We have no tools, no lumber."

"What about going back to Carlin and getting help?" Vyncent suggested.

"It's about a three-hour walk to the city. We might find enough people to help and get it fixed, but the problem is with the water level."

"It's broken." Camille pointed to the fallen waterline, less than half the height it had been. "It's like someone blocked off the source. Olagkoa?"

"That doesn't sound like something it would do. We've only ever seen it destroy. I doubt it could break a river." Savanah glanced upstream. "I mean, unless it built a barricade to block it."

Camille's eyes grew wide. "You don't suppose it's gotten big enough to block the water with its body, do you?"

"If it were that big, we'd see it from here," Vyncent said, his tone somber at the thought. "It could just roll over cities."

"I'm guessing one of the bridges might have fallen in and blocked the flow," Mikel suggested. "Probably Longbridge. But if that's the situation, it must have happened days ago, and we are only feeling the effect now."

"Is it big enough to stop the flow this much?" Savanah asked. They had passed Longbridge at the start of their trip down the waterway, but the wooden structure had not been extended.

"No. And I don't think this water is from the Leosonee. There are a few waterways that feed into it after Zatreus. We passed the Eastern

River shortly before reaching Carlin. Further north, there are the Ibia and Lunenshall rivers."

"So the Leosonee is likely completely blocked," Vyncent concluded, "By something big."

"Or diverted." Realization struck Mikel. "It must be Daymon!" he exclaimed, balling his hand into a fist. "You said he had this mad idea to flood the Banrood Grasslands. If he managed to have the Riverwall destroyed, that would effectively cut off the flow. At least for a few days. Curse that wretch!"

"Then we get help, fix the boat, and wait for the river to return to normal."

"We don't have time for that," he told Vyncent. "I said this morning I wanted to speed up the journey. This has the potential to derail it entirely."

"Then what about borrowing another boat from Carlin?"

"It would have the same problems as this one. The river probably varies in depth over its course. We might float easily all the way to Adradena, or run aground a mile from here."

The valupe shifted, dipping the tip of the mast below the surface. Water surged from the cargo hold door, dragging the remnants of shattered crates in its wake, spilling their contents onto the deck. Among the bits of fractured wood tumbled dozens of red-spotted blue orbs, rolling over the submerged railing before bobbing in the river.

"Kliku fruit!" Savanah cried. Her favorite treat bobbed past her in a parade of wasted sweetness. "We were carrying kliku fruit! I could have been eating kliku fruit the whole trip!"

"Looks like the Duchess has a craving for them, too," Vyncent noted with a chuckle, referring to the noblewoman the major crates in the hold were destined for. "If she's on the docks in Ertonbridge, she might get her delivery after all."

Mikel frowned. "That pretty much puts an end to the idea of repairing the boat in a reasonable time. I imagine there is little left of the hull."

Camille nodded in agreement. "Then our only options are walking to the coast, which makes my legs ache just thinking about it, or getting horses in Carlin."

"On horseback, it will take at least a week. On foot, even longer. Unless Camille wants to share her secret of fast travel." Mikel turned to her, a half-serious expression on his face.

The shapeshifter wasn't about to reveal how she'd flown the last two hundred miles as an owl. They couldn't use that method, anyway. "The secret is to spend less time debating and more time moving. So I suggest we do that."

"You heard the lady." Mikel clapped his hands. "Back to Carlin it is."

"Suits me," Vyncent said, turning toward the campfire. "Maybe we can get a second breakfast. And perhaps a shave," he added, scratching at his forming beard.

Only Savanah remained on the riverbank, staring in disbelief at the retreating blue spheres. They would reach Adradena long before the rest of the group, sweeping into the harbor there and eventually drifting out to sea. She briefly entertained the notion of swimming back to the collapsed valupe to retrieve any that might have been trapped inside. However, she would never hear the end of it if she risked drowning for the sake of a few fruits, however succulent and tasty.

Only when the last orb had passed beyond her view did she turn to their camp with a sigh. She brightened moments later when she remembered they were returning to the city. "If Vyncent gets another breakfast," she called out to the others, "I'm getting more kliku fruit!"

Chapter Thirteen
OLD TOOLS, NEW JOURNEY

L EDA AND THE others spent the night in the clearing, building a
fire as Jai suggested. The weather was unusually warm for spring,
and Erling said it meant their fortunes were turning.

Wynna didn't complain, which they silently accepted as another
hopeful sign. After her outburst in front of Jai, she put on a cheerful face,
but as the evening wore on, her expression dimmed. She sat wordlessly
beside the fire, the smoke curling around her like a whisper, while the
others talked of dinner, weather, and anything but the road ahead.

Her companions noticed her growing quieter, but they were unsure
if she was angry or tired. Silent Wynna was something new to them.
Only Leda had seen her this way before: when her father died during
their childhood, and last year when Tanita was first sick. She understood the woman would come out of her melancholy on her own and
knew she was probably the last person Wynna wanted trying to comfort her.

Graypaw seemed to recognize her mood, too, and nestled against
her side, his slow purr vibrating faintly for most of the evening.

Early the next morning, they were greeted by a grumbling Niggle
bearing a bowl of fruit. Trailing him were Zip and Yop, chirping and

chattering at each other in one of their endless arguments. They put aside their differences to greet Cutie, and the trio had an impromptu air chase, with buzzing wings and shrill chirps, which quickly devolved into a three-way brawl.

Leda chased after them, fearing again for Cutie, but they simply moved higher out of her reach. "What are they always fighting about?"

"My question is how do they participate in combat while staying airborne?" Erling said. "Punching, kicking, and flapping one's wings with the force to keep one aloft must be exhausting."

"Don't strain your head too much over it, horsey. You'll hurt yourself." Niggle set the wooden bowl on the ground, then pointed at the erdi'zal. "She said I had to feed you, but you are not welcome!"

"Then I won't thank you," Erling replied in the same sneering tone. "The fruit is probably rotten, anyway."

"Go eat hay!"

Erling took a menacing step toward him, but Niggle was already retreating to the cottage, his short tail flicking back and forth in time to his mutterings. Only once the erdi'hun had vanished inside did he relax.

"Most enlightened," Shimi Zar teased. "Brings a tear to my eye."

"He started it!"

"Did you have to continue it?"

Erling raised a finger, then reconsidered his reply. "I should not have risen to his goading."

Graypaw let out a loud meow, which could have been a laugh. Malwin and Wynna said nothing as they gathered up their bedding. Leda stepped closer to the pair. "Are you feeling better today?"

"A little," Wynna sighed. "I just..." her voice trailed off.

"I know." Leda caught her eye, and for a moment, the years fell away. They were children again, consoling each other over the loss of their shared father. They had been close then, like true sisters. "And you?" She looked at her towering friend. "How are you handling Shimi Zar?"

Malwin shrugged. "Trying."

Leda nodded. "You are doing very well."

"Good morning, travelers!" Jai strode toward them from the tower entrance as they began selecting from the fruit for their breakfast. "I hope you found the clearing to be suitable accommodations."

"We've slept on much worse," Shimi Zar told her, plucking up a cluster of berries.

"It was most hospitable of you to allow us the space." Erling gave a slight bow, causing Jai to blush.

"I am sorry, again, that we lack beds for you," she said. "We seldom receive visitors, and most don't spend the night."

"We've managed with worse." Leda cinched her bedroll tight and looked around. "And once I get Cutie back, I think we are ready to be on our way."

"I wish we had horses," Wynna said quietly, as if hesitant to say anything negative, but the others heard her.

"I wish we had a wagon," Shimi Zar countered. "Could carry more on a wagon than on a horse."

"A wagon would be useless without a horse." The woman's voice grew stronger as she warmed to the argument.

"There are other animals who can pull wagons."

"Like burrals. I do not want more of those."

Shimi Zar grinned. "I don't think anyone was offering."

"We still do not have a wagon," Wynna told her, crossing her arms.

"That's not true," Jai interjected when the two paused. "There is one here that we use for carrying supplies from the road. It's a bit worn, but it might get you to the Trideen Highlands."

"Won't you need it?" Leda asked, surprised at the turn. She hadn't seen any kind of vehicle in the clearing or the circle of trees around it.

"We have enough of what we require for now. And this is official business, so I'm sure Mistress Nastina would approve. I will have Niggle fetch it." Jai turned and strode across the short distance to the cottage.

"Official?" Wynna frowned. "Official for whom?"

"I believe she means our mission is one which has been approved," Erling offered.

"By who? Nastina isn't here."

"Does it matter?" Leda placed the pit of the blood ceriman she had been eating carefully beside the bowl of fruit. "We might not have to walk the entire distance."

"Some of us still will," Erling reminded her.

Leda nodded. Although they hated the comparison, he was built more like a horse. She was grateful Wynna hadn't suggested he pull the wagon, but it seemed the woman had at least learned that much since her first encounter with the erdi'zal and his companion Holfast last year.

They watched Niggle re-emerge from the cottage and cross to the square barn as Jai walked slowly back to them. "He will get it ready. Then, Malwin, I ask for your assistance in bringing it out."

Malwin nodded, and when they heard a shout from Niggle, he lumbered toward the rickety building and entered through the egyzemorsized gap formed between the two doors hanging loosely off their hinges. A moment later, he opened them wide, being careful not to completely rip them off, and the pair emerged again, with him pulling a shabby wagon in nearly as poor condition as the building and Niggle hovering near its rear. As the vehicle rolled over the uneven ground, its back, right wheel wobbled with an audible creak, groaning with every rotation.

Leda glanced at Wynna, but she was holding her tongue, lips pressed tight in silence.

Erling was not so tactful. "You say this ports your provisions to and from the road? It looks as if it might not make it from that barn to here in one piece."

As if to prove him right, the wobbly wheel twisted awkwardly. At a command from Niggle, Malwin backed the wagon up a few feet until the axle straightened, then continued forward.

"I did say it was a bit worn," Jai reminded them, her expression apologetic.

Erling raised an eyebrow and one side of his eyes blinked as Malwin finally released the cart, letting it rest near the companions. "Perhaps if you have some tools, I could find a way to repair it enough to make it travel-worthy."

"I told you they'd be ungrateful!" Niggle told Jai. He watched the wheel as if expecting it to take off on its own. "It's already fit for travel. Don't you go mucking about it with your prissy paws."

"Don't be rude!" Jai scolded him before Erling had a chance to escalate their conflict again. "You do a fine job of maintaining it and the rest of these buildings, a wonderful job, but perhaps they could benefit from tailoring it to their own needs."

"Hmmph! I'll tell you what they need. A whopping big — "

"Enough, Niggle!" For the first time since they arrived, they saw the woman display something more than a pleasant desire to help. "These people are acting in the favor of Mistress Nastina, and their task is sufficiently difficult without having to take abuse from you. Now, you *will* bring Erling whatever he needs, be it materials, tools, food, or the vest off your back, and you *will* keep your tongue, along with any comments, in your mouth. Have I been understood?"

The erdi'hun looked stunned at her fierce rebuke, as did most of the others. Even the diamurs had stopped their scuffle and were hovering in the air above the group in a hushed silence. Only Shimi Zar and Graypaw seemed unfazed by her outburst. The former could barely keep a smirk from her face, while the latter gave a slow, wide yawn, then began cleaning his tail.

Niggle nodded, not daring to open his mouth even to give an acknowledgment, then waved a hand for Erling to follow him. The pair walked slowly to the cottage without a word, neither willing to risk the woman's wrath if they engaged in further sniping.

"So we have a wagon," Wynna said, finally breaking the silence with her observation. "But like I said before, it is useless without a horse."

Shimi Zar's smirk expanded into a full-on grin. "And like *I* said, there are other animals that can pull it."

Malwin's face suddenly opened, as if an idea had struck him. "You?" he grunted, jabbing a finger toward the false young woman.

"At last!" she exclaimed. "Someone is picking up what I'm putting down. Yes, me! I'm hoping most of the trip will be easygoing, so we shouldn't need too much power to pull all of you along."

Leda's face lit up, too, at the announcement. "You can transform into an animal!"

"I prefer the term 'beautiful beast'." Shimi Zar turned to Jai. "Are you alright?"

The young woman's calm demeanor had returned, but a touch of sadness lingered in her eyes. "I am, thank you. I apologize for what you saw. Mistress Nastina gives Niggle a great deal of leeway in the way he treats others, but sometimes he goes too far."

"I'll say." Wynna shot a scowl toward where the pair had gone. "He was bordering on hostile. Why do you tolerate it at all?"

"Niggle had been through some rough times, though his demeanor can't be blamed entirely on that. He really is caring, along with being a wonderful cook and excellent groundskeeper."

"And I bet he serves as a good deterrent for idle visitors," Shimi Zar added.

Jai nodded. "There is that."

The pair of erdis returned soon with a handful of tools, including a mallet, a small saw, and a few other Leda didn't recognize. Despite the earlier animosity, the two were able to perform the repairs on the wheel without too much bickering. Within an hour, they were ready to leave.

"Thank you for your assistance, and the wagon," Erling told Jai, with a slight nod to Niggle, too. "This should get us to the plains, but I would like to borrow these instruments for our journey in case our work proves to be less than adequate."

The erdi'hun had almost smiled at the gratitude, but that vanished instantly at the request. "No! I need these tools here. This place isn't held together by grass and hope." Niggle folded his arms over his chest. "Get your own!"

"Niggle," Jai said softly. "Remember what I said."

"I assure you, we will return them." Erling adopted an encouraging expression.

But Niggle wasn't having it. "When? You're going to be gallivanting around the continent on a fool's errand. Probably get killed, leaving my lovely wagon out in the wilderness. Or worse, stolen by peasants! And my tools, too!"

"We'll bring them back," Leda said, picking up the mallet and making a show of caressing it. "Promise."

Niggle looked ready to object again, but Jai cut in with a calm, "We know you will. And I'm sure it's what Mistress Nastina would want."

The erdi'hun grimaced, but he didn't protest further. Leda couldn't help but wonder if Nastina would punish him if he didn't behave. For all the talk, she still had little idea about the temperament of the arcanist.

Shimi Zar handed Leda the small bag Jai had given her the night before, then stepped away from the group. "Time for my thing," the shapeshifter said, shaking out her arms like a fighter loosening up.

"Have you chosen what form to use?" Jai asked. Her tone suggested she was asking for dinner preferences, not a feral metamorphosis.

"I have. A horse is too dull, and a burral is too slow. I want something with a punch, yet elegant. An adartigra!"

Erling's and Leda's faces lit up at her choice, but Wynna looked puzzled. "Is that like a donkey?"

"They are enormous cats who roam the grasslands," the erdi'zal explained. "Very rare. I've only seen one once, when I was a youth."

"And we've seen a model of one. Remember, back in the Sleeping Cat Inn? Reginard had that giant woven statue in the main room."

Shimi Zar nodded. "I've had two encounters."

Leda raised an eyebrow. "What were you doing in the Trideen Plains? Didn't you need to stay with the hammer?"

The shapeshifter straightened her neck. "I can go anywhere I want. That's what the orifereg were for."

"I look forward to seeing your replication," Erling told her.

"Just remember not to be scared. They are intimidating creatures, but this one will still be me."

Wynna frowned. "Why can't you tell us all this after you change?"

"Because tigers don't talk. And I'll have huge fangs which aren't made for conversations."

"But it is still you, right? Can't you be part tiger, part you?"

"Of course!" But the female paused to consider the suggestion. "At least, I should. I've never tried. Do you want me to change, or to continue pestering me with questions?"

"Go ahead."

The others watched as the body of the young woman began to transform into the animal. Her form thickened, muscles blooming beneath her skin as her limbs reshaped into padded paws. Black-striped fur erupted in waves, her boots melting into the shift. Her head narrowed and rounded, long hair vanishing as tufted ears rose, and her brown eyes turned golden. Her jaw stretched open, revealing six-inch fangs as she dropped to all fours. A tail lashed behind her, and a crown of bone spikes arched from her spine.

The metamorphosis complete, Shimi Zar-turned-adartigra walked slowly in a wide circle, simulated muscles rippling with each step, as she showed off her new body to the others. When she completed her circuit, she opened her teeth-lined jaw in a low roar that made Leda shiver. The bisegus had been right to warn them. If she hadn't seen the transformation herself, she would have panicked at being in the presence of the formidable hunter.

"Beautiful job, Lisell!" Jai clapped her hands, then corrected herself with a chuckle. "Sorry, Shimi Zar. Your shifts are always a marvel to watch!"

The horned tiger nodded slightly toward her, then faced the others for their reactions. Malwin's expression was unreadable, but Erling's face was lit up like a child during a Sunpoint festival. "Remarkable. Astonishing! You look identical to the one I saw, except it had a torn right ear. But do you have its power?"

Since she couldn't answer verbally, Shimi Zar walked with fluid grace to the erdi'zal, her tail swaying easily in time with her steps. She brushed along Erling as she sauntered past, their bodies nearly the same height. After a wide turn, she moved to stand beside him again, then, with a sudden swing of her back end, knocked the erdi'zal sideways, causing him to stumble. "Hey!" he cried out with a laugh. "Maybe you do."

"You aren't sure?" Leda asked. She had heard both Shimi Zar and Camille explain about their transformations before and how they couldn't really significantly affect their weight. If she understood right, this tiger wouldn't be much of a match for the real creature in a fight, because she would still have the same mass spread out over a larger form.

"I never had one of the noble creatures rub against me and get playful," Erling explained. "So I have no point of reference."

"Can I pet it?" Wynna hadn't taken her eyes off Shimi Zar during the entire transformation and show of strength. Her voice revealed a sense of awe Leda had rarely heard from her.

"She is still a she," Jai corrected her. "And you will have to ask her."

As if to prove the woman correct, Shimi Zar sauntered a few steps over to Wynna and stared up into her face. Wynna was speechless. She should have been terrified, but she held a tentative hand out and touched the tiger's ear. When that didn't provoke an attack, she caressed it gently. Soon, she was stroking the large orange head as its owner leaned into the petting as Graypaw sometimes did.

Maybe she is learning to like animals, Leda thought, watching her friend enjoying the connection with the huge cat. "It certainly is an amazing ability."

"This is something you will someday learn." Jai's eyes were on her. "Not into an adartigra, of course, but a voladorm. Your true form."

Her words were not an inspiration to the woman. "True form? You make it sound as if this body is a fake. It's the only one I've ever known."

"It is, in a fashion. Created to hide you."

Leda still didn't like the idea. "But if Shiftlings only have two shapes, why can't they both be their true forms? Leda the human is very real, with her own life. I don't know this other version."

The suggestion seemed to surprise Jai, as her eyebrows lifted and her lips parted. "Why, I had never thought of it that way. Most Shiftlings are found when they've only had their human form for a few months or years. Your case might be unique. I will have to discuss this insight with Mistress Nastina when she returns."

"Safe?"

The companions turned to Malwin. Like Wynna, he hadn't stopped watching Shimi Zar during her change, but his expression showed he wasn't sure what to think of it. When she revealed she was a bisegus, it invoked an ancestral fear, passed down over many generations. This was the more immediate concern of a deadly predator within striking distance.

"Of course it is safe!" Wynna stared at him as if he were the one who had changed into something completely different. "She said not to be afraid, and she is even letting me pet her." As if to back up her claims, Graypaw joined the women beside the replica of his oversized, distant cousin.

"It is still Shimi Zar, Mal." Leda moved to his side and placed a reassuring hand on his arm. "The same person who was the egyzemor, then the young woman, and now this animal. She'll be pulling the wagon that'll take us to the Trideen Plains."

He wasn't convinced. "Deadly."

Graypaw gave a soft trill and flopped dramatically onto his side, clearly demonstrating what he wanted the tiger to do.

Leda understood his action. "Good idea! Shimi Zar, lie on your side."

The adartigra glanced at the cat, then gingerly copied his movements. It was an unnatural and potentially dangerous position for a predator, and one this hunter wasn't designed to ever adopt, as it left the belly exposed. She shifted the curved spikes into soft, flexible ridges, just enough to let her lie down without stabbing the earth. Or herself. But after a moment, she and Graypaw had nearly matching poses.

"See! She's quite harmless," Leda said encouragingly. "Trust me."

Malwin still looked pained, but he nodded. Egyzemors were the bravest of the races on the whole, but he was fighting two fears simultaneously and probably the first of his people to ever have this particular situation.

With that settled, for now, they loaded their packs and Shimi Zar's pouch onto the wagon, then Leda, Wynna, and Malwin climbed onto the wobbly, worn plank that served as its seat. The narrow vehicle forced the trio close together, with the egyzemor in the center so as not to overbalance it on one side and cause it to tip. Graypaw hopped into the rear, tail flicking as he turned in a circle, then curled among the bundles with a contented huff.

With the help of Niggle, Leda was able to separate Cutie from the other diamurs who had once again fallen into a brawl. She had no idea how they survived as a species if most of their time was seemingly devoted to beating each other.

Two poles extended from the sides of the wagon to the front, where a horse would normally be harnessed. The space was tighter for the wide-bodied adartigra, but she fit with enough room to allow her to maneuver. Jai had Niggle fetch the rigging necessary to bind her to the cart. After only a little protest about how the doomed travelers were likely to demand the vest off his back next, he produced the leather harness. It needed to be adjusted several times to accommodate Shimi Zar's greater bulk, but within a few minutes, they were ready to set out.

Wynna turned to Erling, who was standing beside the vehicle. "Back in the mountain, you mentioned another large cat with long fangs."

He nodded. "Yes. A hortziak."

"What is the difference between that and this?" She waved a hand toward Shimi Zar's tiger form.

"Just about everything. The hortziak has no horns, first of all. It is smaller, less muscular, and a light shade of brown. They are also more common. I've seen a few dozen in my time. Perhaps you will have the chance in the next few days."

That brought out a frown. "I would rather not. I have had enough wild animals. I will stick to these false ones."

Niggle and Jai came to stand near the other side of the cart. Leda waved to them. "Thank you again for everything. We will return when we can."

Wynna nodded shyly. "Yes. Thank you."

Malwin grunted and waved a beefy hand. Erling crossed to stand before the pair. "We are in your debt, fair lady and smelly cretin," he said with a bow.

"You are most welcome." Jai returned the gesture.

"Bring back my stuff soon, you stinking nag," Niggle added, contributing a gesture of his own which Jai quickly scolded him on.

Erling padded to the side of the wagon and looked expectantly at its passengers. "Let us go now to the plains!"

He meant it as an encouraging cheer for the journey, but the vehicle didn't move. Leda and Malwin exchanged glances as they held up empty hands. "We don't have any reins. How do we make her go?"

"Now you two are being silly," Wynna chided them. "You just say 'go Shimi Zar'!"

That did it. The adartigra sprang forward, yanking the wagon with it and almost tossing its riders into the back. The trio struggled to regain their balance as they were carried along by Shimi Zar's sprinting form.

It only lasted a few seconds, as she quickly reached the edge of the clearing and needed to slow to navigate the forest, but it was an effective demonstration of the bisegus's power as the tiger, and Erling laughed.

They were finally on their way.

LIGHTREAVER SCANNED THE document, her lips thinning with every line. She was equally displeased with the armed delegation before her who had delivered it.

"Is Daymon serious about these demands?" she asked them, shaking the paper angrily. "He can't destroy the property of Zatreus, then tell us we can't retaliate."

"*Lord* Daymon is requesting an end to hostilities between both kingdoms," clarified the woman who appeared to be their spokesperson. The diplomats, four stern-faced women, were flanked by five male soldiers, all human and reeking faintly of oiled leather and steel, clearly handpicked to intimidate.

They arrived at the western gate an hour earlier, demanding an audience with the High Monarch. Curious to learn Ludholm's current position, she agreed to have them enter under heavy guard. A dozen of the city's own soldiers — a mix of human swordsmen and erdi'zal archers — circled them even now, in case their presence was a trap.

Jaron stood a short distance away, axe in hand. The sight of the burly man casually gripping the weapon did more to keep things civil than the surrounding guards ever could.

"*Lord* Daymon should not have destroyed our Riverwall if he sought a peaceful co-existence," Lightreaver told the female before her. "What is your name?"

The woman appeared briefly taken aback by the request. "Rithi. Rithi Brightsayer." She gestured toward the female beside her. "This is Yafra, and behind her — "

The High Monarch silenced her with a dismissive wave of her hand. "I only requested yours. Rithi Brightsayer." She leaned back on her cushions, letting the document dangle from her fingers and taking her first proper look at the woman. She was a few years younger, her slender frame barely obscured by a chestnut-colored dress. Ashen-blonde hair framed a face that was striking in its sharpness — high cheekbones and full lips that spoke of hidden strength. A simple band of leather encircled her neck, catching the older woman's eye in its understated simplicity.

Her eyes caught the monarch off guard — irises that shimmered with shifting colors like oil on water, unnerving in their constant liquid shift. Lightreaver glanced away before she could stop herself. "If you had any knowledge of the history behind your name, you would denounce your king's actions against us. Infiltrating our city using shapeshifters to perform acts of destruction is dishonorable."

"Do not presume to know me," the woman said, her voice unwavering in the face of the accusations. "We were at war."

"War is waged on the battlefield, not within city walls," Lightreaver replied calmly, willing herself not to be intimidated by the woman's strange gaze. She'd never met anyone with similar eyes, but a memory tickled at the back of her mind she couldn't quite recover.

"If you had only shared the waterway, there would be no war," Rithi countered. "Our place as the northern port was stolen from us!"

"So you claim. Now you wish to reclaim that title by destroying Zatreus."

Rithi's voice grew sharp. "No. Lord Daymon desires a resolution of peace, sharing access to Leosonee Lake and the river."

"And use our boats as well." Lightreaver's lips curled into a faint, disdainful smile as she shook the document. "There will be no lake. No sharing. And no peace. All you have achieved in the destruction of our wall is a temporary victory. We will rebuild it, then destroy Ludholm once and for all. I suggest all of you find a new home, as your precious city will not last the year."

The three diplomats shifted uncomfortably, their eyes flickering between one another, a shared unease settling in. The air thickened with the unspoken realization, and even their guards, standing stoic yet alert, seemed to bristle at the chilling prospect of their city's destruction. Rithi's jaw tightened, a faint pulse ticking in her temple, but she refused to flinch. "Threatening to attack now, are you? With what? You realize our armies were destroyed, do you not?"

Lightreaver paused, considering how much to reveal. The woman's comment highlighted a flaw in the Matron's claim. If the creature was aiding Ludholm, would it have destroyed their army, too? "I have discovered that, yes. Do you know how they were destroyed?"

"By the same beast which threatened Zatreus," Rithi said. "It struck Ludholm, too, but we turned it back."

The answer surprised and irritated Lightreaver. If the creature had moved on to Ludholm, then perhaps it had given up on her city. The woman before her knew it had laid siege to Zatreus and eventually gained entry. That suggested there must be more spies among the population who relayed the news, giving credence to Nilado's claim. But how were they able to repel it when it proved to be such a task for Zatreus? The High Monarch was unaware of Savanah's group meeting with Daymon, or Eris's part in aiding Ludholm's defense. "Do you know where the creature is now?"

Rithi shook her head, her voice cold. "No. But we do know where it was heading."

"Care to enlighten me?" Her eyes drifted to the trio behind the woman, but none of them spoke. They appeared to only be there for moral support.

Rithi's gaze hardened, a quiet confidence radiating from her. She stood unyielding, as if she needed no one's assistance to stand her ground. "Not particularly. If you plan to attack Ludholm, why should we give you anything you might use against us?"

"I never said we would attack your city with force. Keep your information. We, too, have repelled the creature, and will do so again if required. As to your demands..." Lightreaver held the document up for all to see, then tore it cleanly in half. A second rip made quarters of it. She let the pieces drift to the floor like shed skin.

Rithi's eyes narrowed as she watched the fragments flutter to the ground. "Perhaps you will keep the beast from your city. Perhaps. But if not, do not bother seeking our aid. Will you release us now to convey your rejection in person, or is your intention to kill us here and dispose of our bodies in the Hightower Woodlands?"

The High Monarch briefly met the eyes of several soldiers standing guard, their shared glance a silent exchange. Then, with deliberate calm, she fixed her attention once more on the rainbow-eyed woman before her. "You are free to go, as long as you go peacefully. My guards allowed you to keep your weapons, but do not, for a moment, think you would last more than a few seconds if you attempt to use them."

"Then, in that, at least, we are in agreement." Rithi briefly turned toward her delegation, as if just now registering their presence, before her gaze sharpened on Lightreaver once more. "However, take heed. You have rejected our offer to share the river. That was your one chance. Mark my words, we won't come with parchment and proposals next time."

SAVANAH'S GROUP RETURNED to Carlin under a brooding sky, a dull hush following them. The only trouble they met came at the river, now shrunken and littered with stranded boats like the skeletons of beached whales. Workers swarmed the docks, swearing and sweating, as they tried to salvage their craft, but a few still found time to ferry the companions across.

Those they spoke with were as much in the dark about the reason for the waterway's ailment as Savanah's party. According to one, the city's monarch had dispatched a pair of riders north to track the cause. Until the situation was corrected, they would have to return to traveling by land for trade.

Once within the city walls, Camille volunteered to purchase horses for the four of them, and Mikel had agreed, handing her several Auger Head coins, the highest value currency from Zatreus. Savanah offered to go with her, but the woman said it wasn't necessary before darting off.

While the men found a barber shop, the archer drifted around the marketplace, making good on her vow to purchase a selection of kliku. She added a few nibe fruit as well, their elongated pink forms complementing the blue and red orbs in her sack as well as a pair of blood ceriman.

When they were done with their respective errands, they mounted the new steeds and trotted out of Carlin's gates. On the aptly named Old Road, Mikel led them into a gallop. The crash and return trip to the city set them back nearly five hours, and the man was eager to make up for lost time. The run didn't last long, the path's deep ruts and loose stones jarring their mounts to a hurried trot.

Despite Mikel taking the initial lead, Camille rode a hundred feet in front of them, claiming to be scouting out any trouble. Savanah, however, suspected it was to avoid conversation. There was no plausible explanation for her keeping up with their trip on the river after her disappearance. The men had not pressed it further, but that didn't mean the topic would remain at rest.

She's also avoiding speaking with me. How can I apologize if she won't talk to me?

They rode on for another hour before reaching where the Swift Salvation lay broken in that remained of the river. It had moved a few more times since they left it, allowing water to flow over it easily now. Camille took the opportunity to say a few words of thanks to the vessel that earned its name before galloping forward again. The others only looked on in regret. Their fastest means of travel would carry them no further.

It was mid-afternoon when Camille shouted. She had strayed further and further until she was barely visible on the road again. Her companions spurred their horses into a run when they saw her leave the path and head onto a patch of farmland.

They had passed several homesteads since leaving Carlin. Not everyone chose to live within the safety of the city walls. Outside, more land was available to raise crops and livestock.

As they drew closer, they could see the simple cottage and weathered barn of a farmer. Beyond it lay a fenced-off field populated by a small herd of cows and a trio of horses. To the left of that stretched an expanse of furrowed ground. Lines of seedlings could already be seen poking up from the dark soil.

Near one corner of the barn, Camille and an older man spoke animatedly while her horse munched grass a dozen feet away. The companions approached warily, guiding their animals up the dirt path to the buildings.

When Camille spotted them, she waved for them to approach. "I think we've solved our river problem. My uncle has a small boat he can loan us."

Mikel raised an eyebrow, but the gray-haired farmer nodded. He wore the drabbest of dirt-stained shirts, baggy trousers held up by a frayed belt around his plump waist, and thick black boots.

Despite his shabby appearance, his beard was trim and his green eyes sparkled. "It's not much to look at. There's a bitty hole in it. The rudder is shaky. The rigging needs repairing. There's a — "

"It will need some work," Camille interrupted before he could continue his litany of problems, "but he thinks it should handle the shallower water."

"Have you done much sailing in it?" Mikel asked.

The man shook his head with a chuckle. "Naw. I stay on dry land whenever I can. The boat came with the farm."

"And how long have you had the farm?"

"Oh, I'd say about forty years, give or take a month."

Camille moved to stand between him and her mounted companions. "That doesn't matter. It's a boat! Uncle, can we see it?"

His eyes lit up as if the idea just struck him. "Oh, right. That would be the next step, I'm supposin'. Follow me."

The man led them around to the back of the barn, where a pile of old lumber leaned against the body of a broken boat. With the farmer's help, Savanah and Camille retrieved the mast from inside the building, where it had been used as a drying rack. The sail, patched and worn, covered a horse stall now. "I suppose Stella will have to do without her private shade."

His comment surprised Savanah, and she looked around the interior. The roof had been repaired many times, as evidenced by the missing chunks of paneling, which had been boarded over, but there were no holes large enough to let in an uncomfortable amount of sun. "We're in a barn. Why would a horse need extra shade?"

"Stella is a goat," he corrected. "She's sensitive to moonlight."

Savanah decided not to pursue that line of questioning further, instead focusing on removing the canvas without damaging it further. It had a few small tears and a bit of chewing around one edge, no doubt Stella getting some extra fiber in her diet, but looked otherwise intact.

The trio carried both items out back to where the men had cleared the lumber and were busy examining the craft. The 'bitty hole' was large enough to stick a head through, but it appeared repairable to Savanah. "What do you think?"

"If your uncle... I'm sorry." Mikel straightened and addressed the farmer. "We skipped introductions. I'm Mikel, this is Vyncent and Savanah. Camille, you already know, of course."

"You can call me Morf," came the reply. "You'll be needing some tools. Camille, would you please help an old man fetch them?"

Once the pair left, Mikel pointed to the boat. "This is a venki. A much smaller version of a valupe. It is designed for gentle rivers and ponds. I've only heard descriptions of them, as we don't use them for trade on the Leosonee. It could carry the four of us, our gear, and nothing else. There is no room for walking around or sleeping, unless we do it sitting up."

"So you think you can repair it?" Savanah asked.

"With some help, yes. And it should be able to navigate the remains of the river. There is just the one sail, so it is easy to handle. I bet even Vyncent here could manage it."

"Your praise is overwhelming," Vyncent responded, but he wore a smile.

Savanah noticed that he tolerated teasing from the man but not from her. He used to chide her for not taking her role in the Sovereign Guard seriously. That changed when she was chosen to lead it. So had Vyncent. "Then we will have to leave the horses with Morf. It looks like they will be well cared for, though."

Mikel followed her gaze to the nearby field where the other livestock grazed. "He probably raised them originally. We were fortunate to meet Camille's uncle. In all of Wayela, we stumbled across his farm."

Savanah thought she heard a touch of suspicion in his tone. It was an amazing coincidence, and she suspected there was more to it, but couldn't let the others question Camille's situation further. "It doesn't surprise me. She is always going on about having an uncle in one place or another. This is clearly not the one who taught her to sail."

Vyncent added his assent. "That's true. Her parents must have a lot of siblings."

"I suppose so," Mikel relented with a shrug and rolled up his sleeves. "Let's strip this thing clean, and see how many more surprises it's hiding. I'd rather not discover another hole halfway to Adradena."

He paused, eyes on the warped planks. "For the first time in days, we have a real shot."

Chapter Fourteen
THE FAVOR OF THE ACCUSED

L EDA GASPED AT the devastation of Longbridge.

After following the route from Ludholm to the Old Road, Shimi Zar shed her tiger form to avoid scaring the citizens. After what they had endured, the people of the devastated settlement would likely not have noticed.

Despite Eris's advice, the villages returned to their shattered homes. The buildings on the outer perimeter suffered the least damage and had already undergone rudimentary repairs. Scraps from other rubble had been employed in temporary shelters and makeshift fencing set up to hold the recaptured livestock.

The survivors looked just as broken as their village. While most worked to salvage what they could and tend to the half a dozen camp-fires, many openly wept, some with faces buried in dirt-streaked hands. Others rocked in place beside smoldering fires. A handful knelt beside their fallen statue, offering prayers for aid and lamenting those who had perished in the fight.

"What happened here?" Leda asked aloud, more in shock than in expectation of an answer. She had an idea, but didn't want it to be true.

"The Abomination," Shimi Zar said. "We hoped it would leave Longbridge alone, but that was probably wishful thinking."

"We?" Wynna turned to the bisegus. "What does that mean?"

"Jai told me about the creature's presence nearby. It passed the tower two days ago."

The women stared at her. Nothing like that had been discussed the day before. They were on a mission to stop Olagkoa, but the last they knew of it, it was laying siege to Zatreus. Now it roamed Wayela freely. "What about the city?"

"Still standing," Shimi Zar reassured her. "It did get inside, but was driven soon after. Then it fled to the Banrood Grasslands."

"What is that?" the blonde woman asked.

"An expansive, sunken plain situated between Zatreus and Ludholm," Eris explained. "None of my people live there, but the armies of both cities have adopted it as a battleground."

Wynna's eyes grew wide. "Then they would have fought it! It could not have survived that."

"But it obviously did." Leda pointed to the ruins of Longbridge and its struggling citizens. *It wasn't that long ago when we were in a similar position.*

"What of the armies, then?" Erling asked.

Shimi Zar shifted her gaze to the far side of the road. The bridge remained extended, though it had a significant sag in the middle. "That's not important. We need to get across the river and into the Trideen Highlands. Since it lives, we still have our mission. Come along."

She took a few steps forward, gesturing for the others to follow. They didn't move. Even her pleading expression as she looked back at them earned her nothing but frowns. "What?" Malwin grunted.

Her shoulders drooped. "Can we just go? It's a long journey, and we must get moving."

Wynna folded her arms and adopted her most stubborn stance. "Tell us."

"It would be best if we knew all the facts of the matter," Eris added.

"Alright." Shimi Zar straightened, hand going to her hip. "But remember, this changes nothing." When they continued waiting silently, she sighed. "Jai doesn't know quite what happened, whether the beast attacked them or the armies did it to themselves, but they were all killed. There! I said it!"

Her words washed over her companions, but they kept silent. The reality of her explanation was too great to absorb immediately. None of them, except Erling, knew much about the war, but the loss of so many lives had a chilling effect on them. Such a tragedy almost made the scene before them seem trivial. Even Graypaw seemed to grasp the importance, as he sat still at their feet, neither cleaning himself nor meowing an opinion. Only Cutie, snoring quietly amid Leda's frizzy curls, remained unbothered.

Leda looked at Shimi Zar, hoping the female might take the words back and say she had been mistaken. Instead, she saw her face tense. There was more. "Tell us the rest."

Her command brought the others out of their contemplation, but Shimi Zar shook her head at their questioning gazes. "Jai only knows this because the two armies marched before the Abomination when it passed the tower. But the soldiers were no longer..."

"Olagkoa made them into its servants, like we met in the mountain," Erling finished as her voice trailed off. "So now we have confirmation of its actions."

Leda's heart pounded. She looked at Wynna, hoping the woman had not understood the implications. The former barmaid had expressed before the possibility of using the creature to bring her mother, Tanita, back from the dead. Until now, such an action had been hypothetical. With this seeming to prove it was indeed Olagkoa behind it, she expected Wynna to seize on the idea again.

Instead, she appeared to be working herself into another of her rages. "Why did you not tell us this before? Not only is the monster roaming about nearby, but it has thousands of grotesque servants now, too!"

"I didn't want it to distract you from our task!" Shimi Zar argued in defense.

"Distract?" Wynna yelled, her voice momentarily drawing the attention of some of the citizens. "How distracting would it be for us to stumble into their midst? We could have died!"

"No, you wouldn't. I'd have said something before then. This doesn't change what we must do. If anything, it makes it more urgent."

"You hid the truth from us," Wynna snapped, fists clenched. "Again! Maybe your kind is just as deceitful as the stories say."

Shimi Zar's expression shifted from apologetic to angry in a flash. "And you're proving why we have to be. I trusted you with that secret, and here you are, shouting it out to the world!"

"What world? That miserable lot over there?" She aimed a dismissive finger at the people scrounging among the town's debris. "They are too busy picking at scraps to care that you are — "

Malwin's enormous hand over her mouth and another one to her back, holding her in place, silenced Wynna's outburst. She tried removing the offending palm, but she might as well have been trying to push a burral uphill. Kicking the egyzemor's shins did nothing but bruise her toes. Finally, she calmed enough to let the others speak.

"There are not 'thousands' in the combined army," Erling told her. "There may have been a single thousand with the forces combined, but no more than that." He finished his correction with a slight smile, apparently enjoying having his say without her immediately arguing back.

"She is merely demonstrating why Jai and I thought it best not to fill you in on the gruesome details." Shimi Zar folded her hands against her dress. "I honestly did not do it out of deceit."

"I believe you," Leda said. "And you are right. It doesn't matter. I mean, not to our mission. We are searching for the items we need to stop Olagkoa. Even if it has an army at its command, we still have to find them. Until we do, it will only continue to grow more powerful."

"I agree with the assessment," Erling told her. "Now that we are aware of the greater danger, we may also take more precautions in our travel. We can assume they crossed the river. Is there any information on which direction they went?"

"No," Shimi Zar replied. "I am hoping it isn't the same as ours."

The erdi'zal nodded. "As am I."

Leda's eyes widened at the realization. "You don't think they are heading toward the Highlands, do you? What if it knows an artifact is there?"

"Then my people will handle it the best they can, as they do any challenge."

Erling's words carried the pride of his kind, but Leda sensed a tone of concern beneath them. It wouldn't be the first time an army invaded the Trideen Highlands, but no one had ever faced an enemy like this.

A muffled protest drew her attention to Wynna, still being gagged by their larger companion. "You can let her go now, Mal. I'm sure she won't raise a fuss again." The last was said with a stern gaze directed at the woman.

Malwin removed his hands, causing Wynna to nearly stumble from the abrupt absence of support. She recovered quickly, though, smoothing her dress and returning Leda's stare. "*She* will raise any fuss she likes. But I do not wish to stay here, so I agree we should resume our journey."

Shimi Zar led them to the waterfront, with Malwin pulling the wagon. The village folks watched them idly but made no move to stop them. Their one purpose, to extend the crossway for travelers, had already been done forcefully. They couldn't retract it in its current condition if they wanted without causing major damage and possibly destroying the construction. For now, their only concern was the rebuilding of their town.

When the companions reached the riverbank, they encountered another shock. "Where did the water go?" Wynna demanded, seeing the great Leosonee reduced to a flow less than half its normal size.

"Blocked or diverted, it seems," Erling observed.

"Oh dear," Shimi Zar said, shaking her head slowly. "It's worse than I thought it would be."

Wynna's face contorted in anger. "You *knew* about this too?"

"No!" Shimi Zar snapped. "Well, not completely. The Riverwall in Zatreus has broken, and the Banrood Grasslands are flooding. I guessed there would be some drop in the river, but not this much!"

"We can still get across," Leda said quickly when she saw Wynna drawing in air to begin another rebuke. "I mean, if the army did, it should be safe for us, right?"

Erling scratched an ear as he surveyed the bowed walkway. "Perhaps. But I would feel better if there was some way to shore up its structure. If the townsfolk don't mind, we might borrow some of the larger debris and fashion at least one pillar."

"Why not have Shimi Zar here just change into one?" Wynna asked with a smirk at the bisegus. "Or maybe become a new bridge?"

"I could," came the reply, complete with a sneer of her own. "But you wouldn't like that. I'd drop you in the river."

Not again! Leda threw a hand between the pair. "There will be no dropping anyone in the river. And she can't risk changing in front of the villagers. You know that."

Wynna crossed her arms again. "Then what's she good for?"

Shimi Zar smiled slowly, licking her lips. "I can still eat your soul."

"Kindly suspend your bickering until we have reached the other side," Erling told them, his tone taking on an unusual edge.

"Agreed," Malwin grumbled.

Shimi Zar glanced at them, then nodded. "Alright." She turned her eyes back to Wynna. "But once we have, I am so sucking out your soul."

The woman stuck out her tongue, but the sides of her lips curled upward in a slight smile. "I'd like to see you try."

THE KNOCK CAME just as the last dish was set aside. Hamund stilled and flicked a glance toward Pirro, where she rested on her cot. He accepted that his role made him susceptible to requests at all hours, and expected one of Talidith's citizens to be on the other side of the door when he opened it.

Instead, the High Monarch stood framed by moonlight, her guards looming behind her like shadows. "I received your request," she said before he could speak. "Forgive me for taking so long to grant it. You understand, I'm sure."

"Of the demands of leadership? I have become acutely aware of the... honor, in these months, yes. But you did not need to come here. I could have gone to Wolfsight."

He ushered her in, and with a single glance at the soldiers, she stepped inside, alone. "I have other issues I wish to discuss with you, away from the ears of rumor, which linger there," she explained. "It is also good to get out at times, and remember there are lives outside its walls."

Pirro sat up, exchanging curious glances with Hamund, but he could only shrug as he pulled up a chair for the High Monarch. She took it without question. He settled into another beside the cot.

The residents of the cottage turned their attention to Zatreus's ruler, waiting for her to continue. After a brief survey of the modest room, she met their eyes. "First, why I have ordered your people to be confined. The head of our guilds and trade has leveled some serious allegations against you and those of Talidith, which I must investigate."

The news took Hamund by surprise, but he masked it behind a composed expression. "Naturally. We are strangers and not to be wholly trusted. You made that claim before, though, so I am curious what has caused your renewed mistrust."

"It is related to the creature. How it breached our defenses and gained access is still unclear. We know there were others aiding it. Have you had any dealings with the voladorm known as Sarvendor, or an erdi'zal named Linda?"

The man leaned back. He didn't immediately recognize the names, but he'd interacted with hundreds of people since taking on the role of leader. "Until Jaron arrived in Talidith, most of our citizens had never even seen a voladorm or erdi'zal, let alone had dealings with any."

It wasn't an assurance, and Lightreaver's frown said she wasn't ready to accept it. "You've been here for months, though. Could one of your people have joined with them in an attempt to overthrow me and take the city for yourselves?"

Pirro's eyes went wide at the suggestion, and even Hamund struggled to keep his composure. "The notion is incredible," he told Lightreaver, his tone clipped. "We lost our home, but you provided us with a new one. Why would we have any desire or need to control it? As for working with the creature, no one from Talidith would ever consider siding with that monster. Do you understand the devastation it caused my people?"

"What about the fisherman who led it to our gates?"

The man gave a slow, deliberate shake of his head. "Until he showed up, we believed him dead. He was a good friend of mine. When Talidith came under attack from a horde of vornuks, everyone outside Castle Shieldarrow fled to it, hoping to wait out the siege. That is when I first met him. No experience with weapons." An affectionate smile crept onto his face. "Or women, though he did fall in love with one, and she returned it." His expression darkened as he remembered Leda's heartbreak. Everyone who knew Aedan had mourned the loss. "He helped Savanah drive the creature back into its cave, risking his life to protect us all. When he didn't return, we thought him lost. If any of Aedan still survives, he is being controlled by the beast."

The High Monarch looked on, taking in his story without question. "You think there is a chance to save him?"

"I do," he replied immediately, "and so do others. There must be. He does not deserve this. You sent Savanah, Vyncent, and Camille to find a way to stop the creature. We sent another one. Leda, Wynna, Erling,

Malwin, Graypaw. Two women who were also his friends, an erdi'zal who works for you, an egyzemor soldier, and Aedan's cat."

A flicker of astonishment crossed Lightreaver's face. "You sent a cat?"

Pirro nodded. "Leda says he is a special cat."

For a moment, the High Monarch blinked. Then her mouth curved — not mockery, not derision. Something softer. "There's no one ordinary among you, is there?" Then the smile vanished as she straightened. "You've assuaged my concerns. I'm confident you are not working with the creature, nor attempting to overthrow Zatreus."

Hamund visibly relaxed, letting his shoulders slouch at her words. "I am glad of that. We wouldn't have driven it out of the city if we were."

"I never did thank you personally for your efforts in that. We couldn't have evicted it without you, though I still don't fully understand what happened."

"To be honest, I'm not completely sure either. Our plan to smoke it out of the cemetery wasn't working until one of our soldiers went in and drove it out. One of your citizens accompanied him, a barmaid named Tal."

"I've heard the name. She was with a man who followed the beast from the city. Is that correct?"

"Yes. Eris and Tal. They should still be with the creature, along with two women from here, Farla and Ranin, who were also instrumental in repelling it. Holfast went with them." Hamund paused, his lips tight. "I have bad news for you. The armies from both cities have been killed and turned into Shells."

Lightreaver nodded. "I already knew that. Shells?"

"The walking corpses," Pirro explained. "Tal called them Shells, as in they are empty."

"Sounds like an interesting barmaid." The High Monarch straightened. "We are straying from the topic, though. As valiant as the efforts of your people are, I am no longer confident in their success. The creature now has an army under its control and has already attacked Ludholm. At least they claim so, and to have fended it off. They will not tell me where it is traveling, and there is no guarantee it won't head back here."

This time, Hamund didn't try to hide his surprise. "How did Ludholm deter it?"

The woman's tone sharpened. "They will not say, which makes their claim even more dubious."

"But if their claim is true, how they did it could give us a clue as to how to defeat Olagkoa, or at least protect Zatreus," the man countered. "Such a possibility would be worth pursuing."

"Not for the price. Daymon wants us to share the river and provide them with boats for trade." Lightreaver's anger deepened with every word she spoke. "After they threatened us, then destroyed our River-wall, that villain Daymon has the gall to make such demands."

"What is the importance of the Riverwall?" Pirro asked. Even after her recent illness, she remained fully attentive.

"The land abutting the harbor was damaged centuries ago," the High Monarch explained. "The Riverwall was built to shore up the region and prevent further erosion."

"And destroying it does what?"

"Flood the adjacent Banrood Grasslands." Lightreaver reached back and gave her ponytail a firm tug. "Daymon and the citizens of Ludholm have this foolish notion that there was a lake there once. That breaking the barrier will restore it and their rightful place as a port city. All it will do is destroy the river, hurting everyone from here to Adradena."

"What if they are right, though?" Pirro pressed, echoing Hamund's questioning. "Is it possible that there once was a lake there?"

"Zatreus has been here for seven centuries. There is no record of there ever being so much as a puddle in the grasslands."

"That's not likely." Pirro glanced at Hamund, who gave her a nod to continue. The pair had developed a mutual understanding of perspectives, and while she occasionally took the lead in their inquiries, she consistently deferred to his judgment. "Do you really mean there isn't a single stream or pond in all that land?"

"Not a one," Lightreaver confirmed. "It's little more than barren land, with barely enough moisture in the soil to sustain the sparse vegetation clinging to it. Even if it was a lake a thousand years ago, we control the river now, and there's no chance we're handing it over to that miserable little kingdom. Their demands weren't just about the waterway, though. Something else is coming."

"I believe it would be better if you tried to make peace with your neighbor," Hamund told her. "There may come a time when you need their aid. I know our people would be lost if not for the generosity of our southern friend."

The compliment fell on deaf ears, unheeded in the High Monarch's indignation. "Then we would turn to Drulon. Or Kridmont. Or Stegate. By the stars, I'd go to Begesh before asking for so much as a crust of bread from Ludholm. And before you say anything, they feel the same way about us."

The intensity of her words caught both Hamund and Pirro off guard. "All this hostility over water rights?" the man asked.

At the question, most of Lightreaver's anger abated, and she sighed in resignation. "No. Our feud runs deeper than rivers or walls. Zatreus joined the Empire and profited. Ludholm rejected it, and fell into ruin. They blame us for that. This war is just the newest in a long line of grievances. That is the other reason I am here."

Hamund nodded, thinking he understood her meaning. "You think a neutral party might be able to negotiate a peace."

She stiffened again. "There will be no peace. We will repair the Riverwall and restore our trade. But Daymon involved the bisegus, having them infiltrate the city to destroy the wall. If he is striking partnerships with such dangerous allies, then there are no lows to which he will not stoop. They sent a delegation with their demands. When I rejected them, their spokesperson warned it was our last chance. I believe their next action will be an attack on the city directly. Perhaps with the creature."

Hamund's posture sagged, the weight of her words settling on him. "If they try to tame Olagkoa, they will find themselves in far greater trouble than a war. We fought it in Talidith and barely got out alive. We fought it here and nearly lost. So if you came for more advice on how to battle it, I have told you all I know."

"What I ask of you, and I understand the immense irony of the situation, is that you dispatch the soldiers you have to fortify our defenses. Our army is gone, and our city guard is already stretched between manning our gates, protecting our harbor, and maintaining order in the streets. Even stationing a few here has been taxing."

She managed to catch the pair by surprise once more, and Hamund paused to carefully consider his response. "When we arrived in Zatreus, you wanted us disarmed. Only when we swore not to raise our weapons against you were we allowed to keep them. Still, you forbade our soldiers from joining yours. Now you wish them to flock to your call?"

Lightreaver raised a hand in acknowledgment. "I know, I know. And I would not even consider making such a request if the situation were different. I accept that your people are not responsible for bringing the creature to our gates, but just as it threatened your kingdom with its actions, Zatreus is in peril. You have made the city your home. Will you now refuse to defend it?"

"It is not that simple. The Sovereign Guard never numbered more than a few dozen. We only protected a few hundred souls. We lost many in our conflict with Olagkoa. Most of those remaining chose to lay down their swords and retire here."

The woman's expression softened as she leaned forward. "Could they be persuaded to pick them up again, do you think?"

"Possibly. But you also sent our commander, along with our greatest bladesmith, on the quest to locate something to defeat Olagkoa. Malwin, Camille, Farla, Ranin, and Eris are also absent in an attempt to stop it. Nor can I spare Pirro here."

Lightreaver slumped, disappointment settling on her. "I understand. I had to ask."

"And I have not said no," Hamund reminded her. "I am not turning down the request. But it is not my decision alone. Each person must decide for themselves."

"You could order them."

"Perhaps. And they would likely obey. But they chose me to lead them because they had no one else, and I do not wish to test that allegiance."

The High Monarch bowed her head. She held that pose of defeat only a moment before rising. "Then I will not press the issue further." Her tone was devoid of anger, but her dismay was unmistakable. "Thank you, Hamund, for taking the time to hear me out. You've quieted my doubts. I only hope your people remember where loyalty lies when the gates begin to fall."

Hamund stood too, but gestured for Pirro to stay on the cot. "And I hope a peaceful resolution might still be found between the two cities."

Lightreaver gave him a soft smile. "I wish you and your wife a good evening." Without waiting for another reply, she moved to the entrance and passed through to the attentive guards outside.

When the door closed, Hamund retook his seat. "I apologize," he told Pirro. "I did not mean to suggest to her we were married."

"You didn't. She assumed." She placed a hand on his arm. "We are a man and woman living in the same quarters."

Hamund looked at her, never having considered what their situation might look like to outsiders. "But that is for convenience, so that we may receive information together."

"Of course. I'm sorry." She withdrew her hand, as if that might also suggest something more. "Do you think there is anything wrong with the arrangement?"

He smiled. "I have no complaints."

"If it feels improper... we could find another arrangement."

"Were you proposing something?"

She looked away. "Not exactly."

"Pity." He took her hand. "Well, I have a proposal. We could remove any suggestion of impropriety."

She brought her shy gaze back to him. "How?"

He leaned in, closing the distance between their faces. When she didn't retreat, he seized the moment, his lips gently brushing hers. A spark of warmth spread through him as the contact lingered, soft and tentative, then he pulled away. "By making the relationship more... formal."

She grinned. "Ah. Well, if we must be formal...." Her hand gripped his shirt, pulling him closer, resuming the kiss. His arms wrapped around her, and soon all thoughts of soldiers and monsters faded from their minds.

"KEEP IT STRAIGHT!" Camille yelled, her fingers digging into the slick, splintered wood as the landscape lurched sideways in a dizzying blur. "I'm getting dizzy!"

"I'm trying!" Vyncent shouted back, frantically working the tiller in a desperate attempt to hold the vessel steady. Despite his efforts, the small venki spun into a tight circle, sloshing cold river spray into their faces and threatening to dislodge its passengers.

The four sat aboard the craft, the women in front and the men in the back. Mikel called it a smaller version of a valupe, but even that

219

felt generous as Savanah clung to the central pole, arms aching with every lurch.

The thing barely qualified as a boat with just a thin hull, a crooked mast, and a crawlspace below crammed with their gear. The original rudder had been lost long ago. In its place sat a poorly carved copy, which did little to control the boat's direction, as they learned soon after climbing aboard.

Their trip from Morf's farm had been swift, wet, and terrifying. While capable of moving easily in the lower level of water — gliding more over the river than in it when the sail filled — the vessel never held a heading for more than a few seconds.

If the weaving wasn't bad enough, the venki had the dizzying habit of slipping into a spiral as they sped along, forcing its riders to cling with white-knuckled grips or risk being tossed into the churning water.

The next tower loomed above them as the craft finally straightened, though Vyncent's handling of the tiller hadn't changed. "Steer us into land. We can spend the night here."

"Tell that to the boat! It won't listen to me!"

Mikel grabbed the lever and a grateful Vyncent surrendered it easily. "Everyone, brace! Lean to the left and hold on tight! This is going to be rough!"

They did as he ordered, latching onto the hatch, mast, and anything else secured to the deck before throwing their weight sideways while Mikel released the sail and shoved the tiller hard to the right.

The venki trembled as if attempting to break free from their control, then suddenly changed direction, causing its starboard side to momentarily rise above the water before slamming down, nearly dislodging its passengers.

It cut a diagonal path through the rapids, hurtling toward the exposed embankment. Just before it struck, Mikel pulled back on the tiller, trying to slide them onto land. The craft didn't respond in time, however. The bow slammed into the soft riverbank, mud sucking at the hull as the vessel skidded to a shuddering stop.

Savanah immediately jumped out and yanked the mooring line, holding the venki steady for the others to scramble off.

"That thing is going to kill us long before we reach Adradena," Vyncent yelled as he slogged through the shallow water, slapping the boat's deck before moving to aid Savanah.

Camille followed, sliding into the muddy flow before climbing the embankment. "For once, I agree with Vyncent. I'd rather crawl the rest of the distance than board that again."

"We just need to find a way to stabilize it." Savanah let Vyncent help her bring the venki further to shore. She recognized that, unlike their visit to Stegate, his intentions were genuinely aimed at helping, without any romantic undertones. "But Mikel is right. We must speed up our progress."

"We do," the man agreed, tugging the rear of the craft to match the front. "However, I also don't want to rely on this further until it's safer. With the sun nearly gone, we should set up camp and eat. Then we can have a go at fixing the boat."

The venki, much lighter than the valupe, moved easily over land, but they couldn't port it over the imposing bank to the grassy ground. Instead, they found a few larger rocks to block the underside from drifting back into the waterway. Unless the Leosonee were abruptly restored, it wasn't going anywhere.

The watchtower looming above them appeared almost identical to the one they had stayed at after Stegate, but the surrounding area seemed to be better maintained. Mikel explained that the stone building was often used as a meeting place for people traveling between the cities.

"Have you ever traveled to the coast by land?" Savanah asked the man once they were seated around a fire. They had brought nothing to cook over it, but its flickering heat warmed their spirits as well as their damp clothes. Even with the boat, they managed to soak themselves.

"Only twice," he answered, reaching into the supply of food he purchased that morning and distributing it among the others. "I was assigned to protect a trade caravan from Zatreus. I was new to the city ranks and often got the jobs no one else wanted. It taught me a great deal about the route, though. That's when I learned about the towers."

"What about the creatures we encountered?" Vyncent asked, breaking off a chunk of bread from a hard loaf that flaked crumbs into his lap. "When did you learn about those?"

"What creatures?" Camille asked. "I didn't encounter anything."

Savanah frowned, then bit into a kliku fruit to hide her expression. She had heard Camille lie before. Deceit was what kept a bisegus safe. However, the archer didn't understand why she would lie about seeing the beasts. *Even if she didn't encounter them directly, she must have seen them from the air.*

"How could you miss them?" Vyncent asked, voicing her thoughts. "There were over a dozen of them. Huge, hairy brutes. Teeth. Claws. And howling. They nearly killed us all."

"He isn't exaggerating." Mikel took a bit of bread for himself. "From the descriptions I've come across, they were carcass beasts. Have you ever heard of them before?"

"No." Camille snatched a bite of fruit. "Why should I?" she mumbled as she chewed.

"I didn't think you did. Too many in Wayela don't know enough of their own history. It doesn't surprise me you don't know Begesh's."

"Yes." She swallowed. "Forgive me for not knowing about what happened in another part of Rapria over the last several thousand years! I'll stick to making stew."

Her outburst surprised them, especially Savanah. Her friend had deftly deflected the questions about her time away from them, but an inquiry into a bit of history angered her. *Is this about her ancestor?*

Mikel shrugged it off, though his gaze lingered on her a moment longer before he turned his attention to the fire. "I merely wondered if you wished me to repeat the explanation I told the others."

Rather than apologizing, Camille's expression darkened, and Savanah feared she might storm off again. "Does it matter? We are in Wayela now. I'm sure whatever history lesson you have can wait until we've solved our current problem." Camille crossed her arms and turned from the fire, lips pressed tight. The moment cooled into silence, thick and awkward.

Vyncent nodded eagerly, swallowing his mouthful before speaking. "That is what I said! We need to focus on our mission."

Mikel shook his head wearily. "Once we finish eating, let's see what we can do with the boat. We have a few more hours of moonlight to work by before we sleep. After that, as you wish, we can get an early start on the river. That's the fastest route, so I'm sure you won't complain further about the boat."

"I wouldn't count on that," Vyncent said, a chuckle in his throat. "Never underestimate our ability to grumble. Someone's got to keep morale low."

Chapter Fifteen
RACING THE DEAD

S WINGBRIDGE DID HAVE boats. More importantly, a small barge enabled Eris's party to cross the river with relative ease. It took time, however, as did the ride northwest to meet up with Olagkoa.

Just past dawn, the group found their first sign of the creature's passage. A village unfortunate enough to be in its path lay in devastation, a wide swath of destruction cut through its center.

Most of the settlement's scattered straw-and-wood houses had been beaten into splinters. A line of simple stalls for a market stood in ruin, their contents crushed into the mud. Clothes hanging on extended lines to dry were now strewn about in the grass. Only the fencing holding livestock and the stone fragments of a wall remained untouched.

The sight of the damage caused Tal to cry out, nearly falling from her horse in her scramble to dismount. The others quickly followed, drawing their swords. This much devastation could only have been inflicted by the Shells and Olagkoa. But their training told them to be alert for any danger that might yet be lurking.

There was no one, though. Ranin and Farla checked out the few structures still standing while Eris and Holfast scoured the perimeter for any signs of life. Shocked by the level of wreckage, Tal ran about, calling for anyone to answer her. Grief soon overcame her, and she dropped to her knees next to a cloth doll, lost by a little boy or girl in the attack.

When the rest were confident the danger had passed, they rejoined her. Ranin knelt beside her to comfort the woman, but Tal recoiled from her touch. "The whole village is gone," she sobbed, tears streaking her cheeks. "They slaughtered everyone!"

"Hey! We don't know that," Farla said, sheathing her sword. "There are no bodies. Not even blood."

"They turned them into horrible Shells!" she yelled. Her fingers wrapped around the toy and brought it to her chest. Its edges were frayed, and it had no eyes, but she stroked it as if it were a child itself. "Everyone's dead," she murmured through her tears.

"Farla's right. We don't know that." Ranin looked up at Eris and Holfast. "We don't, do we?"

"We didn't find anyone to confirm that," Holfast replied. "We can't even be certain this was done by the beast."

Eris appreciated the erdi'zal's attempt to ease the woman's worries, but the recent destruction was undeniable. If another force existed with the same devastating power, their troubles had just doubled. "There is a chance they survived and fled. It would be hard to miss seeing the creature and an army from a distance. The stench and sound would be enough warning for them to be gone before the soldiers arrived. If they escaped, they may not know which route the creature's taking. The next village won't be so lucky unless we alert them."

His words didn't explain the rampant destruction of the buildings, which he guessed had been done in pursuit of any hiding villagers. He kept that thought to himself.

Tal's sobbing eased. The suggestion that the population hadn't been wiped out seemed to calm her, and she dried her cheeks. She raised her head to him. "Do you really believe that?"

The man hesitated. He felt she'd earned the right to hear the truth, but her breakdown reminded him she wasn't used to death or trained to handle it. "I do," he lied. "Which means they have likely fled to the nearest settlement. If that is in the creature's path, they will need us to warn them."

His logic contradicted the claim that the villagers would have seen Olagkoa and the Shells coming, but Tal latched onto the suggestion. She tucked the doll into her belt alongside her hammer and returned to her horse. Eris and Farla did the same.

Ranin tore down several slats from the fence, allowing the chickens, pigs, and cows to roam freely. "They should be easy to recapture once the villagers return," she explained as she climbed on her mount. "But if they don't — "

"They will," Tal said, cutting her off before she spoke the grim alternative. "And I'll give the doll to its rightful owner personally." As if to show her conviction, she kicked her horse into a trot, signaling the others to follow.

Eris hoped her belief was merited. Their delay in crossing the river had possibly cost the people of the settlement dearly. It would be a welcome change if that toll proved to be lighter than expected.

They rode for an hour before they spotted the Shell army ahead. Holfast had led the companions on what he believed was the most direct course to Kridmont, and the sight of the undead force marching along that route verified the city was its next destination.

Since emerging from the mountain pass, the army had picked up its pace. The settlement had been in a wooded region. The area they were traversing now featured more clearings, indicating it had been settled recently enough that the trees had not yet fully reclaimed the land. It allowed for easier passage, but he doubted that it was the cause of their increased speed.

Eris signaled for the others to stop. "We will have to get past them, but they must not see our group. If Olagkoa senses our presence, it could attack with its mind, and I don't want Ranin overtaxed in saving us. Since they are making for Kridmont, we can swing wide around and move ahead of them. Holfast, can you bring us back on this route when we do?"

"My people spend their lives navigating the plains with few landmarks," the erdi'zal replied with a grin. "This will be easy."

"Good."

"What's in Kridmont, anyway?" Farla asked, looking past the line of Shells. "What could the beast get from there?"

"More soldiers," Eris suggested. It had entered Zatreus to make more undead from the cemetery there, then moved to the Banrood Grasslands to slaughter and raise the fighters there. Seeking out more bodies seemed the obvious reason. "Maybe it wants to expand its army."

"To what end?" Ranin asked. "It nearly destroyed Talidith on its own. What does it need soldiers for?"

"Revenge." Everyone turned to Tal. She began to fidget under their stares, then raised her voice in defense of her statement. "Leda said it had been trapped underground. That must have been deliberate. If someone did that to me, I'd be a sour-sore."

Ranin nodded. "That's as good a goal as any. I hope it isn't something more sinister."

"You think Kridmont had a part in imprisoning it?" Eris asked.

"Might have," Farla answered for her.

"Wouldn't that implicate Ludholm, too? It attacked them first."

"I suppose."

"It's on a rampage," Tal interjected. "Does it matter?"

Farla lifted a brow. "Probably not. But it is interesting."

"Then consider it while we ride," Eris told them. Ranin's comment about it possibly having a more nefarious purpose made him uneasy. Whatever its goal, they had to make sure it failed to achieve it. "Holfast, will you lead us?"

With the sun still low on the horizon, the riders didn't need to travel too far out to remain out of sight of the army. As a result, they were able to reach the next village in under an hour. Though three times larger than the previous settlement, it seemed tiny compared to the cities they had left.

"I figured there would be a lot more folks living out here," Farla commented as they approached. "There can't be more than a few places like this between here and Kridmont."

"It does seem like a fair distance since the last village," Eris admitted.

Holfast chuckled. "When I first met your people a year ago, I said you were inbred and ignorant. The former may have been an insult, but you are living up to the second."

Farla turned in his saddle to glare at him. "What is that supposed to mean?"

"We are perhaps twenty miles from the mountains. Wayela is more than thirty times that distance from west to east, and even more from your little kingdom to the Hafugung. You humans think everything's just down the road."

"Hey! I was only curious."

Holfast wasn't done with his disparagements. "Humans live in cities. These would be safer behind stone walls."

"Is that why you live in Zatreus?" Ranin asked, adopting an innocent tone to hide the implied barb.

"I do not rely on walls," he huffed, puffing out his chest. "I am a warrior."

"We are all trained fighters," Farla reminded him.

"Human fighters are not the same as erdi'zal warriors."

"Want to test that?" Farla nudged her horse closer to the erdi'zal.

"Relax," Eris told them both. "We have to let these people know of the threat. You two can prove your skills later."

The pair exchanged challenging glares, then resumed their ride forward.

As the companions approached the settlement, they saw it was already alive with activity. Several women were trying to corral their children into cottages while a few dozen men were loading up carts with bags and trunks. Others were hitching up horses and gathering livestock together.

Tal kicked her horse into a gallop, riding up a wide, worn path to the first line of buildings. "You are all in danger!" she shouted, pulling her steed to a halt. "You must leave here immediately. An army is heading this way!"

A man with shoulder-length black hair and a verdant cloak, carrying a large sack to one of the wagons, scowled at her. "You think we don't know that? We are packing as fast as we can."

His reply caught her off guard. "How did you know?" She craned her neck to look around, but the creature and its followers were still too far away to be seen through the various vegetation.

"Folks from Fernwick arrived here a while ago in a panic," he explained as the others came up behind. He tossed the sack on top of a large chest before continuing. "Their story sounded wild, but when you live out here, wild is the norm."

Tal's expression brightened. "They're here? Where?"

The man pointed to the far side of the settlement. "Resting over yonder. The folks must have run the entire distance."

Without a word to the others, Tal nudged her horse into a trot, navigating around the busy villagers as she made her way to the refugees.

"Whatever they told you, it's true," Eris informed the cloaked man as he watched Tal leave. "We didn't reach them in time to give a warning. How many survived?"

"Most," he said, striding over. "They lost nearly a dozen in the attack. What I'm not understanding is why soldiers be attacking us folks. Is this an invasion?"

"Of sorts. There's a tentacled beast leading an army of the dead. They're marching for Kridmont and crushing anything in their way."

The man's expression tensed. He shifted his gaze left to Ranin and Farla. "Is he in jest?"

Farla grimaced. "Afraid not."

He clicked his tongue. "That's an even wilder tale than the others spun. But seeing as how we don't want to end up dead and all, I'll see if I can speed up our retreat."

"Where were you planning to go?" Holfast asked as the man began to turn.

"Kridmont. It will take a bit of walking, but the threat don't seem to be in too much of a hurry. What you reckon?"

"Head north," the erdi'zal suggested. "If the army is going to Kridmont, you don't want to be there."

"But Kridmont's got soldiers. And walls."

Holfast gave a snort. "You humans and your walls. You won't need either if you aren't in the army's path."

Timoth frowned, then nodded. "Fair point. I'll talk it over with the others. Who should I say advised this?"

"I am Eris," Eris told him. "This is Holfast, Farla, and Ranin. The other woman is Tal."

"I don't need all them names. Just one. I'm Timoth. And this is Hearthglen, if you're looking to know." He paused, a frown turning his lips. "How much time you reckon we gots?"

"Less than an hour," Holfast informed him. "No more than half that."

"Then I best get moving." Timoth waved a hand vaguely in the direction of the rest of the village. "Make yourselves at home, as it were."

They watched him walk calmly toward a few more substantial buildings on the left to consult with whoever acted as the decision-makers for the homestead, then continued on their way. While Holfast went to help a few men with getting the larger livestock secured for travel, the three humans dismounted and led their horses along the same route Tal had taken.

She greeted them with a smile when they arrived at Hearthglen's other side. A little blonde girl in a lemon dress stood beside her, clinging to the woman's leg. Her eyes grew wide as she watched them approach. "You were right. They fled here safely!"

"Who's your friend?" Ranin asked.

Tal patted the child's shoulder. "This is Delia. It was her doll. See?" She pointed to the girl's hand where the cloth figure was clenched in her tiny fist. "I said I would return it."

Eris looked past them both. "We don't have much time. This settlement is evacuating. Its people were heading to Kridmont, but Holfast told them to go north, out of the creature's path. Have you found who the leader is among these folks?"

The woman's expression turned to disappointment. "No. I just — "

"Mind my horse." He thrust the lead into Ranin's hand, then pushed past Tal and Delia toward the citizens of Fernwick. While those of Hearthglen were calm, almost resolute, about having to flee, these people were traumatized. Couples and families huddled together, finding seats on logs, crates, and the grass-covered ground.

Many sobbed quietly. Others murmured empty reassurances, their faces betraying disbelief. A few had collapsed from exhaustion. They'd lost everything, and Eris had nothing to offer but a warning to keep going.

The sight reminded him of the evacuation of Talidith's population from the Undercastle. They, too, had been forced from their home, then the stronghold, with little more than the clothes on their backs. Jaron had arrived with aid in that dark hour, but the situation could have turned dire if he hadn't.

Eris's attention was drawn to a single man, maybe twenty years his senior, with a graying beard and wide nose. He walked between the scattered refugees, speaking with each and visibly lifting their spirits. The soldier recognized him as Fernwick's leader, as Hamund had done the same for Talidith, which eventually earned him the role of king.

He waited until the man had finished speaking with a family before approaching. After a brief conversation, Eris felt confident he would lead his people northward as well.

"Why did you do that?"

Eris spun to face a scowling Tal. "Because if we are right that the beast plans to attack Kridmont, it will be safer to not be there."

"Not that. You ignored me."

"I didn't ignore you. I had my priorities, and you should have, too."

"What'd I muck up now?" Tal threw her hands into the air. "I found the folks."

"And focused on taking a toy to a child," he said, his tone growing sharper. "Do you think that will matter if the beast catches up with them?"

"Then tell me, *oh wise one*, what I should have done."

"Find the leader. See how you can help."

"I knew how to help," she snapped. "I returned the doll."

He shook his head. "Try to see the bigger picture. Your personal gratification can't be your first concern."

Tal's eyes burned with fury. "Like you? You freed the monster to impress a woman!"

"Exactly!" he yelled. "I have to live with the guilt of that mistake every day of my life." His voice fell to a hushed murmur as he stepped closer to her. "If I could go back and change my actions, I would. But I can't!" Eris inhaled deeply, realizing his hands were trembling. "So learn from my mistakes, and don't compound them!"

His fury left Tal stunned. She watched him pace, the angry energy not yet spent. "I'm sorry. That was wrong of me."

"It was." He stopped before her, holding out a pleading hand. "You insisted on coming along, so I will do my best to prepare you for what we might face. You need to do better than me."

"Doesn't sound like too tall an order." A smile tugged at the corners of her lips.

"You're not a tavern server anymore, though," he reminded her, glad she was handling his outburst more capably than he would have expected. Perhaps she could learn some lessons more effectively than he had.

"I guess I'm not," she said, almost wistfully. "What am I, then?"

"A monster hunter. Or at least a monster chaser." He grinned. "The pay is terrible, but you get to travel."

Her smile blossomed into a full laugh. "I'll take it."

"Good. Now let's see what we can do to help these people with moving."

Fortunately, the threat of an oncoming army was enough to motivate the folks from both homesteads into action. Within the time Holfast had estimated, the citizens of Hearthglen and Fernwick were heading northward, the former with everything they could pack and the latter with only what they had as they escaped. Tal gave Delia a hug and made her promise not to lose the doll again. The girl appeared too young to fully understand the situation, and Eris hoped that as she grew older, it would be remembered only as an odd day when her family went for a long walk.

"So when do I get to see this tentacled beastie you spoke of?" Timoth asked, waving to the departing mass. Once he had spoken with the settlement's decision-makers, he offered his services to the companions, and they accepted gratefully.

"I'm hoping you don't," Eris told him. "We will be riding ahead of it to warn any other villages or towns on the route, then on to Kridmont itself."

"Alright." The man tugged his hair together at the back and pulled it into a single knot. "I don't see how some animal is a threat to the city, even with a bunch of soldiers to support it, but I'll take your word on the matter."

"It's more than any animal," Farla replied, standing to his right, holding the lead to her horse behind her. Ranin and Holfast had rejoined them as well. "It drove our people out of Talidith, broke into Zatreus, and attacked Ludholm."

Timoth pursed his lips as if he had bitten the sour end of a nibe fruit. "Is Talidith one of the northern towns?"

Farla shrugged. "I guess you could call it that."

"Then I'm sorry for you folks," he told her with a somber nod. "That's a boulder in the field, alright."

"How many settlements are there between here and Kridmont?" Eris asked him.

"Well, let me see." Timoth held up a hand and began ticking off names. "There is Smyrna, Eustis, Kendusheag... no, wait, I think that's further south. And Palmyra, though that place ain't too big. Caratunk, Molunkus, and Meddybemps. Mosswick and Redmere might be along the way. Oh, and a handful of folks were going to start their own town somewhere between Palmyra and Caratunk. A couple of families didn't like each other, and one's dog got the other's pregnant. Or was that their kinfolk?" He studied the fingers extended on both hands. "Anyway, that makes about eight."

"You are known to each of them?"

"Oh, sure." A broad grin spread across his face. "Everyone knows ole Timoth. Actually," the pursed lips returned, "I'm not certain about that new town."

"It sounds good enough to me," Tal said from Eris's left. "Let's get going, or you might see the creature after all."

They mounted up, Timoth having acquired a horse for himself. With a last look behind them to see if they could spot Olagkoa in the distance, they set out again, toward Kridmont.

At a gallop, they reached the first settlement, Smyrna, in a quarter of an hour. Not quite as large as Hearthglen, it still boasted a host of houses and buildings, including a simple church and community hall. Even a tiny militia of half a dozen sword-wielding men stood guard as the companions rode up.

Timoth's boast proved true. They passed the border unchallenged, and Eris quickly relayed the danger to the settlement.

However, despite the urgency of their story — along with a few shouts of frustration from Tal — the people didn't believe them.

"Come on," Farla finally told her companions. "If they won't leave, let them find out for themselves. We can't save all of them, but we still have time to warn the others."

"You can't let them die," Timoth protested. The argument had drawn a crowd of villagers, and many among them now wore worried expressions at his suggestion.

"It is up to them," she replied, not missing the crowd's faces. "Fernwick and Hearthglen had enough sense. Maybe they can salvage the remains of this place once the army has wiped out the population."

"Yes," Tal joined in. "You will all be deaded. Quite sad. Perhaps someone will remember you. Ready to go?"

By now, the gathered citizens were growing agitated and talking furiously amongst themselves. Finally, a middle-aged woman with thick brown hair raised a hand. "You are strangers. How do we know you are telling the truth?"

Timoth smiled softly. "Harriet, is it?"

She appeared surprised that he knew her name, a slight blush coloring her cheeks. "That's right."

"While they are indeed strangers, I am not. We have been neighbors for what — seven years?"

"Eight, come this summer," she corrected gently.

"Eight fine years we've had, living in peace and plenty. Eight grand years in this fair land. My folks have headed north for a spell, till this trouble blows over, which my new mates here assure me it be but a few days." His voice took on a sorrowful edge. "But it saddens me to think when they come back, they'll find their dear, sweet Harriet and her fine Smyrnian neighbors are gone for good, swallowed by a great ill, all 'cause of plain old foolish stubbornness."

Harriet looked at the other citizens. She was met by anxious faces urging her to accept the story and warning. "I guess it wouldn't hurt to have a little trip north, too," she said, facing Timoth again. "How far would we have to go?"

"Only a few miles," Holfast answered for him. "Three should be far enough."

A murmur went up from the crowd. "That's reasonable," Harriet said with a nod. Soon the villagers were busy packing up as many belongings and animals as they could.

"Nicely done," Eris congratulated his companions when they couldn't be overheard. "You convinced them without us having to threaten them."

"That was next," Farla said with a mischievous smile. "Good thing you remembered that woman's name," she told Timoth.

"I didn't," he admitted, his lips curling into a grin. "I heard one of the other women call her that."

They all laughed, enjoying a moment of levity during the tense situation. It wasn't over, though, and once they were sure the people of Smyrna were safely on their way, they continued toward Kridmont.

The next two homesteads, Eustis and Palmyra (Kendusheag, as it turned out, lay further south), were more towns than villages, with the latter being larger than Timoth remembered. They recognized him and accepted the news about the approaching army easily. The people governing these settlements were more practical and knew to take a warning seriously.

It was nearly midday now, and the companions took the opportunity to have some lunch. A generous Palmyra baker gave them each a meat pie she had baked, saying she couldn't take them along. The group accepted graciously. It was a magnanimous gesture to reward harbingers of doom with fresh pastries. They washed it down with ale purchased at the town's single tavern before the owner stored everything away in an underground cellar. The settlement might be destroyed, but the liquor would probably survive.

Once rested and sated, the companions mounted up again at the town's perimeter. Holfast estimated Olagkoa and its army to be about halfway between Smyrna and Eustis. "If they haven't wasted time demolishing it and Hearthglen. And if they haven't sped up again."

"You noticed that, eh?" Eris frowned.

"Slower than a wounded burral through the mountains, then human-paced after that. Or at least after it crawled its way through Fernwick."

"Any idea what caused the change in speed?" Eris asked. "I thought it might have slowed from having to control so many Shells, but that doesn't seem to be the case."

"Indeed," the erdi'zal agreed. "Out on the plains, an animal speeds up when it is rested or it knows it is being hunted. This beast never appears to rest, so perhaps it realizes we are tracking it."

Tal pounced on his conclusion. "And it's scared! I like that. We're proper monster hunters now!"

But Eris shook his head. "The only times I've seen Olagkoa showing fear is when confronted with fire. Remember how it bolted when we circled it in flames?"

"That got it razzled!" the woman announced gleefully.

"I doubt our presence has worried it too much. If it has sensed us, it has not attempted to stop or even slow our pursuit."

Farla frowned. "Makes us more monster gebits, then. Annoying insects buzzing along behind it. We are racing the dead."

"What if it got energy from attacking the village?" Ranin mused. "A rush of enthusiasm?"

"Smashing things does seem to make it happy," Farla noted. "Like a puppy chewing on your favorite boots."

Eris ran a hand through his cropped black hair. "If that's true, then it may take the opportunity to destroy the settlements. That might buy us more time."

"To do what?" Tal countered. "According to Timoth, we've got only four more villages to warn."

"Five," the cloaked man corrected. "Or three. I'm still not sure about Mosswick and Redmere."

"We alert them, then Kridmont. I doubt the city will listen to us, at least not at first." Eris sighed, aware of the challenges that lay ahead of them. "It may take some time to convince them. Timoth, do you know anyone there who might be receptive?"

"By the roots! I'm afraid not. No one important. I've only been there once. There was a good tavern, forgot the name. The bartender was polite — forgot his name, too." He straightened in his saddle and grinned. "The wench was Sylvara. She was very nice, if you catch my meaning."

"Unless she is in charge of the city's defenses, that doesn't really help us," Farla laughed.

Eris grew somber. "You do not have to come with us to Kridmont, Timoth. You have been quite useful, but that could turn dangerous."

"I know that," the man replied. "But I might get a chance to reunite with Sylvara. 'Sides, I came this far. Might as well see this beastie you keep yammering about. I'm sure I'll be safe behind that city's walls."

Eris saw Holfast open his mouth, likely to say something more about humans and their walls, and cut him off. "We are grateful for your continued company, then."

They found no indication of the other settlement Timoth recalled — just another long ride through wind, silence, and unease — until Caratunk rose on the horizon. This homestead was more town than village, with a sprawling spread of sturdy buildings over almost fifty acres. Eris spotted a tavern — *The Golden Plow* from the hand-painted sign over the door — a church with a carving of a male archer, likely Bonimen, on its roof, and even two stores, as evidenced by the barrels of fruit and grains out front.

No one challenged their entry, and they had to ask for directions to the population's leader or leaders. That came in the form of an elderly woman in a dull red robe who refused to leave the round building acting as a town hall. Eris took only Ranin with him to speak with the mayor, figuring she was the least likely to lose her temper. After twenty minutes with the official, though, even she had let loose with several profanities before he dragged her back outside.

Farla couldn't miss the anger in her companion. "I'm guessing she didn't believe you."

"No," Eris confirmed. "She is a bit inflexible in her thinking."

Ranin had stronger words. "That ungrateful harridan said we were 'fostering unrest' and that we should leave her dirt-covered town before her mead-soaked militia forced us." She cast a glare of rage at the structure. "I hope her nose grows three times its size and smells nothing but dung!"

"So that's it?" Tal asked as the pair took back the leads for their horses. "We just take off?"

"Not quite." Eris pulled his steed behind him as he walked away from the building to a busier intersection. Townsfolk strode casually along a few gravel roads, going about their errands without paying too much attention to the visitors. That was about to change. "Listen up, everyone!" he shouted, looking around to draw in as many people as he could. "We came here to warn you that a monster leading an army of unkillable soldiers is on its way here. It will be here in about six hours. That's how long you have to live." He paused, letting his words register with the crowd. "Your mayor ignored our warning. I hope someone here shows more sense. I wish you luck."

He mounted his horse and gestured for the others to do the same, then turned back to where they had entered the homestead.

"You might not want to have done that," Farla said as they walked. "Your friend doesn't look happy."

Eris glanced around to see the mayor standing on the porch of the town hall while a dozen citizens approached her. She ignored them, though, instead moving to a bell attached to the wall. She seized the thick rope and swung the clapper inside the heavy iron shell. Deep, resonant clangs sounded through the square.

At first, Eris thought she was calling the populace together to discuss the news. Then he saw a dozen men charging at them, swords drawn. She had summoned the Caratunk militia.

The companions bolted into a gallop out of the town and another mile before they slowed. "We can't leave them like this!" Timoth protested.

"We can't do anything else," Eris told him. "They've refused to listen and driven us away. They may yet come to their senses, or my message might resonate with enough folks to force an exodus. At any rate, their fate is their own now."

Holfast nodded in agreement. "'He who will not listen may find his cries fall on equally deaf ears,'" he recited. "Sage Seredic predicted correctly."

Tal grimaced. "Who?"

"A famous erdi'zal philosopher. Very wise."

"Too bad he wasn't running that town," she said. "I don't like everyone there being in danger because of one person's stubbornness." The moment Tal spoke, she realized her mistake and turned to Eris.

But he ignored the inadvertent criticism. *It's no worse than what I've thought myself.* "Come on. We've wasted too much time here. We still have two more towns to visit, then on to Kridmont."

Chapter Sixteen
THE WEIGHT OF PROOF

DASIA STROLLED THROUGH one of the lantern-lit upper hallways of Wolfsight, her spirits lifted for the first time in days. The shift in her mood reflected in her attire. She wore her favorite outfit of a long red coat that brushed her knees, paired with a fitted white shirt and trousers. Her calf-high black boots moved softly over the stone floor, each step exuding quiet confidence.

Her full curls bore a deep orange hue, the first time she had changed her hair color since killing Mamatay. The burden of that action had weighed too heavily for her to take joy in such a simple delight. But after the talk with Nilado, she recognized her proper course.

The clothes weren't real, only the *nagdami* morphing fabric worn by all bisegus. It reshaped with a thought, mimicking shirts, robes, or jewelry, depending on the body it adorned.

Dasia provided such clothing to Nilado the year before, under pressure from her boss. She had given in too easily, she realized now. Nagdami could be dangerous in the hands of a *malditano*, a non-bisegus. If the secret of their construction were ever discovered, not only would their abilities be abused, but a way to identify bisegus might be found.

She needed to get it back. Mamatay had tracked her down to make her stand trial for the betrayal, though he seemed more eager to kill her. If others of her kind learned what she did, they would also come for her.

More than that, she needed to clear her conscience. Retrieving the nagdami was a step in that direction. There were far more black marks on her past that this action alone wouldn't remove, and her next move would help to soften those, too.

"Jarontaldor Berkenshire," Dasia addressed the rugged man before her. She'd spent the last hour searching the castle before finally finding him.

He gave the trio of soldiers with him a few parting words, then watched them depart before turning to her. "Yes?"

"I am Jada Dasia, from the Council," she said, then briefly considered whether she should show him more deference. His rank was sergeant, though she rarely heard of him in charge of any guards. She was a civilian, so did that matter? She finally decided a quick bob of her head would be sufficient courtesy.

He stared down at her, his eyes showing weariness despite the early hour. "I know who you are. What do you want?"

"A few minutes of your time. May we speak in private?"

The man made a show of looking around the hallway. It stood empty, devoid of both people and the sound of footsteps that might suggest someone nearby. "We are."

"You can't believe that." She strode past two wide oak doors and opened the third. After a glance inside, she motioned for him to follow. "This should do. Come."

Jaron frowned, but followed her in. It was a small study, with a high glass window letting in a shaft of morning sunshine. Still, Dasia lit a candle and carried it around the room, investigating the shelves of books, decorative items, and even the thick, padded chairs. Finally, satisfied no one was listening, she set the light down on a table and strode back to the man. "Yes, we won't be heard here. You are searching for information on the Matron."

He stared at her. "What makes you think that?"

"I have ways of finding things out. I am offering some of that to you."

"Like what?"

Dasia might have inhaled deeply as she prepared her argument if she had lungs. Instead, she subconsciously shifted a slight amount of her mass from one leg to the other. "First, there are terms which need to be met."

Jaron gave a vehement shake of his head. "I will not be black-mailed, and you are wasting my time. We are dealing with many issues right now, as you should be aware, including a threat against the High Monarch's life." He pivoted toward the door, ready to depart.

A cold knot tightened in her core as she felt her chances slipping away. She darted forward, her boots scuffing on the smooth floor, as she reached out to intercept him. "There is no assassin!" she blurted out. "That was a ruse."

He halted abruptly, his gaze dropping to meet hers. "We thought as much. But how do you know?"

"As I said, I have information. Will you listen?"

He tugged at his ear. "Alright. What do you want in return? I'm not promising anything, but I will hear your request."

Dasia tensed. She'd always known this moment would come, but standing here, ready to reveal herself, her nerves unraveled. "You must promise to remain calm. I am about to tell you something you may find terrifying. I need your oath that you will not harm me."

"You're yanking my beard."

"Please. It is important."

A weary sigh rumbled from Jaron. "By my sword and my honor, I swear that I will do you no harm for the duration of our conversation."

"Only for our conversation?"

"I would be a fool to swear to never harm someone who might one day prove to be an adversary. I'm a soldier. Causing harm is one of my specialties."

"It'll have to be good enough. Brace yourself." She stepped back twice, then paused as one more crucial detail came to mind. "Oh, and you can't tell anyone else."

"No," came the blunt reply. "I would also be a fool to let myself be bound to secrecy over information I don't yet know. You might be telling me something so vital that I must act, like confessing to murder."

If only he knew. I've no choice but to trust him. I'll never get close enough to the High Monarch to tell her myself. "So be it. I am a bisegus." Her hands flew up in self-defense as she uttered the last word.

Instead of the violent blows she anticipated, Jaron simply regarded her with puzzlement. "That's it? You made me take an oath for *that*?"

She mirrored his confusion as she lowered her guard. "Aren't you terrified? Don't you want to kill me?"

Jaron folded his arms tightly, his glare fixed on her. "Terrified, no. As for the killing, I reckon I might if you don't stop stalling."

Dasia couldn't let it rest, though. Bisegus had always been feared. Hated. But the man before her didn't act like it. He should have been attacking or retreating, but instead, he stood still, his anger evident, but lacking the edge of violence. "Why aren't you surprised?"

"I already knew. I have my own sources for information." He nodded toward the door. "I'm not sure you'll have anything more to offer."

"I promise, I do. Much more!"

"Then spill."

She had one more chance. If she didn't get to the point, he would leave the next time he lost interest. "You must promise — "

He interrupted her with a sharp shake of his head. "We aren't going through that again."

"This is the condition for my information. I'm not the only bisegus in the city. You must promise once I tell you what I know, me and my kin in Zatreus will be allowed to stay and not be revealed."

"Seeing as we have no way of identifying your kind, that shouldn't be a problem," Jaron told her. "We are aware there are more of you. The High Monarch fostered that relationship years ago. The Matron took over that correspondence now, so perhaps you should be discussing your continued anonymity with her."

"After I divulge my information, I fear she will be actively attempting to reveal my people."

"I think I understand." The man's voice had softened. "I promise to do what is within my power to prevent any harm from coming to you or your kin."

"And I want the cloth I supplied back," Dasia added, jabbing a finger at him. "Those suits that can change appearance. They are bisegus property."

That put him on edge again. He moved to the large chair and dropped into it. "Whatever information you might have on Nilado had best be worth it to demand that high a price. Yes, I will do what I can. That is all you can ask of anyone."

Her certainty crumbled. She'd thought the truth was enough. Dasia believed what she knew could get her everything she wanted, but all she'd heard were pledges of possible action. With no other route, though, she pressed on. "That's fair, I guess. As I said, the assassination rumor was a ruse, meant to divert our attention to that rather than the Riverwall."

"Which we already guessed, as *I* said. Tell me something new."

Give him what he really wants. "It was the Matron who had Hamza Lightreaver killed. She felt he was challenging her too much."

Jaron slammed his fist onto the arm of the chair. "I *knew* it! We've reckoned that was what happened, but we haven't been able to prove it." He quickly stifled his enthusiasm, replacing it with a sharp glare. "You are certain of this?"

"Yes," she replied, her spirits lifted by his reaction. "And more. The Matron also caused the war. She provoked Daymon when he sent envoys here, then tricked the High Monarch with a fake. All to prevent the river and trade route from being shared with Ludholm."

The large man's composure wavered, the shock of the revelation written on his face. "That's a greater treason than murdering a High Monarch! It puts not just the ruler at risk, but the entire kingdom as well. And you have proof of this?"

Dasia's confidence sank. "I have my testimony."

"That makes it your word against hers."

She flinched. *I thought that would be enough.* There had to be something to substantiate her claims. Or someone. "There is another who might be able to testify to more. Linda of the Bronze Boar. The Monarch had her arrested a few days ago."

His mouth twisted into a grimace. "That won't work. She escaped, along with the other prisoner. At least that's what we were told."

Dasia nearly cried out in frustration until she remembered her last conversation with Nilado. "No. The Matron has only taken her to one of the older holding cells below the dungeon. That's where she puts anyone who crosses her."

"I will look," Jaron said, but his tone sounded doubtful. "I still need something more substantial. I doubt she keeps records of her crimes, but anything written we might use as evidence would help."

The bisegus had spent the last few days searching Wolfsight for that very thing, but she had come up empty. She figured they must be in Nilado's office somewhere, but that search had also proved fruitless. Even the enormous desk the Matron liked to prop her feet up held nothing incriminating. But she knew her boss kept records of everything, as she had demonstrated a few times at meetings, bringing up infractions and issues from years before. There had to be something! "I haven't found anything yet, but I will continue looking."

"Good." Jaron planted his calloused hands on the chair's arms, the wood creaking beneath the shift of his weight as he rose. "I'll check into your other claims and report them to the High Monarch. I reckon her reply will be the same as mine, though."

She nodded, masking her disappointment as best she could. Deep down, she understood how unbelievable her story must sound. If their roles were reversed, would she believe it herself? "Thank you. I am glad you do not fear or hate my kind."

He shrugged. "I've met many odd folks, especially this past year." He tugged his ear again. "The way I see it, being good or bad comes down to the individual. We've got to decide which path we walk."

Dasia took in his words. *Am I walking a good path now?* "Very wise."

That drew a grin from him. "No one's called me that before. I'm just a soldier doing my job. Which I do have to get back to." The smile faltered, morphing quickly into an expression of concern. "Will you be safe from Nilado?"

"She can't hurt me personally," Dasia replied, surprised at his consideration. The Matron commanded fear through her power and position, but even if she were a skilled fighter, bisegus were notoriously difficult to wound, let alone kill. "It is more the fate of my people that I am worried about."

"I'd say that makes you a good person," he said quietly.

If only it were that easy to wipe away my sins. Despite her misgivings, his words sparked a glimmer of hope within her. "Maybe one day."

JARON LED THE way into the dungeons below Wolfsight, his mind going over what Dasia had told him an hour before. He had already guessed some of it. He never suspected, however, that the Matron started the war. Despite all he had known of the woman's manipulative ways, that action seemed beyond even her malevolence.

243

So while Dasia couldn't provide proof for any of her claims, Jaron still had the means to investigate one of them. He needed help, though, which is why Steelfang, the head of the city's guard, and a pair of trusted soldiers, followed him into the castle's underbelly.

The current dungeon of Zatreus were not a wholly terrible place to be thrown into, as prisons go. Torches, lanterns, and proper drainage ditches in the floor kept them well-lit and dry. High ceilings were supported by thick oak beams. The immense chamber had been split into multiple aisles, lined with iron-barred cells. More such cells sat in arched recesses around the perimeter.

Not a rodent or insect scurried away as the foursome passed through. There were also no prisoners to raise their heads to the soldiers. On the whole, crime in Zatreus was infrequent, almost never requiring someone to be cast into a cell.

Jaron visited the dungeons just a week ago, when Savanah, Vyncent, and Camille were imprisoned by order of the High Monarch. Their sentence was commuted when Olagkoa attacked the gates, and Lightreaver decided they'd be more useful outside the city.

Jaron, Steelfang, and the soldiers came to a halt when they reached the rear of the chamber. A windowless iron door sat recessed into the wall before them, its exterior so scuffed and worn that it barely stood out against the stone around it.

"Are you certain you want to go beyond it?" Steelfang asked as he drew a long key from his pocket. Like the soldiers with him, the man showed signs of exhaustion, with bloodshot eyes and his black hair in disarray. Though four days had passed since the Riverwall's destruction, most of the city's defenders had been doing double and triple duty at the walls and in the streets.

Jaron wouldn't have bothered him with the request to enter the old dungeon if not for Dasia's revelation. If her claim bore truth, he wanted witnesses who could be trusted. "I am certain I *don't* want to, but this is important. Like, city security important."

"If you say so, but I think this is a waste of time. No one has been down to this old level since Wolfsight's expansion. They only left it intact for storage, and it isn't even good for that."

He didn't know whether to wish the captain was right or not. "Then this won't take long."

Steelfang stared at him a moment more, then shrugged, too tired to argue further. With a dull click, he turned the key in the door's lock and returned it to his pocket. "Grab some torches," he ordered the guards behind him, then tugged the door open.

A fetid stench of mold and rot rolled out, thick and wet in their nostrils, clinging to the back of their throats and triggering a sharp recoil. Jaron waved a hand to clear the air. "I'm no expert on matters of dungeons, but I don't think it would stink this bad if it were empty. Do you?"

Steelfang scowled but kept quiet. He grabbed a torch from the first guard, a thin human male, and brandished it into the opening. A narrow passage stretched ahead, sloping downward, its stone steps slick with moisture, forming a precarious path forward. On either side, the remnants of an iron railing clung to the walls, secured by rusted spikes. One shifted as the captain gripped it, but didn't fall.

Jaron took a torch and fell in behind him, ducking to get through the low doorway. At first glance, it certainly didn't appear as if anyone had been here in years. But in his mind, the key turned too easily, and the door swung open with little effort and not a squeak.

The four quickly reached the bottom. The stench had grown much stronger, but they still inhaled sharply at the sight. Smaller than the chamber above, the primitive room wasn't even as large as the library where Jaron spoke with Dasia. At least it didn't appear that way from what little they could see in the light of their torches. The ceiling stood barely a hand span taller than Jaron, and the damp surface of the wall behind gave a shimmering reflection of the flames.

"Spread out, and be careful," Steelfang ordered. The warning was unnecessary, as none of them wanted to stumble and be lost in the oppressive darkness. While only a level deeper than the more comfortable chamber above, the mass of Wolfsight seemed to press down on them in the gloom.

After a few seconds of exploring, Jaron regretted bringing light to the grisly vault. Most of the cells remained intact, though their iron bars were rusted and coated in what he could only hope was mold. They were not all empty, however. The first he stumbled upon contained a few elongated bones, likely the arms or legs of an egyzemor. *The dungeon has been used since they closed it up!* Apart from a few cloth remnants beside the remains, he saw little evidence there had ever been more of a body. He couldn't tell how long they'd been down there, either.

His next discovery was more gruesome. Patches of scaly skin adhered to the thin bones of the skeletal remnants of a hafu. One bony hand clutched the bars of its cell, a final grasp at the freedom it never received.

A few gasps from his companions told him they had found similar bodies. *How many were sent down here? Are they all the work of the Matron?* "Still believe no one has been down here, captain?"

"Blood and ash!" came the harsh response from Steelfang. "Someone's been using this pit for butchery! Have you found anyone alive?"

A muffled groan from the far end seemed to answer him, and the four rushed to locate the source. They passed other corpses, some recent, as the stench became almost unbearable. Finally, in a closed cell at the opposite end of the chamber, lay a female erdi'zal, stripped bare and covered in blood.

She winced as the torchlight struck her, flinching away as if it burned, three of her eyes slamming shut. Where the left front eye should have been, only a shallow hole remained, stained red from bleeding. Despite her disfigured face, Jaron recognized her. "It's Linda!"

He reached to help her up, then drew his hand back in shock. Her entire front right leg was gone, as if someone had cleaved it with a sword. The severed flesh looked cauterized, but badly. The charred edges curled away from the raw center, reeking of burnt hair and blood, probably cauterized with a hot iron. He cursed and pointed, alerting the others to her missing limb.

Steelfang grimaced, then turned to the two soldiers. "Fetch blankets. Strong ones. We need to get her out of here!"

The pair nodded, then retreated toward the stairs, the glow of their torches bobbing in the gloom. "Don't tell anyone what we've found," Jaron called after them.

"A crime has been committed here!" the captain growled at him once the others left. "Multiple crimes, by the look of it. The murderer must be brought to justice!"

"We have no proof of who that is," Jaron replied calmly, scanning the wounded erdi'zal. After her initial reaction, she slipped back into a semi-conscious state. Her ears twitched at their words, and her bare chest moved just enough to indicate she still breathed, but apart from that, she looked like any of the dozen other corpses they'd found. "I had hoped Linda might be able to corroborate some information, but she is in no shape to speak."

"You have an idea of who did these barbaric acts?"

"I do. And so should you. Few could have accessed this level without drawing too much attention."

"All my guards are loyal and would never play a part in this."

Jaron didn't reply. Someone helped Sarvendor escape and moved the erdi'zal down here in secret. At least one of the jail attendees had to be working for Nilado. But how do you uncover their identity without tipping them off that you're onto them?

Linda's mouth twitched, and both men brought their focus to her face. After a long moment, her remaining front eye slitted open. She appeared to be trying to look at them, but her gaze remained unfocused.

"Who did this to you?" Jaron asked, afraid to miss the opportunity. He believed he could trust the captain, but at present, that didn't extend to the guards he'd brought. Once they returned, he might not get the chance to confirm his belief.

Her eye shifted rapidly left and right. "Don't hurt me," she murmured through cracked lips. "Please.... Please..."

Her upper torso began trembling with what Jaron could only guess was terror. He gripped her shoulder gently to calm her. "We aren't going to hurt you. I'm Jaron. You are safe now."

The last part wasn't strictly true, but it seemed to have a soothing effect. She tilted her head slightly, allowing her to see more of his face. "You have to get me out!" she rasped, breath coming fast and shallow. "Now! Please! Before they come back!"

Jaron leaned in. "Who? Who did this?"

Linda lost focus, and her eye began its rapid shifting again. "The Matron!" she whispered, as if saying her name too loudly might cause the head merchant to appear. "The Matron." Her breathing quickened. "Before she comes back... please..."

Steelfang shifted closer, voice taut. "Who else? Was it one of my soldiers?"

But her eyes fluttered, and her lips parted in a silent breath. Her body went slack.

"Linda," Jaron coaxed, but she didn't move. He released her shoulder, his hand tingling where her clammy skin met his. Sorrow and anger welled up inside him. Dasia had been right. Nilado had brought the erdi'zal here, and while he had no proof she also caused the deaths of the other corpses, he saw no reason to suspect otherwise.

But did that prove true the rest of what the bisegus had claimed? He still didn't know. But did it matter? Mass murder was a serious enough crime to have her tossed into the dungeon, along with her victims. The High Monarch would have to decide that.

"I had no cause to doubt my guards before. Now, one of them is likely an accomplice to murder," Steelfang said softly. "I wish I had never come down here."

"I'm sure she felt the same, as did the rest of them." Jaron shook his head. "Let's get her out of this place. She has suffered enough."

DEMZI LIGHTREAVER SAT like a coiled storm in her padded chair, a jeweled goblet of *akkum* clenched tight in her fingers. "You had no right to agree to those terms."

"I made no promise." Jaron stood near the canopied bed in her personal chambers. The last time he visited it, he wore a disguise to hide his identity from anyone who might question why the High Monarch would be meeting with her sergeant in private. His discussion with Dasia and the discovery in the dungeon seemed important enough to risk impropriety. "I told her I would bring her information to you and see what could be done. That is all."

His explanation didn't ease her mood. "You should have brought it to me before even the suggestion of action was made."

"She wouldn't tell me what she knew until I agreed to consider it."

"Then you should have walked away!" Lightreaver didn't answer immediately. Her grip on the goblet tightened. "We have far too many issues to deal with already to worry about protecting a certain segment of the population. The entire city is at risk."

"What about the clothing?"

"Impossible. Until we know what Ludholm is planning, we can't give up what little strategic advantage we possess. I would have sent the spies back to learn more if we weren't so short-handed."

Jaron's shoulders sagged. He sank onto the edge of the bed, its stiff mattress creaking beneath his armor. Though he hadn't promised Dasia he could grant her wishes, the thought of her risking everything to betray Nilado gnawed at him. It didn't sit right that he couldn't repay her. "Will the people of Talidith help?"

"No. Hamund said we sent some of their best fighters away, and the rest are retired." Lightreaver took a sip from her goblet and winced.

The rejection didn't come as a surprise to the sergeant. "You did make it clear that they were not welcome in our ranks."

"Another point Hamund made, thank you," she told him, her tone matching the bitterness of her drink. "I stand by that decision, however. We were at war. We still are."

Jaron recognized her mood. The exhaustion from the past few days and recent setbacks had taken their toll, making her argumentative and bitter. "Yet the decision changed."

He should've known better than to provoke her. Her eyes bore into his, fixing him with an unmistakable glare. "Are you now questioning my actions? Yes, the decision has changed, because the situation has changed." She paused, returning her attention to the goblet. "We will manage without them. Our guards will just have to remain extra vigilant."

"That might be a problem," he said, undaunted by her ferocity. They had been friends since they were youths, and part of what sustained that lasting relationship was their honesty with each other, especially when it hurt. "What we found in the old dungeon suggests the Matron had help from one or more soldiers. If she has split the loyalties of even a few, there could be an uprising if we take action against her."

"So you believe Dasia's account now?"

The man shrugged. "What she said about Linda proved true, and we have long suspected the Matron's hand in the murder of your father. As for her starting the war, well, I don't know how she managed that."

"She is already dealing with the bisegus. Having one impersonate an envoy, as Dasia suggested, would be a simple matter."

Her calmness regarding Dasia's words puzzled Jaron. "You don't seem terribly upset about this news."

The glare returned, though it remained fixed on her goblet this time. "I am furious. Nilado has, at the very least, slaughtered many of our citizens in brutal ways. If the rest holds true, she stands guilty of committing multiple acts of treason." She downed the remaining akkum in a single gulp.

The man nodded, thinking he understood. Even if they believed it, they still had nothing to back it up. "We just need more proof before taking action."

"Proof? With all of Zatreus at stake?" Lightreaver jumped to her feet and hurled the goblet across the chamber. It struck the wall with a shrill metallic crack, then clattered to the ground. "I have endured this evil woman for too long. She has spoken her last lie." Raising a fist, she stared down at the still-sitting soldier. "Bring her to the throne room. Her three days are up. Double the guards as well." Her tone softened when she realized what she was ordering. "I know it's a strain, but it will only be for a few hours."

Jaron nodded again. "I will be at your side."

To his surprise, her expression grew darker at his statement. "If you had done so as you promised, you would not have accepted Dasia's terms so easily."

He stood to match her stance, refusing to accept the reproach. "You made it impossible when you forbade me from accompanying you to see Hamund."

"You've grown too attached to them," she said, her gaze tracking him as he rose and stood just a few inches taller than her. "I needed to talk with him without your loyalty clouding the room."

"If I had gone, I might have been able to persuade him to lend us his soldiers."

"Do not forget your place, Jarontaldor Berkenshire," she snapped, jabbing a finger into his chest. "I am High Monarch, and my decisions are not to be questioned."

His expression went from shock to anger. She had never made an issue of their different ranks. "Should I bow next time, Your Radiance?"

"Save it until after this matter is resolved." Lightreaver walked toward where the goblet had landed, dismissing the man's sarcasm with a wave. She turned on her heel, leaving him standing in silence. "The only one I expect to see groveling now is Nilado."

Chapter Seventeen
UNMASKED

JOICE NILADO BURST into her office, panic driving her now where rage once had taken her.

The deadline for her to provide Lightreaver with proof of the alleged activities of Sarvendor and Linda passed hours ago, and she expected soldiers to be coming for her. Dasia not only failed to present her with someone who could pose as Linda and confess to the allegations, nor did she offer a bisegus willing to remove the High Monarch altogether. Nilado hadn't seen the shapeshifter all day and suspected she might have developed enough of a backbone to betray her.

The Matron hurried to the desk as fast as her short, plump legs would take her. Burral skin boots replaced the slippers she normally wore around Wolfsight. The rest of her attire had been swapped out as well, leaving her dressed in trousers and a long-sleeved tan blouse. She despised the common clothes, but she knew her escape would be aided if she blended in with the other citizens.

Her errand into the streets took longer than she had hoped. The merchant she hired to take her beyond Zatreus's borders had to use the promised wagon to move his goods south, forcing her into a last-minute search for a replacement. She found one in a local farmer who planned to head back home at midday. A bit of money persuaded him to stay a few more hours and transport her to the Lunenshall River.

That gave her precious little time now to get her affairs in order. Nilado had already ensured her most valuable items were sent on ahead through discreet channels, but she needed one more thing from her office.

The mahogany table, with its decorative, gold-edged side paneling and carved, grimacing faces, was among her finest acquisitions, and one she would be forced to abandon, one of her few regrets. It served as her place of business for many years, as well as a reminder of the wealth she had accumulated.

Nilado dropped into the chair behind it, slid open the top right drawer, and crammed her pudgy arm into it. Her fingers pressed a recessed button inside, causing a slight click and a shift in the desk's inner workings.

More than merely a surface on which to work, the table contained a cleverly hidden compartment, large enough to conceal the detailed records of all her transactions over the last decade and a half. Among the papers were the names of people she bribed and had killed, including the woodworker who built the piece.

Until a few days ago, she doubted anyone could find the bundle in its niche. But shortly before the destruction of the Riverwall, she discovered someone *had* accessed it, disrupting the documents and leaving the panel protecting it unlatched. Even if she didn't plan to ever return to Zatreus, she couldn't let it be found again. There was enough incriminating information in the records to ensure Lightreaver would order her hunted down wherever she went.

The Matron retracted her hand, then rose and moved to the left side. Slight pressure on a hidden panel there produced another click. One more to go.

Abrupt pounding at the door startled her. She hastily backed away from the desk, afraid her position might give a clue to the table's secret. *They've come for me! But I need more time!*

She would have to accompany them and ask for an extended deadline. There was no other option. The only way out of the room was through the soldiers on the other side. Nilado took a moment to compose herself before raising her voice. "Enter!"

The latch clicked, and the door swung inward. Sure enough, a pair of guards, both human males, stood in their blue and gray uniforms. "The High

Monarch requests your presence in the throne room," said the man on the left, his voice unexpectedly soft beneath the thick beard covering his chin.

Nilado exhaled in relief. The mood remained cordial. "Thank you, boys. Please convey my apologies, but I am a bit busy at the moment. I will contact her later to arrange another time."

The two guards looked at each other. They had never had someone decline a summons. "While the message is polite, it is an order, not an invitation," the beardless soldier told her.

Drat! "Then lead the way, and I will follow close behind."

The pair exchanged glances again. "We can't allow that. We are to escort you."

The Matron relented. If she put up too much resistance, they might grow suspicious. "Very well. You may be my escorts."

Happy that she was finally accepting her role, the guards led her through the halls to the throne room. Inside, Nilado saw the number of armed individuals had increased. *That had better be just for the assassin scare!*

Lightreaver sat on the silver chair ahead of her. A short distance from her stood Jaron. *She's got her pet with her again. Does she think she is fooling anyone with their act?*

The men flanking Nilado guided her closer to the ruler and sergeant, then stepped back to join the other soldiers on the side. Nilado didn't know if that was a good sign. They at least didn't regard her as a threat at the moment. "There really was no need for an escort."

Lightreaver gripped the arms of the throne as she addressed her. "Were you planning to go somewhere?"

Nilado smiled pleasantly. "Only to come see you."

"Dressed like that?" The High Monarch waved a hand to indicate her simpler clothes. "You look as if you are preparing to do manual work. We know that would never happen, of course."

"Sabastian asked me to try on some of the outfits he is designing for farmers," Nilado lied easily. "I will tell him you approve."

"I doubt you will have the opportunity." The throned woman grew stern as she straightened. "You were given three days to bring me justification for the jailing of two citizens. Do you have it now?"

"I was in the process of gathering it together when your escorts arrived. Give me a few hours more, and I promise you will have all the proof you need."

"I think not. We cannot have you attempting to flee your responsibilities. Or our city."

The Matron tensed, but she had no choice except to continue the bluff. "High Monarch, I — I serve only you and Zatreus. What reason would I have to go anywhere else?"

"Perhaps news of our discovery reached your ears." She casually ran her hand over the throne arm. "It turns out Linda did not escape, after all. We found her in the old dungeon, beaten and maimed."

Rust and ruin! How could that have happened? What do they know? "That is outrageous behavior from your soldiers! Why would they do such grievous harm to one such as her? How is her condition?"

"Dead," Lightreaver told her flatly, fixing her with a hard stare. "But not before she revealed who had done that to her."

The Matron's composure shattered, her eyes widening in alarm. "She must have been half out of her mind. I am certain you would not put your trust in the words of someone in that state!"

"She said *you* put her down there, where you tortured her. We found the remains of others as well. How long have you been tormenting my citizens?"

"I have done no such thing!" Nilado protested. "You cannot believe anything Linda says. I told you before, she is a Ludholm spy, here to overthrow you."

"She also revealed that it is you who started the war," Lightreaver continued, ignoring the repeated claim. "Care to tell me and the soldiers in this chamber why you deliberately put their comrades in danger, as well as risking the entire city?"

The plump woman cast a wary glance at the armed men and women stationed around the room. Their faces remained neutral, yet she could have sworn she caught a few scowls lurking beneath their stoic expressions. "High Monarch, you met with the Ludholm envoy yourself. How could I — "

"Linda also revealed you were the one who had my father killed." Lightreaver leaned forward menacingly. "I suspected this to be the case, but now we have Linda's testimony, and can — "

Realization struck Nilado. "That's impossible! She didn't know about your father. This is Dasia's hand! She's the one who told you these things!" She cast about frantically, searching for the curly-haired bisegus. "Where is she? Show yourself!"

The High Monarch stood, drawing her attention back to the ruler. "You have committed treason against the people of Zatreus, involved us in a conflict against our neighbors, and tortured your own guild master. Any one of those would see you put to death. But my father..." Her voice caught in her throat, but she swallowed the pain. "For that, I will make sure that your demise is agonizing and slow. In the end, you will beg me for forgiveness. But your pleas will — "

Panic flooded Nilado, constricting her chest. There was no talking her way out of this situation. Her crimes were out, and a punishment announced. She had only one choice left.

Run.

The short, overweight woman who had known only a life of leisure for the past two decades lacked both the coordination and strength for anything that could resemble running. She managed a sprint of about ten feet before the guards moved in. Surrounded, she gripped her pendant, her first and only means of defense. If any attacked her, a quick invoking of the artifact would knock them to the ground.

Even that proved futile, as they merely closed in around her, their swords leveled and unwavering. She still had one last diversion. "Dasia is a bisegus!" she shouted. "She is a spy! She will destroy you all!"

"Take her to the dungeons and keep her under heavy guard," Lightreaver ordered, smoothly intervening before the guards could react. "If she keeps spouting lies, you are to cut her tongue out."

Her panic morphed into dread, then anger. How dare she threaten the Matron! "Your father crossed me, and he paid for it," Nilado snarled, glaring at the tall redhead. "You will, too. I swear by my last breath, you will suffer!"

Strong hands seized her shoulders, yet she kept her gaze locked on her opponent. The power struggle between them had reached its peak, but she refused to concede defeat.

It was not her decision, though. "You are mistaken," the High Monarch told her with disdain. "With you gone, my suffering eases. Get her out of my sight!"

WITH A FEW hours of daylight remaining, Mikel guided the venki into the remains of Fircrest's port. While not much bigger than Carlin's series of docks, the boats that would normally be berthed there had already been moved onto land. The companions had their choice of berths, but they all stood far above the river now, forcing the travelers to drive the craft into the shore again.

They had set out early from the tower after rigging the vessel with a tightened tiller and braced sapling for stability. It wasn't elegant, but it cut the tailspins.

"As much as I dislike stopping, we should spend the evening here. It isn't safe to sleep on the venki," Mikel explained, sliding off the boat's deck to the muddy embankment.

"Thank you for that." Savanah climbed down from her side, the planks slick beneath her soles. "I don't think I could relax on it, anyway."

The man patted the tiny craft. "It is safer than it was, though. And it's faster than horses."

"Nothing wrong with horses," Camille chimed in. "I'm sure my uncle will look after ours until we return."

Vyncent frowned. "What makes you think we'll be coming back this way? The other items could be anywhere."

"Just a hunch."

After securing the boat, they headed into the city. Sawdust hung in the air as they navigated the bustling streets. Fircrest earned its name from the dense forests flanking the riverbanks. It thrived as a lumber town, evident in the robust timber structures dotting the landscape and the abundant piles of wood instead of typical merchant stalls. The scarce stands they encountered offered woodwork goods, ranging from hand-carved whistles to ornate jewelry boxes.

A few of the simpler items caught Savanah's eyes until Mikel reminded her how unreliable their transportation had been of late. Whatever she purchased, she would have to carry every step of the way to Adradena and beyond. She begrudgingly agreed, but she made a silent promise to herself that she would return someday.

Their first stop was dinner. *The Maple Leaf* tavern offered a limited selection of dishes, so they selected the Axeman Platter. It included an array of cured meats, aged cheeses, soft bread still warm from the oven, and savory pies that steamed when cut. While little different from what they normally carried as their own rations, the cozy atmosphere of the alehouse vastly improved the meal.

After washing it down with a bit of Kane ale — a decision Savanah soon regretted, as it stung her throat and brought tears to her eyes — the group resumed their search for lodging along the streets. The inn they finally found, *The Birchwood Lodge*, had an abundance of vacant rooms, allowing them to rent two for the night. The men took one, leaving the other for the women.

Savanah considered the arrangement less than ideal. She had longed for a chance to speak with Camille in private, to find a way to repair their strained connection. However, faced with the opportunity, she would have traded almost anything to have more time. They couldn't split the foursome in any other way that wouldn't cause more problems. Vyncent and Camille would be at each other's throats by morning, and she wasn't sure she wanted to share a room with the man, given her clarity on their relationship.

Once the oak door was shut behind her, she watched her friend stroll around the close quarters, unaware of Savanah's trepidation. *It has never been this hard to talk with her. Maybe I can ease into it.*

The archer crossed to the nearest of the two beds, placed her pack, quiver, and pair of bows against the wall, and lowered herself to the lumpy mattress with a creak of its worn supports. It stood too high for her to sit properly, however, and she pushed herself further up onto it, leaving her feet dangling a few inches from the floor. "Tell me about your uncle Morf," she prompted. "Are you close?"

Camille frowned and walked to the second bed. "You know he was a complete stranger to me."

"I know nothing of the sort." Savanah tightened her lips to hold back a smirk. "We were just incredibly fortunate to stumble upon one of your relatives when we needed him."

"Stop. Morf and I are not related, at least not that I'm aware of." She sat on the edge of the bed, directly across from Savanah. "Yesterday was the first time I've met him."

257

The archer nodded. She suspected that. Meeting a family member when they did was too big a coincidence for her to accept. "Then why did you call him your uncle?"

"My kind has 'aunts' and 'uncles' everywhere," Camille told her, idly running a hand over her bed's cover sheet, feeling the stiff straw underneath. "While our most fundamental law is never to reveal another bisegus, we still work to aid each other, as Morf did. But since we rarely understand the full conditions of another's situation, it is easier to refer to them as a vague family member."

"So those other uncles you've mentioned before aren't related to you either?"

"No. Just strangers I've spent time with. Sailing on a river, drinking in a tavern, selling clothes in a merchant caravan."

Savanah remembered that the last was how they met. She once perused a sample of items from a seller and spoke with a tall, red-haired assistant. While she knew now the shy female had been Camille, she had never considered the burly trader might also be a bisegus. "We do similarly. An uncle or aunt might be just someone close to the family."

"Exactly." Camille's face brightened. "Ours just doesn't have the requirement of being known at all before we meet. It allows us a fellowship without attachments or questions. A sort of secret family."

"That does sound nice." Savanah opened her mouth, then paused. The event that had caused her friend to flee had hung over the group since her return. If they were ever to regain their friendship, it had to be addressed. "Camille, you always have a sister in me," she began, her voice hesitant. "I know we aren't related, but I trust you more than anyone." She inhaled. *Just say it!* "When you left that night, I felt like my insides were torn out. I didn't want to leave you! But those things came, and they did nearly kill us, and I — " Her words caught in her throat as she broke into tears.

Camille hurried to her bed, took a seat, and wrapped her arms around her, cheek pressing into Savanah's hair. "I am *so* sorry I left. And for what I did. I was wrong to take advantage of your feelings like that. You love Warne, and I understood that."

"I should have recognized your feelings." Savanah wiped her cheeks. "Instead, I went on about Vyncent and his father. I acted like a lovesick little girl."

"No!" The shapeshifter took Savanah's chin and turned her head to meet her gaze. Two nearly identical faces stared at each other. "You loved him, but didn't tell him in time. You can never fix that. Maybe that is why I... you know."

"Kissed me? You wanted me to understand how you felt?"

Camille gave a brief nod. "You can never be with the man you love. Does that mean you have to live without love?"

"It isn't that simple." Savanah shrugged out of her friend's arm, which still clung to her shoulder. "I can't switch my feelings from one person to another."

"Why not?" The inquiry was tinged with a blend of pain and frustration.

"Can you? Can you shift your affection from me to someone like Mikel?"

"I don't think of Mikel that way."

"Exactly." Savanah gulped, then grabbed the other woman's hands. "I adore you, Camille, but as a friend. A sister. You are precious to me. But that doesn't extend to the kind of love you want — the kind you deserve."

Camille's hands slipped from Savanah's grasp. She rose slowly, shoulders tight, and turned her back to the room.

Savanah watched her, unsure of what to say. She dreaded this moment, but as she needed to be honest that night about her feelings for Vyncent and Warne, she had to speak the truth about those for Camille. "Are you angry with me?"

"I can never be angry with you," came the reply, but she still didn't face her. "Especially when it comes to emotions. And you are right. I can't expect you to feel what you don't. And now I've ruined our friendship."

Savanah jumped to her feet, wrapping her arms around the shapeshifter from behind. "No. No, you haven't," she murmured into her ear. "You've strengthened it. We understand it better, now. We truly have no secrets from each other."

Camille gently withdrew from the embrace, shaking her head as she turned. "I will always have secrets from you. That's the curse of my people. I told you before, our relationships are built on lies."

"Or complete trust. You said there were two kinds."

"Which I can never have. My own people — those who know about my ancestors — would never trust me. Nor could anyone in the other races."

"You mentioned that before, but I still don't understand what you mean." Savanah softly guided her to take a seat on the bed before settling in beside her. *I want answers this time.* "What sets you so apart?"

Camille exhaled wearily, as if preparing to tell a story she would rather forget. "How do you feel about arcanists?"

"I don't know. I've only met one. After *The Parting*, they vanished. Or, I guess, they went back to being normal. You can't be manipulating arcana if the arcana has gone."

"But they were the reason the Skorgan Empire rose to power. Without their artifacts, it could not have expanded. With them, they took over most of this continent and waged war against the other races. When that failed, they summoned Olagkoa."

"But they weren't all bad," Savanah told her. "Those like Nastina vowed to use their power for good."

"Good is relative," Camille pressed. "King Sakur Dunni wanted to unite Wayela with arcana, the Union of Arcany. He thought it would be better for everyone. And each ruler believed they were doing the same."

"I know this argument. You can't force people to join, even if you think it is best for them. That's where the empire turned evil. What has this got to do with you?"

"What did you learn about Emperor Redshard the First and Vasi Taksil?" Camille asked, ignoring the question.

Savanah sighed. "That Redshard wanted to enslave all non-humans, and Taksil was the arcanist helping him. That is evil. Something went wrong, killing Redshard while Taksil escaped. No one knows what happened." She waited for another question, but Camille was uncommonly quiet. "If you don't want to tell me about it, I understand. I'm your friend, and I won't — "

"Taksil is *lindugo*," Camille whispered. "My ancestor."

Savanah blinked.

"I share his *bagasa*. His evil." Her voice cracked. "It lives on in me."

Savanah's jaw dropped. She actually believed that about herself? "You aren't evil!"

"Not yet," she cried. "Neither was he, at first."

"And the others blame you for what he did?"

"He betrayed our kind, and that of all *malditao!*" Shame and anger surged up, years' worth of both. Camille had been worried when her friend discovered her true nature, as humans hated and feared the mimics. Trusting her with the knowledge that made her own people shun her was a whole other magnitude of anxiety.

Savanah didn't understand her words, but got that intent. "But you aren't him. It isn't right..."

"It is the way it is, though. But it doesn't stop there. Vasi wasn't the only one in my family to betray others." Camille hesitated, then steeled herself. "Vasi is my great-great-great something uncle. *His* great-uncle was Viscardi Taksil. Also known as Viscardi the Mad."

Savanah's breath caught in her chest. To have one arcanist who turned to evil in your ancestry could be forgiven. Two would suggest the bloodline itself had a tendency toward villainy. If the other bisegus believed Vasi betrayed them, it made sense that they would think she would do the same. According to Mikel, Viscardi deceived the other arcanists and used their power against the population. If her kind thought Camille would repeat his crimes, then no one could trust her. "Is that why you traveled to Talidith? To find a place away from anyone who might know your heritage?"

"It was a consideration," Camille admitted. "Our moving to Zatreus brought it all back. Now, if carcass beasts are loose here, it will bring Viscardi's legacy into scrutiny again. I'll never get out of the shadows of my arcanist ancestors."

Anger flared up the archer's neck, her skin prickling hot. *To think her own kind outcast her for things she never did! Those cowards!* "Well, I don't care what anyone in your past has done. I know what *you've* done and who you are, and that is all that matters."

"Thanks. I mean that. I am grateful for your support." Camille's expression eased, though her eyes stayed heavy. "But I can't shake the feeling that my past is catching up with me."

"Not tonight, it isn't!" Savanah declared, snaking an arm around the other woman's shoulder. "We've got warm food in our bellies, sturdy beds to sleep on, reasonably dry clothes, and our friendship. So I'd like to spend the evening with my favorite person. Can we do that?"

"Only if I get to spend the same time with my favorite person!" A grin split Camille's face, dissolving the last lingering bits of pain in it. "And no more talk of missions or arcanists or uncles!"

Savanah reached out and took Camille's hand. "Deal," she said, her voice firm. "Sister."

Chapter Eighteen

THE GATE OF DOUBT

"IF WE ARE all in accord, we may proceed to finalize this judgment."

Lord Durant Tallsky looked to his fellow Triune members for confirmation. To his left, Lord Kain Redgrove gave a slow nod, his loose, brown curls bouncing with the action. To his right, Lady Morwen Sunmore did the same, though her straight charcoal hair barely moved.

"Then I hereby pronounce that on the matter of recalling our outward dwelling citizens from the lowlands to the inner fortifications on account of these strangers, we vote nay."

The trip from Caratunk to Kridmont had not gone well. Leaders in both Molunkus and Meddybemps also regarded the companions' warning as fiction, though they did not drive Eris and the others from their borders, which was at least more polite.

As Farla had noted however, politeness held little value when you were dead. Or undead.

With no other means of convincing them, the Shell Patrol had proceeded to Kridmont, arriving shortly after sunset. To their surprise, they were allowed entry through the city's immense iron doors and past its fifty-foot-tall stone walls with little hassle. Even seeking an audience with the governing body overseeing the major decisions for the population had merely required a request to the right officials, and they were swept up to the Grand Conclave, the capital building and inner fortress.

Convincing the Noble Triune — the two noblemen and one noble-woman, who wore richly colored robes with ridiculously high collars, standing before them — of the approaching danger was turning out to be much harder. Once presented with the warning, the trio took nearly an hour to deliberate in private before returning to what they called the *Consultation Chamber*.

"But you can't just ignore what we're saying," Farla protested. Five of the companions were seated comfortably in cushioned chairs, while Hol-fast had been given an *alki* — a short, padded stool used by erdi'zal to rest their backends. Their seats were organized in a straight line to opti-mize their view of the three thrones. Closer to the rustic style of King Va-leria's chair than the pillow and silk-covered silver seat of High Monarch Lightreaver, the high-backed chairs were no doubt positions of power.

"Why can't we?" Lord Durant asked. The apparent eldest of the three, with his voluminous white hair, the one unkempt aspect of his otherwise prim appearance, served as both head and spokesperson for the trio. "Despite your fanciful story and adamant tone, you have prof-fered no evidence of the veracity of your claims."

"I believe them," Timoth offered, hesitantly holding up a hand.

Lord Durant fixed him with an inquisitive stare. "Have you seen it?"

"Well, no." His arm fell back to his lap. "We fled before it got there. But refugees from Fernwick arrived in Hearthglen. They saw it."

"Then perhaps one of them should have accompanied you," Durant told him.

Eris began to raise his hand, then caught himself. "We five have seen it."

"And where are you from?" Kain asked. While polite, his simple question still carried an overtone of disdain.

"Tal and Holfast are from Zatreus," Eris replied, pointing to each. "Me, Ranin, and Farla are from Talidith."

Durant's head tilted in a subtle shake, signaling that the response fell short. "The words of foreigners carry no weight in this matter."

Holfast blinked both sets of eyes at the pronouncement. "I'm no for-eigner! I'm originally from the Trideen Highlands, which lie to your west, no further away than Fernwick. My kin are your neighbors."

Lady Morwen clasped her hands together, as if she were speaking to a child. "Then perhaps you should take your tale" — she paused, not intending the reference to his hindquarters — "forgive me... your story, to them, as they must surely be in danger as well."

Anger rose in Eris's chest. How many times did they have to explain this to people too stubborn to listen? "The creature and its army are coming *here*."

"How do you know this?" Durant looked up and down the line of travelers. "Have you spoken with this beast?"

"It doesn't speak," Eris replied. "Not like we do."

"Then one of its minions, perhaps?"

"They are all dead," Ranin chimed in.

Durant nodded as he glanced at his fellow nobles. "Quite convenient, wouldn't you think?"

"It attacked Zatreus." Eris struggled to keep his voice level as he spoke through a clenched jaw. "It attacked Ludholm. You are the next closest kingdom."

Morwen's face brightened, and she leaned forward, a spark of discovery in her eyes, as if she'd uncovered a flaw in his logic. "Ah, but are we? Our recent survey of the region quite clearly shows Stegate is closer to both those cities by at least a mile. Perhaps two."

"That doesn't matter!" Eris shouted. "It is coming here. We've been warning the towns and villages on its route so they can evacuate."

"And they believe you?" Kain asked, his expression growing as eager as Lady Morwen's had been.

"Not all, no." Eris's voice dropped in volume. "The closer towns were as stubborn as you."

"As clear-eyed." Kain grinned, then leaned toward the older lord. "Haven't I said the smaller settlements were too gullible in dealing with foreigners?"

"You have, indeed," Durant replied, a slight smile slipping across his lips. "Relish your confirmation."

"I am."

"We have heard your pleas and rendered our decision." Durant raised a hand to gesture toward the entrance. "Now, if you will please — "

The door to the hall suddenly swung open as an older woman, the same one who led the companions to the Consultation Chamber, rushed in. "Forgive the intrusion, Lords and Lady, but a situation has arisen."

"Let it bother you not," Durant told her, rising to his feet. "We are finished here." He directed both the last comment and his gaze toward the visitors.

"It's the outer communities. They are coming here."

"Please explain," Morwen ordered. "In what way are they 'coming here'?"

The woman stared at her. "The people are approaching the city from the east. Our sentries estimate they number in the thousands, though it is impossible to tell until they draw closer."

Kain stood. "For what purpose? We have not planned any events, have we?"

Farla understood the meaning first. "It's the towns! The army must have driven them here!"

"Fiddle-faddle." Durant waved her off with a flick of his hand. "They are obviously confused. Have a message sent instructing them they are to return home. There is nothing to fear."

Once more, the woman's expression twisted in confusion. "Sir, sent to whom? There are thousands of them."

"If they are coming, Olagkoa can't be far behind." Eris jumped to his feet and stepped in front of the trio. "You may have decided to ignore us, but you can't ignore them!"

Lord Durant seemed to finally listen as he considered their options. He caught the eye of the other nobles. "I have a proposal. Strictly as a measure of gaining additional information and to learn the cause of this influx, I propose we relocate this discussion, on a purely temporary basis, to the eastern battlements."

Morwen also paused to think. "Would such an action not run counter to our previous judgment?"

"I believe there is precedence for two conflicting actions," Kain told them, running a hand through his curls. "If we retreat to the study, we can — "

"Let's go. They will be here for another hour." Eris's boots scraped hard against the stone floor as he pivoted toward the woman and beckoned for the others. "What's the quickest way to where they said?"

Following her instructions, the Shell Patrol and Timoth collected their weapons as they left the capital and headed into the street. Kridmont was not as populous as Zatreus, but its location along the Ibia River facilitated a steady flow of trade between Drulon to the north and Stegate to the south.

Now, the entire population poured forth from their houses and businesses to gather outside, making the air thick with overlapping voices and the warmth of too many bodies in narrow streets. News of the approaching townships had spread, and with it came the same confusion about the cause as the Noble Triune. Kridmont's walls protected its outer city and the settlements beyond in times of great danger, in the same way Castle Shieldarrow had acted as a stronghold for Talidith's people who made their living off the land.

But such occurrences were rare. The last had taken place a few hundred years before, when an exceptionally harsh winter drove a nearby colony of wood vornuks to attack several towns in desperation. Once the citizens were safe in the city, Kridmont's military had moved in and driven the vicious humanoids out, even tracking them to their breeding grounds and wiping them out permanently.

The vornuks' possible return was the worst rumor Eris, Tal, and the others heard as they worked their way through the streets toward the gate, but it wasn't the only one. A plague infesting the poorer hamlets, driving the survivors to seek a cure. A drought draining the ground of all water, causing crops to wither and livestock to die. A wildfire sweeping westward, consuming everything in its path.

The last was closest to reality, only these 'flames' were intelligent and impossible to extinguish.

It took the companions nearly an hour to navigate the crowd and press their way to the nearest tower. A pair of human guards, dressed in gray uniforms with gold trim, blocked the base of the spiral stairs, allowing no one through.

"We were sent by the Noble Triune, on orders from Lord Durant himself," Eris told the pair, hoping a little name-dropping could facilitate their passing.

"On what business?" one guard demanded.

"We have information about the approaching populations of Caratunk, Molunkus, and Meddybemps." Eris pointed to Timoth, who nodded. "This gentleman is from the villages himself."

The second guard raised a hand. "Hold up. We don't know enough yet to confirm where these folks are coming from."

"We do, which is why we were sent. Do you intend to go against the judgment of the Triune?" Eris didn't know how much power the trio of nobles exerted over the city's military, but he figured it couldn't hurt to invoke them.

Apparently, they had a fair amount of influence, as the pair of guards paled at the suggestion. "Certainly not." The first one stepped aside, gesturing for his partner to do the same. "You may pass."

Once the companions reached the top and strode out onto the torch-lit ramparts, they saw what the messenger had been so concerned about. The rising moonlight revealed hundreds of people trudging through the farmlands and entering the rural dwellings of the outer city. With them were dozens of wagons drawn by horses — and in some cases, cows — bearing boxes and sacks, along with small children. Most of the refugees were human, but several erdi'zal and a few egyzemors could be spotted among the ranks. Even atop the wall, curses and sobbing drifted up on the wind, carried like prayers no god would answer.

"I guess Caratunk's mayor changed her mind after all," Farla said. "Maybe your speech worked."

"More likely, the creature reached their borders," Ranin replied. "She's not the type to admit she was wrong."

"Then they must have fled to Molunkus, then to Meddybemps." Eris scanned the crowd, but determining their numbers from this distance remained impossible. Definitely sufficient to fill three settlements, though. "Question is, how many survived? Were the people of those towns smart enough to recognize the threat when its victims appeared on their borders?"

"Hearthglen was." Timoth stroked his cloak proudly. "We may not be big, but we've got sense."

None of the other soldiers on the wall questioned their place together. The turmoil brewing outside, combined with the mounting disorder within, was more than enough to consume their attention.

The refugees had nearly reached the gate when the Noble Triune finally joined Eris and the others, still dressed in their high-collared robes. Surprise filled their faces as they gazed down at the multitude below.

"Do you believe us now?" Farla asked as the trio whispered among themselves.

"They appear to have," Lord Durant replied. "However, all we can see is a populace approaching. No doubt they're frightened, but panic spreads fast. That doesn't make your creature real."

Tal threw her hands up in frustration. "Unbelievable."

"Precisely."

"No," she snapped, then flung her arm toward the masses below. "An army could waltz up your backside and you'd think it was a pleasant breeze until it was too late."

"We do not act in haste," Kain insisted, unbothered by her outburst. "For that is folly. It is best to know all the facts before making any judgment."

Ranin gestured over the edge, indicating the crowd unmistakably advancing toward the entrance. "You'd better start deliberating, then, because the populace wants in."

Lady Morwen followed her gesture and frowned. "That does appear to be the situation."

By the time they reached a decision and passed it on to the gatekeepers, the displaced townsfolk were banging their fists on the iron doors. Before they could be opened, however, the city's guard needed to clear the citizens inside who had pushed forward in curiosity, which delayed the process by several more minutes.

Then the refugees poured in. Most continued their weary trek further into Kridmont, wagons, belongings, and all. Many huddled against the inner wall, too tired to continue, just grateful to have protection.

Their fear was obvious, but even then, the obstinate trio of nobles refused to accept that there was actually anything to be afraid of. "They are merely excitable," Kain explained. "Perhaps one was startled by a wild sced."

As more refugees came, the courtyard below swelled with people. Still, hundreds were outside, pressing forward like water behind a dam in the hopes of finding protection from whatever had driven them from their homes.

In addition, those living in the dwellings immediately beyond the walls and extending further for a few miles understood something was amiss and began their own trek toward the city.

"If you listened to us hours ago, you might have been prepared for this." Eris knew lecturing the ineffectual leaders would be useless, but right now, he could do nothing else as exhaustion dragged at his limbs. The other companions had found places to rest along the ramparts, their day of riding finally catching up to them.

Weariness tugged at Eris as well, but he refused to turn away from the sight below. Rage kept him upright as the Triune vanished into the crowd. Not just at them, but at himself. For believing he'd left the worst behind. For letting himself hope.

In this moment, however, the fury inside found a new target. When the creature first appeared in the Undercastle and killed Warne, the Commander of the Sovereign Guard, along with fellow soldier Thamas, Eris had refused to believe the threat. He had contested Savanah's claim to the position, sought King Grisk's approval, and had removed the silver bow from its place in the newly revealed cave.

The last act ended the beast's imprisonment, though no one knew that until Eris led a group of eager guards into the cavern to kill it. Instead, it nearly slaughtered them. Only with Ranin's surprise ability to fight back against its psychic powers did any of them survive.

So he understood the disbelief that each explanation of the creature drew. The High Monarch of Zatreus had not accepted the nature of the threat at the gate. General Harid Rushad, head of Zatreus's military on the field, had not believed them, nor did Knight Keven Balbiscu, commander of Ludholm's forces. Both men had paid for that with not only their lives but the lives of the soldiers they led, becoming Shells themselves in the approaching army.

I am responsible for releasing Olagkoa and the death of my fellow soldiers, including Kehnin, the woman I loved. I will bear that burden to my dying day.

The anger tightening in his chest hardened into resolve. *But I will not shoulder the responsibility of every person since then who has failed to listen. My mistake is my own. Theirs must be, as well.*

Eris drew in a deep breath of damp, city air tinged with soot and sweat and released it slowly. To his surprise, the anger and tension had faded. For the first time in months, he felt as if he could enjoy the simple act of breathing again, and he inhaled.

Tal appeared beside him. "How are you faring?" she asked, bringing her face close to his to be heard over the wall's noise. "Come and rest. Holfast thinks it will be another few hours before the army arrives."

He turned to her. She had shoved, argued, bullied, and manipulated her way into his life, and he still didn't understand why. She stood an inch taller than him, with a slender frame, betrayed only by wide shoulders and a full upper torso. With her sharp eyes and the same stubborn grace, she reminded him too much of Kehnin. Without thinking, he reached out a hand and brushed his fingers across her cheek, the skin cool and soft beneath the pad of his thumb. "Thank you."

Her eyes narrowed. His tenderness seemed out of place in a relationship that mostly revolved around arguing. "If we had the sense to bring any akkum, I'd say you've had your fill."

He smiled, but withdrew his hand. "I need to rest."

She guided him to a section of the walkway where they sat, their backs supported by the parapet. A little further along, Holfast was similarly kneeling, his upper torso propped up by the stone barrier as he slept. Timoth lay on his side, tucked into a ball, snoring. Farla and Ranin huddled together, the former's arm curled around the shoulders of her slightly taller partner. All of them had been riding, or in the erdi'zal's case, running, most of the day, and while they weren't wholly safe yet, they needed to take the opportunity to regain their energy.

Tal leaned against him, her head settling on his shoulder, her hair brushing the side of his neck. Eris felt his own remaining reserves draining, and his eyes began to close, suddenly becoming too heavy to remain vigilant. After a moment, he shifted, and wrapped an arm around her, letting her rest more comfortably against his chest.

Then he slept.

A piercing scream from below jolted them all awake sometime after midnight. Holfast was the first to his feet, urging the others to do the same. They scrambled to the crenels to peer through the gaps to the scene below.

The moon still cast its glow over the region, though its light waned. It reflected off the weapons and helmets of the army on the outer city's perimeter. Even if the night had become completely dark, the regular thud-thud of a thousand marching individuals would have been enough to raise the alarm.

And raised it was. Bells tolled through the city, alerting all within and those miles beyond to an approaching threat. The warning rang out — hours too late, in Eris's mind. The arrival of the terror-stricken hordes from the townships should have been sufficient notification.

Shouts arose from the men and women along the wall. Eris doubted any of them had ever witnessed a force even a tenth the size of the one now approaching. He felt his own heart pounding at the sight, and he had been part of the defense against the vornuk army that assaulted Castle Shieldarrow. Those foul creatures, at least, could be slain. The same couldn't be true for those advancing through the brick-paved roads below.

"I guess rest time is over," Farla noted wryly. "Hope everyone slept well, because this is going to be a long night."

Ranin gave her a playful nudge on the shoulder. "I want to see the faces of those three fools who decided we were lying."

"I believed you," Timoth said as he stared in awe at the lines of undead marching in unison. "But I didn't think there would be so many!"

Tal squinted. "Where's the creature?"

The others changed their focus to search for the horror. "It must be in the rear, like at Ludholm," Eris suggested.

They stared into the gloom, eyes stinging with the strain, hearts thumping as the regiment stretched on and on, but no mass of tentacles emerged. The Shells marched four abreast down the road, their ranks stretching out for a quarter of a mile, making the tail barely discernible in the distance.

Holfast spotted it first, the jerky movements of its immense appendages as they shoved it forward just visible among the shadows. He pointed it out to the others, but it was several tense seconds later before they saw the beast. "Olagkoa might be intelligent, but it lacks courage," the erdi'zal told them, puffing out his chest as if attempting to intimidate the creature. "A leader travels at the front of his fighters, not at the rear like a *koldra*."

"It is strange that it holds back," Farla agreed. "It can heal its wounds, is big enough to crush houses, and has an unstoppable company at its command. What is it afraid of?"

Timoth's expression hovered on the verge of a disappointed pout. "I still can't see it."

Beside him, Tal shook her head. "You don't want to. Trust me."

"I doubt fear has anything to do with its tactic," Eris said. "The people here don't know about its abilities, and it is using that to its advantage. Keeping itself hidden so the true threat remains unknown."

"The townsfolk would have seen it and told others," Ranin reminded him.

"Who would have trusted the tale as easily as all the rest we've warned. Not at all," Tal noted. "Misted blank-brains."

Eris grinned at the woman's assessment, feeling a bit more confident of his own realization and glad she wasn't leveling the description at him for once. "Fortunate for them we've come, eh?"

"I said I believe you," Timoth protested, leaning over the stone barrier. "But all I see are shapes in shadows."

The bells had stopped, and soon the army's advance did, too. The lines parted, and Tal gasped. From between the soldiers' ranks, several village folk emerged. With their hair in disarray and their clothes torn in multiple places, they stood out from the uniformed Shells around them.

A broad-shouldered soldier strode out behind them. His bushy black locks showed signs of graying, and his thick beard had streaks of white, but he walked with the confidence of a much younger man. He wore the blue and gray uniform of Zatreus, though his remained intact and unstained, as if he had never been on a battlefield.

Eris's throat constricted as blood rushed to his head, reddening his cheeks and throbbing in his ears. He felt the same rush of panic and confusion when he saw the same face last year. A face so similar to his own, one he had known for most of his life. His father, Rikard Duskmore.

His father — dead six years — now standing alive before him, delivering threats.

"Open your gate and surrender, or we will slaughter your townsfolk one by one." The commanding voice coming from the figure remained the same as Eris remembered, though he knew the man would never have made such a threat.

Farla nudged him. "Isn't that... "

"Yes," he told her, before she asked the obvious question. "His appearance, at least."

Tal overheard the interchange. "Who?"

"My father," Eris replied, his throat tightening again as he spoke it aloud. "But he died several years ago of a sickness. He had been in the Sovereign Guard before he retired."

The woman stared at him in horror. "The creature turned your father into a Shell?"

"What? No! This is Olagkoa, playing one of its tricks. Remember the fight outside the cemetery, when it projected itself growing? It must have stolen the memory of my father when we attacked it in the Undercastle. It used his image to trick us then, too."

"Do you think they will fall for this ruse?" Holfast asked, catching the end of the explanation.

"They have to!" Tal cried out. "No leader would let his own people die, even the witless trio."

"They would if it meant saving the lives of many more," Ranin replied softly. "And right now, the lives of a handful of villagers are nothing compared to the thousands behind these walls."

"What is your business here?" A few hundred feet further down the wall, a uniformed woman with cropped white hair and a sword strapped to her side shouted a reply to the illusionary soldier below. To her left were the three nobles, huddling for what Eris guessed was a drawn-out proposal on what to do next, followed by counterarguments and hypotheticals. *The city is doomed.*

Rikard's fake face split into a grin, which caused a shiver of fear in each of the companions. "Only to enter into your city and seek reparations for the crimes committed against Olagkoa, obedient servant of the Exalted Nizlan, God of Power and Bringer of Turmoil. Open now, or I shall begin with these." The last was accompanied by a slow, sweeping gesture toward the hostages, whose bowed heads and slack limbs showed they had already surrendered to the promise of death.

"Who is he talking about?" Timoth whispered. "Is that someone else's dead father?"

"Olagkoa is the creature's name," Farla explained. "No idea who Nizlan is meant to be."

"Sounds like a nasty god," Ranin muttered.

"Why aren't they moving?" Tal asked, pointing to the front of the army below. "The villagers. They aren't moving. Shouldn't they be crying or trying to escape or something?"

No cries. No flinching. No fear. Eris's gut twisted. They weren't hostages at all. "The creature got them! They're Shells! The whole thing is a trick!"

"We need to warn the Triune!" Tal was the first to sprint toward the trio and the cluster of soldiers gathered at the center of the wall, with Eris and the others close on her heels.

Two armed men, swords drawn, stepped forward to block the companions, bringing their advance to an abrupt halt. "We need to warn them before they open the gate!" Tal protested. Her hand went to her own weapon, ready to force her way through when Eris grabbed her arm, staying her attack.

"The Noble Triune is presently engaged in sensitive negotiations," the first guard told them. "Rest assured, all matters are being handled appropriately. Return to the streets. You may seek an audience with them at a future date, when they are less occupied."

"There won't *be* a later!"

Beyond them, the nobles had come to an uncommonly quick decision, which the woman reported to the army below. "We do not recognize the authority of Olagkoa or Nizlan. Release our people now."

Eris briefly reconsidered forcing their way through to the Triune, but the companions had pushed their luck too far already. They had been fortunate to gain access to the ramparts. Another action against the city's defense could see them driven from the walkway. "Your people are dead. So is the army. Don't fall for its deception!"

The second guard wrenched his sword from its sheath, the blade partially emerging in a menacing display. "Keep silent. You have no place in these deliberations."

"Don't I? That's my father giving the demands!" It was a risky claim, as he could be blamed for the conflict, but he hoped it might add some clout to his position. Anyone who took a moment to compare the faces of the two men would immediately see they were related.

However, the need for further pleading vanished. "As you wish." The figure of Rikard stared up at the defenders on the wall, abruptly giving in to their demand to release the townsfolk. "You have convinced me."

The words set Eris's mind reeling in confusion. "What did he say?" Farla asked behind him, showing he wasn't the only one surprised.

Below, the fake Rikard gave a sweeping gesture, as if telling the hostages to move ahead, and they did. Eight men and women shuffled forward stiffly. If there had been any doubt before about their status, their sluggish movements dispelled them. Tal's shoulders slumped at the confirmation. She had hoped all of Fernwick's people had escaped in time.

On the ramparts, the nobles shared congratulations, apparently believing they had won the negotiations. The female soldier who spoke for them appeared less certain, her eyebrows furrowed in thought. Beyond them, two dozen archers stood ready, bows in front and arrows dangling in their fingers, poised to be nocked and released on command.

Inside the walls, the refugees and citizens crowded together, waiting for the outcome. They had heard most of the shouted interchange but couldn't see either party to judge who might be the winner. Even with the hostages freed, an army and a monster still remained beyond. No one was safe. Not yet.

Eris and the other companions, unable to get past the pair of guards, watched the ambling villagers approaching the entrance. That's when more of Olagkoa's plan became clear. While the demand to have the gate opened failed, releasing the hostages now forced the city's guards to open it anyway to allow them in. It wouldn't have to be much, but even that brief relaxing of their defenses could be enough for the army to surge forward and gain entry.

"Don't open it!" Tal yelled, having worked out the trap as well. "They'll get in!"

The second guard unsheathed his sword completely this time, advancing toward her with purpose. Eris swiftly stepped between them, hand on his hilt, his gaze sharp as he glared at each soldier in turn. "The enemy is down there. We came here to warn your city, but your leaders ignored us. Don't be as foolish as they are and do the same."

His words failed to have the calming effect he intended. "One more word," the guard growled, "and you'll be flying, not walking." His blade rose a finger higher, enough to catch the moonlight.

Eris glanced past him to where the other guard had drawn his sword. The companions outnumbered the pair six to one. Even so, he had no idea how well the unarmed Timoth or the untrained Tal would do in such close-quarters fighting. Even if they fought their way past the soldiers, it was unlikely the Triune would listen to them, especially given how their previous attempts were dismissed.

A booming clang interrupted the standoff, echoing through stone and bone alike. Eris thought he recognized what the sound was, and his stomach dropped. The guards before him knew and quickly lowered their swords as they rushed to peer over the parapets.

The gate was opening.

No, no, no! Eris whirled about and called to the others. "They've done it. They are letting them in. We only have one chance left."

Tal's face twisted into a deep scowl as she raised a fist at him. "You're not going to attack the creature directly again, are you?"

"You have a better plan?"

Her hand dropped, and she nodded to the two women behind her. "Have Ranin use her power to strike it mentally."

"Hey!" Farla snapped, grabbing her shoulder and yanking the much taller female to face her. "Don't go volunteering my friend!"

"It doesn't matter," Ranin told them softly. "I don't think I can. Every time I've pushed back against it, it attacked first."

"You can try!" Tal encouraged.

Farla glared at her. "Stop it!"

But Ranin had closed her eyes, apparently willing to test the idea. She held the position for only a moment. "Nothing. I don't even know how I'm supposed to find its mind."

"I suggest we act swiftly on whatever you have planned," Holfast told them. "Our time is short."

Eris nodded vigorously. "Yes. We must retrieve our horses and get out of the city. Our best chance is to circle around the army and deal with Olagkoa directly. We have to break its concentration and hope the city's guard can do the rest."

"And if we can't?" Timoth asked, struggling to follow the conversation.

"Fire!" Tal exclaimed. "It worked back in Zatreus."

Eris gave another nod and turned to the man. "Timoth, do you think you could convince some of Kridmont's soldiers to join us at the rear of the army with torches? As many as you can."

He offered a reluctant shrug. "I reckon I could try. I was thinking I'd see your beastie, though."

"You will," Eris told him, suppressing a chuckle. "That's who the torches are for. The one true weakness we've found is fire."

The villager's eyes brightened with childlike wonder, a grin spreading across his face. "By the root! Then you can count on me."

Chapter Nineteen
ARROWS AND ASHES

WITH THE AID of a soldier too overwhelmed by the events of the last few hours to question their intent, the Shell Patrol found a postern gate to the outside. The small opening was normally used to allow escape during a siege or to launch a counteroffensive without risking the city's defense. It would serve their purpose perfectly.

"May luck be with you," Timoth told the companions as they led their horses through the doorway.

"To you as well," Eris replied. "Remember, whoever you convince to help us, do not engage with the army. The target is the mind controlling them."

"I'll remember."

They remounted their horses on the other side and rode along the southern path between the wall and the river until they came to the outskirts. The moonlight waned, making it harder to navigate the roads and buildings, but they eventually found a route that seemed to go straight through to the border.

Behind them, the soldiers on the ramparts sprang into action. The gatekeeper had been ordered to open the doors sufficiently for the village hostages to enter. Something had gone amiss, however, and the iron barriers continued swinging on their immense hinges until a gap large enough for the entire army easily march in had been made.

Eris's suspicions proved false. The Shells didn't need to surge forward to gain entry. Olagkoa, lurking in the rear, needed only to nudge the minds of those physically moving the doors to keep opening them until they were cast wide.

Once the controlled villagers were inside, they joined in keeping the gate open, even as others moved to force it closed. A battle of strength erupted as the undead soldiers marched forward.

They didn't advance unchallenged, however. The archers atop the wall who had been waiting for orders finally got them and unleashed their arrows on the hosts below. Most struck true, as their targets made no attempt to defend themselves. It did no good, though, as the projectiles simply lodged in arms, shoulders, chests, and necks, going unnoticed by those they pierced.

Terror surged through those gathered inside the walls. Screams and shouts filled the night air as they scrambled to find shelter deeper within the city. The panicked citizens were the first to withdraw, leaving the townsfolk struggling with their belongings and family members. Merchants abandoned their carts, spilling goods across the streets. Children wailed as their parents dragged them toward safety.

A few braver individuals rushed to aid the refugees, ordering them to abandon their possessions and animals so they could flee. Nearby, a priest clutched his *alar-orakon* — the wooden prayer wings sacred to the followers of Diovola — his fingers moving feverishly over the carvings as he whispered urgent prayers for their salvation.

Above, on the ramparts, the archers continued their volleys, nocking arrows as fast as their hands could manage. It did no good. If they didn't get the gate closed soon, Kridmont would be overrun.

"There it is!" Holfast called out, outpacing the others' horses. As the companions drew closer, it was hard to imagine how they could have missed seeing the looming monstrosity from the ramparts. It towered over most of the surrounding buildings, a ball of tentacles and hate just as wide around as it was tall, massing more than two dozen egyzemors. Stopping it with swords and arrows was impossible.

Eris signaled the others to dismount a fair distance away. It wasn't far enough to avoid the stench, though, and the putrid odor of the foul creature caused their eyes to water. Even Eris and Tal, who had been up close with the beast more times than could be considered healthy, struggled not to gag.

It didn't react to the humans and erdi'zal. Most of its claw-tipped limbs hung limp, though a few smaller ones still writhed in the air. Most of its focus lay bound up in the activity ahead.

"Now what?" Farla asked, her face buried in the crook of her elbow. "Our weapons won't do much good, even if we got close to it."

"We irritate it," Eris said. "Don't strike the main body. You'll get a nasty jolt if you do. We don't need to land a solid blow there, just its limbs. That should break its concentration and hopefully buy the city some time."

"And Timoth is the backup, if we fail," Tal finished for him.

"Right. Holfast, I want you to stay back here and use your bow on the upper parts. Give us a shout if you see a change in the army or it."

"I'm all eyes," the erdi'zal replied with a grin.

"Move out!"

The three women and one man advanced on Olagkoa, swords held before them. Although the creature lacked a discernible face or front, they instinctively moved toward the side farthest from the city, relying on the tactical logic of striking an enemy from behind.

Farla and Ranin continued around the beast, allowing the group to attack it on two fronts. The enormity of it almost felt as if they were dealing with a large force instead of a single entity.

Once in place, they attacked.

At first, their slices, jabs, and arrows got no reaction. They barely penetrated the mottled grayish-blue flesh, but where they did, its brownish-orange blood oozed out. They were like the gebits Farla had mentioned — irritating and sharp, but ultimately harmless.

Suddenly, the tentacles lashed out with terrifying speed, forcing the four to scramble backward to avoid being struck. The abrupt shift in the battle demanded a fresh approach, requiring them to weave defensive actions into their offense, dodging and striking in a desperate dance. They pressed the assault, blades flashing, but the creature showed no sign of faltering.

Then Ranin caught a lucky blow, opening a long cut along one of the appendages. Ichor sprayed wildly as the tentacle yanked away, forcing her back. But the true retaliation came when the familiar burst of pain drove the other fighters to their knees in crippling agony.

They weren't the only ones affected, though. The Shells froze like statues, halting mid-stride and giving the defenders a chance to act. Seizing the moment, the few refugees still in the courtyard sprinted deeper into the press of shops and houses as the city's defense surged forward. The undead at the gate stiffened. A handful were hauled aside by panicked guards as the doors reversed their path.

It all happened in only a few seconds, the brief time it took for Ranin to gather her psychic response. It slammed into the creature, causing it to shriek from some unseen orifice.

She wanted to scream, too, but too much was at stake to give in. Gritting her teeth, she pressed on with the assault. In her mind, a steel spike formed — sharp, gleaming, deadly. She gathered every ounce of energy around it and drove it forward.

Olagkoa convulsed, its appendages flailing momentarily before it went limp. Ranin collapsed to the ground. Her last blast had wounded it deeply, but it also exacted an immense toll on the woman.

The mental shockwaves rippled through the Shell army, sending it into turmoil. Both inside the walls and beyond, the undead warriors became disoriented, breaking ranks and roaming about. Kridmont's soldiers struck hard, stabbing and slicing the walking corpses, their blows going undefended and unreturned. They could drive the invaders out!

Farla was the first of the companions to recover, and immediately rushed to her fallen friend. When the others rose, they found her cradling Ranin's torso, sobbing. "She fought it," she told them around tears.

Holfast sprinted up to them, pointing back toward the city. "Look to the army."

Tal and Eris spun to witness the disoriented Shells staggering about like drunks leaving a tavern. A few stumbled, and one slammed into the side of a nearby house.

Beyond that, they could see the movement of the gate as those inside worked to close it against any further assault. "We did it!" Tal shouted, shoving her fist into the air. "We stopped them!"

Farla's scream disrupted her celebration, though. Olagkoa had begun moving again, reaching its appendages forward and driving its rear ones into the ground, just twenty feet from where the pair of women were. It was heading for Kridmont!

While the companions rushed to hoist Ranin onto Holfast's back, fresh fighting broke out in the city. With Olagkoa regaining its senses, the Shells recovered as well. The one-sided beating from the city's soldiers changed in a flash to a desperate struggle against revived opponents. Worse, the fighters realized almost all the damage they inflicted on their foes had been useless. The undead fought on, no matter how many times they were stabbed or sliced.

For a few fleeting seconds, Kridmont's defenders held their ground. Even though they outnumbered those who had gotten past the gate, there was no way to stop an enemy for whom injury meant nothing. The soldiers were forced to fall back.

Outside, the Shells there had recovered as well. Not bothering to return to formation, they surged at the entrance again with a force large enough to shove the iron doors, no matter who stood in their way. A fresh wave of arrows rained down on them from above, but they had no more effect on the uniformed undead than the other volleys had.

"Zounds! That is a big beastie!"

Timoth sprinted toward them from the southern side of the outskirts, a torch raised in his grip. He wasn't alone. Nearly two dozen of the refugees ran behind him, all wielding similar flaming brands. Exhaustion etched their faces, but they had come just the same.

Hope resurged in Eris as the brigade reached them. In the heat of the battle, he had forgotten the backup plan. He hadn't expected this kind of assembly. "This way!" he called to them, breaking into a jog toward the advancing Olagkoa.

They followed with a surge of energy, their enemy finally in view. Eris shouted more instructions, and soon the band had spread out, forming a semicircle around the back of the creature. "Now!"

As if they had trained for this moment, the fire-wielding mob tightened about the beast and shoved flaming brands into its limbs. Deafening shrieks filled the air, and it halted to redirect its tentacles toward the attackers, swinging the immense appendages wildly.

Three of the townsfolk were sent hurtling backward, their torches falling to the road below. Two more had their brands knocked from their grip but were otherwise unharmed. The rest dodged and retreated before the creature could strike them, too.

However, the assault had only paused Olagkoa's advance. Once it was no longer being attacked, it began moving forward again. The fire scorched it deeper than their blades ever had, but the beast stood strong.

"Eris! Ahead!" Tal shouted from somewhere off to his right. "The carts!"

Fearing there might be some new threat, the man ran ahead, scanning the region before the creature. The army still lay a few hundred feet ahead, marching relentlessly toward the gate. Then his eyes fell upon what she had meant. On the side of the road sat four wagons stocked with hay, likely brought in from some outer field for the horses in the city. A blockade!

Snatching up one of the fallen torches, he ran full out toward them. Tal got there seconds before him, and began tugging the nearest into the creature's path. He did the same with another, yanking it one-handed into the road.

Olagkoa's towering form was nearly upon them when they shoved the last two into place. Eris thrust his torch into the dry piles of each, leaving it in the fourth, then the pair sprinted to a safe distance.

For a few tense seconds, little happened as the fire crept hungrily through the hay. Then, just as the beast plowed into them, the fire roared to life, engulfing the straw in an instant. Heat and smoke billowed as flames leapt upward, licking at the monstrosity's tentacles and flesh.

A shriek of rage or pain tore through the air, but momentum carried it forward, straight into the heart of the inferno. The stench of burning flesh added to the plume as Olagkoa blazed.

Behind it, Timoth and the refugees ran to add their torches to the pyre, reveling in the chance for vengeance. Tal wiggled beside Eris in excitement, and even he felt a rush of euphoria.

The response of the Shells was far more pronounced. While the last assault on it had caused them to lose focus, this attack seemed to crystallize it. Every one of the animated corpses, including those winning their battle within the walls, spun and launched itself at the screaming beast. They ran in wild, jerking motions, like puppets on strings, ignoring all else in a frantic pitch to obey the psychic call.

Tal noticed the change before Eris. "Run!" she yelled, grabbing his shoulder and pulling him into a sprint. Her warning reached Timoth and the refugees as well, and they hastily abandoned their idea of revenge for one of retreat, casting their torches toward the burning monstrosity before fleeing. Even if the Shells seemed intent on rescuing their master, they might still seek retribution on those nearby.

So the companions and townsfolk ran, assisting the three who had been struck and joining Holfast, Farla, and Ranin. The latter remained draped over the erdi'zal's back, but she had opened her eyes and showed signs of recovering.

After they retrieved their horses, she was transferred to her animal and strapped on, freeing Holfast to guard their retreat. Timoth led the villagers toward the city — taking a wide route around the outskirts to avoid the army — with the Shell Patrol bringing up the rear.

As they moved past the many buildings, they lost sight of the Shells' attempt to aid Olagkoa, but the frequent screeching said it was still in flames.

When they came into range of the entrance, they saw the last of the undead had been repelled and the gate shut again. They had stopped the beast and saved the city. At least for now.

Once back through the postern — the soldier who had let them through it before thankfully thought to keep watch for their return — they were able to catch their breath. The riders dismounted, easing Ranin down with great care. Her eyes were open but she remained frail and unsteady. Farla slipped an arm around her, guiding her gently to a nearby bench where they sank together, too tired to speak.

The refugees wandered back into the city, seeking their families to spread the word of what they had done as Eris turned to Timoth. "You did it!" he exclaimed, clapping the man on the shoulder. "I'm guessing the soldiers wouldn't come."

Timoth grinned. "Naw. They were pretty busy handling the crowd. Then I thought, 'I bet some folks would like to get a little payback'. This lot jumped at the chance."

"I'd have expected more," Tal said, eyeing the group. Of the thousands who arrived at Kridmont's entrance a few hours prior, they represented a very small percentage.

"There were," Timoth replied, his smile not fading at her comment. "But I figured you wanted the hardiest of the bunch."

Eris appreciated the man's reasoning, though if those who had volunteered were in the best shape, then the refugees were in even worse condition than he had feared. Still, they had come and played a critical role in the fight.

Kridmont's guards were battered as well. Their confrontation with the Shells had left two dead and a dozen wounded with slashes to their faces and limbs. While the bodies of the deceased were dragged out of the area to await burial, the others did their best to staunch their wounds while remaining vigilant. The first wave might be over, but that didn't mean they were done.

Atop the ramparts, the members of the Noble Triune, no longer cowering behind the parapet, were taking the opportunity to congratulate themselves on a battle well fought. Nearly every decision they made had been wrong, but that didn't quell their enthusiasm. For them, they were in charge when the fight was won. Therefore, they must have been the ones who facilitated it.

The other soldiers manning the wall didn't see it that way. They were too busy trying to work out exactly what happened. Why their arrows failed to even slow down the enemy remained a mystery, as did the nature of the monstrosity below and why it was in flames. Eris and Tal's contribution, along with Timoth and the refugees, had gone unnoticed in the fury of battle.

While those within the walls recovered, the undead army rallied around their otherworldly commander. Without its intelligence to guide them, they could only race toward it as if they were kandrel moths, drawn to the greatest source of heat.

Olagkoa lurched backward, stumbling over the abandoned torches before veering sideways to escape both fires. Its flailing appendages clawed desperately at the flames, but with little success. Each frantic swipe did more harm to the approaching Shells than to the blaze itself.

But the mindless soldiers continued coming, forcing themselves against the burning flesh in their compulsive attempt to heed its summoning. Several caught fire themselves, but that didn't stop their relentless press.

Their cause wasn't wholly futile, however, as their bodies helped smother the blaze. Whether a vestige of intelligence lingered in their heads or the creature had regained enough control of itself to communicate a new command, the soldiers in the rear began climbing over their comrades. Boots shoved into backs, shoulders, and necks as they formed a second tier around Olagkoa, working to snuff out its remaining burning flesh.

When the last trace of flames was extinguished from its body, the beast calmed enough to order the Shells to back away. They tumbled to the ground, mostly unhurt, except for those still engulfed. At a special mental command, the latter lumbered out of its range before collapsing, as the fire destroyed their cohesion. Those dead were finally allowed to rest.

The others, however, received new orders. Though blistered and blackened, with a few tentacles nothing more than withered husks, Olagkoa wasn't finished with Kridmont.

Just as it had drawn the army to itself, it now willed them to attack.

And they obeyed. This was no orderly march in formation as before. Nor was it another attempt at trickery. They rushed the iron doors, trying to shove them open by brute force.

On the ramparts above, the guards shouted to those below about the oncoming assault. Both teams braced themselves for the collision of corpses and metal.

Bones cracked as a dull thud echoed throughout the courtyard. But the gate built to withstand battering rams and siege engines was not going to give way to the unaided strength of men, alive or dead. Especially not when the dual crossbars had been shifted into place. Even the animated egyzemors and erdi'zal corpses made no difference. Thankfully, the undead voladorms had either lost their ability to fly in death or the creature hadn't realized their potential yet.

At Olagkoa's whim, the undead hurled themselves at the barrier again and again. Those not on the front line pushed against the Shells ahead of them. That force dispersed over multiple others and the width of the gate itself resulting only in more damage to themselves.

Those on the ramparts watched with morbid fascination at the display. Eris and Tal rejoined them, unimpeded this time. The sight shocked them too, but their concern lay more with the beast beyond.

Olagkoa had been scorched before. It had once fallen for a trap in the Undercastle, entering a room, only to have the contents set aflame. When it broke free, it had seemed almost dead. Then its regeneration abilities activated, and its flesh began to slowly mend. The same happened after Eris and Tal surrounded it with fire in Zatreus's cemetery, though its wounds weren't this pronounced.

Still, it had healed, and from what could be seen in the low light, it was doing so again.

"What in Zaljaka's name are they?" asked the uniformed woman Eris assumed was Kridmont's commander of its defenses. Despite the starkness of her hair, he realized she was much younger than he originally thought, perhaps a few years his junior.

"People, once," he explained. "Now dead, just shells of what they were."

The soldiers whirled about at his words, ready to defend their leaders against the strangers, but the woman ordered them to stand down. "What do you know about them?"

"Now you want to know?" Tal snapped before Eris could stop her. "We told your trio before, but they didn't believe us."

The commander looked at the Triune. Only Durant met her gaze. "Captain Althar, they arrived in Kridmont several hours ago, speaking of an approaching army and a monstrous threat. Their claims seemed unfounded and lacking credibility," he recounted, his tone dismissive. "We saw no need to take action in the face of so obvious a lie."

"Is *that* a lie?" Eris pointed to the Shells throwing themselves at the gate. "Or that?" His arm shifted to indicate Olagkoa further out.

Althar followed his gestures, then turned back to the nobles. "Why didn't you inform me of their claims?" she demanded, her tone icy. "We could have prepared, even if they proved to be false."

"They provided no proof of their tale!" Kain protested, daring to face her anger after all.

"What did you expect them to bring? One of those..." Althar thrust a finger toward the undead fighter still attempting to gain entry, then looked to Eris, realizing he hadn't fully explained them.

"We call them Shells," he said. "A few days ago, they were the soldiers of Zatreus's and Ludholm's armies. Then *it* drove them into battle until every one of them was killed. Using some power we haven't figured out, it healed their wounds and turned them into walking corpses, obeying its commands."

"And what is *it*?"

"It calls itself Olagkoa, but we don't know much more than that. It has great mental capabilities and can read minds and project images as well as pain. That man you argued with before was an illusion."

Durant pounced on the explanation, his blood-red sleeve flapping as he gestured wildly. "See how preposterous their entire story is?"

The woman glared at the noble, and he hastily withdrew his arm. "Yet we've witnessed it, which inclines me to believe it." She turned back to the pair of strangers. "Now, who are you?"

"I am Eris. This is Tal. We arrived with four companions. One is a villager from Fernwick. The others are two women, Farla and Ranin, and Holfast, an erdi'zal male. We are the ones who set the creature on fire, with the aid of some of the refugees."

"I see." Althar stared down at the soldiers, then at the beast. With its flames extinguished, it had gone still, its tentacles hanging limp and lifeless.

Tal, who had brightened when the commander seemed to be listening, now folded her arms in frustration. "She doesn't believe us. She's as misted as the rest of them."

"It isn't that," the other woman argued. "You've just presented us with a great deal to consider."

Eris appreciated that she hadn't dismissed his words as nonsense, though it helped that the proof had quite literally shown up at her door. "I know how incredulous it sounds. Trust me."

"What do you suggest we do, then?"

Morwen trembled with rage, her voice shrill. "You cannot be seriously considering seeking advice from these strangers!"

"I can!" Althar fired back. "They gave us a warning and provided proof. Their word means more at this moment than yours."

The trio looked stunned by the rebuke, hands clasped in front of them, their expressions dark. "Triune, I propose a new order of business," Durant intoned. "Captain Vespera Althar should be stripped of her duties immediately and replaced, pending an interview process to be begun at sunrise."

Kain bobbed his head once. "I second the motion. All in favor?"

All three raised their hands. Once the vote was counted, they returned to their smug posture. "You are relieved of your post, Althar," Durant announced, loud enough for those along the wall to hear.

Despite his words, the commander's expression remained calm, with only the flare in her eyes giving any hint of the fury beneath. She didn't lash out, however. Instead, she lifted her voice, scanning the length of the rampart to ensure every soldier heard her words. "Listen up! You have heard the case. The Noble Triune withheld information vital to the security of Kridmont, endangering the lives of its citizens as well as those in the outer settlements."

Durant's smug expression fell, replaced by one of concern as he realized how their actions might be interpreted. "That isn't what I meant when — "

"Now they wish to remove the leader of the city's defense while it is under siege without naming a successor, leaving us impotent in the face of danger." Althar paused, letting the importance of her words register with every guard. "Will you be obeying those orders?"

"No!" The reply thundered from every throat, a unified defiance that shook the air.

The captain tried to keep her expression stoic, but a hint of a smile betrayed her feelings at the result. "Will we be taking further orders from the Triune while Kridmont is threatened?"

Again, the response came in the form of a single syllable. "No!"

Now the grin pushed through, widening her lips and lighting up her eyes. Althar ran a hand over her gray outfit, then lifted her voice again, this time addressing the trio. "Lords and Lady of the Triune, you have heard our judgment. Lieutenant, take a couple of your men and escort these three back to their Grand Conclave. Perhaps there they can deliberate on their mistakes and reach a better conclusion."

Morwen and Kain looked despondent as a gruff-looking man approached them, flanked by four soldiers, hands gripping their hilts. Durant glared at their captain, but she shooed him away with her hand, and he went with the others.

"Blades above!" Althar exclaimed, spinning back to Eris and Tal. "That felt incredible! I've been waiting far too long to do that."

"That was amazing!" Tal chimed in, enthused to see the trio put in their place. "But won't you get in trouble? You just turned against your rulers."

"Those clods?" she laughed. "No, they are our decision-makers, and today is another example of how they are no longer fit to serve. They are the ones who will soon have a reckoning. With them gone, perhaps we can be productive."

The pair explained as briefly as they could the events of the past few days while the Shells continued their futile assault. The bizarre siege lasted nearly an hour before Olagkoa ordered it broken off.

"That seems to be the end of it," Althar commented as the army retreated clumsily. "Or do you think they will attack again?" The three had tried to get some rest while they watched, as did the other soldiers, above and below. Water skins had been passed about to relieve their parched throats, along with blocks of cheese, hardtack, and strips of smoked meat to ease their hunger.

Eris went over their various encounters with Olagkoa in his head. "The creature is stubborn. Its tricks failed, so it fell back to force. I believe it may try to shove itself through the gate."

"Do you think it could succeed?"

The man exhaled. "I wouldn't dare answer that. It has surprised us too many times. I suggest you shore it up with anything you can."

"And hit it with fire!" Tal chimed in enthusiastically. "That really razzles it!"

"Yes. Hit it with anything flammable," Eris advised. "Do you have any *pulveld*? You could apply that to your archers' arrows."

"We have some. But I don't understand how it's still alive." Althar nodded to where Olagkoa remained dormant. "You burned it. It should be ashes now. Instead, even the damage it took seems to have faded."

"It can heal itself, the same way it heals the bodies before making them walk."

The captain's face tightened. "So you are saying if we wound it, it won't stay wounded."

"Not for long," he admitted.

Althar shook her head in disbelief. "You've been dealing with this — "

A shout drew their attention back to the scene below. While the soldiers had dispersed randomly, Olagkoa was shoving its way forward. Its flesh remained scorched and blistered in some areas, while the burned tentacles were regaining their grayish-blue hue. As Eris predicted, it planned to assault the gate directly itself.

Althar started shouting orders while Tal and Eris pressed themselves against the parapet to watch. By the time the beast reached the entrance, a jar of pulveld and a pair of flaming torches had been fetched to the top of the wall. There, the archers smeared the sticky, slow-burning paste onto their arrows. Below, men and women scrambled to find anything that might be lodged against the doors.

The gate shuddered as Olagkoa slammed the iron barrier, but showed no further sign of strain. The same limbs that propelled the immense mass of flesh over the ground lacked the strength to both shove it and the gate with enough force to do any damage.

It wasn't giving up yet. Hooked tentacles played over the countless panels and massive bolts that made up the portal, searching for purchase among the seams and cracks, eager to find a weakness to exploit.

But the craftsmen who built it long ago had done their job well and centuries in the elements hadn't weakened it enough to fall to the probings of the beast.

"Attack!"

On Althar's order, the archers let loose their flaming arrows from the ramparts. They couldn't miss, not with a target this big and close. The first volley got Olagkoa's attention. The second and third enraged it. Even without finding a weakness in the gate, it flailed its tentacles against it, attempting to beat it down where finesse had failed.

The dozens of small fires in its flesh were taking its toll, though, and it began focusing some of its appendages on the burning sections. A score of Shells surged forward to aid, but whether they intended to extinguish the flames or launch a fresh assault remained unknown.

They never got the chance for either. Two guards above tipped a barrel over the wall's edge. Thick, yellowish oil poured out, coating the monstrosity. A pungent, greasy stench reached those on the rampart, causing them to wince, but their eyes never left the beast, tracking every movement.

Once the barrel was emptied and pulled back, the archers lit their arrows for one last volley. As the fresh flames hit the tallow, they ignited in an instant, rapidly engulfing the creature's form and lighting up the night. Black smoke billowed upward, carrying with it the stench of old fat and burned skin.

Cheers rose along the wall as Olagkoa shrieked and shoved itself backward. But the fire stayed with it as it crashed into the Shells it had summoned. It staggered back, flames clinging to its body, while the undead surged forward.

As its puppets worked to suppress the fires, Timoth, Holfast, Farla, and Ranin rejoined Eris and Tal to witness the triumph. Ranin remained fatigued, but her grin was the brightest among them as they watched Olagkoa burn. After the last few days, it felt good to see their fight had actually mattered.

"I hope it doesn't have any more ideas of getting in here," Althar said. "You don't think it does, do you?"

"It still might," Eris told her. "Have your guards keep an eye on each other. It may try to control one or more of your people and have them open the gate again. If it does that, fill it with more burning arrows."

"Feel free to do that even if it doesn't," Farla added, giving Ranin a tight hug that made the taller woman gasp. "We are off duty."

Althar's expression softened into a quiet smile. "You've more than earned it. We couldn't have defended the city this far without your help."

"You can fill that Triune of yours with arrows, too," Tal told her. "What are you going to do with them?"

"That isn't up to me," the captain said. "But I am certain they won't be making any more decisions for us. Is there anything we can do to thank you?"

"Stay vigilant," came Eris's blunt reply. "With luck, the creature will realize the futility of attacking here and move on. When it does, we must follow and warn whoever it attacks next."

"Not me!" Timoth stepped forward to address the group. "If it's all the same to you, I'm staying here. I've had my fill of monster hunting."

"Done with adventures, eh?" Tal teased, giving him a quick hug.

"Not quite." He glanced down, suddenly bashful, as he looked into the courtyard below. "I'm going to ask Sylvara to share a drink with me."

Chapter Twenty
TERMS AND CONDITIONS

DEMZI LIGHTREAVER FOUND Jaron in the armory, which sat on one of the lower floors of Wolfsight. The pair had barely spoken since Nilado's arrest, and while the High Monarch told herself they were merely busy with their various duties, she couldn't shake the feeling that he was actively avoiding her.

The armory housed the weaponry for Zatreus's soldiers, though it had largely been depleted to supply the war effort. Now, in the light of a dozen lanterns throughout the room, she was relieved to see efforts had been made to replenish the forged weapons. If they were to rebuild their army and stand against any action taken by Ludholm, the armaments could mean the difference between victory and defeat.

The chamber doubled as a meeting area for the city's forces, and Jaron was speaking with a trio of guards now. The soldiers, two humans and an erdi'zal, wore the signs of exhaustion like so many since Olagkoa first arrived at the main gate, but their expressions were relaxed, almost upbeat. She prayed to Diovola it was a harbinger of a change in fortune.

Lightreaver waited until the guards left before advancing to address Jaron. The big man saw her first, and a scowl crossed his features as he looked away. She needed him, however, and had no patience for his pouting. "Jaron, we need to talk."

His jaw tightened, but he turned to face her. "Of course, your eminence. How may I, a lowly soldier, be of service?"

His aloofness stung, but she knew it wasn't unwarranted. "That will do!" She pulled in a measured breath, tempering the edge in her voice. "Look, I am sorry for my words before. You were right to listen to Dasia, and I'll try to find a way to honor the agreement. Just stop looking at me as if I am a stranger."

"No," he told her, his expression remaining hard. "It was good that you reminded me of my place. We were becoming too familiar."

"Jaron, that —"

He grunted, cutting off her plea, and turned to a rack of swords. Their blades reflected the lantern light flawlessly, as if they had never seen use. "We've experienced a turn of fortune. I've been going over our inventory. With the aid of *Forge Ahead* and a few other swordsmiths, we should have sufficient weaponry to defend the city from Ludholm or the creature. If our weapons have any effect on either, of course. We are still working on obtaining more spears, bows, and arrows."

The woman nodded. She hadn't realized how deeply she hurt his pride and knew it would take more than a few words to smooth that over. "That is good news."

"There is more." He scratched his beard. "The river has been mostly blocked, with only a little seeping through. It should be enough to rebuild the Riverwall, and work will begin shortly."

Lightreaver nodded once more. "Well done. If you have the time, I need your assistance on a related issue."

"There is nothing more to do down here," he told her, his jaw tightening again. "What is your new assignment?"

"It isn't an assignment," she said with a sigh. *Why must he be so stubborn!* "With Nilado removed from her position, the Council has no head. Despite her betrayal, she was probably the only one capable of wrangling those quill-scratchers into a functioning unit."

Her description of the guild heads elicited a slight smile from Jaron that peeked out between his mustache and beard. "So you wish them to join her in the dungeon?"

Lightreaver shook her head, not entirely sure his suggestion was in jest. "We need to find a new Matron. I summoned them to their chamber to discuss it. I would appreciate your backing on this."

The man's broad shoulders sagged at her plan, but he had already said he had no other pressing matters. "Lead the way."

Figuring his response was the best she could hope for, the High Monarch did just that. They didn't speak as they walked up two wide flights of stone stairs, the echo of their boots sharp and hollow in the silence. At the top, they marched down a long hallway and through a few arches to a set of closed, ornate iron doors.

There they stopped, and Lightreaver turned to Jaron. "Since Dasia did not disclose who aided Nilado in her betrayals, any or all of those inside could be co-conspirators. Until we learn the truth, let me do the talking."

"Don't you always?"

Jaron's expression remained neutral, so Lightreaver was again left wondering about the seriousness of his words. Rather than try to argue, though, she inhaled deeply, then pulled the doors open.

The chamber for the Council of Influence and Affluence stood a third the size of the throne room, but it contained several trappings of wealth to compensate for the disparity in size. The gold-colored silk curtains of twin tall windows were drawn back to reveal the struggling harbor, but they were the least impressive items in the hall.

A pair of three-foot-high vases made from the rare *enek ezus*, or singing silver, sat in one corner. They were adorned by pastel gems known as *doaku*, or flowstones, causing the surface to glisten with a dozen colorful teardrops.

An ornate iron table in another corner held four simple-looking boxes with colorfully painted patterns — intricate puzzle boxes crafted by skilled voladorms. Other priceless items rested on pedestals, with a few in protective glass cases. Even the walls were richly decorated, with various tapestries and the pelt of an adartigra, black horns jutting out from the fur.

The most opulent item, however, was a life-sized wood carving of Zaljaka, the erdi'zal god specializing in wealth and chance.

Five council members sat around an intricately etched metal and stone table. The mumblings between them quickly halted as the pair entered.

Jaron moved to the side while Lightreaver approached the head position where Nilado would normally sit. She ignored the plush chair there, choosing instead to stand for what she had to say. "I have no doubt you are wondering why I called this meeting."

"We know why," a male erdi'zal with rust-colored fur and hair at the center of the left side said sharply. He was Marroc of the Twisted Stream, head of the weavers guild and coordinator of land travel-related issues. "You arrested the Matron. What we don't know is on what grounds."

"Yes," concurred a human male on the opposite side. Sabastian Thurlow was head of the tailoring guilds, though his particular interest lay in headgear, which he displayed at every opportunity. Perched atop his head today was a short crimson hat, its brim extending nearly two feet on either side, enough to jab the eye of anyone sitting beside him. Fortunately for the others in attendance, both those seats were vacant. "We demand you make your position known to us that we may judge its merit."

A voladorm to Lightreaver's immediate left nodded in agreement. The petite Adfina handled the apothecary and related professions guilds. "You cannot arrest her without cause."

The High Monarch knew each of their names and purposes, as well as which would likely give the most complaints, so their protests were expected. "I have plenty of cause. She had a merchant arrested, as well as Linda — one of your own — and failed to provide me with a reason. She is also the one who started our current war with Ludholm."

Gasps circled the table. Even Dasia, seated between Marroc and a hafu, couldn't resist a show of surprise, though Lightreaver knew it for the act it was. Marroc ran a hand down his puffy, ornate shirt, signaling the others to keep their composure. "I am certain she had her justifications."

"I am certain she did, too. But her justifications are not necessarily good for others or the city." She planted both hands on the table and swept her gaze around those seated. "Did any of you know about her betrayal?"

Sabastian shook his head, causing the brims of his hat to flap with the motion. "You have not yet proven she has committed said betrayal. Release her at once, so we may judge for ourselves."

The woman locked her eyes with his. "You seem to misunderstand how things operate. I blame that on the Matron, as she has spent far too many years attempting to muddy the issue. She and I are *not* joint leaders of Zatreus. *I* am the High Monarch. My decisions are final in all matters."

Marroc blinked both sets of eyes. "But we — "

"Answer ultimately to me," Lightreaver finished, shifting her glare to him. "Nilado is ... was your immediate superior, but she still answered to me. Don't let her petty maneuvers convince you otherwise." She swung back to stare at Sabastian. "Moreover, because my decision is final, I never have to answer to you. *Never.* If I share details of a situation, that is at my discretion, not your demands. Similarly, the merchants of your various guilds answer to you, and not the other way around." She straightened, resting her fingers softly on the table's cold surface. "Have I clarified the power structure for you?"

They remained silent, but their chastened expressions suggested they accepted her explanation. For now. Adfina drew in a breath. "So when will the Matron be returning?"

"Returning?" Lightreaver's eyebrows shot up. "She committed treason. She's never returning to her former position. *Ever.* Punishment for that crime is execution. A man would be hanged, drawn, and quartered. But I may be merciful and stick merely to burning her in one of the city's squares."

Jorah, the brightly colored male hafu at the other end of the table, gasped. "But that is — "

"Deserved. She started a war to protect her wealth, endangering the lives of two kingdoms and their populations. Can you think of a more egregious crime than that?"

Marroc held up a six-fingered hand. "But nobody has died."

"Then your castle spies have failed you," Lightreaver snapped. She had expected pushback over Nilado's arrest, but those assembled seemed to be in complete denial. "Both armies are gone. A thousand soldiers, dead."

Adfina shrugged, sending a ripple through her folded wings. "They are only soldiers."

Jaron, who had been silently listening, stepped forward at her disparaging words, hand on his hilt. "They weren't just nameless soldiers! They had families," he said, his voice thick with rage. "Children who will never hug them again. Parents who have lost their loved ones. Do not dismiss their deaths so lightly!"

"*And* they were citizens who contributed to your economy," Light-reaver added pointedly, eyeing the council members. "With the River-wall destroyed and our trade in peril — more casualties of this needless war — you cannot afford to lose even one potential customer." She gave a gentle nod toward Jaron, and when he relaxed, she turned her full attention to the group. "If you are still unimpressed with her lists of crimes, look to what happened to Linda."

They stared at the empty alki to Sabastian's right, as if noticing her absence for the first time. "Where is she?" the hatted individual de-manded. "If she was falsely arrested, then release her."

"She is dead," Jaron replied bluntly. "Nilado tortured her in the depths of our dungeons. From what we found, the Matron has done the same to others. How many people have you noticed gone missing?"

The guild masters drew sharp breaths, their shock rippling through the chamber like a sudden gust of wind. Discussing the death of a thou-sand soldiers meant nothing to them, but the violent passing of one of them was almost unimaginable. "We cannot have an empty position. It must be filled immediately."

A hollow feeling spread through Lightreaver's chest. Their lack of com-passion saddened her to the core. She had expected at least some sign that their lives had not been completely corrupted by power and money, but even Dasia seemed impassive. The ruler hoped that it was also just a de-ception to hide her knowledge. "That is part of the reason I summoned you here. You will need to find a replacement for her and the Matron."

The five looked at each other uncomfortably. "How will we do that?" Jorah croaked.

The High Monarch stared at him, confused by the question. *How much did Nilado need to do for them?* "Just pick someone. How about you? Why don't you be the new Matron?"

The hafu gasped again. As head of the fishmonger's guild and coor-dinator of all water-related issues, he had at least some of the skills needed to handle multiple tasks, but he didn't appear happy about the nomination.

The others bristled at the suggestion. "That would be most unfair," Sabastian explained. "He'd focus only on his smelly fish."

Frustration filled the void in Lightreaver's chest. "Then you."

Adfina's slight frame trembled with outrage. "He'd have everyone wearing his foolish hats!"

"Hats are not foolish!" Sabastian growled, gripping his own protectively. "They are versatile accessories, providing both a function — "

"Alright then, Adfina," the ruler said, cutting him off. "You lead them."

Now Jorah protested, the gills lining his neck flaring. "She'll put her herbs before all else!"

"They smell better than your stinky fish!" she shot back.

"Have you ever *smelled* wettifrass with that little nose?"

"What would a salt sucker know about aromatics?"

"Stop!" Lightreaver slammed the table. "Are there none of you who could be tolerated as the new head of the guilds?" They glared at each other, but shook their heads. The ruler briefly considered handing the job to Dasia — the only one among them to show any sign of a conscience — when she remembered Nilado's assistant. "What about Ven? Where is he?"

Again, the members looked about before Jorah spoke up. "I haven't seen him in days."

"Anyone else?" A glance around the table told Lightreaver the others had the same experience. She guessed he fled, sensing what was coming for Nilado. *That, at least, is one problem I don't need to deal with.* "Then for now, you answer to Jaron here."

This time, it was the sergeant's turn to be shocked. "You wouldn't!"

The others weren't happy with the choice, either. "What does he know of the rules of commerce?" Marroc demanded.

"Does he know the seven principles of supply and demand?" Jorah called out.

"Has he ever negotiated prices for importing fruits from another city?" Adfina asked, adding her own question.

"What is his opinion on the optimal height of a hat?" Sabastian inquired, tapping the top of his.

Jaron stepped toward the table, hands raised to calm them. "I am sure we will figure everything out. Just not at this time." His eyes wandered over their faces, each eager for answers. He had none, so he reached for the one topic he knew anything about. "How is the rerouting to land routes going?"

That sparked another wave of heated arguments among the members, each clamoring to have their services prioritized over the others. The sergeant attempted to reassure them, insisting that everyone would have their turn, but his words only poured fuel on the fire.

Voices rose, overlapping in a chaotic din until, with a frustrated grimace, he finally slapped his hands over his ears to block out the storm of demands.

The moment Lightreaver sensed their guard had slipped, she slammed her fist onto the table. The sharp crack silenced them at once, and she fought back a smirk at their startled reactions. As she leaned in, Jaron slowly lowered his hands, his attention fully on her as well. "One more piece of business," she said, her voice so soft they had to move closer to hear. "I know the Matron is responsible for the death of my father, the former High Monarch. That is also treason." She paused, looking at each of them in turn. "If I learn any one of you played a role in that crime, this Council will be searching for your replacement along with the others."

Her words met no argument or denial, only the soft rustle of robes and a faint swallow from Sabastian, loud in the sudden stillness. There might have been more resistance if she hadn't already pointed out Nilado's likely fate, but they seemed to grasp the gravity of her warning. She stood straight, then turned to Jaron. "They are all yours."

He tried to protest, but the shouts of the others drowned him out, and soon he added his own voice to their contentious discussion.

Lightreaver didn't stay to learn the results, choosing instead to head for the door and quieter quarters. The Council would have to remain leaderless for a while longer. She had higher priorities than finding someone crazy enough to want to handle the lot.

LORD PARNECUS DAYMON sat on a splintery farmer's stool in the drafty chamber that passed for his throne room. The chamber hadn't held a proper monarch's seat since long before he took the office of Ludholm's ruler, and he had no intention of seeking to replace it. He liked to think the lowly furniture kept him grounded.

Grekorn sat on a simple chair a few feet in front of him, arms crossed. A second chair stood empty. Its prospective user, Rithi, paced nearby, the anger from her meeting two days ago with Zatreus's leader still surging through her. Fury filled her striking eyes, somehow making them even more intimidating.

299

She reported the entire exchange on her return to Ludholm. Despite the closeness of the kingdoms, it had taken her and the delegation two days to journey between them. With floodwaters rising across the grassland, that shortcut became impassable, requiring them to take the road out to Longbridge, cross the river, and then travel up the western side.

That trip was further complicated by the town's condition. Rithi learned from the recovering citizens that the creature and its army of undead had come through, smashing their beloved statue and forcing the bridge open. Since the attack, the townsfolk had reinforced the wooden span with beams, making it barely safe to cross.

"Lightreaver grows bold, denying us access to the river's mouth," Daymon said, addressing the pair. "I hoped she might have learned how determined we are by now, but this insolence cannot stand. Rithi, I want you to lead a return envoy, much smaller. You need not enter the city. I will prepare the document."

"Why?" The woman stopped her pacing long enough to protest. "She made it clear she wouldn't share. Instead, she threatened to destroy Ludholm."

"Because I wish this to be done formally," he replied, straightening his back. "The lowborn of Zatreus may resort to murder as a means of negotiations, but we will not. You'll be presenting a formal declaration of our pledge to end that city's role as a trading port."

She threw her hands wide in frustration. "Not to sound confrontational, but I ask again. Why?"

"Rithi," Daymon began, his lips curling at the ends in the start of a smile, "I doubt there has been a moment since you were born that you weren't confrontational. I am offering Lightreaver a final chance to reconsider her stance. If she interpreted our request for compromise as a weakness, perhaps she is too brutish now to understand anything but threats."

"And if she calls our bluff?" Grekorn asked. He didn't take the news well either, his silence cutting deeper than Rithi's fire. Unlike the woman, he displayed his irritation by shutting down.

"It won't be a bluff," the ruler said quietly. "When our spies infiltrated Zatreus, they discovered a compound there called *robantuz*. It has a force like a lightning strike, but does more damage. They used it to destroy the Riverwall."

Rithi's anger shifted in an instant, flaring into excitement. "We could use that on their city! Did they bring any back?"

"No. They could only steal enough for their purpose. But they did learn where it came from. The egyzemors in the Eastern Heights." He looked at the knight. "Grekorn, send an envoy to the assembly there. We must convince them to provide us with the same. Perhaps a few of the egyzemors from here could act as ambassadors."

"Fosco and Bertrada are still here," the man said, relaxing his arms now that a retaliatory plan was being discussed. "I'll speak with them."

Rithi's arm shot up. "I volunteer for the mission to attack Zatreus with it. Lightreaver needs to know they can't dismiss us."

But Daymon shook his head. "That is not how I intend to ruin them."

"Why not?" Anger surged back as she lowered her arm, her hand tightening into a fist. "Haven't they caused enough trouble to deserve it?"

"We can't risk another physical war. We've lost nearly five hundred of our best fighters and devastated our male population. Our goal was always to restore Ludholm's place as the northern trade center. That is how we will ruin them."

"You heard what I said, right?" she pressed, her voice growing louder. "They refuse to grant us access or boats. So how will we punish them?"

"We create our own," Daymon told her flatly. "Or rather, recreate."

Confusion softened Rithi's ire. "I don't understand."

"Our records show what we use as our route to the Old Road used to be the channel to the river. It would take months to dig that out. If we can secure robantuz, we could greatly speed it up."

The young woman deflated at his explanation, finally dropping into the empty chair. "So no sundering their walls?"

"No sundering their walls," Daymon confirmed. "That would only spark another war we can't afford. Get some rest while I draft the declaration. You can head back to Zatreus tomorrow. You are dismissed."

Rithi stayed put, sulking in her chair as Grekorn rose. "I will dispatch the envoy to the Eastern Heights tomorrow as well."

Daymon nodded, and the knight strode from the chamber. The remaining pair sat quietly as they listened to the sound of his boots receding. When they were gone completely, the ruler leaned forward on his stool. "There is something else bothering you."

She didn't look at him, instead boring a hole in the wall with her eyes. They didn't damage the stone, but she kept trying anyway. "What's the problem with my name?" she finally grumbled.

"Rithi? There is nothing wrong with that."

"And my last? Brightsayer."

Daymon shook his head. "I don't see anything wrong with that one either. What has upset you?"

She shifted her stare to him. "Lightreaver made some remark about the history behind it. Said if I knew it, I would denounce your actions against Zatreus."

"I doubt there is any truth to her words. She was merely trying to rattle you during the discussions." He understood her concern, though he knew of no other way to ease it. She was the only person in Ludholm with her kind of eyes. Even her parents didn't have them. They took some getting used to, but Daymon never saw anything malevolent in her gaze. Her name had never suggested a deeper meaning — not to him, at least.

His reply didn't seem to satisfy her, though, as she resumed her attempts to stare down the wall.

When he realized she might stay for the remainder of the day, Daymon rose and brushed some mud off his boots. She didn't take the hint, so he sighed and headed for the door.

A young man, perhaps fifteen years old, nearly collided with him as he sprinted into the chamber. "Forgive me, my lord, but I have urgent news!"

Daymon placed a hand on the youth's shoulder to calm him. "It is alright. What is the news?"

"The water," he choked out, his breath sharp and uneven. "As far as we can tell, it has stopped rising!"

The ruler straightened calmly as he considered the information. "So Zatreus has found a way to dam the river. Interesting."

Rithi didn't handle it as well. "They can't do that!" she yelled, jumping to her feet so forcefully that her chair went tumbling behind her.

"They can," he gently corrected her. "They have to in order to repair the wall."

"But that will stop the lake filling, too! They have won again."

"Not yet." He tapped his chin, then fixed her with a somber stare. "Do you still wish to sunder something?"

Her fists clenched. "Do you have to ask?"

302

"Very well. Once you have delivered the declaration, send the rest of the delegation back. The blockage must be north of the city. I want you to locate it and see if you can find a way to remove it, or at least open part of it."

Rithi started to speak, then remembered his earlier words about retaliation. "Doesn't this go against your idea of fairness, though?"

"Destroying the Riverwall was an attempt to restore the land to its former state. This will be no different. Do you disagree?"

A grin split her face from ear to ear. "Not at all! It will be an absolute pleasure."

"THIS IS FUN," Camille called out as she, Savanah, Mikel, and Vyncent were led through a stone corridor of Starlight Citadel, the seat of Ertonbridge's rulers. Their entourage consisted of six soldiers, clad in snug attire of violet, green, and gold. Each carried a barbed polearm, no doubt meant to intimidate any visitors. "We're being brought before another city's ruler. That's never happened before."

"I bet it is to praise us for all we've endured in the name of saving Rapria," Savanah responded, matching the woman's sarcastic tone. They had faced too many threats to be cowed by a few pointed sticks.

"Must be. Maybe we'll be honored for our service." Camille elbowed her friend in the side. "Or better yet, made nobles! Duchess Camille doesn't sound too bad."

Savanah shook her head with a smile. "I'd prefer to be a baroness. Less hassle."

Mikel leaned between them as their boots clomped across the worn flagstones. "Quiet, both of you. This is a serious occasion. You should feel privileged."

"Hear that, Vyncent?" the redhead called over her shoulder, her voice bouncing off the vaulted ceilings. "How much of a privilege have you felt when some monarch summons you for questioning?"

"The only privilege I've had is sampling their hospitality behind iron bars." While the man's expression remained somber, his tone mirrored their mocking demeanor. "None have the grace of King Talidith, may he find eternal rest."

Mikel stood upright and glanced at him. "Alright. I understand your encounter with Daymon may have soured you on the ruling class, but I don't — "

"Wasn't just Daymon. Your favorite redhead tossed us in her dungeon before sending us to find you," Camille told him.

"I am sure that was with the best interest of Zatreus in mind."

Savanah gave him an exaggerated nod. "Then she decided later that we were the best hope for Zatreus. That is why we doubt this king's intentions."

"We aren't meeting with a king."

A frown creased Vyncent's forehead. "Then who — "

"Silence!" the soldier to his right snapped, striking the floor with the butt of his weapon. "You will show respect for our magnates!"

The designation surprised Savanah. She learned a few forms of governing when she attended school in Adradena — with the city's own council republic being the fairest — but had only heard the term 'magnate' when she set out on her travels. The city of Tromont, situated on the west coast between a swamp and a desert, had only recently removed such a person from his position of power.

The wily individual had wormed his way into the upper tiers of noble society through various transactions, both legal and criminal. After he tried to influence the decisions of their monarch, he nearly cost the kingdom a year's crops. When he tricked the noble houses into violent infighting to distract from his mistake, everyone agreed it was time for him to go. He was shamed in the public pillory for a week before being finally chased out of the city at sword point.

Is that who leads Ertonbridge? A group of power-hungry swindlers? While the city was a close ally with Adradena, she had never heard anything ill said about its leader, though at the time, she understood it to be governed by a single figure. *Who are we meeting?*

Her question found its answer moments later as the escorts led them into a circular throne room. Short windows around a tall, domed ceiling filled the chamber with natural light while unlit torches lined the solid, gray walls. While not as large or grand as the one occupied by the High Monarch in Zatreus, it was definitely built to impress both citizens and visitors.

Set slightly back from the center of the room, a pair of carved oak chairs adorned with azure cushions supported two figures. On the left sat a dark-skinned man in a sleek red suit, tailored to perfection over his slender physique. Gray streaks threaded through his tightly curled black hair, while faint lines hinted at the onset of wrinkles on his chiseled face. His partner on the right couldn't be more of his opposite. Her long, blonde locks complemented her pale complexion, while her plump pink lips, deep green eyes, and matching layered dress added bursts of color to her otherwise monochrome appearance.

The lead soldier stepped ahead of the group, his exaggerated steps reflecting a practiced formality. He turned abruptly and struck the floor with his polearm, sending a crisp ringing sound echoing about the chamber. When it faded, he puffed his chest as his voice boomed out the pair's titles. "All hail Lord Philip Dunnil and Lady Madeline Marsk, supreme sovereigns of Ertonbridge and the outer enclaves. Bow before their wisdom and compassion."

The travelers eyed each other nervously for a moment before hesitantly bending at the waist in deference. Despite their earlier sarcasm, they still bowed. Words aside, they knew how to show respect to a throne.

Lord Philip spoke first, his voice soft and welcoming. "We appreciate your willingness to meet with us."

Lady Madeline nodded curtly. "We would not interrupt your travels if it weren't such an urgent matter."

"We didn't have a choice," Camille replied bluntly. Their trip from Fircrest aboard the venki had been relatively uneventful, though the roughness of navigating the rapids had left all of them nauseated. An hour after they moored in Ertonbridge for the night, a dozen soldiers had accosted them, saying they were wanted for an audience in the capital. Despite their insistence that they had done nothing wrong, the four were escorted to the stronghold, still gripping their weapons and supplies.

"Our soldiers meant you no harm," Philip explained, ignoring her brusque tone. "It seemed the swiftest means to ensure this discussion."

Mikel cleared his throat. "You want to know about the river. Is that correct?"

"Indeed." Lady Madeline straightened, apparently pleased someone had broached the subject. "You traveled here on a craft capable of traversing the reduced flow."

"We didn't start that way. A few hundred miles north is a crashed valupe sitting in the water."

Lord Philip inched forward in his seat, clearly excited by the revelation. "So you were on the Leosonee when it collapsed? Did you happen to see what caused it?"

"It isn't anything local," Mikel told him with a shrug. "We believe something has happened in Zatreus. That is where we came from."

"Please, tell us your theory on this disaster."

"Yes," his pale companion agreed. "What could have caused this?"

Camille raised her arms, adopting her favorite pose to mimic tentacles. "A giant creature covered in limbs that crushes you and reads your mind."

"It does the mind reading before crushing you," added Savanah. "After would be too late." Despite Mikel's warning and her own experience serving in Talidith, she found it difficult to take their questions about the river seriously, especially when the companions were focused on thwarting a threat to Rapria.

Lady Madeline placed a hand against her chest, her fingers splayed tight over her heart as if steadying its pace. "Gracious! What an outlandish idea!"

Lord Philip's eyebrows dropped into a grimace. "We would appreciate you taking this inquiry seriously."

"What they say is true," Mikel told him, shooting the women his own glare. "The High Monarch sent us on a search to find a way to stop it. That is what brings us to your fair city."

"And how would this beast inflict the observed harm on the waterway?"

Savanah swallowed her retort. *They are wholly obsessed with the river!* "We don't know. But it was attempting to enter the city when we left."

"Your explanation is a difficult one to accept." Lady Madeline's expression matched her disbelieving tone. "A hitherto unknown creature destroying Wayela's primary means of trade."

"It's not the only possibility," Mikel cut in. "I believe the Riverwall may have been destroyed. It prevented the river from spilling into the adjacent grasslands."

Lord Philip tapped his chin, signaling to Savanah that at least one of the sovereigns was finally paying attention. "Could this limbed beast have caused that? You said it was destructive."

"We hadn't thought of that!" the archer exclaimed. "Perhaps it entered the city that way."

But Mikel shook his head at the suggestion. "It wouldn't have to. It could just swim into the harbor through the river. There would be no benefit I can see in it destroying the barrier."

Lord Philip's expression faltered as he looked from one companion to the other. "You are wholly serious about this creature?"

"Is there a chance of it coming to our fair metropolis?" Lady Madeline added, running a nervous hand over the arm of her seat.

"It would have to travel several hundred miles," Vyncent chimed in.

"Ah!" Lord Philip held up a finger. "Not if it swam."

Mikel shook his head again. "We are speculating wildly here. It's likely that Daymon's soldiers were responsible for breaking the River-wall. That seems to have been his intention all along."

The male monarch cast a disapproving gaze in his direction. "Are you referring to Lord Parnecus Daymon of Ludholm? Please address him with his full title."

"Indeed." His partner tensed on her throne, showing signs of agitation as well. "Such informality is unbecoming of a soldier."

Their abrupt change in attitude surprised Mikel. "What makes you think I'm a soldier?"

Lord Philip gestured toward him. "Your bearing. You hold yourself with an air of authority, yet you presented no titles for yourself. That marks you as a protector. The High Monarch Demzi Lightreaver would not entrust a mission of such import, as you state, to anyone of lesser station."

"Your female companion holds a similar ranking," Lady Madeline pointed toward Savanah. "Though she speaks little, there is a calm in her stance. She knows her authority without flaunting it. Her brother and sister would be wise to follow her lead, so they may also attain such poise one day."

Savanah raised her eyebrows at the praise. *Is that true? Do I stand calmly* She looked down at her body, at the leather pack gripped in one hand, holding the remains of her supplies. At her sword and scabbard hanging from her belt. At the strap across her back, securing a quiver of arrows. At the pair of bows, mundane and magical, looped off her shoulder. *With all I'm carrying, I'm probably unable to stand any other way.*

Vyncent had a stronger reaction. "Excuse me? First, I am not her brother. Second, up until a few months ago, I was her superior officer. I am Vyncent Warne, Lieutenant of the Sovereign Guard of Talidith, finest swordsman in the kingdom."

Lady Madeline raised her eyebrows at his outburst. "My apologies. I did not mean to cause offense," she told him, though her tone suggested she wasn't truly concerned.

Camille laughed at the man's protest. "Despite his lack of sophistication, what Vyncent said is true. The three of us were all soldiers of Talidith before it was destroyed. Our people fled to Zatreus. Mikel here is a proper soldier from there."

"You have our deepest condolences on the loss of your kingdom." Lord Philip bowed his head, which Savanah took as a sign of sympathy.

"We heard it had fallen," Lady Madeline added solemnly, "but the cause was unclear."

Savanah gave a mental sigh, wondering how many more times they would have to explain what happened the year before. "A horde of vornuks overran our castle, and we fled underground. There, we found the tentacled creature we spoke of. With aid from Zatreus, we attempted to trap it, but it escaped and followed us."

Lord Philip's expression morphed from empathy to dread. "This is dreadful! How does one destroy such a monstrosity?"

Mikel's eyes widened at the question. "We would rather not — "

"Artifacts!" Camille gushed, missing her companion's hesitation. "We need to find a bunch of arcana-infused objects created to send it back to its world. There is one in Adradena. Actually, we think the hafu have it."

"Gracious!" Lady Madeline exclaimed. "You certainly spin a wild tale."

"One which we should not be boring you with," Mikel interjected. "Your inquiry was into the river. I believe Day... Lord Parnecus Daymon sent agents to destroy it. We've been at war with Ludholm for months over rights to the waterway."

The magnates' demeanors resumed their businesslike appearance. "I see." Lord Philip tapped a finger against his armrest. "If this is indeed the cause of the waterway's distress, how quickly do you believe it could be rectified?"

Lady Madeline gave a rigid nod. "Yes. We must resume trade as soon as possible."

Savanah shrugged. "We left Zatreus several days ago. We have no way of knowing what the situation is there."

Lord Philip turned his gaze to her. "Then I implore you, return immediately and aid the High Monarch Lightreaver in resolving this crisis."

"We will do no such thing!" Vyncent yelled. "We have our own duty to complete, and it doesn't involve us being your errand boys."

Mikel grabbed his arm to restrain him. "Vyncent, please — "

"No. He's right." Camille took a step toward the magnates, who cringed at their raised voices. "No matter what happened to the river, it affected us too, but we don't have the time or the means to go back just because your supply of iceberry pies and Raudona's late for whatever masque you're throwing."

"Such insolence!" Lord Philip's brows furrowed deeply, his eyes narrowing with simmering frustration at their raised voices.

Lady Madeline's thick frame shook as well. "We merely made a polite request, and you swiftly turned hostile."

Mikel contorted in panic. "Please forgive my companions," he said hastily, making a deep bow before the seated leaders. "Our mission is highly time-sensitive, and we have already endured several hardships on our journey. To turn around at this point would not only set us back weeks, it could put all of Wayela in danger."

His words seemed to calm Lord Philip. "You place so much importance on your task?"

Savanah pulled Camille back to her side. "This creature killed our friends and kinfolk, then destroyed our kingdom. Now it's attempting to do the same to the rest of Wayela, perhaps all of Rapria. If we don't stop it, even Ertonbridge will feel its wrath."

"So if you want the river fixed, send your own people!" Camille added gleefully. "We're busy!"

The archer put a hand on her shoulder. "That's enough."

On their thrones, the regal pair seethed, their eyes locking in a silent exchange of shared frustration. Then, with a brisk nod from the man to his companion, they redirected their attention to the assembled company. "Then will you deliver a missive to Adradena's council? Is that too great a request?"

Mikel quickly nodded at the inquiry. "We most certainly can. However, if you wish to ensure we reach the city with your message intact, would you consider aiding us in repairing our vessel? We have done what we can to provide ourselves with a safe and swift journey, but I am certain you have far more capable boatwrights at your disposal."

"Indeed, we do," Lady Madeline assured him. "Are you intending to stay the night in Ertonbridge?"

"That was our plan. A meal, then overnight in an inn."

"Then continue on that course." Lord Philip waved a hand towards the entrance to the hall behind them. "We will have your boat seen to while we prepare the missive. You will find both at our docks by morning."

"Your generosity overwhelms us." Mikel gave another low bow. "I wish your city good fortune and pray to Zaljaka that the Leosonee is soon restored."

Lady Madeline straightened, a smile splitting her face. "And we wish you luck. May your journey to your final destination be expedient."

The half dozen soldiers who escorted the companions into the chamber sprang to life at a look from Lord Philip, marching ahead of them, creating a barrier between the magnates and strangers. Understanding that their audience was over, Savanah and the others allowed themselves to be led back out of the citadel.

"What was the point of all that?" Camille snapped once they were clear of the stronghold and the soldiers had marched back inside. "Now we have an extra chore. When did we become everyone's lackeys?"

Mikel glared at her. "We gained their good grace, which we desperately need after yours and Vyncent's outburst. If you were this rude with Lightreaver, I can see why she tossed you in prison."

Savanah had never seen the man this angry. While the others had been discourteous, it wasn't entirely unjustified. "Demanding we return to Zatreus *was* outlandish."

"Agreed," he said in a lighter tone. "But from their viewpoint, their city has been largely cut off from the goods they want."

"So are Carlin and Fircrest," Vyncent reminded him. "Neither place treated us like this. And they can always use the road if they are that desperate. It would take them as long as us to make the trip, and they could bring back whatever they needed."

Mikel held up a cautioning hand. "I'm not arguing that they were justified. However, I am saying you must learn diplomacy. It gains you more than aggression. For example, in return for transporting a bit of paper, I secured us an improved boat."

"Until we're gone from here, don't anyone mention our former cargo," Camille warned. "Those crates were supposed to be delivered here. If that pair was already upset about delayed goods, they'd likely be more enraged if they found out we broke some."

"Don't remind me!" Savanah groaned. "All those kliku fruit, gone!"

A smile appeared on Mikel's lips. "I am sure Adradena will have plenty to keep even you satisfied. Let's find some rooms for the night, then head out as early as we can. If our luck holds, we will be there the day after tomorrow."

"If our luck holds?" Vyncent laughed. "When's that ever worked out for us?"

Chapter Twenty-one
FLEE, FOLLOW, PREACH, AND SHIVER

OLAGKOA LAUNCHED SEVERAL more assaults against Kridmont that day and into the night, each one repelled in bursts of fire. Even when it sent the Shell army to scale the wall, archers rained flaming arrows down on the beast. A stalemate settled between them.

Despite the relative ease with which they kept the monster at bay, those within the walls and the guards on the rampart fretted over each fresh attack. Though the gate held, they were still under siege by an unknown enemy with no idea when it would end.

Captain Althar and her soldiers planned for the worst. Even if Olagkoa never breached the gates, its presence blocked land trade and cast a shadow over every decision.

But Kridmont had one advantage: the Ibia River. Though narrower than the Leosonee, it served as a supply line to Stegate, Drulon, and the trade towns between. The waterway also gave them an avenue of escape. Fortunately, the creature had not attempted to find another entryway, or it would have discovered the small harbor on the western side. Althar had ordered extra men to guard the access point when the army first arrived. As long as that was secure, they had a means to sneak away the most vulnerable, like children with their mothers or the critically wounded, in the hopes of reaching Stegate. A messenger could also be sent by boat to seek aid from that city or by horse to Drulon. Their fleet of boats paled in comparison to Zatreus, with only five large enough to carry a dozen people, but it remained an option.

The Shell Patrol rested against the parapets. They spent most of their day atop the wall, keeping watch over the monster and its army, sleeping in shifts. Farla, Tal, and Holfast slept now, huddled against the wall, while Eris and Ranin slumped against the stones as they stared at those below. The man had insisted she get more rest as well, feeling guilty about her having to counter the beast again, but she refused.

"I thought this thing was supposed to be smart," Ranin noted as they watched it healing itself. The last futile assault had ended nearly two hours before, leaving it scorched by oil. Now, most of its flesh had returned to its usual ugly self and was no longer blackened or blistered.

"It is. I think it's made this personal. It doesn't like failing." Eris thought of his brief interaction with the creature when the beast projected the image of his father to their group in the Undercastle. That had been a ruse, though, allowing it to get close to them and not true communication. The only way they could learn what it was thinking was by observing its actions, and even those were questionable at times. The relentless assaults on the gate suggested it refused to give up, but he wished they had better insight into its reasoning. "When you... do your thing to strike back at it, do you see any of its thoughts?"

"No," Ranin said, wincing at the memory. "It's more like punching someone who is punching you. You try to hit them harder, but you don't notice anything else around you. I think I can only do it when it strikes first because it is opening its mind to ours. Next time, I'll try to see more, if I get the chance."

The man chuckled. "Don't let Farla hear you say that. I'd rather you didn't have to punch back again, especially if it draws her ire."

"She's not so tough. Just fierce when it comes to people she cares about."

Eris nodded. "Tal is the same way."

"And you?" Ranin fixed him with a questioning stare. "Tal told me you've been taking on the creature directly."

"She talks too much."

"She's worried about you. Farla and I were there, remember? We all followed you into that cave. We all wanted to avenge Captain Warne. We still do. You weren't alone then, and you aren't alone now."

Eris told himself the same thing, but it rang hollow. "You weren't the one who removed the sole object holding it captive. You didn't cause the death of so many of our people. The death of... "

"The woman you love?" she finished for him when his voice trailed off.

"So Tal told you that, too." Eris couldn't really be mad at her, but he never intended his personal struggles to be a topic of conversation. He glared down at Olagkoa. The creature hadn't created all his problems, but it definitely compounded them.

"Yes, but we already knew your feelings for her, and hers for you. Neither of you was very subtle about it. But throwing yourself constantly into danger won't bring her back. Not any of them."

"You think I don't know that?" he snapped. "I can't undo what was done, but I can make sure more don't die. I'm trying to be the leader Kehnin thought I was."

"Oh, Eris!" She gripped his shoulder and forced him to face her. "You already are. But a leader doesn't sacrifice themselves. That only makes sure those they led suffer." She could see he wasn't listening, at least not with the intent to understand, but pressed on. "Do you think Valeria planned to leave us without a king? Or Warne to leave us without a commander?"

"A leader must be willing to die for those he protects," he countered. It was part of every soldier's basic creed as well.

"Be willing, yes. But not wanting. Kehnin saw you as a leader, not a martyr. We feel the same."

It doesn't matter what you feel. This is mine to fix. Ranin wouldn't release him, however, so he diverted the subject. "Have you had this talk with Tal? I've tried my hardest to dissuade her from coming with me, but she's stuck to me like a shadow since I met her."

She glanced at the sleeping woman and dropped her hand. "She's looking for adventure. And something else, I think. For now, she hopes to find that with you."

Eris grumbled, regretting walking into the Crosseyed Eggy that day. Below, tentacles twitched, then swayed. "Looks like Olagkoa is beginning to move again. Better wake the others."

"Why? Do you think it might be more successful this time?"

"No." Eris allowed himself a slight smile. "But it is satisfying to see it continue to fail after all it has put us through."

They watched as the wall of flesh shoved itself into motion. But it didn't head toward the gate. Instead, the Shells, which had gone dormant as well, began moving again.

Ranin leaned out farther, jaw dropping. The creature wasn't attempting another assault. It was marching southeast, following the river. Behind it, the Shells reformed in tight ranks, four abreast, save for the egyzemor and erdi'zal corpses, which took up two places. The eight undead townsfolk fell into formation at the back.

Olagkoa led them away from the city. Kridmont's soldiers tensed, believing it might be preparing to test the city's walls for another way in. But it continued on, its army marching behind it.

Althar ordered the archers to the rear wall while Eris and Ranin shook the others awake. They scrambled to their feet, with Tal sprinting to the crenellations to look below. "It's moving off!"

Farla and Holfast quickly joined her. "It is!" the latter shouted. "We defeated it!"

"More like outlasted it," Ranin said. "But I'm willing to take the victory!"

Holfast watched the creatures retreat, his mind running through calculations. "It appears to be making its way down the river. If its goal is indeed to gain more soldiers, the next stop will be Stegate."

Eris's lips tightened in resolve. "Then that's our destination, too."

"Warning everyone in its path again," Ranin added.

He nodded. "That is the mission."

Farla huffed, then clapped her hands. "Rest time over, people. Ranin and I will get the horses."

"I'll inform Althar of our intent." Eris turned and scanned the upper walls for the captain. "Perhaps she will have some advice for the route."

Tal smirked. "Monster hunters. Heroes of the Siege of Kridmont. The Shell Patrol rides again!"

The man grinned at her levity. *Maybe Ranin was right, and she seeks adventure.* The mission stood clear. This offered them an opportunity. The Abomination still lived, but it no longer besieged the city. They would pursue it. They would warn Stegate. And then, they would face it again — on their terms, not its. "Go!" he commanded, his voice firm as he pointed southeast. "Stegate awaits."

JOICE NILADO LAY sprawled out on the cot in one of Zatreus's dungeon cells, the stiff straw mattress making her back itch as she muttered to herself. Not that it mattered. There wasn't a soul left to hear her, even if she shouted. The former Matron, for the first time in decades, had no one hanging on her words, awaiting her orders, or looking to her for guidance.

Her abrupt plummet in status, from the city's second most powerful individual to an imprisoned criminal, would have demoralized most. But Nilado hadn't reached her position by giving in to bouts of pity or self-doubt. Since her incarceration, she had kept her spirits aloft by coming up with revenge scenarios to enact against the High Monarch. In the last two days, nearly fifty different ideas had passed through her mind, each explored in loving detail.

Her latest and current favorite imagined the woman growing so rich off bisegus cloth that she bought all of Zatreus and banished Lightreaver to the Racina Mire. Most of the others involved inflicting torture or death upon the High Monarch, but this last one left her only exiled in the deadly swamp. Nilado relished the image of her boss sinking into the muck, calling for help while she laughed from the bank.

Despite all her mental bravado, reality crept in during quiet moments, and with it a chill. She had perpetrated multiple acts against the city which Lightreaver now knew. She had also committed at least a dozen criminal acts during her tenure in Zatreus. The torturing of those who defied her was among them, but not the worst. Nilado understood the High Monarch would order her execution as soon as she found the time.

Her inevitable demise was just an item on an agenda.

She sighed, a low, heavy sound of regret that rumbled through her plump flesh. A thick arm flopped over her eyes, more from hopelessness than to block out the dim light.

"I never thought I'd see you giving up."

The voice startled Nilado, and she pulled herself to a sitting position with a grunt. At her cell door were two guards, a human female and a male erdi'zal. "I'm merely resting my eyes, Bathilda," she told the woman. Only then did she notice the immense ring of keys in her hands. "What took you so long? I've been stuck in this pit for two days!"

"We couldn't just barge in, Your Opulence." Bathilda fumbled through the keys. "We needed time to plan."

"I doubt that," Nilado snapped as she watched the guard struggle to open the door. "There isn't enough intelligence between the two of you to fill a thimble."

"Always so kind, she is," Denis simpered. "We must move fast. There is a cart waiting for us down the street."

"What about the guards?"

"Gone, but not for long," Bathilda said, trying another key. "We told them Ludholm was attacking from the eastern gate. That emptied the prisons, but they'll be back." The lock clicked, and she yanked the door open with a grin.

Her success received no praise from Nilado, who shoved her way past the pair and headed for the entrance. "Then what are we doing here yammering? Take me away from here." She stomped her feet furiously against the stones as she spat out one last curse. "We're finished with Zatreus. May the city fall into the abyss."

AS THE SUN dipped below the trees, Leda, Wynna, Erling, and Malwin sat around a fire, gnawing quietly at their rations. Cutie snored softly from somewhere deep inside his mistress's hair, while Graypaw curled up in the egyzemor's lap. Shimi Zar, in her female human form, dropped down beside them, her face somber. "You were right. The wolves are back."

They had reached the edge of a dense forest, larger than any of the other clusters of trees they passed during their journey. With a small stream nearby providing fresh water, it seemed like a comfortable place to camp for the night. The location provided some cover from rain and, if needed, shelter from the wind. It did nothing to deter the augur wolves, though.

The pack had followed them for three days, ever since they crossed the river at Longbridge. Wynna didn't need Shimi Zar's confirmation of their presence. She could sense them nearby. Most of those nights, vivid dreams plagued the woman. Terrifying dreams. "I told you," she grumbled. The recurring visions left her so weary, her usual fury lay smoldering.

"It seems the auger wolves have expanded their hunting grounds westward," Erling observed. "I wonder what is the cause of this change."

"Maybe they are running away from the creature," Leda suggested, "like those groups of villagers." During their trek west, they had approached a caravan of a few dozen farmers and fishermen with their spouses and children. Shimi Zar had quickly changed to her human form, certain that seeing her as an adartigra would have terrified them and had Malwin pull their cart for a while. Erling padded ahead and learned they were fleeing their homes. Some were from the outer settlements around Zatreus, some were from the city itself. All of them wanted to be far from the monstrosity that had come down from Talidith, as well as the war.

The companions didn't stay with the refugees, though. They avoided most villages, sticking to the more isolated routes. Tiger Shimi Zar would be a horrific sight. The fact that the huge cat was really a bisegus would probably have been even worse.

Wynna knew why the wolves were there, but kept her mouth shut. They were there for her. When the group initially became aware of the gray beasts, she feared they had come to devour them, taking the chance they missed when they first crept near several nights ago.

After a night of their presence, she wished they *would* eat her.

More nightmares than dreams, her visions were filled with the same figure in a hooded cloak from her initial vision a week before in the Headwaters Forest. There was no clue as to who they were or even if they were male or female. But in every scene that played out, the individual tended to a wounded or nearly dead person. After a brief time, the prone body would abruptly open its eyes, sometimes sitting up, its wounds gone.

Then Wynna would wake, shaken to her core and terrified of what it might mean. She didn't know why the images scared her. Her main reason for coming on the journey was to find a method to revive her dead mother. Wasn't that, in some way, what she was seeing?

She hated it, though. Every second of it. The figure, whoever it was, was evil. She sensed it, even in the dreams.

"Mal, can you add more wood to the fire?" Leda asked, breaking the woman out of her thoughts. "Wynna is shivering."

"I'm alright," she lied as the egyzemor shoved one of the branches they collected when they made camp into the flames, moving carefully to avoid waking the cat. She wasn't about to tell them the cause of her trembling had nothing to do with the chilled night air. They were the weird ones, not her.

But Shimi Zar mistook her shaking for something else. "Don't be afraid. I'm guessing they are keeping their distance because of the tiger. Even if they don't see it, they know there is one among us."

"Could you fight them off if they did attack?" Leda asked.

"Malwin would probably be better for that," the bisegus replied, drawing a smile from the egyzemor. "I'm more for show, but he has real strength."

"As I explained before, they don't usually attack people," Erling told them, a bit of irritation creeping into his voice at his word not being believed. "Besides, we are almost to the Trideen Highlands. We should be there by the evening, two days from now. I am nearly certain they will not follow us there, not with so many other predators roaming about."

"Nearly certain," Wynna muttered. "That is *so* reassuring." She felt they would never stop following her, so his words offered no comfort.

A low growl rumbled from outside the clearing, a sound so deep it vibrated in Wynna's chest. It wasn't a challenge, not exactly. More like an acknowledgment. The firelight flickered, revealing nothing in the dense shadows beyond the trees, but Wynna felt their eyes on her, burning like embers in the darkness.

"They're closer than before," Shimi Zar whispered, sounding uncommonly nervous, considering her ability to shapeshift into a fiercer creature.

Erling, finally sensing the shift in the atmosphere, stood up, reaching for his bow. "Perhaps a watch is in order," he said, his voice taut. "Two-hour shifts. I'll take the first."

Leda nodded, pulling a worn blanket tighter around her shoulders. Malwin, ever alert, gently shifted Graypaw from his lap and rose to his feet, stretching his massive frame.

Wynna remained seated, staring into the flames. The growl confirmed her worst fears. They weren't merely following. They were waiting. Waiting for her. The hooded figure in her dreams, the one who healed the dying, was somehow connected to these wolves. She didn't explain how, but she knew it in her heart.

"Wynna?" Leda's voice was gentle, concerned. "Are you alright?"

The woman forced a weak smile. "Just tired," she mumbled. She couldn't tell them the truth. They wouldn't understand. They would probably fear her, just like she feared herself.

She pulled one of her blankets close and lay down on her side, not wishing to move further from the protective fire. As Erling took his position at the edge of the clearing, his silhouette a dark sentinel against the dimming light, Wynna closed her eyes. Sleep would bring no rest, only more nightmares. She could already feel the familiar pull of the dream, the hooded figure, the dying.

She shivered again, icy dread gripping her heart. She was the key, she realized with growing horror. The sacrifice. The wolves weren't just following her — they were leading her somewhere. To the mysterious individual. To her destiny. A destiny she felt in her soul lay steeped in darkness.

The fire crackled, a small defiant spark against the encroaching night. But Wynna knew, with a certainty that chilled her to the bone, that the darkness was coming. And it was coming for her.

ANOTHER CARAVAN, LARGER and slower-moving than the one Leda's group had seen, lumbered toward Drulon's eastern gate. A dozen wagons creaked under salvaged possessions while horses strained with exhaustion.

Coming up at the rear, Sarvendor of the Winged Slopes, still wrapped in the oversized cloak he wore as a disguise, encouraged the animal pulling his own cart forward with the others. His devoted follower, Ki Kamaz, lay curled up in the back, her tiny blonde-haired form hidden under the canvas tarp. Squeegy, her fierce, feline-like companion, snuggled up at her side, emitting soft, rumbling snores.

Ganu Burein, a former citizen of Talidith before Hamund banished him, slumped beside the voladorm, his expression etched with the weight of exile and revelation alike. His eyes, once alight with the pride of his homeland, now smoldered with something darker — a mingling of sorrow, resentment, and the cold certainty of truth. After Sarvendor tricked him into poisoning Talidith's population in Zatreus, the two had fought. The man lost, but was brought along on their journey, with the cult leader hoping to still find a use for the broken individual.

Sarvendor was in a better frame of mind. During the long trek from city to city, he had taken a rare introspective view of events. His introductory meeting with the creature had been less glorious than he expected, but he walked away from it under his own control and aided Olagkoa's escape from Zatreus. That assistance, however, led to his humiliating arrest and imprisonment. With the aid of a fellow cultist, he escaped first the dungeon, then the kingdom, with most of his belongings, as well as enough supplies to bring them to Drulon's border.

The entire ordeal ought to have enraged him, or at least broken his morale. For a time, he'd been angry. When they found and joined the caravan, however, he saw his chance to start fresh. The refugees, with their despair and displacement, were ripe for the message he carried. It shouldn't take too much to convert them to Nizlan's cause.

To keep the refugees uncomfortable, the voladorm hid his supplies, doling them out carefully among himself, Burein, Kamaz, and her pet, while the other travelers needed to ration what little food they had brought among them.

The group stopped in several villages and towns along the way, sometimes begging, sometimes bartering, for food and spreading word of the horrors they had seen. Many were of the mind that the explosion meant the return of the monster. Sarvendor watched with self-satisfied delight. The work had begun without him.

As they waited for the city's authorities to emerge and deal with them, Sarvendor saw another opportunity. "Come," he said to Burein and the stirring Kamaz, then dropped the reins and hopped down.

"Good people of Drulon and Zatreus, rejoice, for I bring you grand news!" he began, raising his voice so all could hear as he strode to the head of the caravan. The more who could see him directly, the more he might persuade. "Time of retribution is upon us all! For too long, you have suffered in silence while privileged few hoard wealth and power! They feast while you starve. They live in luxury while you toil in squalor. But I tell you, time for justice is at hand!"

He did not receive an immediate response from the bedraggled travelers, but he was just getting started. "I am but a humble servant of

Exalted Nizlan, God of Power and Bringer of Turmoil. Highest Lord Nizlan has seen your suffering! He has heard your cries! He has sent Olagkoa, his powerful yet lowly servant, to deliver his divine retribution upon those who have wronged you!"

His omission of the definite article—a common voladorm trait—didn't seem to confuse the crowd. A few had already begun to warm to his words, leaning forward in their wagon seats or moving to the front to see the cult leader more clearly. Meanwhile, Sarvendor's companions had come up behind him. Kamaz and Squeegy flanked him on the right while Burein held back on his left side.

The man scowled at the speech, recognizing it as nothing more than a web of lies and manipulation. Once the respected steward of Shieldarrow, Burein now served a glorified faith hustler — and he knew it.

"Join me, brothers and sisters, in sacred Coven of Venerated Gift!" Sarvendor continued, raising his arms wide. "Embrace power of Olagkoa, and together we shall cleanse this land of wicked! Wealthy shall be stripped of their riches, powerful shall be brought low, and those who have mocked and oppressed you shall know true meaning of fear!"

"I'm just here to get away from those corpses what invaded Zatreus!" shouted a bearded man from a wagon a few positions back. "I watched a guard stab one clean through the heart and it kept going. Didn't even bat an eye."

"I saw them too!" chimed in an older woman in a maroon cloak from a cart on the right. "Dreadful creatures!"

The Shells were Olagkoa's creation, but Sarvendor didn't falter. "Wise and Nurturing Nizlan extends his blessing and protection to all his followers, even against dead who refuse to rest. With it comes a brighter and more bountiful future for devout."

"Why?" From the back of a rickety wagon that looked as fragile as he did, an elderly man thrust his gnarled walking stick toward the voladorm. "We're nobody. Why would your Nizlan help us?"

"Why? Why, you ask. Because he knows your pain! Who else will come to you in hour of your greatest need? Bonimen? Nay, he is too obsessed with his great hunt. Diovola? She dare not sully her pretty feathers. Zaljaka? He is on side of the wealthy! Even Szemist, goddess of protection, has not one ounce of time to aid your plight. Only Courageous and Generous Nizlan is brave enough and kind enough to grant you, me, us, what we need." His diatribe against the other gods wasn't just part of his proselytizing. The prayers to the voladorm goddess over his dead love, Narikana, had gone unanswered, setting him on his current path. He assumed others had been similarly ignored.

"How come I ain't never heard of Nizlan?" the bearded man asked, apparently not yet swayed by the speech.

The normally innocent-looking Kamaz adopted a fierce stance, her eyes glowering at the questioner. "Shut it! Squeegy here doesn't like your attitude." Hearing her tone, the animal bared its sharp teeth, tail twitching as it loosed a noise between a growl and a hiss.

Sarvendor held out a calming hand. "Let them speak, Kamaz. Hallowed are ignorant, for they shall be shown light. Other gods are jealous of Nizlan's benevolence and do not wish for you to share in his divinity. They would rather see you suffer and struggle your whole miserable existence."

The older woman jabbed her finger toward Burein. "If it's so wonderful, how come he don't look happy?"

"Right!" chimed in another woman with a tattered blanket wrapped around her shoulders. "Why's he lookin' like he lost his best cow?"

The sudden attention caught the former steward by surprise, and he struggled to find an answer that wouldn't sound like Sarvendor forced him along. Burein could have told the truth and thrown himself at the mercy of the refugees, but he wasn't sure Kamaz wouldn't send her pet to rip his throat out.

"This is Burein," the cult leader intervened smoothly. "One of most devout to our order! He has personally seen power of Olagkoa first hand. He has seen its divinity and it has moved him — body, mind, and soul."

That got a reaction from his audience, with several murmurs of admiration rising from the crowd. Sarvendor knew he had them now. "He watched as Redeemer cast down wicked, as flames of its judgment swallowed unworthy, and as its will shaped fates of those who dared defy it. Burein has felt its voice in his bones, a whisper of truth no king nor priest could silence. He stands before you as proof, a man reborn in purpose, stripped of doubt, and armored in faith!"

It was an impressive buildup, with a rhetorical flourish elevating the exiled man to a position of near divinity. Of course, it conveniently left out that part where he fled from Olagkoa, leaving a sick woman and her daughter in its path.

323

A few of the wayfarers not atop wagons approached Burein, wishing to get closer to him. They didn't speak to him, instead simply casting their eyes over him as if searching for a visual sign of his sanctity.

At first, he shied from the scrutiny. After his exile, being anyone's focus made him uncomfortable. As more came forward, a surge of pride welled up in him. It was a feeling he hadn't experienced since the vornuk assault on Talidith. He was appreciated, even if the reasons were fabricated.

"Do you feel fire in your hearts?" Sarvendor preached to those still with their wagons. "Do you yearn for a world where fairness and equality reign? Then join us, and together we shall usher in an age of divine justice! Let earth tremble before might of Nizlan, and let his wrathful servant Olagkoa deliver vengeance you deserve!"

The voladorm wiped perspiration from his neck with the sleeve of his cloak. His kind didn't usually sweat, but when the fervor of a sermon seized him, it felt as though a fire had ignited within him.

Alerted to the presence of the refugees, four guards emerged from inside the city's courtyard. Two were male humans, their uniforms featuring a long dark gray coat with bronze trim, layered with reinforced shoulder guards and forearm bracers of polished bronze and silver, and white gloves and boots in matching hues. The pair of male erdi'zal wore a similar ensemble with matching colors.

The foursome looked beyond bored, having already processed two caravans earlier that day. Apparently, Sarvendor's performance had not gone unnoticed, as one of the men gave him a hard stare. "Hear, hear. Enough of your rabble-rousing. You lot from Zatreus?" A chorus of voices from the new arrivals confirmed the assumption, and he nodded. "Alright. When you enter the gate, head to your left." He waved in that direction with his right hand. "You will be processed there and are to remain in that area until we find temporary housing for you. Understood?" Another refrain made it clear the instructions were grasped. "Good."

One of the erdi'zal guards leaned toward Kamaz. "Little girl, get that animal under control," he told her gently.

She nodded hesitatingly, as if his size intimidated her, then the innocent expression slid back into place. Even Squeegy had swapped his demeanor, looking no more dangerous than a house cat. "Y-yes, sir."

As the refugees returned to their respective wagons and began rolling forward again, Sarvendor looked at his traveling companions, a rare smile spreading over his face. "We have made a good beginning. Within a week, they will all be devout followers. Then we will begin converting rest of city." Smirking, he sat back and flicked the reins. "Time for living in shadows has ended."

Chapter Twenty-two
SALT AND SUNDER

THE TRIP OF the venki down the reduced river from Ertonbridge went surprisingly smoothly, much to the relief of its passengers.

Under the magnate's orders, the vessel underwent a transformation. It now boasted new stabilizers meticulously installed with a robust crosspiece spanning its width and a sturdy barrel securely fastened at each end. The single sail was also patched up, leaving it free of holes.

In return, a long, waterproof tube containing the required missive from Lord Philip rested tucked away in Mikel's bundle, along with the changeable *nagdami*.

The sun hung low, bleeding warmth across the water as the companions searched for a place to camp for the night. Even with the smooth sailing, communication between them had been reduced to raised voices and shouts. Most of those yelling came from the females sitting on the front, warning about potential hazards in the waterway. When the river was at its highest, most menaces were safely out of the way in the depths. Now, those had become perilous.

"It looks like shallows up ahead on the right!" Savanah called out, pointing to an area where a tangle of plants was plainly visible on the surface, their weedy stems stretched out in the current.

"I see them. Hold on!" Mikel pushed the till away from him, and the venki veered smoothly in the opposite direction. Their benefactors in Ertonbridge had even fixed the rudder to obey commands properly.

"Rock!"

Camille's shouted warning came too late, and the starboard float struck an exposed stony outcropping. It was a glancing blow, but the lateral beam it attached to snapped nearly in two, rendering it useless.

The sudden loss of its right stabilizer caused the boat to veer towards shore. Mikel shoved the till again as the others clung to the deck, but it did no good. "Vyncent! Fell the sail!"

While Vyncent had no experience with boats before they started down the river, he had learned enough to heed the command and pulled at one of the rigging's ropes. The cloth remained full, however, and he yanked harder.

The mast snapped with a dry, splintering crack, sending the heavy pole and voluminous sail hurtling toward the men at the stern. Both Vyncent and Mikel slid off the sides before wood or canvas hit, leaving the craft without guidance.

The lack of a sail didn't slow the venki, however, as it careened rapidly with the current. Camille and Savanah screamed. Stuck on the front of the boat, they had no means of steering the vessel and didn't dare join the men in the water at the risk of getting struck by the out-of-control craft.

Their terror was brief. After fifty feet, the bow plowed into the exposed river bottom that now acted as an embankment, bringing the vessel to a definitive stop. Stunned, the women barely had time to recover before sliding off into the shallow water to aid the others.

They used the fractured mast to pull Vyncent and Mikel from the swift current, guiding them safely onto the muddy riverbank. There, all four took a few minutes, panting and soaked, to regain their breath.

"I'm guessing we aren't fixing the boat this time," Vyncent said, wringing water out of his waistcoat. He had purchased it in Forden to replace the one he had sacrificed in their escape from Ludholm.

Mikel shrugged, rubbing his drenched hair. "We could probably fix the stabilizer if the broken part wasn't currently floating down the river. It will reach Adradena before we do, now. I can't say the same for the mast."

"Am I the only one thinking that all happened a little too easily?" Savanah asked, staring at the crashed boat.

The men paused and Mikel looked at her. "What do you mean?"

"She's right," Camille added. "I saw it. We barely touched that rock. The support should not have snapped like that."

Vyncent nodded. "Or the mast. I'm strong, but that thing is solid. Or was."

Mikel cast a skeptical eye on the others. "Are you suggesting the magnates had our boat sabotaged?"

"I'm not suggesting it. I'm saying it." Camille nodded in the direction they had come. "Those vornuk-kissers wanted to send us to the bottom of the river. And they almost succeeded."

"Now, we have no proof of that," he told her.

"Don't we?" Vyncent sloshed through the water to the venki and pointed to the remaining shaft extending a few feet above the deck. While one side displayed the splayed fragments typical of a broken branch, the other was flat and smooth. "Doesn't that look cut to you?"

"The crosspiece is that way, too!" Camille shouted, pointing to where the second barrel had been. "After all we did for them!"

"The only thing you two did for them was get angry when they suggested we return to Zatreus." Mikel let out a disappointed sigh. "But I admit, that seems to have been enough to want you incapacitated."

"Incapacitated?" Camille sputtered. "They wanted to make us fish food! I'd say we go back and dump them in the river."

"That would only slow us down further. As it is, it will probably take us until morning to reach Adradena." Mikel pushed up a soaked sleeve. "If we head off now, we can get a few hours of walking in before stopping for dinner and a brief sleep. With an early start, we could arrive in the city soon after dawn."

Camille fumed. "I'm glad we smashed their cargo. I hope the Duchess gives them a royal earful!"

"They'll just blame us," Savanah said, sloshing into the shallows to join Vyncent, who was already crawling onto the deck to retrieve their items from the hold. "They might even claim we're dead."

"Let them think that!" Vyncent called out. "If we come back this way, we can make a pointed visit to remind them we aren't."

"I want more than that," Camille replied. "When the river gets fixed, I want to find a way to make it completely miss their stinking city."

Mikel's expression darkened into a scowl. "That sounds like something an arcanist would do."

"Then they'd better be grateful arcana is gone," she told him with a grin, "or one of them just might!"

"WELCOME TO ADRADENA!" Savanah beamed as she led the others along the building facades lining the wharf. "The largest port city in Wayela, home to sixteen thousand fishermen, sailors, merchants, farmers, and tradesmen, and the gateway to the rest of Rapria!"

Unlike cities set further inland, stone and brick provided the base of most buildings, while the upper levels were a combination of wood and mortar. Most also had at least three floors, the city having long ago run out of space in its center to expand horizontally. Many of the tallest were topped with a smaller lookout room and a wooden or iron spire. Above them all sat an expansive building with an enormous gold-painted dome.

The road the companions followed had passed by miles of farms before meeting with the brickwork docks extending to the watercourse. A dozen oak piers jutted into the river where it widened to flow into the harbor. Those further up the waterway were empty, their boats having been moved to the ones nearer the sea. Despite the drop in water level, the Hafugung had flowed in enough to buoy the crafts there.

From their position, they couldn't see the southern docks, which catered to the ocean-bound vessels, but they could make out the masts and riggings of a few ships peeking between the shorter buildings.

Beyond that, a rock breakwater wall extended from the other side of the river, curving into the depths and providing some protection for the harbor against storms. At its tip sat a stone tower, oddly reminiscent of the old watchtowers the companions had visited on their trip down from Zatreus.

As the group neared, bird chirps gave way to the steady murmur of a city in motion. Though the sun had only recently climbed above the horizon, Adradena's citizens and visitors had already begun their busy day. The thick, salty ocean air clung to their skin, cool and damp, mingling with the sharper scents of burning fires, baking bread, and the briny tang of fresh fish. While the change in the river might have a major impact on most of Wayela, it hardly seemed to be noticed here.

"It is a fine city," Mikel agreed, stepping aside to let a bearded man with tanned, bulging arms wheel a sealed crate past. The entire expanse of the landing was a chaotic dance of goods being moved between storage and transport. Shouts bounced off stone walls, carts clattered over brickwork, and the heat pressed close, thick with the musk of sweat.

Most of the wares were enclosed in boxes, barrels, or bags. A few, however, defied conventional packaging, such as a seven-foot-tall statue of a woman dressed in a robe and holding a torch and book, carved entirely out of gray wood, standing near an open doorway.

"The finest," Savanah agreed. "No disrespect to Zatreus, of course."

"Zatreus rules the river. Adradena rules the sea," he told her, acknowledging the hierarchy. "At least on this continent."

Camille grinned as she looked up at Vyncent. "So, what do you think? Bit of a change from Talidith, eh?"

He didn't immediately answer. The man hadn't stopped staring at the throng of people and towering buildings since they arrived within the city's limits. He had taken a while to acclimate to life in Zatreus after leaving the solitary northern kingdom. A week in the wild, with only a few stopovers in other cities along the way, hadn't prepared him for the sheer magnitude of the seaside metropolis. "It's big," he mumbled, his words barely audible over the commotion.

Camille heard him, however, and laughed. "That is an understatement, but accurate. You get used to it, though."

"You've been here before?" Mikel asked.

"A few times," she told him. "I prefer my city of Vellena, as it's a tad quieter, but Adradena is a good place to get lost in."

A crease formed between his eyebrows at her assessment. "That's my fear. We need to stick together. Getting here was just the first part of our mission."

As if to punctuate his solemn words, a loud bell rang out twice, its tone echoing over the metropolis. Vyncent looked about, searching for its purpose. Both Talidith and Zatreus used bells to alert the population to threats. When no one around them seemed to pay the sound any particular notice, he relaxed. "I admit, after our last crash, I doubted we would ever reach this place. But we are here!"

"And we couldn't have done it without Mikel's aid!" Camille cheered. "Thank you."

The man nodded at the praise. "As I said, it is in my interest, too. Even if Zatreus repels the creature, it remains a threat to the continent, and that means my city is still in peril."

"So let's take care of that!" Camille appeared even happier to be in the city than Savanah as she bobbed along the street. "How do we contact the hafu?"

Before answering, Savanah led them to the corner of a building as they stepped out of the wharf section and into an enormous plaza. Much like Zatreus and Stegate, stalls lay scattered about, their owners shouting out the workmanship of an item or the tastiness of a selection of food. A few wagons rolled through, their iron-bound wheels rumbling over the brick-covered streets, pulled along by horses or the antlered *orinib*. A trio of burrals loomed over the crowd at the far end, their backs laden with sacks and barrels, waiting to begin their trek to the outer reaches of the city.

The only structure taller than them was a twenty-foot statue looming over the center of the plaza. *Mwariwa*, the androgynous hafu god of the sea, watched over its people and their allies with arms reaching toward the domed capitol but wide eyes looking to the ocean. Unlike the aquatic dwellers below, its tail remained whole, curled in a loose circle along the ground, giving the sculpture an expansive enough base to support its immense weight.

"We need to find passage on a ship to Redemption Point," Savanah explained, once they were out of the flow of traffic. "It's a series of islands off the coast set up as a rendezvous between hafu and non-hafu. I remember my father explaining a meeting between the city assembly and the local hafu tribes when I was a child. There was all kinds of talk about ceremonies and etiquette."

"Can't we just convince one of the city's hafu to do the meeting for us?" Vyncent gestured to a few of the sea dwellers strolling by. Nearly half of the figures populating the crowded streets were the ocean-living race, their colorfully patterned scales glistening in the morning sun. The other half were mainly humans in skin shades ranging from pale, like Vyncent, to a nearly coal-like darkness, a few tones darker than Savanah and Camille. It made for an odd contrast between the two races, with one kaleidoscopic and the other

331

monochromatic. Among them moved a handful of egyzemor, adding elevated texture to the palette.

"That's part of the etiquette. If a hafu is asked to make a trip to the land, the other party must travel to the sea. The islands are a compromise."

The man shook his head in disbelief. "Seems like a lot of hassle."

"Not when you consider our customs," Mikel interjected. "When strangers wish an audience with the High Monarch, they are brought to the throne room in Wolfsight. We should be grateful that the hafu don't expect us to meet their leaders in their underwater strongholds. If they have such things."

"Leaders?" Vyncent looked at them both. "How many will we need to meet with?"

"I don't think we will be speaking with any, at least not directly," Savanah said. "We will meet with what we would consider an ambassador who will take our case to the current leader. At least that's how I remember the descriptions."

Mikel nodded. "You are correct. That's the way it was handled when I visited the islands. I had an assignment years ago to escort a merchant who wished to set up a new trade agreement with some hafu farmers. The negotiations were successful, which is why we now have *magirini* in the marketplace."

Vyncent's expression of confusion transformed into one of astonishment. "That comes from the ocean? I thought it was fruit."

Savanah raised an eyebrow. "Not quite. Magirini is gandari eggs."

His cheeks turned a shade of green as he tried to recall every time he had snacked on the semi-translucent gray orbs. "Ew! That's disgusting!"

Camille laughed. "Maybe the hafu will have some fresh ones for you! So, how do we get passage?"

"I will find a few who can escort us." Mikel drew a decorative scroll holder from his pocket. "First, I had better deliver the message we carry."

Camille's mirth vanished. "After they sabotaged our boat? Toss it in the harbor. That's all those traitors deserve."

"We made a promise, and I intend to keep it."

"Look for one of the Legates," Savanah told him. "They are the ones with the ridiculously tall hats. We've passed a few already. They act as the eyes of the city council and will deliver it to the capital."

"Good idea. While I locate guides, can you secure us passage?" Mikel looked toward the ocean. "It might be a few days, but the sooner we find a way, we can acquire lodgings."

"I can. Where do you want to meet?"

"The last time I was here, we visited *The Nautical Nook*. It's a tavern near the southern harbor."

"I know it. That's where I learned to drink." Savanah turned to the other two. "Who's going with me?"

Camille bounced on her toes. "I am! Mikel can help those villains, but I won't."

"Vyncent, go with them," Mikel told the other soldier before he could voice his opinion. "I can handle finding the escorts. Meet me in the tavern in an hour."

"Sounds good to me," came the reply.

Once Mikel had given them a few coins and disappeared into the crowd, Savanah led the way to the harbormaster. The southern docks extended nearly twice the length of the Riverwall in Zatreus, requiring them to walk for several minutes until they reached their destination. The comparatively small building looked like it had been disgorged from the ocean itself, its wooden frame weathered and warped from exposure to the damp sea air.

Inside, the archer spoke with a gnarled older man whose skin matched the building's facade. One of his green eyes remained stuck in a permanent squint while the other bulged as if to compensate. After consulting a thick, open tome on a tilted desk, he informed them *The Silver Wind* departed at fifth high. It normally passed near the islands, and for a fee, the captain would make a stop.

After thanking him, the trio headed toward the Nautical Nook. As they dodged and weaved through the seemingly endless tide of people, Savanah gleefully pointed out the various sights. Here sat the bakery where she would buy sweet cakes as a child. There stood the armorer where she got her first sword at the age of nine. Across the way lay the shop where her mother bought her a dress once, a garment she adamantly declined to wear. Every description came alive with the same bright enthusiasm, as if the event had occurred just yesterday.

Camille nudged Vyncent. "I think she's happy to be home."

"What gave it away?" her companion asked. "The huge grin plastered on her face or the nonstop chattering?"

Savanah grinned at them both, executing a half-twirl that made the arrows in her quiver rattle. "I am *very* happy to be home. I didn't realize how much I missed it."

Camille returned the smile. "Do your parents live nearby? Do you want to visit?"

"Their house is about twenty minutes that way, closer to the center of the city." A subtle shift overcame her face as the vibrant smile receded, leaving a trace of wistfulness. "I don't think I should see them, though. Not on this trip. We've had enough distractions to slow us down."

"I understand that. Visiting my family in Zatreus was more trouble than a heartwarming reunion."

Vyncent walked behind them in silence, his expression a sullen mask.

Soon, they reached their destination. The Nautical Nook stood taller than any drinking establishment they had encountered in Zatreus. The three-story structure, painted in a rich crimson hue, drew the eye amid the muted surroundings. An iron weather vane, shaped like a long fish with a curving tail, topped one end of the roof ridge. Instead of the usual square windows, wide portholes punctuated every storey, giving the tavern a distinctly maritime appearance.

The naval aesthetic continued in the interior. Worn planks, recovered from decommissioned ships, made up the floor and walls, while thick beams spanned the ceiling. Fishing nets draped from the corners, lanterns hanging from hooks, and weathered barrels set among the sturdy tables and chairs completed the atmosphere of being below deck at sea. Only the total lack of rocking with the waves dispelled the illusion.

Savanah ordered at the bar for the three of them, which had been designed to look like the bow of a ship stretched wide, while Vyncent paid with a few of Mikel's coins. Camille led them to a vacant round table set among the bustling tavern patrons to wait for their food. Even at the early hour, the establishment was nearly full. They placed their packs under the table, with Savanah resting her bows and quiver beside her chair.

Vyncent frowned at the variety of currency in his open palm. "Why are the coins so strange?"

"They aren't. We are in Adradena. The city has its own currency. I'll show you. Give me your hand." Savanah picked over the coins, fanning them apart. "Alright. This gold-colored one with the old man's head is an 'andar'. That is our biggest coin. This silver one with the boat and oars on the other side, see, is a 'carsing'. You need a lot of these to make an andar. Do you have a — yes, this one with the gold center and silver rim is a 'pitar'. It's worth about twelve carsings, and it takes fifteen to make an andar. And this little one here — "

"Enough," Vyncent interrupted. "Just tell me their worths compared to augers. Now that system, I understand."

"There isn't a direct link between them," she replied. "An andar is worth more than an augur head, but not by much, so it is mostly ignored. That makes a paw about three times the value of a pitar, but a tail is only worth about a third more than a carsing. It is harder to convert a gimpar, but it's worth only a bit less than an augur ear. Comparing it to a gim is easier."

Camille leaned in to admire the coins. "I've never heard of a gim."

"We don't use it often. It's a holdover from before the Skorgan Empire, and the gimpar replaces it. See, a carsing is worth twenty gimpars, but only nineteen gims. That makes conversion easier when dealing with other currencies, like Zatreus augurs and Cartegian ringits. Now there are some complicated comparisons. For that, one andar is — "

Vyncent abruptly closed his hand around the coins and pulled it from Savanah's grasp. "I don't want to know anymore. You can take care of paying for things next time. I just gave the bartender two heads."

"Which is why you got one back in the form of an andar," Savanah explained. "That is way too much."

Camille glanced toward the entrance. "Should we have ordered something for Mikel?"

Savanah shrugged. "Maybe, but we don't know how long he will take. We were fortunate to complete our task so quickly. He can get what he likes when he's found us escorts and has the letter delivered to the council."

"About that," Vyncent began. "What is this council about? Is it anything like the one in Zatreus?"

"Oh, no. I don't believe so. In Talidith, we had the wisdom of King Valeria to govern us. In Zatreus, it appeared to be a joint ruling between the Council and the High Monarch. Here, the Assembly of Adradena makes all the decisions for the city, at least the major ones. Its members are elected by the citizens, so there is little chance of any single individual gaining too much power."

"There was no problem with that in Talidith."

"I wasn't implying there was," Savanah reassured Vyncent. "But even there, your ancestors learned it was best to have a chosen leader, not one by bloodline."

"Dirstim Shieldarrow started that, I know, after he overthrew Sarlan Talidith." The man's tone sharpened. "You don't need to teach me military history."

"Well, the Assembly isn't military. We have our own soldiers whose leaders work with the Assembly, but aren't controlled by it."

"Sounds like they've got it backward. The ones with the strength should be in charge, not a bunch of civilians."

Camille gave him a hard stare. "Because that worked so well for the Skorgan Empire, right?"

"That's different. They didn't — " He cut himself off when one of the servers, a tall blonde woman adorned in a snug blouse and baggy breeches, approached their table with a tray of three dishes and a trio of high mugs. She distributed the items, along with a selection of iron cutlery, and then quickly left. Vyncent stared at the food, wincing. A steaming slurry of cooked mushrooms, carrots, and potatoes covered with thick slabs of turquoise-tinted flesh filled the platter, smelling of brine and lemon. "What did you order?"

"Pickled veshomi." Savanah grinned. "It's like a small gandari. With herbs and vegetables. Don't make that face," she scolded when his expression twisted into a scowl. "Camille and I are having these. Considering the way you reacted to the magirini, I ordered a fish pottage for you." She swapped the dishes around, leaving a less intimidating meal before him. "Normal fish, probably trout or cod."

His countenance didn't change as he sniffed at the pale flesh in a stew of grain and greens. "Why fish at all? I had enough fish in the Undercastle to last a lifetime."

"Because Adradena is the seafood capital of Wayela, and I've missed having it." Savanah adopted a frown to match his. "Just eat it. When we are back on the road with only dried fruit and meat, you'll miss this."

He picked up a spoon and prodded one of the fish slices, its soft, pale flesh flaking under the pressure, a faint steam rising with the scent of salt and dill. "Can't I miss it now?"

"By Diovola's bow! You are such a child sometimes!"

"Stop it!" Camille hissed. "We're being watched."

"I don't care. They can mind their own business." Vyncent craned his neck to catch a glimpse of where her gaze was fixed.

As he did, a man rose from a nearby table where he and his companions had been observing the trio. He crossed between a few groups of patrons until he stood near Vyncent.

"Can we help you?" Savanah asked, not knowing why anyone would take an interest in them. She didn't recognize the older figure before them, but a thick gray mustache and beard covered the lower part of his face while a round, flat cap concealed most of his hair.

The stranger's eyes never left Vyncent. "Eternal circle, right?" He spoke with a slight accent, a shifted emphasis on his syllables, suggesting Waylan wasn't his native tongue.

Savanah didn't recognize the words. Neither did Vyncent. "Excuse me?"

A chuckle escaped the man's cracked lips. "It is alright. Here, you are among friends." He placed a bronzed hand on his chest. "My name is Kadin Fademar. My ancestors... that makes no matter. We, my companions and myself," he gestured to the table where Savanah could see the other men still watching, "only know of the medallions by legend."

Savanah brought her gaze back to the man, searching for anything that she could identify. His attire was little different from what many in the tavern wore, apart from the strange flat cap. Then her eyes found a tattoo on his neck. Three circles linked into a triangle, matching the High Monarch's marking and the design on the pendant she had given the group.

Just as puzzled, Vyncent looked down at his chest where the ornament rested. He had donned it to help make contact with Mikel when he was undercover in Ludholm and hadn't thought of it since. He brushed it now with his fingers, feeling the worn wood against his skin. "Lightreaver."

He spoke the High Monarch's name to himself, but Kadin heard it as well and grinned. "A noble appellation. I will leave you to eat in peace now. I merely wished to say it was an honor to behold one of the oldest families here. If you need anything, simply ask." He gave a curt bow to Vyncent, then a nod to the women before returning to his table.

"What was that all about?" Camille hissed, leaning forward to make herself heard over the din of the room. Her eyes followed Kadin to where one of his companions still watched them. She offered him a weak smile before turning back to the others. "That was strange, wasn't it?"

"Definitely," Savanah replied. "Did you see his tattoo? Lightreaver had one just like it on her neck, and it matches Vyncent's pendant."

"It's not my pendant. You can take it." He began to pull it off when Savanah grabbed his arm to stop him.

"Keep it on," she said. "They think you're someone important because of it. Let's keep it that way for now."

Vyncent met her eyes, then dropped the pendant back to his chest. "You might be right." He let out a heavy sigh. "Why do these things happen to me? First, those creatures tried to kill me, then strangers are offering to help me."

Camille's mouth dropped open. "Happening to you? Last I checked, we've all had our misfortunes on this trip."

"Did you nearly get killed by a pack of savages?"

"Stop it." Savanah shoved a hand between them, breaking their stares. "I am tired of you two always competing. Put aside whatever grievances you have and focus on our goal. In a few hours, we will be negotiating with the representatives of the hafu leadership for an artifact that we need in order to stop Olagkoa and rescue our friend, Aedan. We don't need your petty rivalry on display then or now!"

"I completely agree." The three looked up to see Mikel standing at the table. Beside him stood a pair of hafu. Their colorful markings showed they were male, with one covered in garish yellow and green swirls, the other mostly various shades of red with a single patch of orange covering his left shoulder. "Savanah, Camille, Vyncent, let me introduce you to Krill and Borcus. They have agreed to be our escorts. Were you able to secure us transportation?"

"The Silver Wind will take us to Redemption Point for a fee," Savanah replied. "It leaves today at fifth high. We have another hour before that."

Mikel exchanged a glance with the hafu, and one made a small gesture with a webbed hand — a subtle curl of fingers they used in place of a nod — confirming the arrangement was suitable. "What about the return?"

"We forgot!" She slapped the table in frustration. "We can look to see if another ship will pick us up afterward. Do you think we'll need longer than one night?"

"In the meeting I was part of, it took two. I'm certain this won't take more than a day." Mikel looked at the hafu again. "Can you arrange that for us?"

The nearest, with the orange shoulder, made the gesture again. "One day. Yes."

"Thank you." Mikel nodded toward the entrance. "I am sure you have other tasks to attend to. Meet us at the port before fifth high." The pair repeated the gesture, then shuffled out of the tavern. Once they were gone, he pulled up a chair and deposited his bundle at his feet. "I had the letter delivered, so we are all set to go." His gaze went to the dish before Savanah. "What is that?"

"It's disgusting," Vyncent told him.

"It's pickled veshomi. One of my favorite dishes." Savanah lowered her eyes. "I'm sorry we didn't order for you — "

"I didn't expect you to. Dig in. I'll order my own." Once Vyncent returned the change to him, Mikel stood and headed toward the bar.

"What is fifth high?" Vyncent asked, poking at the stew again.

Savanah picked up a knife and began slicing into the slightly bluish flesh on the dish before her. "Timekeeping. When we arrived, we heard a bell toll twice. That was *two high*. It rings every hour." She plucked the sliver of veshomi between her fingers and slipped it into her mouth, savoring the crisp brine that burst over her tongue before she began chewing.

Vyncent glanced at her plate, then quickly looked away. "So the more chimes, the later the hour. Got it."

"Not always," Savanah said, shaking her head as she swallowed. "There are two bells that mark the hour. A lower-toned bell starts at midday. Up to six rings for each. In the evening, it will be the high bell again."

Camille chewed on a bit of her own food. "And in between those are the half-hour bells, which have an even higher tone and ring three times. We have a similar system in Vellena."

"Yes. When you have so many travelers coming and going, keeping accurate time is critical!"

"I guess." Without any further questions to distract him from the inevitable, Vyncent finally scooped a spoonful of the pottage into his mouth. His wince changed to a look of surprise. "This isn't too bad."

The smile returned to Savanah's face. "We know how to do seafood right in Adradena."

Camille stabbed at a hunk of veshomi, her fork easily penetrating the soft flesh. "Let's hope the rest of our time here goes as well."

Chapter Twenty-three
THE ENEMY WITHIN

SALT AIR WHIPPED her braid and stung her cheeks as Savanah leaned on the upper quarterdeck's rail, watching Wayela shrink to a distant shadow.

The group picked up some extra provisions before boarding the Silver Wind as the bell tolled five times. Their hafu escorts met them on board, bringing nothing except the loose breeches their kind commonly wore on land and fluorescent green sashes across their chests. Used to the cold climate of the depths, most land temperatures didn't bother them. The pants were only worn to appease humans and the other races who had adopted clothing. Even the females went topless, as they were devoid of any upper mammary glands. However, there were none of the taller, less colorful sex among the crew.

Nearly half the thirty-person crew were hafu, with the other half composed mostly of men. The few women aboard wore the same close-fitting shirts and puffy trousers as their male counterparts, their hair either cropped short or tied back in a ponytail like Savanah's.

Both races worked together to handle the vessel, though many were only there to aid in loading and unloading the cargo. While Mikel had paid the necessary fee for their passage, Savanah had inquired about the ship's route. After dropping them off, it would harbor briefly in Samos' port of Kania, move on to Lokvi in Begesh, then head down to Duchari. The entire circuit took a month, barring any unforeseen issues or violent weather. In comparison, their week down the river seemed like a holiday trip.

The ship, however, was a much sturdier construct than either the venki or valupe. Savanah had spent enough time as a youth watching the harbor to recognize it as a northern design. Its hull was rounder, with a raised quarterdeck in the rear and a lower one at the front. The rigging was simpler than the sailboats, with only a single, large, rectangular sail to propel it.

Once they were underway, Mikel and Camille retired to the lower decks to catch up on some sleep. They had gotten only a brief rest the night before and had another seven hours before arriving at their destination.

"We should be at Redemption Point before sunset," Savanah told Vyncent as he approached.

He gripped the carved oak railing and looked down at the water. While they were sailing at about the same speed as their trip on the river, it felt much slower. The only reference point they had for gauging their rate of travel was behind them. "Why is it called that?"

"Hafu mythology. They believe all life began in the ocean, as created by Mwariwa. That was the huge statue we saw in the city. Those who ventured onto the land were corrupted by it, turning away from their god and losing their ability to swim." She recited the explanation like an old classroom lesson. "That's how they explain humans, egyzemors, and everyone else. We've all lost our way, so they pity us. At least the ones who never leave the ocean. The rest treat us like voladorms do. As beneath them."

Vyncent shifted his gaze to the main deck below and the handful of sea dwellers watching the horizon. "So why have anything to do with us at all if they think we are worthless?"

"Because their religion teaches that we are not without hope. We may yet find our path back to the water. The islands are an unsubtle jab. Anyone who visits them is nearing redemption, in their eyes."

He continued studying the crew. A few of the human members adjusted the rigging while a lithe female scaled the ratlines to take a position in the crow's nest. The hafu paid them no attention. "I guess that explains why they act so aloof. I thought maybe we did something wrong."

Her eyes trailed the direction of his stare. "We did. We're different. That's the sin of all races." She sighed. "Sometimes I wonder how we learned to live with each other at all."

Vyncent turned back to face her. "It helps that we didn't try to wipe them out, like the bisegus did to us."

She bit her tongue. *Would he ever accept the truth about Camille if he knew?* "But we did. The Empire waged wars on everyone. The egyzemor, the voladorms, the erdi, and the hafu. The Empire didn't attack any bisegus homeland because they don't have one."

"They never attacked the hafu."

"I didn't think you would know about that." She struggled to keep the sarcasm from her voice. "I doubt that event would be considered a military offensive."

"I don't see the point in studying history which doesn't help me now."

"As we are heading into a hafu homeland, you had better know it," she said tersely. "When the Skorgan Empire turned against the other races, they tried to control them, too. It didn't go well for either side, like the other conflicts. Ships full of soldiers wielding lances and bows traveled deep into hafu territory, killing its citizens and dumping garbage over the sides. In retaliation, the hafu began sinking their ships, punching holes in their hulls, and sending creatures to devour the survivors."

"That's horrible!" Vyncent exclaimed, recoiling at her description.

"I think so. But which part are you shocked at?"

He stumbled for an answer. "The killing part, of course."

She fixed him with a skeptical stare, unsure which side he thought was the aggressor, but didn't press him to clarify his response. "When the Empire fell, Adradena worked hard to rebuild its relationship with its people. Now, every vessel needs permission to sail in these waters, and must stick to established routes. At least two hafu who aren't part of the crew must accompany each ship as well, which is why we need Krill and Borcus." She turned to the deck again, this time focusing on the pair who stood at the bow, their gills open to take in the mist churned up by the ship's thrust.

"Can we trust them?" Vyncent asked, following her gaze.

She gave an uneasy laugh at the odd question. "Why not?"

"Because of all the stuff you just told me."

"That was hundreds of years ago. They don't blame us for what our ancestors did. We've made amends." *Haven't we?*

"The bisegus still hate us, and that was thousands of years ago."

Savanah stiffened. He always seemed to come back to them. "And you hate them, though not a one ever wronged you. Maybe you can learn from the hafu."

He didn't immediately respond, instead shifting his attention to a group of the ocean dwellers washing a section of the deck. They moved stiffly compared to their human shipmates, dragging their mops in jerking strokes, the water drawn from a single bucket sloshing wildly against the planks. "How do you... I mean, they are so..."

"Different?" Savanah offered.

"Strange. They look like a human mated with a fish, and an ugly one at that."

She let out a sharp, surprised laugh, more shock than amusement. "Don't say that around them. Seriously. They are born to live underwater. I wouldn't expect them to look like us. If you're wise, you won't mention that comparison within earshot of them."

"Do they have ears? And why do they live on land if they consider it so corrupting?"

Savanah shrugged again. "You'd have to ask them for yourself. I imagine the same reason the other races mingle with humans and we mingle with them. Curiosity." Despite Vyncent's earlier claim of them being aloof, one of the swabbers turned in their direction. Savanah brought a hand to her head, palm out, then extended her arm. The hafu returned the gesture. "You get used to them. You might even learn some of their language."

The man shook his head. "No, thank you. I did my best to avoid them in Zatreus. I don't want to indulge them now."

Her frustration with him resurfaced in an instant. "Why didn't you say you felt this way before? You've known for over a week we would be meeting with them."

"I figured someone else would do it," he admitted. "And I didn't expect there to be so many."

"You didn't think Wayela's biggest port city would have many of Rapria's water-dwelling race in it?" This time, she couldn't hold back her mocking tone. "Didn't you learn to anticipate an enemy in training?"

He met her gaze. "Then we agree they are a threat."

"That isn't at all what I said."

"That's what I heard." He glanced up at the sun as it approached its midday position. "I'm going below to try to get some sleep. I do remember one should be well-rested before heading into battle."

She watched him descend the stairs to the main deck before returning to look across the vast expanse of water. Since his father's death, the man she once knew had been slipping further from sight, clinging to force, rejecting everything Warne stood for. He stuck tenaciously to the idea that soldiers were always the solution, that might meant right, even as he tried to reject that life.

He's holding on to what he knows. Would I react any differently if my reality were torn away and I were forced into a world I didn't know? He's had a sheltered upbringing compared to the rest of us. His father had shared that existence, though, and not become so close-minded.

Her mind filled with the image of her former commander. She could see his dark blue eyes set into a rugged but clean-shaven face staring back at her. *My dear Rhashar, I am doing my best to look after your son, but I'm afraid he is going to meet a truth he can't cope with. I hope he can find your strength.*

She lingered by the railings a while longer, trying to focus on the path ahead instead of what they lost, until weariness overtook her, and she finally sought a berth below deck.

A while later, Camille jerked awake, the sling swaying under her as if the ship itself had shifted. She had chosen a hammock stretched between a wall and a post, letting its gentle swing rock her to sleep, but something had broken that spell.

A glance about the quarters told her Vyncent and Savanah had finally succumbed to exhaustion and lay asleep in a pair of bunks. Mikel had left, though.

Unable to fall asleep again, Camille climbed quietly to the floor and ascended to the main deck. She spotted the man at the ship's bow, conversing with the two hafu he recruited. She watched their lively conversation and expressive gestures, but they were too far away for her to understand their discussion.

Communication between hafu in their natural environment involved three different languages, depending on distance. Only *wemuta*, a variety of hand and head signals, could be used normally outside of water. There, it was employed along with Waylan or a pidgin tongue to approximate their underwater vocalizations.

She moved to the gunwale and stared at the waves. After five hours at sea, they were too far out to see land in any direction. The only sign of life besides her fellow shipmates was a handful of petrels soaring on the wind currents, their pale, orange bills and mottled gray plumage the only color against the hazy blue sky. A few landed on the ship's deck, boldly searching for any scraps of food until one of the crew shooed them off.

It's so peaceful out here. No one questioning your motives. No need to lie about who you are. She drew in a lungful of the salty air and exhaled it slowly. *No one to break your heart.*

"It's a bit bigger than the river, but I believe this ship is solid enough to handle the trip," Mikel called out, striding toward her.

"I hope so. I don't have an uncle out here we could borrow another boat from." She looked past him to the front of the vessel where Krill and Borcus had returned to their ocean bathing. "How are our escorts?"

"Enjoying the trip." He reached the edge, then glanced back at the pair. "I think the only reason they accepted my request was so they could ride at the bow. I was just asking if they had seen anyone transporting strange creatures into Wayela."

"You mean like the carcass beasts you encountered?"

"Exactly. They've spotted some unusual animals making the trip, but nothing resembling them. It doesn't prove they weren't brought by ship. A few might have found their way onto a boat heading back from Begesh."

Camille looked across the water again. It was the most logical assumption, but every mention of them acted as a reminder of her past. "If they are as vicious as you described, I'm sure someone would have noticed."

"Possibly," he told her, following her stare. "But for the same reason, I don't think anyone would have tried transporting them overland."

She forced a casual tone, hoping to redirect him. "Maybe you were wrong. Maybe what you encountered was just some other wild beast. There are a lot of animals we don't normally see in the wilderness, like sceds, vornuks, and basura."

"I hope I am," he admitted. His voice dropped, hesitant. "But if I'm not, it could mean the return of Viscardi."

"From what I've heard, he died centuries ago. How could he be around now?"

"One of his titles was 'Viscardi the Deceitful'. No one ever saw him die, and we've seen that arcanists can live for centuries."

Camille looked up at him, angered by his line of reasoning. "We've met *one* arcanist who has lived that long. It isn't normal. All others are extinct."

"There is no way to be sure of that. We only know about Nastina because she makes it known she is an arcanist." His tone darkened. "What if more of them are still alive, just in hiding? They could be among us now, waiting for a chance to regain their power."

"What power? Arcana is gone, remember? Nastina explained how Olagkoa blocked it from their use."

"But if they are deceiving us, do you think she would tell us the truth? She's one of them." His voice rose with the accusation. Realizing his volume, he dropped it to a murmur. "What if they actually have full access to it and are secretly preparing to bring back the Empire?"

Camille stared at him, dumbfounded at how far he had taken the argument. "Why would you think that?"

"Look at what they've done in the past," he hissed, taking an ominous step toward her. "The Skorgan Empire only rose to power because of their abuse. Viscardi terrorized a continent. Two kingdoms nearly wiped each other out in the Artifact Assault of Samos."

Unable to answer, the woman turned away. *Why is he telling me all this? Does he suspect my heritage?* "You believe arcanists are evil?"

Mikel seemed to sense her shock, letting some of his enthusiasm wane. "No. I believe arcana taints them, driving them to do evil things. We wouldn't be in the position we are in now if a group of them hadn't abused their power. For that, they deserved what happened to them."

His claim only drove her concern higher. "Even Nastina? You think her wings were crushed as punishment? She *was* trying to prevent it from happening."

He hesitated before answering. "I don't know. But don't you find it ironic we are tracking down powerful artifacts for her?"

"To stop the creature."

"So she says."

Camille glanced at the stairs to the lower deck. She had never heard the man speak like this, and wanted him to stop. The woman wished Vyncent and Savanah were there to hear it. Was it because the others weren't present? Or did he somehow know who her ancestors were? "We won't be sure until we find all the artifacts."

"And what happens if, when we do collect them all, she uses them to take control of the creature?"

"To do what?" she challenged. "Send it rampaging across the countryside? It's already doing that."

Mikel paused again, then dropped his voice. "There are those who believe it is an emissary of a god, sent here to punish all those who have asserted dominance over others. She may fear it is coming for her."

The news didn't surprise Camille. There were as many groups who held beliefs in retribution from the gods as there were who believed in eternal bliss. She was more concerned by the sudden conspiratorial turn their conversation had taken. "Nastina isn't still alive because of arcana, and I'm sure her intentions are good."

"How do you know that?"

"I just do," she snapped. "As for the rest, it sounds like you need to decide if you truly want to be on this mission. Savanah trusts Nastina, and so do I. If you don't, then we must talk with the others when we return to Adradena."

The man went silent, moving back to the gunwale. For a moment, only the splashing of waves against the ship's bow and the calls of the crew broke the silence between them. He tilted his head toward her. "My apologies. It seems the stress of the last few days has affected me more than I knew. Please forgive my foolish ramblings."

Camille couldn't bring herself to face him. *Those weren't the words of exhaustion. Is this the first time he's showing his true feelings?* "We are all weary of this mission already. It's forgotten." She stared deliberately at the entrance to the lower decks. "I'm hungry, too. This sea air gives you an appetite. I'm going to grab a bit of fruit from our supplies. Can I get you anything?"

"No. Thank you. I'm going to speak with our captain to see if he has any knowledge of the creatures."

Camille shrugged. *He won't let that go. At least there is no way he can learn my connection to them.* "Suit yourself. Good luck!" she wished him, then headed for the entrance, grateful their discussion was over. She needed something bitter. One of the nibe fruits would do. It would take time to process all he had told her, and at the moment, she wanted to forget it.

AS THE SUN bled orange across the horizon, the Silver Wind creaked closer to the shadowed islands. A pair of sailors — a man and a hafu — rowed the companions, their escorts, and their supplies in a dinghy to a long, worn pier jutting from the shore of the largest island, then returned to the ship. The four watched the vessel hoist anchor and continue east.

"Does anyone else feel like we're not seeing that ship again?" Vyncent asked, frowning at the waves.

"We won't," Savanah said. "I told you, its journey will last a month. We'll be taking a different ship back. Is that correct?" She directed the question at the hafu.

"Two days," confirmed the one with the bright shoulder, who Savanah decided was Krill.

"Then we had better take care of our business as soon as possible." Mikel bowed toward the pair. "Please inform your leader of our intentions and what we are seeking, as we discussed. We will be waiting here for an answer."

"Understood." They turned stiffly, stripped out of their trousers, and waded out into the ocean. When they were waist deep, they dove in. Back in their own environment, they quickly disappeared beneath the waves.

"At least they won't be trapped here," Vyncent remarked, his expression unchanged.

Camille chuckled and patted his shoulder. "We won't be either. Have some faith."

The group moved further up the beach, the sand cooling under their boots, to an overgrown section of forest. On its edge sat a collection of felled trees covered in slick, sponge-soft growth, stacked together in what may have been a formidable shelter once. Now, it could barely protect a rabbit against a rainstorm.

"That hasn't changed," Mikel proclaimed. "Except perhaps for a bit more moss since I came. This grand dwelling is where visitors of the hafu are meant to take cover."

Vyncent looked it over, then shook his head. "And be crushed underneath when it collapses? I'd rather sleep in the open."

Mikel grinned at his assessment. "As would I. But this island isn't large, and we are more exposed here to the ocean's wind. It'll get much colder after sundown than it did on the shore of the river."

"Then let's make an effort to repair it," Savanah offered. She didn't believe it looked completely hopeless. "We have a little more time before nightfall."

"I was about to suggest the same." Mikel stepped toward the construct and ran a hand over the nearest log. "You and I can repair it while Camille and Vyncent collect wood for a fire."

"Collect wood," Vyncent said. "That's a surprise. We're *always* collecting it. Come on, Camille."

An hour later, the shelter stood upright again — still crooked, but no longer threatening to collapse — while a campfire was blazing in a hole of sand nearby. The travelers brought nothing to cook over it and resorted to their simple supplies for supper by the flames.

"I said you'd miss that fish pottage," Savanah teased Vyncent as he bit off a piece of tack.

"I miss having a roof over my head more," he told her around his chewing. "A solid, moss-free one, not surrounded by endless water."

Once they finished, Camille, Savanah, and Mikel set up their bedrolls under the overhanging protection. Despite their efforts, Vyncent refused to join them, instead selecting a flat section of ground near the campfire, claiming he would keep it fed until morning.

Sometime after midnight, the man woke to a chill. He opened a single eye and saw the flames had died to embers, leaving billowing clouds of black smoke in its wake.

He groaned and considered rising and feeding it as he had promised, until he spotted a strand of seaweed among the coals. Someone had smothered the fire!

A splash offshore, just loud enough to be heard over the lapping of waves, confirmed his suspicion. Adrenaline surged through him as he shoved himself out of the twin layers of his bedroll. Tall silhouettes were creeping toward the shelter and his companions. "We're under attack!" he shouted.

A sharp sting bit into his neck, and a moment after, warmth bloomed from the puncture — followed by the slow pull of darkness. The dart that embedded in his neck held a mild poison. Larger doses could take down an adult gandari. This quantity merely rendered Vyncent unconscious, causing him to slump onto the sandy ground.

A few seconds later, his companions fell to the same attack.

It was over an hour before he awoke, his soaked clothes clinging to his skin. The soft beach beneath him was now rough stone. The gentle tide caressing the shore turned to loud dripping that echoed about the cave. The cool breezes were replaced by dank, mineral-heavy air, thick with the scent of algae and salt, glowing with an eerie blue tint.

Vyncent prodded where he had been hit as he tried to stand. The dart had vanished, leaving a throbbing ache in his neck and a pounding in his head.

"Go slow." Camille appeared, kneeling beside him. "It looks like you took a bigger dose. And we've got company."

His gaze drifted beyond her shoulder. Four hafu formed a rough circle around Savanah and Mikel, long bone daggers gripped in their webbed hands. Another pair, similarly armed, stood near him, poised as if ready for a fight. Unlike the ones in the city, these wore no clothing. Instead, a few were adorned with jewelry made of bones or pearls. Vyncent's hand went automatically to his hip but found only his damp clothes.

"They took our weapons and supplies," Camille explained. "Whoever they are, they knew who we were."

"I knew it!" he growled, struggling to his feet with her help. "They turned on us!"

"I suggest you not insult them when they are armed and outnumber us," Mikel told him. He and Savanah matched their captors' stances, legs spread apart and arms out to their sides, prepared to act if the standoff escalated into a fight.

"What do they want with us?" Camille asked. "They left everything we have behind."

Mikel caught the eye of the nearest one. "You heard the lady. What is it you want?"

"Maybe they don't speak Waylan," Vyncent offered when no immediate answer was given.

"We speak your land tongue fine," spoke one of the pair near Vyncent. By her taller frame and duller scales, Savanah recognized she was a female of their species. Around her neck, suspended by a length of seaweed, hung a solitary orange flowstone. Its interior seemed to ripple like liquid with each graceful movement she made. "You want spear."

Vyncent sneered. "We know what we want. Maybe you don't speak as well as you think."

"Nyara!" The hafu beside her, an older male by the looks of his faded colors, snapped, striking the man's head with an open palm. "Riva speak!"

Vyncent stumbled under the blow, briefly stunned. He reached for his sword again, and when he found nothing, he raised a fist and took a step toward his assailant.

"Don't," Camille mumbled, blocking his path. "They haven't hurt us yet. Don't give them a reason to."

He glowered, his body tense, but her words penetrated the rage, and he let his hand drop.

"Smart." Riva turned to Mikel, the gills on her neck pumping away in irritation. "Spear is *chinba*. You seek other chinba. We want all. Give!"

Apprehension knotted Savanah's stomach. *How do they know about them? Have we been betrayed?*

Mikel appeared unfazed by the request, though, as he straightened to his full height and shook his head defiantly. "We can't give you those. We need them to stop a monster terrorizing Wayela."

Riva blinked, a twin pair of eyelids — one scaly, one transparent — closing and opening in the space of a second. "Land can die. Already corrupt. Give us chinba!"

"Even if we agreed to that, we can't give you what we don't have," Mikel responded. "So, unless you release us, there is no way for us to retrieve them."

Savanah stared at him, her stomach tightening further. *Was he thinking about accepting her demand?*

"Then you stay. And her." The hafu whirled a finger toward Camille. "Others find and bring here. When all chinba have, you go."

"You can't keep us here," Camille protested, adopting her own rebellious stance. "It could take months for them to locate all the artifacts. We need air and food."

Riva pointed to a shaft sloping upward from the ceiling near the center of the cavern. "Air you have. Food we give. Chinba you bring. One week, or you breathless."

"We are not taking orders from you." Following the other's lead, Vyncent squared his shoulders. The female stood a few inches taller

351

than him, forcing him to lift his gaze to meet hers. "You will release us now!"

"Nyara!" The hafu swung a furious hand once more, aiming to strike Vyncent for his insolence.

But the soldier anticipated the blow and caught the sea dweller's wrist in his grip. "I will not be quiet. We are trying to save the continent and our friend."

"Don't provoke them!" Camille cried out, tugging at his shoulder. "Let him go!"

But Vyncent had had enough of orders. He shoved her aside and stepped forward, forcing the male hafu's arm back. Then his scaled opponent exerted his own strength, locking the pair into a test of power — one trained in swordplay, the other forged by the currents. They were nearly perfectly matched, a point each refused to acknowledge as they fought to overwhelm the other.

"Zvak!" Riva shouted. She raised her bone knife, aiming it at the trembling limbs. "Enough!" The white blade dropped.

But it never reached its target as Camille jumped forward and blocked the hafu leader's forearm with her own. The bisegus packed more raw strength than her much taller adversary, and the blow failed. *"Kudza kuvhi!"*

Riva's head tilted in confusion, but she gestured with a free hand a sign of acquiescence and withdrew her arm. Satisfied her directive was understood and obeyed, Camille similarly stepped away.

Her friend's command of their language surprised Savanah, too, until she remembered how bisegus were masters of mimicry. She didn't recognize the phrase, but it sounded like a challenge — a call for honor, perhaps, or to let the combatants fight without interruption.

Can we use it as a distraction? She glanced at the four hafu guarding her and Mikel. While their weapons remained aimed forward, their attention was on the struggle for dominance.

Seeing their chance, Savanah slapped Mikel's shoulder and nodded toward their distracted captors. He understood her intent, but frowned and shook his head. *Too risky,* he mouthed.

His reluctance puzzled her. While there were more of the sea dwellers, the companions were four trained fighters. Surely they were more than a match for the hafu on land, even if their own weapons were elsewhere, especially while their captors were distracted. So why not act?

Vyncent seemed to have the same thoughts. When he glanced toward the surrounding spectators and saw no one taking action, he pushed hard and let go. The male hafu stumbled back a single step, but didn't attempt to re-engage. Instead, he held his left fist with his blade in front of him, then swung his right hand over it, as if grasping the air above it.

That appeared to settle the matter as Riva and the other four hafu returned their attention to Mikel and Savanah. When she spoke, her tone was calmer. "You earned time. Daybreak to decide. Bring chinba, or all die."

"That isn't a choice!" Camille protested, but the hafu were already retreating, slowly easing away from the companions but keeping their blades high. The one who had clashed with Vyncent flashed him another hand signal, moving his palms vertically and away from his body.

Unsure what it meant, the soldier repeated the gesture back. The hafu bared his teeth in a grin, satisfied. He turned and strode away from them, apparently unafraid of retaliation.

"Let them go," Mikel called out, though none of the others had made a move to stop them. The hafu tightened their group until they nearly reached the wall of the cavern. One at a time, they slipped into a narrow trough of water and disappeared.

Riva was the last to leave. "Daybreak," she said, repeating the deadline, before vanishing with the others.

With the immediate threat gone, the four regrouped near the shaft in the ceiling Riva had indicated. It extended nearly vertically for almost twenty feet before darkness shrouded it.

Despite the lack of visible light, the cavern glowed faintly, with pale blue veins in the stone casting a watery shimmer across the walls. The steady dripping of water from a handful of hanging outcroppings and shimmering reflections from the trenches lining the wall made it seem to the companions as if they were underwater, though they could breathe.

It didn't take long for them to examine the rest of the grotto. The entire space could have fit inside the modest throne room back in Shieldarrow, though that hall had taller ceilings. These would force an egyzemor to stoop.

"I would say this complicates our mission a tad," Camille announced as they returned to the center.

"We aren't going to let it," Vyncent told her with a rare tone of certainty for the man. "We just need to find the way to get out of here, like the route they used to come in."

Mikel met his suggestion with a frown of disapproval. "That could be dangerous. We don't know how deep we are, or how far it is to shore."

"It's worth trying, isn't it?" Vyncent insisted. "It's either that or give up on saving Aedan and Wayela. Unless you and Camille are willing to spend the rest of your lives in here."

But Camille had a similar countenance to Mikel. "We can't swim out of here. This is a *bekone*. It will be deep underwater and miles from the islands."

Vyncent rounded on her. "How do you know that? And how did you speak their language?"

"Because I've spent time among them, and more than a casual acquaintance," she answered. "Look, this isn't normal rock. It filters air from the water and exhales it into this cavity, like hafu gills. That, and the twisting nature of the tunnels into here create a natural cave non-hafu can live in."

Now Mikel stared at her. "Why didn't you tell us you've lived among them?"

"Because it is none of your business!" Camille glared at the men, not happy with the attention on her past. "That was another lifetime. And it wasn't with these tribes, so I couldn't give you any more knowledge on how to handle them."

Savanah understood the source of her friend's irritation. There were bigger things at stake, though. "But your experience might help now. If you've been in one, you must know how to get out."

Camille exhaled. "I already told you. The twisting tunnels the others used. But none of you would survive that route."

Vyncent leaned in toward her. "And you would?"

She hesitated before answering, allowing some of her ire to disperse. "This isn't about me. We need to escape or convince them to let us go."

"I think we should do as they say."

The companions turned to Mikel, puzzled by his suggestion. "We can't," Savanah told him. "You said it yourself. We need to stop Olagkoa."

"And I am *not* staying down here for months hoping the others find the artifacts," Camille added.

"You wouldn't have months," Vyncent corrected. "That hafu said one week."

She nodded. "It took us longer than that just to get here. So we can't give in to them."

Mikel took the rebukes in silence, not arguing with their statements. Savanah's curiosity spiked. Why hadn't he fought earlier? Did he know something they didn't? "Why are you proposing that?"

The man looked at her, his eyes almost pleading for her to see his side. "Because we *don't* have a choice. Camille says escape is impossible. Our best hope is you and Vyncent finding the artifacts and earning us some leverage."

"If we can't find them, that leaves you and Camille dead at their hands," Vyncent reminded him.

Mikel shrugged, as if their fate wasn't a concern. "Then at least we still have a chance of stopping the creature."

Savanah could not believe his suddenly fatalistic attitude. "Not without the spear, which they will still have."

"If they have it all," Vyncent said. "We still don't even know for sure this Riva has it."

"Oh, she has it," an airy voice called from behind them, its sweet tone echoing off the curved walls. "And I would appreciate your aid in retrieving it."

The four jumped and spun toward the unexpected voice. In a narrow trench of water near the wall appeared the upper torso of a female hafu. Her pale blue scales nearly matched the cave's interior, making it difficult at first for the others to see her. She might have blended in completely if not for the sparkling pink eyes and amber kelp wound around her neck.

She blinked at their abrupt reaction. "I'm sorry. I didn't mean to startle you."

Mikel looked the most unsettled by her arrival, his brows furrowing with agitation. "Who are you?"

"Oh, I'm Kyla," the hafu answered lightly. "Are you the humans asking about the spear? I heard some were captured, but couldn't be sure which bekone they had been taken to."

"That's us," Camille piped up. She stepped toward the female, neither seeming troubled by the other. "I'm Camille. We are trying to collect all the artifacts. Olagkoa has been freed, and we need them to defeat it. Can you help us get out of here?"

Mikel's face contorted in rage. "What are you doing?" he demanded. "You can't tell this stranger about our mission?"

"Why not?" Camille snapped at him. "You told Krill and Borcus. That's the only way Riva could have known about it."

Her response gave him a moment's pause. "They had to know to plead our case."

"And she needs to know so she can help us!" When Mikel retreated, Camille turned to the hafu. "Can you help us?"

"I think so," Kyla said, giving her a brisk nod. "But I need your aid first to get the spear back. I failed and let it fall out of my hands."

Her meaning finally registered with Savanah. "Are you one of the guardians Nastina employed to hide them?"

Kyla's pink gaze turned to hers. "Not originally, but I am now. Or was." She returned her attention to Camille. "So, will you help me?"

"No," Mikel ordered. "This could be a trap. Riva might have sent her to test our resolve."

But his logic sounded hollow in the archer's ears. "Then she will learn we are committed to finding the artifacts," she told him before addressing Kyla again. "We will do what we can."

The hafu brightened. "Oh, thank you. But I was talking about her." She raised a webbed hand towards Camille.

The red-haired woman needed no convincing. "I say yes!"

"I said, don't trust her!" Mikel roared, reaching for Camille as she strode forward.

The woman dodged his lunge, but he didn't avoid Savanah's. "Come with me now," she demanded, yanking at the man's arm. "Vyncent, you too. I need you."

Mikel scowled, but let her lead them a short distance from Camille and Kyla. When they were out of earshot, she released him from her grip, but not her fury. "You need to tell me what is going on here," she spat. "Camille is right. Riva and her crew could only have learned about our mission from Krill and Borcus. Who are they?"

"No one special," came the growled answer, obviously not happy about being ordered about or questioned. "Just some hafu I found in Adradena to escort us, like I said I would do. I'm more concerned about the appearance of this stranger."

"A stranger who claims to be one of the guardians," she said, her gaze fixed on the man. "Did you mention anything about them to our escorts?"

For the first time since they had met, the soldier looked genuinely uncomfortable. "I might have."

"Of all the — " Vyncent threw up his arms. "You try to stop Camille from telling the leaders of Ertonbridge about our task, but have no trouble blabbing it to unknowns you find in the street?"

"Because we needed their help!" Mikel insisted. "The magnates helped us without that knowledge."

Vyncent's eyes blazed with outrage. "Their help nearly sent us to the bottom of the river," he reminded him, his words strained through clenched teeth.

"Only because you never know when to keep your smart mouth shut."

"It wasn't my mouth that got us kidnapped. The entire mission is at risk because of you!"

"So we accept their terms and find a way out of it later," Mikel concluded. "They are a threat we know. She is not!"

Camille's serene voice broke through their dispute. "She is not a threat."

Mikel snapped his gaze to her. "How do you know?"

"I just do," she replied simply, as if her word should be good enough. "We have a plan to steal the spear, but it will take some time. If we aren't back before Riva returns, you will have to stall them."

Savanah opened her mouth to speak, but Vyncent beat her to it. "Back? Where are you going?"

"I just said. To steal the spear."

"But where?" he pressed. "You said there was no way out of here except underwater. She can do it, but you can't."

The archer placed a hand on his chest. She knew how her friend intended to leave, but it put her secret at risk. "Vyncent, drop it."

"I'll manage it," Camille told him.

Vyncent wasn't ready to accept that, though. Too many things had been kept from them already. "Then tell us how, so the rest of us can get out of here, too. Or is Mikel right, and this is some kind of trap? Are you working with them?"

"Vyncent," Savanah repeated, more forcefully this time, "I said to drop it."

A twisted smile split Mikel's face. Apparently, he enjoyed watching someone else squirm under questioning. "No, Savanah. Let's hear her explanation. Tell us, what is this plan of yours? Why does she need you, specifically?"

Camille saw his smirk. In less than an hour, their mission had broken down, the companions turning on each other. One man, whom she had served with for years, believed her a traitor. The other man, who had led them through multiple perils and guided them on their trip, now mocked her. All because of the secrets they kept from each other.

If they already doubted her loyalty, she may as well give them the truth. "Because I'm a bisegus!" she finally shouted. "I'm not limited to your useless human form. Satisfied?"

Vyncent reacted as if he had been punched in the stomach. "A bisegus?" His hand went swiftly to his side, but he still didn't have a sword. The fact only intensified his animosity. "You've betrayed us!"

Camille's eyes performed a slow, exaggerated roll. "Don't be stupid, Vyncent. For once, try to use the brain in that hollow head of yours. You've known me for years and know I wouldn't betray you."

So that was it. The secret was out. Savanah had handled it well when she learned it in Shieldarrow, but understood her reaction was not the normal one among humans. She quickly stepped in front of her friend now, fearing aggression from the men. While she was unarmed, so were the men. "Calm down. You can trust Camille."

"You knew about this?" Vyncent's fury softened into a wounded expression. "How long have you been lying to us?" He turned to Mikel. "Did you know?"

To everyone's surprise, the man appeared strangely calm. "Know? I did not. I suspected it, though."

"Oh, really?" Camille planted her hands firmly on her hips, challenging his claim. "What gave it away?"

"Your appearance. Two people looking as alike as you and Savanah do while not being related is too much of a coincidence for me to accept," Mikel explained, a bit of the smirk returning. "Then you showed up in the river without any sign of how you got there. That sealed it."

Vyncent failed to grasp the man's conclusion. "What are you talking about?"

"I flew, Vyncent," Camille huffed, waving her hands like a bird. "I sprouted wings and sailed across the countryside. All because you insulted my stew."

"You really are a bisegus?" His tone suggested he still held out hope she was merely teasing him.

She snickered. "It's a good thing they took our weapons, or you'd have hurt yourself by now." Seeing neither seemed intent on attacking her or running away, she placed a hand on the archer's shoulder. "Savanah, I know this wasn't the best way for them to learn the truth. See if you can talk some sense into him. If that doesn't work, let Riva have him. As for you," she directed an angry stare at Mikel, "I am going with Kyla. We will find the spear and return soon. Hopefully."

"You are putting your life and ours in danger if you go with her," the man insisted, though he didn't move to stop her this time.

She looked back at Kyla. The hafu, still partially submerged, rested her arms on the cave floor, listening with interest to their argument. She flashed the bisegus a smile.

"You're wrong," Camille told him. "This will save our lives and our mission." Without waiting for a response from any of them, she walked back to Kyla and dropped onto the stone ledge, letting her legs slip into the water. She glanced at the trio one more time as they stared at her, then changed.

Savanah had seen her transform a few times, but this was a first for the men. Vyncent openly gawked, mouth open, forced to accept her claim. Mikel watched with less surprise but a fascination, nonetheless.

Her limbs lengthened, her frame reshaped. What was soft and human turned sleek and aquatic. Plump breasts and posterior flattened. Dark skin, meant to match Savanah's, lightened and changed into a swirl of pale green and gray over smooth scales. Rigid fins sprang from the top of her head and partway down her back. More flexible versions formed at her elbows while webbing crept up between her fingers. Several lines appeared on the sides of her neck, then split open to form gills. The red hair she loved retreated into her skull, leaving just a crimson streak near the tiny holes where her ears had been. Her eyes widened, changing to a deep green and forming a second set of eyelids. The simple outfit of black breeches, verdant boots, and purple tunic she had worn since Zatreus also morphed, compressing and reforming into a necklace of pearls.

Finally, her lower body fused, and her feet extended out into flukes. The hafu they had encountered on land had legs, meant to copy those of humans. In the water, though, those would come together into the fish-like appendages. Being a bisegus, Camille's integration was as thorough as that of a native.

The change pleased Kyla, whose smile only widened upon seeing her new form. "Lovely! Now we go?"

Camille nodded. Without another word to her companions, she slid beneath the surface, and the pair vanished.

Chapter Twenty-four
THE IMITATION GAME

THE FEMALES DIDN'T swim far. While Camille had the appearance of gills, they didn't truly function, forcing her to hold her breath. Bisegus could do that for much longer than other races, but not indefinitely. It was a relief when Kyla led her through a series of tight tunnels into another bekone so she had a chance to refill her lungs.

They hopped onto the floor of that cave, letting their tails swish in the water. Though smaller than the previous cavern, more glowing rocks illuminated it in a similar pale blue.

Despite Camille's defiance, the way she left the others weighed on her. Kyla noticed her troubled expression. "Are they your friends?"

"They are," she confirmed. *At least, they were.* "Two I've known for years. The man who tried to stop me, Mikel, we've only known for a week or so."

Kyla tilted her head in sympathy. When she spoke, her voice dropped to a murmur. "What you did back there was incredibly brave."

Camille sighed and stared into the water. Their tails caught the cave's faint illumination and shimmered beneath the surface. "It was reckless. The woman, Savanah, knew and accepted me. I doubt the others will. Vyncent especially. He already didn't like me."

Kyla watched the light show in the water, too. "Maybe it's better that you told them, then," she said, her tone still shy. "That way, no more secrets."

Oh, if only it were that easy. "I don't believe it matters anymore. We have much bigger problems than what I look like."

"You said the Abomination had escaped. That's why you're here." Kyla paused, her voice retreating once more. "And if you asked me, I think you look quite pretty."

"Thanks." Camille raised her head to meet Kyla's gaze, the compliment coaxing a faint smile. "I haven't taken this form in a long time. Never thought I would slip into it again."

"Why is that? Don't you like it?"

Because I discovered a better place to hide, and a person to hide with. That's over. "I just found another life. One which has brought me here."

"To me," Kyla said, in a way that sounded both hopeful and melancholy. "How many of the Arcane Relics have you collected?"

"Just the silver bow. That's why the creature is free." Camille turned back to the water, but it no longer held her attention as she recalled the events of the past year. "That is a long, sad story. It destroyed Talidith and last we knew, it was attacking Zatreus. We left to find a way to stop it, and Nastina set us on the task of finding the artifacts. She believed one was among the hafu, so here we are."

The other female bowed her head, though this time not in shyness. "Oh, I messed that up. I'm sorry!"

She didn't have the spear. That much Camille knew. "Tell me what happened."

Kyla's tail flicked, creating gentle ripples in the trench that caressed the wall. "Well, I like the hafu. Always have. I thought I would try living among them." She held a webbed hand out and glanced at the other female's fingers. "I suspect you've done the same."

Camille understood the comparison. Bisegus could quickly mimic other people, but those forms would be better matches if they practiced the new body or were around the person often. Kyla's hafu figure was indistinguishable from a true member of the sea-living race. Her own was remembered from another time. "I have."

"It's amazing, isn't it?" the other gushed, abandoning her timidity. "The freedom! The open water! Oh, I don't care as much for the hunts or the tribal squabbles, and I admit, I would love to eat something not soaked in seawater, but still, you can't — "

"The spear?" Camille interrupted her gently. She had felt the same when she first came to the hafu. The ocean bottom offered even more anonymity than the isolated kingdom of Talidith. If not for lack of breathing abilities, she might have stayed.

But Kyla seemed to be unrestricted in that area. Their short underwater trip had been enough to see the other bisegus had either built up a greater capacity to store air, or her gills were for more than blending in with the locals.

"Oh, silly me," she said at the reminder. "Well, I met the previous guardian. He was looking to pass on the responsibility, and since I was already here, I agreed. I learned all about the Abomination and the Arcane Relics and Caster Nastina. I don't know what Talidith is, though. Is it important?"

Her question stung more than it should have. *Just my home for the last five years.* "It was the kingdom built above where Olagkoa — what you call the Abomination — had been trapped."

"Oh, I'm so sorry! Is that where you and your friends come from?"

"Some. Tell me what happened to the spear."

"Well, I assumed the role protecting it. The previous guardian had buried it away in a tiny cave, but I thought that was too risky. What if someone stumbled upon it and took it for themselves? So I dressed it with shells and seaweed and bones. Made it pretty and almost completely unrecognizable, like it was just a bit of sea junk. There is a lot of that about. Then, when I carried it around, the hafu would mistake it for something I found and fancied. Clever, eh?"

"So what happened?" Camille asked again. Despite the urgency of their task, she felt herself drawn to the other bisegus's enthusiasm. Pinning down the age of their kind was a nearly impossible undertaking, even for their own kin, but she didn't believe Kyla was much younger than her. Somehow, perhaps by remaining among the hafu and their hidden realm, she had managed to keep her passion for the world around her. Or had she herself just lost her own when she took on the life of a soldier?

The female's demeanor drooped. "I set it down one day to catch a nap in some comfy sand dunes when someone stumbled upon it and took it for themselves."

Camille blinked. So much for foolproof disguises. There was only one likely candidate for the theft. "Riva?"

"One of her followers," Kyla clarified. "But he gave it to her. At first, I thought she would discard it, but she seems to believe it is special. She has her males guarding it at every hour."

"And now she knows it's an artifact," Camille finished.

"Yes. So before I can give it to you, you need to help me reclaim it."

Then find a way to rescue the others and get back to Adradena. I should have stayed an owl. "I said I'd help, but I'm not sure I can, according to your plan."

"Why not?" Kyla's question was more curious than hurt. "Isn't it good?"

"It will do," Camille told her. "But the reason I didn't stay long with the hafu before was I can't breathe underwater. So I've been trying to work out how you can."

The pink-eyed female tittered, covering her mouth. It was a sound no hafu would ever make. "Oh, *that!*"

"Yes, that. It's why there isn't more of our kind living among them. I had to spend most of my time in the bekones, as other non-hafu do. That's a severe limitation on freedom and no expanse."

"It's simple, though." Kyla bounced with excitement, nearly slipping into the trench. "Well, not really, but it's doable. The last guardian taught me. Come closer."

Camille did as she was told, scooting her hafu posterior nearer to the female. "Closer," Kyla instructed. "You have to be able to see into my gills." After she moved again, the pair were touching hips and tails.

Kyla leaned in, stretching her neck and revealing the pulsing flaps there. "Hafu gills are more complex than we give them credit for but are vital for their survival underwater. The key is to mimic those finer details. Take a look."

Camille obeyed and moved her head nearer the female's throat. Inside the openings, she could just make out a series of fine filaments, similar to fur, swirling with the air passing through with each breath she took. The fluctuating skin folds protecting them made it impossible to see the details for more than a second at a time. "Could you pause your breathing? I can't get a clear look."

"Oh, sorry. It's become such a habit for me, I forgot I was doing it." The flaps froze, and the slits widened, revealing their inner workings. "It will be important to keep that up, otherwise the others will see you aren't a true hafu."

"What would happen if they did?" Camille just revealed her nature to some of her friends, knowing the fallout would likely destroy those relationships forever. The thought of doing it before another race in their homeland sent a chill down her simulated spine.

"I honestly don't know," she admitted, trying to look at her while keeping her neck exposed. "The hafu are funny about things. They think all the other races are cursed by their god, yet many choose to live among them. They tend to treat those who do better, thinking they are working to redeem themselves to Mwariwa, but what they would do if they learned another race was imitating them is anyone's guess."

"What happened to the previous guardian?" Camille asked as she examined Kyla's gills. They certainly were more complex than she had thought. Bisegus were experts at mimicking other life forms, but only what they were able to see. That was usually all that was needed, as it would be all anyone else would notice. It wasn't necessary to reproduce the insides as well. For example, the shapeshifters had their own organs for processing oxygen and could mimic breathing without creating the lungs of a human or egyzemor.

With the hafu, however, their external also affected their internal. On land, hafu gills still functioned, but for a bisegus who could already breathe there, only an appearance of working gills was needed. Underwater, they had to actually work.

"I don't know all of it," Kyla said. "He talked about retiring to the depths, where even the hafu hesitate to go. They didn't kill him, if that's what you mean. So, can you reproduce my gills?"

Camille placed a webbed hand on her neck, steadying her while she focused on the respiratory organs. She felt the female shiver under her touch, but did her best to ignore the reaction. "I think so."

"Good. While I am wholly enjoying our conversation, Riva did issue your friends a deadline. One that ends in their actual deaths."

"I appreciate the reminder. Give me a moment." Camille sat back and closed her eyes. While it wasn't necessary to blot out her surroundings to focus, the action was one of many habits she had picked up from humans. She brought the features of Kyla's gills into the front of her mind, concentrating on the fine details of the filaments, arches, and tissues. Even with her hyper attention to detail and skill at manipulating her own flesh, simulating organs that functioned well enough to sustain her life took some work.

After a few moments, Camille's eyelids slid open, and her gills re-formed. Kyla thrust her face forward eagerly to examine the changes. "Beautiful! You've done a wonderful job. Can you thin the fiddly things a bit more, though? Those are the most important parts." She watched as they flattened further until they were nearly transparent. "Yes! Like that! Now it's time to test them!"

She pulled away, but not before giving Camille a playful slap on the shoulder. "Catch me if you can!" she called out, hopping off the ledge into the trench and vanishing through the tunnels. Her companion followed almost immediately, grinning at her mischievous nature.

Back in the water, the pair raced through the currents with complete abandon. Though the hafu form was not natural for either, its simplicity allowed them to move through the ocean nearly as well as a native.

At a depth of a few hundred feet beneath the sparkling surface, they sped amidst shimmering schools of fish and glided with ease through the undulating fronds of kelp forests. Effortlessly, they skimmed over lush beds of swaying seagrass, like birds gracefully soaring over fields of blooming flowers. Their heightened vision, coupled with the abundance of bioluminescent flora and fauna, enabled them to delight in every spectacle they encountered.

The gills thrilled her most of all. She could breathe! The flow wasn't perfect, and the filtered air had a particularly briny taste, but she knew her time underwater was no longer limited.

Feeling giddy, she sped forward and grabbed Kyla around the waist. The other female collapsed into a fit of silent giggles, letting herself be caught. They tumbled in slow motion over and over through the cold water before coming to rest against the soft floor of the ocean.

The pair embraced each other, eyes sparkling and lips pulled back in smiles no true hafu could make. They remained like that for several moments, enjoying the truest freedom their kind could. Isolated from all others, each knowing the other's identity as a bisegus, their psychological walls were down. That they were still imitating another race didn't matter. Both could let their guard down.

It couldn't last, though. Even that short span of respite stole from their limited window of opportunity. Only a few hours remained until daybreak at the surface, when Riva would be demanding an answer from the trio trapped in the cave.

It is time to go, Kyla told her, using a combination of hand and head gestures.

I know, Camille responded. *You lead the way.*

They released each other and swam toward deeper water. Soon, Camille noticed a dramatic shift in the landscape. The plant life exploded in diversity and colors, with everything from stubby growths similar to grass on land to towering, thick columns of giant kelp that reached for the surface.

Trees grew here, too. Aquatic variants of their terrain cousins. Camille spotted a grove of *hunikuz*, commonly known as swellwood, to their left. Opposite them, a herd of hovhiza grazing contentedly as their flippers guided their sleek bodies easily over the plants. The water smelled fresher here, tinged with the crisp scent of coral blooms and sand.

They encountered several hafu as well, though none paid them more than a slight glance. With a social structure somewhere between the openness of the egyzemor and the tribal politics of the erdi, most conflicts erupted over hunting grounds, not personal space.

This became evident as they passed the hafu equivalence of houses. With no roads needed, residences were placed about haphazardly, with more concern going into the surrounding terrain than relative locations. Some were similar to human homes, with structures made of swellwood or coral, some like erdi huts, woven from kelp and brown alga. Many were simply open areas, like sunfish nests, marked by a few objects around the perimeter. The type of home depended on how much privacy its owner desired.

These hafu were different from those who lived in Adradena, too. Up until this point, everyone they had seen in the city and the bekone walked on a pair of legs, similar to humans. Now, it was apparent that was the exception, not the norm. Those living in the ocean had tails like fish, which is why Camille and Kyla had formed the same. Only those who underwent *nekati*, or 'the halving', gained the ability to travel on land.

As they moved through the water, with Kyla in the lead, the number of dwellings increased, as did the population of hafu. Camille saw that while none wore clothes, most had some adornment. Bone necklaces were the most common, but there were also a lot of flowstones used as pendants or rings. She noticed several had seaweed draped around their necks or shoulders, as Kyla did. A few even flaunted pearl strands, like herself, though theirs were real, while hers were a product of the versatile bisegus cloth, nagdami.

Kyla waved in the direction of a large form in the distance, and Camille followed her toward it. As they got closer, the rear of a sunken ship came into focus. It was smaller than the Silver Wind and probably brought there, as it lay upside down in the mud, with no sign of the rest of the wreckage around it. Barnacles and algae, accumulated over decades, covered the wood, yet despite a few holes that likely hastened its descent, the rest of the vessel remained mostly intact.

Three hafu circled in a lazy patrol before what had once been the door into the lower decks. Inverted and closed, it had to be the only secure location for miles around. Camille recognized it as their target.

The pair stopped a short distance away, pretending to admire a patch of sun coral, their tendrils drifting with the current. *This is the place,* Kyla gestured to Camille.

I gathered that, she responded. *Are you sure the spear is in there?*

That's where Riva puts everything she values.

Then let's get this done. Camille paused while a young male wandered past. They were still using only hand signals, but she didn't want the risk of someone coming close enough to see them. *I just need a little time. Honhur alright?*

A shiver of excitement ripped through Kyla's frame. *Excellent choice!*

Then meet me back at my friend's bekone when you have it.

I will. Good luck!

And you! Camille made a final gesture of farewell before heading upward, her strong tail propelling her toward the surface. That wasn't her destination, though.

Most races on land were limited to travel by ground. That confined them to a very limited region. Even the voladorms, who could take some advantage of the area above through flight, couldn't maintain a lifestyle without a connection to the earth.

Hafu, however, had the unique benefit of existing in a truly three-dimensional space. Not only was the vast floor of the Hafugung theirs to expand into, but every foot above it to the surface. Nothing natural tied them to any plane.

But their kind had learned early in their existence that the seemingly infinite expanse led to a sense of isolation. While hundreds of thousands of hafu made the oceans of Rapria their homes, that was millions of miles to fill. So they had followed the same patterns as humans and erdi, developing smaller communities within the larger territory. This arrangement provided them with socialization and safety. It also reduced their world largely to the singular plane of the ocean's bottom. They traveled in the areas between that and the surface, but for the most part, it remained empty of the sea dwellers.

Which is exactly what Camille needed. The plan wasn't complicated. She had to create a distraction to clear the area around the sunken ship while Kyla slipped inside and retrieved the spear.

They had decided the surest way of clearing out any hafu would be a localized threat. With no walls or other barriers to protect their city, larger predators sometimes wandered into the region or dared the armed guards at its perimeter in the hopes of capturing an easy meal.

Being a bisegus, Camille didn't need to pass through those borders. She could simulate any creature she wanted.

Within reason. Her kind worked best if they had firsthand experience with whomever or whatever they wished to copy. A vague description would never hold enough detail to make a convincing fake. Fortunately, in her previous time in the ocean, she had witnessed a few of the nearby predators up close. She closed her eyes now, recalling the memory, and began the change.

The area far above their dwellings provided not only the privacy she required to transform in secret, it also gave her the space to expand. *Honhuruyerfu*, usually shortened to simply 'honhur', were giant sea worms, related to the mountain-dwelling orifereg. Camille had chosen their appearance because of their size and ease of recognition. They often grew to over fifty feet long and eight feet wide. She decided on something half that length so as not to inhibit her movements.

When Leda accidentally outed her as a bisegus in the Undercastle, Aedan suggested Camille take the form of Olagkoa to battle it. She had explained that her weight remained relatively the same, just spread out over the larger body.

The same issue affected her now. As she poured her flesh into spiny flippers and a pair of giant, barbed claws, she could already feel the

369

current pushing at her expanding surface area. Her eyes fused into a single huge red orb, and a mass of tentacles exploded around her head.

A proper honhur used its flippers and claws simultaneously, the former propelling it through the water, the latter snapping at prey. If Camille had more time to practice with the new body, she might have managed the combination. Now, though, she had to put all her concentration into controlling the enormous shape. Any offensive capabilities would have to be forgotten. Hopefully, they wouldn't be required.

She needed to make one adjustment to the form, however. Breathing was still a concern, and she had no idea how the honhur did it, so the hafu gills she had learned from Kyla shifted to behind the huge claws where they would be hidden.

With the transformation complete, Camille-as-honhur swung her immense frame back toward the hafu settlements below. Her new body felt vast and sluggish, every movement dragging against the water's grip. *If this doesn't work, I've just made myself a very big target.*

It didn't take long for her to learn if the ruse was successful. The first handful of hafu who spotted her swiftly darted away in the opposite direction. They emitted low bellows and wails like whales in their long-distance language, *urikuri*, to send an alarm to the others.

By the time she reached the remains of the ship, most of the hafu in the region had cleared out. A few stayed their ground, though, hoping the threat would pass them by. That included one of the guards at the door. He brandished a thick sword, no doubt obtained through trade with the mainland, as if that would be enough to dissuade the large predator.

Camille spotted Kyla hiding behind a clump of oversized seaweed, waiting for her to complete the first part of the plan, so she turned her attention to the stragglers. With all the speed she could muster, the honhur lunged toward each, swinging her immense claws menacingly.

They scattered, heading for safer water. *That leaves just Riva's male.* Camille writhed in what she hoped was a fearsome manner, then charged at him.

To his credit, he didn't flinch, holding his own defense against the predator. She swung a claw, but he deflected it with the blade. For a moment, she considered trying to bash through the door behind him, but she doubted her dispersed mass would be enough to have an effect. If anyone noticed, it could reveal her true nature.

Then something struck her side. She whipped about to see a dozen hafu flanking her, spears and daggers made of sharpened bones clenched in their webbed hands. *Magtot! I took too long! Let's see if they follow.*

With a final tail swing at the guard, she lunged toward the gathering hunters. They darted out of her way, but not before a few more weapons found their marks. Though she screamed inwardly in agony, she was powerless to dislodge them from her flesh now. Not waiting for more blows, she sped away from the ship wreckage and swam for the outer perimeter of the city.

Kyla watched as Camille vanished into the murk. She'd hoped no one would get hurt. Bisegus were tough, but that didn't mean they didn't feel the pain.

Worse, their plan had fallen short. A single armed male remained between her and the spear, and soon the locals would return to their spot. It was her time to act.

The guard was apparently devoted to Riva, or at least loyal enough to risk his life. That meant only Riva could turn him away.

Still concealed, Kyla began to transform into the larger female hafu. It took her only a few seconds, as she already had a similar form. The last detail required her nagdami to change from the strand of kelp to an orange flowstone necklace. It wasn't versatile enough to mimic the gem's flowing properties, but she hoped the guard wouldn't notice.

Wasting no more time, she darted from her hiding spot and swam toward the ship. The hafu there snapped to attention, lowering his weapon as she approached, accepting at least for the moment, the ruse.

Give way. She added a series of clicks and short whistles, their third language of *Weputar* to her hand signals. It carried with it an extra level of familiarity, and she needed that to pull off her deception. *They are no longer safe here. We must move everything.*

There is no problem. I scared it off, he reassured her, exaggerating his encounter with Camille.

Kyla scrambled for another excuse. *It is the humans. They are coming. We can fight them. I'm not leaving your side.*

She didn't know if he truly was brave, or merely trying to impress Riva. Either way, he seemed prepared to stay, no matter what. She tried a more direct tactic. *Move. Now,* she ordered, gliding closer until she floated only a few inches from him. Nearly a head taller, she thrust her torso toward his face, hoping to further intimidate him.

It appeared to work. He averted her eyes, staring into her chest. But then he noticed the flowstone there, unnaturally still. His gaze shot upward. *What is wrong with your jewel?* he signed.

She abruptly grabbed his arms, pinning them to his sides. Shocked, he lashed his tail at her, but she sprouted tendrils, which quickly secured it. Another tendril snapped out from her neck, covering his mouth before he could wail.

Knowing she could be being watched, she thrust him aside and shoved her shoulder against the door. The knob for it had long ago rusted, and it fell open. She propelled herself with a graceless shove through the entrance, dragging the male along with her.

Kyla shoved the door shut, hoping to gain a little extra time before they were discovered. The cabin lit up with faint blue-green light, startling her, until she spotted a tiny school of glowing lanternfish zipping around the small room, no doubt collected by Riva or her minions for this reason.

Everything of value had long been stripped away. All that remained were the remnants of a table and a half-broken crate perched upon what had once constituted the ceiling. Atop these sat a few items she knew must have come from the world above. A ceramic bottle, faded in color but generally intact, lay on its side. Next to it was a chunk of ore she recognized as *kaserc*, or iron stone. Beside these objects rested a silver crown, elegantly simple in design, exhibiting no traces of corrosion, while an amulet depicting a bird showed the start of decay.

She momentarily fretted, not seeing the object of their entire endeavor. Then she caught sight of it, nearly obscured in a shadowy corner. It rose six feet in height, boasting a cylindrical shaft, while the final two feet flattened into a blade. A solitary blue gem adorned the haft. Devoid of any rust or signs of wear, the weapon looked as though it had just been forged. It also lacked the shells and adornments she had added. That confirmed Riva knew its true purpose.

The male squirmed in her grasp, reminding her she needed to move. Three tendrils formed from her chest. The kaserc and bottle were obviously useless, but the pendant and crown might have value, seeing as Riva had gone through the effort of protecting them. She snatched them up, along with the spear, and tugged them to her chest. It took her a moment to steady herself, as the weapon extended beyond the length of her entire body. Once ready, she yanked the door open.

By then, many of the hafu who had fled before had returned, but she could no longer be concerned about that. She squeezed through the doorway backward, pulling her captive out at last. Clear of the ship, she uncoiled his tail and shoved him away.

The water provided too much resistance for him to travel far, but Kyla only needed a moment to get out of reach of his sword. He didn't bother swinging it, though. With his mouth free, he loosed a series of wails: She has the spear!

Those around them paused their activities to ponder the meaning of his cries, but it was all too clear to Kyla. With a powerful flick of her tail, she propelled herself away from him and toward the outskirts of the hafu city, where she hoped to meet Camille. That was, if her new friend found a way to shake off her pursuers.

Chapter Twenty-five
NO MORE HIDING

CAMILLE CURSED AS she yanked the last bone spear from her side. The bloodless puncture it left began to close as she willed the flesh to fill in. Being highly fluid in nature, a bisegus body was resistant to blades, but that bit of tissue would be sore for a while, like a normal wound.

I'm never doing that again. I was nearly skewered! Even with her ruggedness, she had organs that could be damaged by a strong enough assault. Fleeing attackers wasn't too much of a threat. Despite the vast expanse of the ocean, she still managed to swim headlong into a hunting party. Fortunately, their prey had been a harmless *cryllen*, which only dined on vegetation. If it had been more dangerous, she might have found teeth sticking into her instead of spears.

She'd relied on quick thinking and faster reflexes to avoid it and the armed hafu chasing it. Three times her size, the sea grazer had provided her pursuers with a worthier target, and soon she darted away from them unhindered.

Once out of sight, she transformed into a squid, which posed less of a threat and would be ignored while she de-speared herself. She could only operate a few of the tentacles at a time, so she focused on a single pair to extract the weapons.

This is as close as I ever want to be to mimicking Olagkoa, she thought wryly, remembering seeing the creature similarly yank armaments from its flesh. *But I can see some advantages of the form.*

Once free, she changed into a *hovhiza.* The seal-like animals had far fewer limbs to control, with just the four flippers to propel and steer her way to the bekone. Until she reunited with Kyla, she didn't want to risk drawing more attention to herself.

What if she couldn't get the spear? She mentally chewed a lip she didn't have in this body. *What if she is hurt?* However, the second concern passed quickly. The other bisegus would be every bit as tough as her. Plus, she knew these waters.

The realization that she was lost came suddenly. In her attempts to evade her pursuers by constantly changing direction during the chase, Camille had become completely disoriented.

Panic rose in her sleek chest. *Relax! It can't be that hard to navigate around here. How do the hafu do it? How does Kyla do it?* She rotated her body so she was looking toward the surface. No light from the sun filtered through the depths, telling her at least it wasn't yet dawn. *I still have time.*

So she dove. Nearer to the bottom, there might be a landmark she recognized. It all looked the same, though. Or rather, there were such seemingly random placements of flora and fauna that nothing stood out.

Wait. Isn't that where Kyla and I ran into the ground? It was. The furrow was long enough for her to determine the direction it came from. That gave her the information she needed. From there, her precise bisegus memory would allow her to trace their route back.

She shot forward, her flippers speeding her along easily. Soon she spotted the cave system rising up a hundred feet from the seabed like a stout tree. When she had first encountered the submerged structure, she believed it to be some kind of plant life. Learning that it was truly stone had increased her amazement.

According to legend, Mwariwa planted rocks in the deep sea during the world's creation, which blossomed into magnificent underwater formations. Caves formed on the outer branches, which became the bekones. The plants on land, by comparison, were considered mere imitations of this marine splendor.

Camille's awe turned to shock as she swam closer and spotted a figure heading directly toward the upper region. Though she had glimpsed it only once before, the silhouette was unmistakable. *Riva! And she has the spear!*

She thanked whichever god ensured the hafu was alone as she kicked herself forward. If she could subdue her before her followers arrived, they could proceed with the remainder of their mission. But she had to act now!

Seconds before Camille reached the adversary, she tried to morph into something more formidable, but all she could manage was turning her front flippers into the claws of a honhur. She opened one and swung.

However, the hafu pulled up short, narrowly avoiding the strike. She turned to face Camille, meeting the creature's gaze. Only then did they recognize each other.

Kyla! Camille wanted to cry out in joy, but she couldn't even speak in hand signals with her present body. Only up close could they make out the unique colorations that marked them as bisegus.

Both rapidly changed into their regular hafu forms and embraced. *You found the spear!* Camille signed.

And more. Kyla gestured to the crown hanging from her wrist and the amulet draped around her neck. *But Riva's followers are coming! We have to finish this.*

They swam toward the outstretched caves above them, Kyla leading. Camille found herself grateful for the other bisegus's help. Without her, she couldn't even tell which bekone her friends were in. *Will they still be my friends when we return? Vyncent won't, I'm sure. This gives him a final excuse to be rid of me. What about Mikel? Savanah defended me, but can she continue doing that without risking the mission?*

Before them, the opening to the curving tunnels appeared. Kyla went first, carefully maneuvering the spear in sideways before sliding in herself. *Once they are safely out of here, I'll leave them,* Camille told herself as she followed. *Then they can go on without having to worry about me.*

Even with that decision, she felt a wave of elation when they emerged from the trench into the bekone and saw her companions. The trio had taken the opportunity to rest, with the men lying on their backs, arms behind their heads, and Savanah sitting on the rocky ground, head resting on bent knees. They snapped to attention as water splashed, and the archer jumped to her feet. It took her a moment to recognize that it was Camille in hafu form. A smile split her face. "You're back!" she called out, hastily shuffling over the stone to greet them.

"With gifts!" Kyla replied, waving the spear triumphantly.

But Savanah wasn't listening. She threw her arms around Camille, squeezing her tightly, despite her friend now being a head taller, wet, and covered in scales. "I was afraid I wouldn't see you again," she mumbled, knowing the bisegus would hear her, regardless. "The men were — "

" — being human," Camille finished for her, sharing the embrace. "I didn't expect anything different." She looked beyond to Vyncent and Mikel. Neither approached. *They don't trust me or Kyla, even though we just saved the mission.* She wanted to scream.

"I also found these," the other bisegus announced. She lifted the amulet chain from around her neck and held it up with the crown. "I thought they might be useful."

Savanah pulled back from Camille to examine the items. "You have the spear *and* the crown? That gives us half the artifacts already!"

Her enthusiasm overcame the men's concerns, and they quickly joined her. Mikel immediately reached for the headpiece, which Kyla relinquished easily. "This would certainly make our search easier," he noted, tracing his finger over the metal.

Vyncent's gaze went beyond them to where Camille stood as tall as him. She noticed his stare. *At least he's not attacking me or running away.* "We have to move. Kyla said Riva's followers were in pursuit."

"That's right," the other false hafu chimed in. "We will have to carry them out. Do you want the angry one or the ugly one?"

"Hey!" Vyncent shouted, his voice finally returning. "I don't need anyone to carry me! Certainly not another hafu!"

She tittered. "Oh. It seems he can also be angry."

"Then this is your lucky day, Vyncent," Camille told him. "She's not a hafu either."

"No one leaving. Return chinba." The five spun around to see Riva emerging from the trench on the other side of the cavern. A pair of male hafu already stood ready inside, bone daggers gripped in their hands.

The companions watched as Riva swung her tail out of the water and onto the cave floor. Two creases running its length appeared in the scales on both sides, then twin flaps of skin pulled back, revealing spindly limbs beneath. Her makeshift legs spread apart, enabling the flaps to wrap around each individually. What had been flukes rolled into coils at the ends, bending into basic feet.

She stood with a wobble and took a few steps forward, allowing another pair of hafu to emerge and begin the same process. "You stole from me. Return at once."

Mikel squared his shoulders. "The spear belongs to us. As does this crown. Now leave. You cannot hold us here."

His boldness surprised Camille. *That's certainly a change for him. Wasn't he ready to give in to her demands a short time ago?* "He's right. You've lost. Go."

Riva looked at her, then shifted her gaze to Kyla beside her. Her face contorted into the hafu version of a frown. "You helped them!"

"They helped me," the bisegus replied. She raised the artifact defiantly. "The spear is where it belongs, with me. And I give it to them."

"So we're leaving now." Vyncent's words didn't carry the same level of bravado, yet his nervous posture indicated his need to convey a sense of courage despite his apprehension.

He had good reason to be concerned. While they argued, the full complement of Riva's males from before had reentered the bekone, each armed as before. Two more heads had appeared from the water, signaling more were coming.

The others saw them, too. "Perhaps we shouldn't provoke her," Savanah hissed as the pair split their tails and stood, leaving room for the next two. "Now they outnumber us even more."

"We have weapons, though," Mikel replied, his gaze unwavering from the menacing hafu.

"We have *one* weapon," the archer told him, "Against ten, all with their own weapons."

Despite the odds, excitement coiled in Camille's gut. The others knew what she was now, but still didn't comprehend fully what that meant. She glanced at Kyla. Her new friend's secret could remain intact. "Wrong," she said, then raised her voice so they could all hear her challenge. "You have me, and I am tired of being ordered around."

She'd already chosen her form and began to shift as she stepped past Savanah and Mikel. The ocean teemed with formidable creatures, and it was likely that the hafu were well acquainted with the majority of them. She needed something more terrifying. Something they had never seen before.

Her body withdrew, height changing to thickness. Legs and arms shortened as she hunched on all fours. Hooves replaced fingers and toes, blond wool replaced scales. Her mouth and nose joined and jutted out as ears sprouted from where only small holes were before. Finally, curving horns sprang from her head, ready to do damage.

The ram broke into a charge, straight for the group's leader. Her hooves clattered on the rock floor, echoing around the confined cave. She added a loud bleat to the racket as she slammed into Riva.

Clicks and whistles erupted from her followers as the hafu went down hard. Eyes wide and gills throbbing in terror, they scrambled to get out of the animal's way. But their legs weren't suited for running, and Camille had plowed down two more before her companions joined in.

Vyncent ran toward the prone Riva while Mikel launched himself at a pair of the sea dwellers fleeing nearby, thrusting the crown on his head to free his hands. The ram skidded, then made a dive at a stunned hafu standing in the rear.

Kyla shoved the spear into Savanah's grip. "Use this," she ordered.

The archer took it gladly, but gave the female a worried glance. "Will you be safe?"

Kyla flashed a toothy grin. "It's them you've got to worry about. Go!"

Savanah nodded, then ran into the fray. Three of the males raced toward her, hoping to disarm the woman before she could bring the weapon into play. While most comfortable with a bow, she had also trained in the use of the lances and brought the spear into a broad sweep, keeping them at bay.

Vyncent had tried to grab the dagger from Riva's hand, but her hold was too strong. Halfway to her feet, she lunged at him, swinging wide. He dodged it easily, delivering a blow across her back as she ran by.

One hafu sprawled on the floor while the other wrestled Mikel, dagger raised but blocked by his grip. Another pair of hafu came up behind them, forcing the soldier to strike his opponent in the stomach before retreating.

Camille kicked her own foe in the head as he started to rise, then looked for her next target, relishing the wild chaos the form granted her. It was a simple choice when she thought back to their time in the Undercastle. Leda's adopted pet ram, Precious, had been released among the citizens of Talidith in close quarters to create a genuine commotion and draw their wretched King Grisk out of the throne room. The ruse had not gone entirely as planned, but the chaos had been authentic.

She considered forming only one horn as a tribute to the animal, but felt both were needed in this situation.

A cry from Savanah drew her to the right side of the cave, where the three hafu were attempting to circle the woman. Camille sprang into action, barreling into the nearest and slamming it to the ground.

In the meantime, two more followers had come up through the trench and grabbed Vyncent from behind, each holding an arm. The man struggled to free himself, but the hafu held him steady. Riva approached him slowly, dagger in hand. She made an exaggerated gesture of eying his stomach, then shifted her gaze to his visage. Her intent was evident.

Then she wailed and fell, face forward, barely missing the three before her. An immense orange tabby cat dug its claws from all four feet into her scaly, humped back.

The sight of the feline startled Vyncent, but it surprised his captors even more, and he took the chance to swing one ahead, pulling him off balance. A swift kick to the other hafu's spindly legs sent the opponent to the floor, releasing his arm in the process.

He snatched the bone dagger from the webbed hand and lunged at the first hafu still clinging to him. The male relented, letting go and retreating several steps. Satisfied, Vyncent ran to aid Mikel.

The other man had fallen to a crouching position, arms wrapped around his head, while three hafu stood over him, pummeling him with their fists. Vyncent slashed the dagger across the back of the nearest, causing him to whip about to face the man. Kyla, in the form of the cat, leapt at the leg of another, digging her claws in deep. He swatted at her with his fist, but found his flesh punctured by her sharp fangs. He wailed as Riva had, hopping away and shaking his hand in agony.

As Vyncent struck the hafu facing him, Mikel rose and punched the remaining foe. Both sea dwellers retreated, unsure how to deal with the men. It had been easy to wage an assault when they had superior numbers. That changed when they faced a single opponent alone.

Camille trampled another of Savanah's assailants, but the third had gotten in close enough to grab the shaft of the spear and was attempting to wrest it from her control. Despite the threat to their lives, she didn't want to hurt the male, just stop him from attacking. But the spear was an offensive weapon, and if she didn't use it, the hafu would take it.

Suddenly, the male lost his grip as his body flew backward. He struck the nearest wall, then slid to the ground, unconscious. Savanah yanked the spear away in surprise.

Seeing their leader down, a handful of hafu raced forward, waving their daggers and forming a barricade around Riva. "Get chinba!" she yelled, climbing painfully to her artificial feet again. Blood dripped from the gashes Kyla carved into her back, but she remained determined not to lose the fight.

The other hafu weren't so sure. Only nine of the twelve still stood, with one unconscious on the floor and two more deciding to remain prone, risking Riva's wrath instead of another confrontation with the bisegus animals.

The five regrouped — three humans, two shapeshifters — facing the hafu still standing. Their numbers were better balanced, but that didn't put the odds squarely on one side or the other. There were simply too many variables.

The element of surprise is gone, Camille thought. *Now we need the element of fear.* She couldn't give a warning to the others in her ram form, but she hoped by this point they didn't need it.

Her wool darkened, thickening into fur. Arms stretched, claws split from her hooves, and her maw expanded into a toothy snarl. In seconds, a barlmed, over seven feet tall, loomed where the ram had stood.

Beside her, Kyla had similar thoughts. Her cat had enlarged ten times over and turned a shade of chestnut. The fangs and claws that had been painful on the smaller feline were now deadly. A hortziak.

Bear and tiger advanced on the hafu party, one lumbering and growling, the other slinking and hissing. The effect on the sea dwellers was striking. Three of them immediately fled, shuffling to the nearest trench and dropping in, escaping to the ocean outside. That brought the count back to the original six, with Riva standing front and center.

"We no scared," she announced defiantly. Her remaining followers exchanged uneasy glances, apparently not wholly agreeing with the assessment. "Give chinba or die."

Camille had no intention of doing either. A quick lunge had her rearing on her back legs, towering over the hafu leader. A powerful swing of one of her paws, and Riva flew backward into the males behind her.

The display was enough to send them running. Not even taking time to see if she remained alive, the last five fled for the exits, slipping into the water and vanishing.

Camille lowered herself to the floor. Kyla slunk over to the now unconscious Riva and nudged her with a wet nose. When she didn't move, the pair changed from their animal forms back into hafu.

"That was amazing!" Vyncent shouted. He hurried past the females to disarm Riva and stand over her. Whatever concerns he had about the bisegus temporarily left him in the aftermath.

"He's right. You were both incredible." Savanah stepped forward and looked up at the pair. "Leda would be proud you remembered Precious."

Camille laughed. "I certainly appreciate his viewpoint now. All I wanted to do was knock everyone out of the cave."

Kyla laughed too, her slight, shy giggle, though confusion was evident on her face, despite its fishy look. "That was a funny choice. Who are these Leda and Precious?"

"Friends," Savanah told her, a touch of sadness creeping into her voice. "Precious was Leda's pet ram. He helped us when we — "

"Save it. We've got more company." Vyncent pointed toward the rear trenches where the bare heads of a pair of hafu were emerging. The others looked, and a moment later, Mikel called for them to relax when he spotted their green sashes.

"It's Krill and Borcus," he explained, hurrying over to greet them as they converted their tails to legs. "Have you any news?"

"Forget that," Vyncent snapped. "How do we know they aren't working for this one?" He pointed one of the daggers at Riva. She began to stir, and Kyla moved to restrain her. "How did they find us?"

Krill looked from Mikel to him, as if trying to decide who to answer. "You asked about spear. Mambo Ecthelion knew of presence. Sent *mubatiri* to investigate. Alarm sounded. Followed."

"What alarm?" Savanah asked.

"Oh, that would have been me," Kyla piped up, raising her hand. "My apologies. I had to break into Riva's hiding place, and there was a guard, so..."

"That was my fault," Camille explained. "He wasn't afraid of the honhur." An unexpected sense of elation filled her, and she laughed. They knew, now. For better or worse. But she didn't have to lie anymore. "I mean, me."

"What?" Vyncent looked like he was about to explode in frustration. He whirled back to Mikel and Krill. "Wait, so this king of yours..."

"Mambo Ecthelion," the hafu corrected.

"Him. He knew about Riva and the spear already, and didn't do anything? And you didn't come to help us?"

Krill blinked double lids at him. "Are you not warriors?"

"Mambo wished to see if you were worthy," Borcus said, speaking for the first time since they had met the pair. His Waylan was more fluid than his partner's, and Camille wondered why he didn't speak more often.

"You're joking!" Vyncent called out.

Krill tilted his head, confused by the accusation. "Oh no, he is quite serious," Kyla explained. "We are all *Vaskufani*. Unworthy." When the newest arrivals stared at her, she slapped a hand to her chest. "*Isinachi*. Formless."

That they understood and made gestures to indicate it. "Mambo Ecthelion meet with you morning. Island."

"He intends to meet with us himself?" Savanah asked. "I thought he didn't do that."

"As far as I knew, he didn't," Mikel told her. "Have we done something wrong?"

Camille noticed Mikel had fallen quiet since their questioning hours earlier. The group had fractured, that was certain. How deep did the divide go?

"Mambo explain," Krill replied. "Come."

"Where?" Vyncent demanded, his suspicions clearly not eased yet.

"Back to the island," Camille said. *Doesn't he ever pay attention?* "And we should head there now, before Riva's henchmen decide to see if the nasty animals have gone."

Savanah looked up at her. "You said we can't swim that far. Will you help us?"

"Naturally." *One last time. At least she hasn't changed. Vyncent will barely look at me, though. I figured as much.*

"What about her?" Mikel pointed to Riva. She lay conscious, glaring at the ceiling as if willing it to fall on their heads.

"Leave," Krill ordered. "Mambo deal with."

Vyncent wasn't convinced. "But what if she and the others attack us on the island and kidnap us again?"

Kyla laughed, and Camille found herself falling in love with that sound. "Then they will meet with the teeth of the mighty hortziak!"

After more arguing, Vyncent conceded to letting himself be carried out by Borcus, while Krill would take Mikel. Camille, with her functioning gills, volunteered to take Savanah, while Kyla would leave last, making sure Riva didn't follow.

The humans held their breath as they were pulled through the water and back to the island. There, they collapsed on the sand, gasping for air and thankful to be on dry land again with the open night sky above them.

None of them spoke as they dragged themselves up the shore. The adrenaline had faded. Only silence and exhaustion remained.

They still had a few hours until dawn, allowing them to rebuild their fire and change into fresh outfits while their clothes dried. Krill and Borcus spent the time in the water, a short distance from them, preferring the ocean to the company of the humans.

Her secret revealed, Camille reverted to her normal form, which was still a copy of Savanah's. *When will I find a body that's truly mine?*

She suggested Kyla change to human appearance, but in a moment of solemnness, she refused. "I chose to live as one of them. If I shift back now, I undo all of it." She stayed with her and the humans, but the bisegus pair kept their distance from the others, finding a soft bit of sand nearer the beach. Camille knew neither of them was wholly trusted, and she didn't want to force a confrontation. Not yet, anyway.

Both groups talked among themselves for a while, the space allowing for reflection. Camille and Kyla caught each other up on their escapades, one explaining her flight and struggle with the hafu hunting party, the other detailing how her attempt to fool the guard failed, requiring her to use force.

As she listened, Camille found herself drawn in again to the female's bubbly nature. *I've been a soldier too long,* she thought. *I've for-*

gotten what just living was like. She also noticed Kyla treated her exactly the same, regardless of which form she wore. It had been ages since she'd spent time with one of her own kind and had missed it dearly.

After an hour, Savanah rose and joined them on the beach. She dropped to the sand next to Camille, immediately putting an arm around her friend. "We never properly thanked you. If it weren't for you, we'd be dead."

Camille appreciated the embrace and words, but it didn't ease the fallout of her choice. To save them, she had destroyed her relationship with the others. "Thank you. Kyla deserves most of the credit. She retrieved the spear. I only acted as a distraction."

"Oh, don't listen to her." The fake hafu gestured humbly with a webbed hand. "She was amazing! She drove a whole mess of them away, then led them on a wondrous chase!"

Camille blushed. It was a human reaction, but one she had mastered so completely that she did it now without thinking. "But you are the one who fought one of Riva's guards and broke into her stronghold."

"She has a stronghold?" Savanah asked, a note of concern creeping into her voice. "Is she someone powerful?"

Kyla replied with her shy titter. "Only in her mind. She flirts with a number of males, and they all think she is really interested in them, but it's all hook and no worm." She paused, poking a webbed finger into her chin. "At least it started that way. Now she is looking for something to justify their following her. She somehow figured out the spear has arcana, and began searching for other objects."

"Her 'stronghold' is the rear deck of a sunken ship," Camille explained further. "The doors are intact, so I'm guessing that's where she stores what she finds. Or steals."

"That's it exactly," Kyla affirmed. "Like a *mungani* collecting shiny things for its nest."

"But how does she know about the other artifacts?" Savanah asked.

"Oh, I have no idea," she said. "I can only guess she learned about it from her father."

Camille raised an eyebrow. The other bisegus hadn't mentioned that before. "How would he know? Who is he?"

"Mambo Ecthelion," Kyla replied, as if the answer was self-evident. "I told him about it."

Savanah groaned. "We beat up the king's daughter. No wonder he wants to meet us!"

Camille leveled a stern gaze at Kyla. "Why did you tell him? I thought the artifacts were supposed to be a secret."

"He's their leader," she said. "I felt it would be wrong to bring something like that into his realm without the courtesy of letting him know. He seemed quite keen on having it here."

"Did you also tell him you were a bisegus?" Camille appreciated the female's honesty, but for their race, it could be deadly.

"Oh, no. Do you think I should have?"

"You told Krill and Borcus."

Kyla gasped. "I did!"

Camille stared at the moon's reflection on the ocean's waves. That was the eternal question for their kind. Who could they trust with their secret? So many lives were forced to live in deception, all because of a miscalculation thousands of years ago. Could there ever be a day when bisegus could openly embrace their true selves without fear?

At least Kyla still had the sense to keep her identity hidden from the hafu king. She had revealed herself to her companions when she changed into a cat, though. That put her life in jeopardy now, too.

Before Mambo Ecthelion arrived, Camille had to make them understand how dire the situation could be. She scrambled to her feet, fists clenched, and began stalking up the beach. Surprised, Savanah and Kyla followed as quickly as they could.

As Camille approached, the men glanced up from the fire. Her expression, ablaze with fury, warned them to stay quiet, and they wisely complied.

"You know what I am now," she told them bluntly, coming to a halt a few feet in front of them. "You know how my race is hated and feared by humans. Now you will learn our rules."

Kyla and Savanah arrived behind her but said nothing. With everyone's full attention, Camille continued. "We survive by keeping who we are secret. Your kind forced that upon us long ago. We don't even acknowledge each other, so dire is that secrecy. I revealed myself today, as did Kyla, to fulfill our mission and save your hides." She paused for emphasis. They needed to realize the enormity of the situation. "You will keep our secret. You are never to reveal who we are to another soul. Our lives depend on it, literally. Those are the rules." *I've said it! How they handle it is on them. Why do I feel numb, then?*

She felt Savanah's hand on her shoulder, reminding her that at least one friend stood with her. A moment later, Kyla's webbed fingers pressed into her back. They weren't the ones she needed to impress, though.

Mikel was the first to speak. He still wore the crown Kyla had recovered, the firelight catching it as he nodded. "Well spoken. As I said once before, I've met bisegus before. I have no intention of revealing them, nor you." He gave a soft smile. "Personally, I don't understand the fear. You seem quite approachable to me."

A bit of relief soothed Camille's nerves. "Thank you, Mikel. I'm grateful for your open-mindedness. You give me hope for the future." She turned her attention to Vyncent now, as did the others. *Will he agree?*

The man visibly tensed, but didn't turn away from her. "I appreciate what you did for us, retrieving the spear and helping in the fight. However, you have deceived us. Deceived me. I trusted you, and you have lied to me continuously." His jaw clenched. "I won't tell anyone else who you are, but I will never trust you again."

Camille felt like she had been punched, but she simply nodded. *I didn't expect anything more than that.* "Then I won't put you in that position any longer. Once we are back in Adradena, I'll go my own way."

Savanah's grip tightened on her shoulder as she pulled the female to face her. "You can't! We need you."

"No, you don't," Camille told her gently. "You managed when I was... away."

"You rescued us from the river! We might have drowned."

"You would have made it to shore without me." The bisegus straightened, trying to take a firm stance to match her words. "I'm not discussing this further. I've made up my mind. The men know it's right. They're not arguing."

Vyncent said nothing, but Mikel stood. "If this is what you want, then we will accept your decision."

"We will not!" Savanah exploded. "I thought I had lost you before. You aren't leaving again."

"You always want us to see the larger issues," Camille told her. "That's what I'm doing. We can't continue as a group if we don't trust each other."

"I trust you!"

"But they don't!" Camille threw a hand toward the men. "Look at them. Mikel said he won't reveal us, not that he trusts us. Vyncent flat out claims I deceived him, even though it was to protect my own life." She dropped her arm and with it her tone. "Today showed me how dangerous this mission could be, and we turned on each other in a heartbeat. My staying just adds to the tension. If I stay, we break apart. That's how Olagkoa wins."

Tears pooled in the archer's eyes. "But you — "

Camille grabbed her shoulders. "Savanah. I love you. That doesn't change. But you still don't understand the lives Kyla and I must live. You can't. And I wouldn't wish that on you. Please, don't fight me on this. We knew this might happen someday."

Overwhelmed by sorrow, Savanah could only nod, pulling Camille into a tight embrace.

AFTER A FEW hours, as the sun began its climb into the sky, Krill and Borcus emerged from the ocean near the pier. The companions and Kyla roused themselves when they saw another pair of hafu appear behind them, only their torsos exposed.

"Mambo Ecthelion is coming," Kyla explained, stepping across warm, grainy sand to greet the arrivals. With a shrug, Camille followed, and soon the others came too.

The leader of the hafu did not come ashore, however. Neither did his female escorts. When Ecthelion's face rose above the surface, beads of saltwater clinging to his skin, it was in an area near the front of the dock. The females accompanying him tread water a few feet away on either side. Krill and Borcus kept a much larger distance from their king, and Camille wondered if it was because they had chosen a life on land.

Mambo Ecthelion didn't appear old to her eyes, but there was a stiffness in his movements, even in the shallows, which betrayed his age. His blue and green hues, once vibrant, had faded with time. Like all other sea-dwelling hafu, he wore no clothing, though a circlet of flowstones topped his head, changing with his slightest move.

Savanah and Mikel sat at the end of the pier, legs dangling over the edge. Vyncent remained standing behind them, spear gripped in his hand, while the shapeshifters hung back. *This is their journey now,* Camille told herself.

"Greetings," Savanah called out to the ruler. "Thank you for granting us this audience. My name is Savanah. This is Mikel, Camille, and Vyncent. We came in search of a weapon we believed to be among your people. With the help of one of your subjects, we found it, Your Highness."

The female escorts pulsed their gills while emitting rapid clicking sounds which Camille recognized as laughing. Ecthelion himself wore a smile. "Funny title for hafu," he said, his voice a grainy, baritone. "More low than high. Maybe deepness. Yes. Much better." He paused, signaling the pair beside him to quiet. "Know of spear, I do. Little one told me. Know she *isinachi*."

Kyla's mouth fell open. "You knew about me? How?"

The king emitted a hafu equivalent of a chuckle, consisting of a brief whistle followed by a series of clicks with his tongue. "Smell like *vaskufani*. Tail not move right." His expression turned serious as he faced Savanah. "Now, return spear to Ecthelion."

"But Your... Deepness," the archer began in protest, "We need it to defeat a big enemy that is loose upon the land. The spear was created for that purpose."

"Know," Ecthelion acknowledged with a slight tip of his head. "Your *kukuva* said." He raised a webbed hand towards where Krill and Borcus stood in the water. "Is powerful. So stays."

Savanah frowned. "Is this because of your daughter? Are you angry at us for taking it from her, or are you giving it back to her?"

Mikel stared at her. "Riva is his daughter?"

"Yes. And no, I didn't know until a few hours ago," she replied.

Ecthelion's shoulders sagged, the light in his eyes dimming. "Riva is troubled. *Yaka.* Corrupted by power. Will deal with her, yes."

"Then wouldn't it be better to remove temptation from her?" Kyla asked. "Let them take the spear so that she may find her way back to your ways."

"No," the leader answered bluntly. "Spear belongs to Pedyonema kingdom. It stays here."

"How about only loaning it to them?" the bisegus suggested. Her role as guardian remained incomplete until she handed over the artifact to the party destined to use it. "Just until they take care of their business. Then they return it."

389

"We could do that!" Savanah said, seizing on the proposal. "We won't need it after we defeat the creature. We could bring it right back here."

Ecthelion's head tilted as he seemed to be considering the idea. He glanced at his escorts, but they offered no advice. They were there for company, not counsel. "This possible," he finally said. "One condition."

Savanah tensed. "What is that?"

"You take one of us with you. Protect spear."

"I could go, Your Deepness," Kyla proposed.

Camille felt the sudden urge to hug her. It was a generous offer, but one that the others would never accept. One bisegus would be just as bad as the other. She also had no idea of the perils they might encounter.

Surprisingly, it was the hafu leader who shot it down. "You are not of us. Must be another."

Mikel cracked a smile. Camille had once loved seeing his face light up like that. Now she only felt resentment as he plied his charm on someone else. "Do you mean one of these lovely females beside you?" the man asked. "We would not dare to steal such beauty from you."

That drew a clicking chuckle from Ecthelion. "Not them. I will send him to you. Will be good."

Savanah perked up at his words. "Then we have a deal?"

"Deal. Yes." The hafu leader wiggled in the water as his smile widened. "Now tell, how you get spear from daughter. Must know."

The companions became abruptly silent, glancing hesitatingly at Kyla. Camille realized they were uncertain whether the leader sought the information for punitive purposes or simply out of genuine curiosity. She wasn't sure herself. The bisegus pair hadn't strictly hurt the hafu, but they hadn't been gentle either.

"It was me," Kyla volunteered, surprising the group again. "I pretended to be Riva and fooled her guard."

Ecthelion's eyes lit up. "Must see. Do it!"

Kyla glanced at her fellow shapeshifter, clearly not expecting to transform before the others. Camille gave her an encouraging nod, though, and she made the change. In seconds, Riva was standing on the pier.

"Quite wondrous!" The hafu king clapped and chuckled at the show. "But I heard talk of another. A honhuruyerfu."

Kyla-as-Riva faltered. She had revealed herself to the leader, or rather, had been recognized. Her friend, however, remained anonymous. "You must be mistaken, Your Deepness. There was no — "

Camille saw no problem with admitting who she was here. Half of those gathered already knew anyway, and the hafu didn't seem at all upset. "It was I, Your Deepness. I am also an isinachi."

Ecthelion's eyes locked onto hers. "Show!"

She looked at her companions. The men, at least, wouldn't like seeing her use her abilities. Kyla, however, returned her encouraging gesture. Camille took a deep breath, then morphed her head into that of a honhur, complete with the single red eye, tentacles, and claws.

Savanah beamed, proud of her friend's boldness. Surprisingly, Mikel appeared fascinated by the transformation. Vyncent, however, turned away in disgust.

Ecthelion seemed delighted, clapping his hands again and laughing. "By the shimmering seas! That is splendid! Now do a hovhiza!"

"Your Deepness," Kyla began, hastily changing back to her own hafu form, "I'm so happy you appreciate our abilities, but this makes our human companions uncomfortable." She leaned forward a few inches, which did nothing to close the distance between herself on the pier and the king a dozen feet away in the shallows. "Not all possess the currents of wisdom and depth of enlightenment you do," she explained in a mock whisper.

Ecthelion's expression became somber at her words. "Sadly true."

Camille put a hand to her mouth to stifle a giggle. She touched only tentacles, though, and quickly shed the honhur appearance.

"Your Deepness, when will your ambassador be joining us?" Savanah asked, stifling a similar smirk. However, her male companions scowled at the jest directed at them.

"Am-bass-dor? Oh." Mambo Ecthelion laughed, his expression becoming light again. "You depart soon?"

"We are expecting a ship this afternoon," Mikel told him.

"Will have him then. We keep little one." He gestured toward Kyla. His escorts frowned slightly at his declaration, but quickly covered their disappointment.

The bisegus was completely taken aback. "You mean I can stay after my deceit?"

He chuckled, his tongue clicking loudly in mirth. "You *mudzidzi*. Means much. Plus, help keep Riva behaved."

Kyla joined in his laughter, her own resembling a more human-like giggle. "Oh, I will do my best!"

"And you," Ecthelion nearly bellowed as he shifted his gaze to Camille. "You keep am-bass-dor good."

No. I have to leave the group. "Your Deepness, I'm afraid I — "

"She will do her best to protect whomever you send with us," Savanah finished for her. "We all will." Camille scowled at her friend's intervention, but the archer merely grinned back.

"Then done!" the hafu king declared. "Am-bass-dor will be sent. First food. Will bring you eats for your trip. Plenty magirini!" With the proclamation given, he abruptly dove backward into the shallows, his tail splashing at the surface before also disappearing. The female escorts followed only seconds later, sending more seawater toward those on the pier.

Mikel and Savanah cringed as the cool liquid splashed onto their clothes, but neither seemed truly upset. "That went much better than I expected," the woman said. "Considering the circumstances."

"Speak for yourself," Vyncent grumbled, crossing his arms and staring at where Ecthelion had been. "Didn't you hear what he said? He's feeding us magirini!"

Chapter Twenty-six
BLADES AND BETRAYALS

T RUE TO HIS word, Mambo Ecthelion sent a small feast of seafood to Savanah and her companions on the beach of Redemption Point. A pair of male hafu arrived bearing a wide, high-edged swellwood tray filled with delicacies from the deep.

Kyla explained each item to them, starting with the grape-like magirini. Sliced maku fish, its mottled pink flesh and tentacle-like extensions laid out in a spiral pattern. Other fish, which she guessed were either salmon or cod, wrapped in seaweed, called *hovem*. Fresh crab, steamed by some means she didn't explain, split open, revealing the rich meat inside.

Camille and Kyla took a sampling of the meal and settled a short distance away from the others. Savanah insisted it wasn't necessary, but recognized it gave the two shapeshifters a chance to enjoy the company of their own kind.

Mikel reached for the cluster of magirini and plucked off a few. "We probably could have gotten permission for the crown, too," he noted, popping one of the eggs into his mouth.

"Maybe," Savanah admitted. "But it was still better to stow it with your gear before meeting him. If he doesn't know about it, he can't claim it."

"And now, with three of the six artifacts, we're halfway there!" Vyn-cent selected a piece of maku fish. "This will be easier than I thought."

Savanah bit her tongue. Wasn't he just complaining yesterday about how everything bad happened to him? "We couldn't have done it without Mikel. Or Camille. Don't forget that. We owe her more than our lives."

His eyes narrowed as he held the bit of meat just inches from his lips. "How can you trust her, after she's been lying to us for so long?"

"You are not the sharpest of blades," Savanah snapped. "It's human hatred of her kind that forces them to hide and lie."

"If she had told us who she was when she first arrived in Talidith, I would have accepted her," came the indignant response. He popped the slice into his mouth and chewed vigorously.

"Why would she trust a stranger with that information?" the archer countered. "And why would you trust a stranger who made such a claim?"

"Savanah's right," Mikel chimed in. "We've forced them to live this way. It took a long time for us to convince the bisegus living in Adradena to lend us some of their cloth because of the tension between our two races."

Shock crossed Vyncent's face. "There were more in Adradena? How come I didn't see any?"

Savanah stared at him. "Because they are shapeshifters," she said, drawing each word out slowly. "Did you bump your head during the fight?"

He frowned. "I mean, why didn't you have them marked as bisegus, so others could be warned?"

"Because they are harmless," Mikel replied with a shrug. "Mostly. They just want to survive like everyone else. Besides, part of the deal of their cloth was that they were allowed to remain in Adradena unmo-lested."

Now Savanah looked surprised. "Wait. Would Lightreaver have driven them from the city if they hadn't complied? That goes against what you just said about them being harmless."

"Mostly harmless," he corrected. "Animosity between the two races goes both ways. While I believe most want to be left in peace, a few spend their lives in open revenge on us. Like the ones Daymon sent to assassinate the High Monarch. They must have blown up the Riverwall, too."

"All the more reason to keep their kind away," Vyncent concluded. "What if one day, all the bisegus in Adradena decided to take revenge on the city?"

"Then the city would fall to them," Mikel admitted, taking a bit of hovem.

Savanah grabbed a few magirini. "Are there that many?"

Mikel nodded. "A few hundred, at least."

"Against several thousand?" Vyncent asked in disbelief.

"You saw Camille and Kyla back there." Mikel gestured toward the pair seated in the sand, engaged in their own discussion. "Do you have doubt they could have wiped out Riva's forces if they wanted?"

Vyncent shifted uncomfortably at the question. He shot a glare at Savanah. "Why did you tell their king Camille was coming with us? She said she intends to leave when we are back on the mainland."

"Because whether you accept it or not, she is our friend, and we need her," she replied coldly. Once again, she felt resentment building toward him for not being the same man as his father. *But can I be sure Warne wouldn't have reacted the same?*

"I don't need her," Vyncent declared. He idly snatched up one of the magirini eggs before remembering what it was and hastily dropping it on the tray.

"I hope you don't come to regret those words," Mikel said. His attention went to the water, where a pattern of ripples grew wider and more pronounced. Something was coming to the surface. "Ah, this must be our am-bass-dor."

A pair of hafu heads broke through. After a moment, their bodies followed. One of the ocean dwellers remained in the deeper area, but the other shifted his tail to gangly legs and stood upright. The second bore bright cyan and pink markings, with clusters of yellow dots around his stomach and hips. He blinked slowly as he surveyed the beach. "You are the vaskufani?" he asked when his gaze fell on Savanah's group.

"We are," the archer confirmed.

The hafu turned back to the one in the water and made a few gestures with his hand. When his companion vanished beneath the surface, he faced the shore again and splashed through the shallows, surf swirling around his shins. "Give me the relic," he ordered when he reached the sand.

His bluntness surprised the trio, but Vyncent climbed to his feet with the spear. "Not yet. How do we know you aren't with Riva?"

The newcomer regarded him with a disdainful gaze, his eyes sharp and full of silent judgment. "Do I have the appearance of a *mwanaka-para* to you?"

Vyncent didn't recognize the string of syllables, and a glance at the others told him they didn't either. "I guess not."

"Did Ecthelion send you?" Savanah asked.

The hafu fixed her with an equally dismissive stare. "He offered me the opportunity to join as your am-bass-dor," he replied, using the same broken form of the word. "I am Hali."

"I am Savanah," the archer explained. "This is Mikel and Vyncent." She pointed to where Kyla and Camille were talking, the pair too engrossed in their discussion to notice the hafu. "The redhead is Camille. She is also going with us. The other is Kyla."

Hali didn't look to the others, apparently indifferent to their place in the group. "Give me relic."

Vyncent looked to Savanah again for guidance. "Go ahead," she told him. "Did His Deepness tell you what our mission is?"

"You require it to slay some land-bound cryllan or such," the hafu said, accepting the spear from Vyncent. "It should provide me with firsthand experience of life among vaskufani."

"What does that mean?" Vyncent asked.

"Hali wishes to learn how we lesser races live," Mikel explained with a hint of amusement.

Savanah expected Vyncent to take offense. Instead, he matched Mikel's grin. "I hope we are enlightening, then. Care for some magirini?"

The hafu took some, but ate it standing up while he examined the spear, and the others finished their meal. Soon, they spotted a dinghy approaching with a single human man aboard, rowing heavily. A few minutes later, it reached the shore, the bow digging into the wet sand.

Vyncent and Mikel climbed into the boat, storing their supplies under one of the seats. Borcus and Krill stepped in next, settling in near the sailor from the ship.

"We can never repay you for your help," Savanah told Kyla, taking one of her webbed hands into her own. "Will you be safe here?"

"Oh, I am sure I will," she replied. "Ecthelion is a nice enough fellow. I'm sure I will be happy. Especially since I don't need to guard that spear anymore."

"You do not," the male hafu asserted, then clicked his tongue. "That duty falls upon me."

"And you are welcome to it!" Kyla gently slid her hand from Savanah's grip as she turned to Camille. "I will miss you, though," she said, reaching forward and caressing the other bisegus's face.

Camille leaned into her touch with a smile. "I will miss you, too. But I won't be gone too long. Once all this business is sorted, I'll visit."

"Yes, you will. Or I will go on a quest of my own and find you!" The shy shapeshifter suddenly bent down and planted a soft kiss on Camille's cheek. "That was for helping me."

In response, Camille stepped forward and slipped her arms around the other female's waist. "That gives me an excellent reason to come back."

Hali observed the entire interaction with interest. "Are they bidding farewell or extending greetings?" he asked Savanah.

"Both, I think," she responded.

Once they were done, Kyla remained on the shore while the three moved to the dinghy. Hali looked it over with a confused expression. "Why do we not simply swim out to your ship? It is not so far away."

"Because humans cannot swim as well as hafu," Camille explained. "The boat is easier."

"Can you, isinachi?"

The bisegus grinned. "In the right form, maybe faster than you."

Hali stepped into the dinghy with the spear, taking a seat next to Savanah while Camille shoved the boat off from the sand, jumping in once it was floating unhindered. She settled onto the floor of the bow, her pack and sword beside her.

Once they reached the ship and climbed aboard, a crew member guided Savanah and the others to a common area below deck, where they stowed their supplies. Though smaller than the Silver Wind, the vessel carried almost half as many crew, mostly human men and women, all armed with swords. Not a single hafu among them. *I guess that must be part of the protocol on retrieval trips.*

Hali paced the deck, taking an interest in nearly everything. He gripped the spear in one hand, changing to two hands whenever he neared someone, apparently taking his duty seriously. Devoid of clothing, he looked incredibly vulnerable, even wielding the weapon. Coupled with his lack of supplies, Savanah wondered how much they would have to protect him on their journey. She couldn't tell if they'd gained an ally or a liability.

About an hour into their return trip, Mikel approached Savanah as she stood at the side of the deck, watching the water. "Once we reach Adradena, we can move on to the next artifacts. Perhaps it would be prudent to determine that destination sooner."

"You want me to check from here? I'm sure it will point north."

"I believe that, too. But if two of them made it this far south, there is a possibility others may have traveled even further. It would be wise to confirm that hasn't happened before we head up the continent again."

"I guess so." She took the bow from its sheath on her shoulder. While she had a normal bow and arrows now, tucked away with the rest of her supplies, she still liked carrying the silver weapon. She held it out and closed her eyes to focus on the remaining items. The greatest draw was definitely from the direction they were headed. "I'm getting a very strong pull from the north. It must be the Trideen Highlands, like Nastina said. It feels as though there is more than one, though." She faced south and concentrated again, but felt nothing. "I don't know how far this can detect the other artifacts, but I can't sense anything that way."

"That is a relief. May I handle the bow for a moment?"

"Of course." Savanah passed the weapon to the man, curious as to his intent. He hadn't shown interest in it since they first met.

"Thank you." He turned the artifact in his hands, as if inspecting it. "I appreciate the trust you and the others have put in me." With a sudden flick of his wrist, he tossed the bow to a nearby sailor, who caught it as easily as if he had been waiting. "It has made fooling you all so much easier."

The archer's heart leapt in her chest as her eyes darted between the two men, taking a few hesitant steps back. "What are you doing?" Her raised voice drew the attention of both Vyncent and Camille, who were positioned at opposite ends of the deck.

"I thought that was obvious," Mikel replied, a sneer forming on his lips. "I am relieving you of the artifacts." His eyes snapped to Hali, who had been examining the ship's rigging for the third time since arriving on board. "Now hand over the spear before we have to resort to violence."

"Don't, Hali!" Savanah shouted. "Your job is to protect it from the wrong people. He definitely fits that category!"

"How can you say that?" Mikel asked, a mocking tone of hurt in his voice. "A few hours ago, you said you couldn't have gotten this far without my help."

"A few hours ago, you weren't trying to steal the artifacts," she replied hotly.

"Not try, my dear. I am stealing them quite successfully." He snapped his head to Camille as she sprinted toward Hali. "I wouldn't advise that," he snarled. "You are on a ship in the ocean, completely outnumbered by armed opponents. You have no help and no way out."

"Neither do you," she shot back, but she halted nevertheless, coming to stand beside the hafu. "And you know what I am capable of."

"Indeed, I do." Mikel raised his voice so everyone could hear. It wasn't needed, as all eyes were on him and the companions. Only the helmsman, a burly, bald man with thick muscles, paid them anything less than his full attention as he guided the ship over the waves. "If she begins to look any different than she does now, strike her down."

Hali cast a glance at Camille, his expression contorting as he realized the proximity of their potential target to himself. He extended the arm holding the spear out to Mikel. "This is not anything I am a part of. You are welcome to this."

"No, he isn't!" Camille surged forward, seizing the weapon from his grasp and aiming it at the man. "Anyone makes a move toward me, and I'll put a hole through your boss."

"You must not!" Hali protested, clicking loudly. "The relic must remain pristine. Bodily fluids defile it!"

"You were ready to give it up a moment ago!" Camille growled. She glared at Mikel. "Why did you lie to us?"

"Asks the bisegus," the man laughed. "While I do like redheads, my loyalty to Nizlan is greater. As will be his rewards."

Savanah didn't recognize the name, but it was apparent he followed someone other than the High Monarch. "Does Lightreaver know?"

The sneer returned. "Of course not. She is too trusting. Like you."

That elicited a harsh laugh from Vyncent, who stood near the entry to the lower deck, with two of the armed soldiers on either side of him. "She trusted you, but not us? I wish she were here to see this. Why are you doing this?"

"Because arcana is an abomination, and these items are accursed by it. Our Lord, The Exalted Nizlan, sent Olagkoa to cleanse the world of unbelievers and those who think themselves above others. It represents true power."

"You're from one of those crazy groups you told me about!" Camille accused, remembering their conversation on the way to the island.

"The Coven of The Venerated Gift aren't mad zealots. We are the harbingers of the shattering onslaught, seers of mystic strife. All hail Nizlan. Hallowed are the powerless, for they shall know true power."

Every sailor, along with Borcus and Krill, repeated the litany in unison. "Hallowed are the powerless, for they shall know true power."

"No, that's not crazy at all," Camille remarked sarcastically, still aiming the spear in the man's direction. "Olagkoa is using arcana itself, remember? That was Nastina's conclusion."

"She lies, as do all her kind. They are in hiding, waiting for their chance to rebuild the Skorgan Empire and take control of the world. But we will stop them! With Olagkoa's help, we will finally rid the world of their villainy. Hallowed are the sinners, for they will see his justice."

Again, those around him repeated the phrase. "Hallowed are the sinners, for they will see his justice."

Mikel reached for his sword. "Hand over the spear now," he demanded, "Or we'll take it from your corpses and let Olagkoa turn you into more mindless servants."

Savanah stepped to the side, getting out of the man's range. She had suddenly remembered when she brandished the spear in the cave. "Camille!" she shouted. "It's an artifact! Use it!"

"That is forbidden!" Hali cried. "Only I may — "

But the bisegus had already understood Savanah's call and focused on the weapon. From its tip surged a burst of energy. Unlike the lightning Aedan had wielded, this power was wholly invisible, radiating outward with a force stronger than any egyzemor's blow.

Mikel received the full impact of it, hurtling up and backward against the ship's gunwale. With a yell, he went over the side, barely catching hold of the wood to prevent himself from tumbling into the waves below.

The sudden change in their leader's position stunned the sailors. Vyncent took the opportunity to draw his sword and attack the nearest, forcing the startled man into a retreat.

In seconds, the deck erupted into combat. Two more of the crew-men closed in on Vyncent to help their mate while another ran to Mikel's aid. A trio raced toward Savanah and Camille from the opposite side, with more advancing from the rear.

The companions were outnumbered eleven to four. Despite Mikel hanging off the edge and the helmsman remaining at the whipstaff, Borcus and Krill saw no reason to involve themselves and stayed out of the fray.

Savanah dodged a swing as she drew her sword, moving around to make her own attack. Out of the corner of her eye, she saw the group about to reach her friend. "Camille! Behind you!"

Bisegus and hafu whirled to see the trio of sailors, two men and a woman, descending with their blades held high. The sight was too much for Hali, and he began screaming. Vocal cords meant for under-water communication emitted a sound more like a wounded vornuk than a cry of fear.

Camille braced to fire the spear again, only for Hali to shriek and release a stream of brown, oily fluid in terror. It slicked the deck be-neath their attackers, and seconds later, they lost their footing and tum-bled to the deck.

A blast from the spear sent them sprawling back the way they came. While Hali continued his wheezing cries, Camille spun back to see how the others fared. Savanah had sliced the leg of her opponent, sending him to the ground, but the sailor with the bow was bringing it up to shoot her. "Behind you!"

The woman whirled at her shout, but Camille had already lunged forward. The man's face registered sheer shock as the force of the spear's blast propelled him several feet backward, causing the weapon to slip from his grasp. Savanah sheathed her blade as she dove to re-cover the artifact.

As Camille turned to assist Vyncent, a hand seized the spear. Before her stood an older woman, brandishing a sword aimed at the bisegus's neck. "That'll be enough of that, I think," she growled.

Camille's head shifted without warning, jaws elongating into the barlmed's tooth-lined maw. It snapped at the woman, who retreated in terror, backing into the pair of sailors behind her.

Before they could recover, a projectile of energy struck them, and they howled in pain. Savanah regained control of the bow and put it to use.

Now free, Camille sprinted to Vyncent's aid. The man had just sent one adversary to the deck with a long gash across his shoulder, but now two more assailants were closing in, intent on cutting him down. His prowess enabled him to fend off attacks from both simultaneously, but it was only a matter of time before his defenses waned. Already, he bore several slices along his arms, the crimson streaks visible through tears in his shirt.

The spear's blast sent both opponents slamming into the cabin wall, their bodies sinking to the ground, unconscious.

It took Vyncent a moment to realize what had happened. "I didn't need your help," he snarled at Camille, then yelped, seeing the shaggy bear's head on the woman's body. "You don't have to rub my face in it."

"Put down your weapons now and hand over the spear!"

The pair turned. Mikel stood with a sword to Savanah's neck, his other hand gripping her shoulder. Two sailors flanked him, with the three she had been fighting forming a half circle before her, all with their weapons drawn.

Hali's shriek became a strained moan. "And stop that cursed noise!" Mikel snapped.

Camille's head returned to its normal shape. "Hali! Stop it!" she ordered as the trio she had knocked down earlier moved to surround her and Vyncent, their clothing smeared in the hafu's excretions. A putrid smell reached her nose, and she scowled. However, the screams finally ceased.

"You had your chance to relinquish the artifacts peacefully," Mikel called out to them. "Instead, you attacked me and my comrades. For that, Nizlan demands retribution. Your death."

Savanah strained against the man's grip, but there were too many around her, even if she pulled free. She caught Camille's gaze and gave a faint nod, signaling her friend not to attempt a rescue. If they complied now, they might yet have a chance to turn events in their favor.

"No."

All eyes shifted to Vyncent, who still held his sword high. Blood from the cuts in his arms had begun to stain his torn shirt, with more oozing from the wound in his shoulder, the exertion having opened it anew. But he glared unwaveringly at Mikel across the deck. "You call yourself a soldier, but these are the actions of a coward."

The man gave a harsh laugh. "That is a meaningless accusation from you, the one who sought every opportunity to abandon this mission because it was difficult."

"I have never turned against those I called friends," Vyncent countered.

"Tell that to the bisegus beside you. You can barely look at her."

Camille felt the gravity of his words, her demeanor reflecting the weight of the situation as her features softened. A dozen feet away, Vyncent's expression didn't change, but the muscles in his jaw tightened. The truth of the accusation couldn't be denied. "You've betrayed your monarch, your city, and your world!" he shouted. "For what? To be a servant to a monstrosity and a petty god."

"We are ridding the world of evil!" Mikel proclaimed, his grip tightening on Savanah's shoulders, eliciting a sharp cry from the woman. "Arcana is an abomination. Anything created with it is abhorrent, and those who wield it are the true monsters!"

"By killing how many?" Vyncent took two defiant steps forward, ignoring the glares from the surrounding soldiers. "Hundreds? Thousands?"

"Right now, only four."

Vyncent grimaced at the threat. "Then start with me. But in an even match with you. Not by some lackeys."

"You expect to perform some grand gesture where we cross swords and the winner decides the outcome?" Mikel's voice dripped with contempt, a tone the companions had never heard from him before. "If so, let me make it clear. There will be only one outcome."

"Then prove you aren't a coward and fight me." Vyncent stepped forward again, lifting his sword in readiness.

Mikel shrugged, releasing Savanah and advancing toward the other man. "If that is how you wish to die, I won't deny your request."

"Kudza kuvhi!" Hali shouted as the pair squared off. Tradition overrode his fear, and he watched the opponents with interest. The rest of the crew made space on the deck. One took hold of Savanah while two more latched onto Camille's arms. No one moved toward the hafu, apparently not considering him a threat.

"Honor the hunt!" Camille translated for the others. "This is between them alone. No one is to interfere."

"Hear that?" Mikel asked in a mocking tone. "The women can't step in to save you this time."

"Neither can your followers," Vyncent replied coolly, flourishing his blade. "Nor your imaginary god."

"Nizlan will make his presence known when I drive my sword through your heart."

"I preferred the fake you. He didn't seem so delusional." Vyncent abruptly swung, but the other man parried it easily.

"You're the one clinging to a delusion if you believe I can be defeated so effortlessly," came the retort. Mikel made his own lunge, which Vyncent casually knocked aside.

The two men locked blades again, quickly falling into a pattern of strikes, blocks, and dodges. Each moved with the ease of the trained fighters they were, seeking an opening in his foe's defenses and attempting to take advantage of it. But they were too evenly matched, each attack thwarted by a flick of the wrist, a raised weapon, or a hasty bit of footwork.

A hush fell over the ship's occupants, with only the clangs of colliding swords breaking the air, punctuated by the occasional grunt as one of the fighters exerted himself. These became more frequent as the fight went on, each man pushing his body to perform against an equal opponent.

"Where is your Nizlan now?" Vyncent taunted as the two backed off to recover their breath. "I thought he was supposed to strike me down."

Mikel smirked, not rising to the bait. "That role has been delegated to me."

"Then I have nothing to fear." Vyncent attempted a sword feint, but his adversary didn't fall for the ruse. Instead, he twirled and swung, hoping to catch the younger soldier off guard.

Vyncent barely dodged it, stepping back hastily. "Come on now," he said, masking his anxiety after the close call. "The creature's a better opponent than you, and it's blind."

Mikel didn't reply, instead pressing the retreat, following up with two more swings and a lunge, forcing his rival backward. Vyncent blocked every strike, but with decreasing force. His wounds drained his energy at an accelerated rate, and despite his bold words, the older fighter proved to be highly skilled.

All eyes focused on the pair as they approached the port side, one on a constant attack, the other barely able to match his furor. Then Vyncent faltered, allowing his foe's blade to slip past his defenses and nearly impaling his shoulder.

The sneer returned to Mikel's face when he recognized the fight was almost over. He drew back his sword as Vyncent fell to one knee. "This was always meant to be," the cultist reminded him. "Don't waste your final breath on regret. Nizlan represents true power, and your death will ensure his will is fulfilled." He raised his weapon, blade down, preparing to strike. "Hallowed are the suffering, for they — "

A scream cut off his recitation as Vyncent suddenly swung his sword upward, striking the man's hand. Mikel's sword fell to the deck, along with two of his fingers. He stumbled backward, shoving his wounded limb into his chest to staunch the bleeding.

Vyncent rose to his feet, belying his previous display of exhaustion, and held his blade before him, ready if the man tried to resume his attack. Mikel, enraged and in agony, was in no position to retaliate. "What have you done?" he yelled as blood streamed over his waistcoat.

"Was this the outcome you planned?" Vyncent asked coldly. "Why don't you ask Nizlan to heal it for you?"

Mikel glanced wide-eyed over the deck. No one moved to assist him, obeying the hafu rule against interference, despite most being human. It wasn't easy to live alongside another race and not adopt some of their moral codes as your own.

His gaze found Krill's. The hafu motioned his hands like an ocean wave, then formed them into fists.

The man's lips tightened, recognizing the meaning. He returned his attention to Vyncent, who seemed to be waiting for his next move. "Exalted Nizlan, deliver me upon safer shores so I may serve you again," he chanted. Then, with a final glare at the man before him, he threw himself over the side.

Multiple shouts erupted on deck. Savanah swiftly pulled free of the grip on her shoulder, bringing the silver bow to bear on her former captor. Camille hardened her arms, then swung her body, sending her own captors tumbling to the ground.

Before the others could react, both women got into positions where they covered most of the sailors with their artifacts.

Had they wanted, the crew might have overcome the pair, with only minimal damage to their numbers. However, the sight of their leader fleeing had demoralized them, and at a command from Vyncent, they dropped their swords.

Krill and Borcus had not taken part in the fight and appeared unwilling to participate in the punishment for it. The two hastily followed after Mikel, diving over the side into the roiling water below. Of the crew, only the helmsman remained unfazed by the events on the deck below as he continued steering the ship toward land.

Hali stared around at the battle's aftermath, double eyelids blinking. "Is this how humans normally conduct themselves on long trips?"

Once the sailors had been rounded up, with basic medical attention given to those wounded in the skirmish, Camille escorted them to the vessel's cargo hold and locked them in. The ship wouldn't reach Wayela for several more hours, and the friends couldn't risk letting the fanatics roam freely, in case some of them decided to avenge their leader.

After a brief talk with the helmsman, Savanah learned he had no loyalty to the Coven of the Venerated Gift or Mikel. He was aboard the ship in Adradena's harbor when the cultists swarmed it, tossing the few crewmen overboard and ordering him at knifepoint to sail to Redemption Point.

"So we took down a group of religious fanatics and recovered a stolen ship!" Camille bounced across the deck, a grin plastered on her face. "Plus, we have three of the artifacts! Overall, not a bad trip."

"Except for the part where Mikel betrayed us," Savanah told her, rubbing her shoulder where the man's fingers had dug in. "How could we have been that blind?"

"Lightreaver recommended him," Vyncent said, shaking out his arms. The bleeding had stopped, but the cuts still stung, and his muscles ached from the duel. "So he fooled her, too."

"He is an excellent spy," Camille noted. Some of the exuberance faded from her face. "Was, now, I guess."

"Good," the man replied. "He would have had us killed. We didn't need him anyway."

Savanah shook her head sadly as she looked over the railings and across the water they had traveled. Somewhere beneath the depths, the soldier who led them from Ludholm now rested. "He helped a lot. We still wouldn't have gotten here without his aid. I'm finding it difficult to believe he was lying to us all this time."

"Not about everything," Camille said, following her gaze. "Only his reason for joining the mission. It is possible to be wholly honest on most things, except for your true nature."

Whether Camille meant it for Vyncent, or was just voicing the constant ache of being a bisegus, the words hit hard. For most of their trip, she and he had been at each other's throats. Her recent revelation had opened a chasm between them.

He walked hesitantly over to the women, moving to stand in front of them. Even then, it took a moment to find his voice. "Camille, I know you meant well. You can't help who you are. Mikel was right that I was turning against a friend." His shoulders stiffened. "But I can't simply accept the deceit. Or that you can.... change. It will take time for both."

Camille bit her lip, her eyes watering at his confession. "And I shouldn't have expected you to handle it as well as Savanah. All I ask is that you give it a chance."

"I'll try," he replied with a nod. "So what now?"

Savanah's heart swelled. His accepting Camille as a bisegus wouldn't be easy, but he seemed genuinely willing to make the effort. It was the first step to getting back to the way they had been. *Perhaps he inherited more from his father than I had realized.* "It will be late when we reach Adradena. I suggest we find a place to spend the night, then head out early. From what I could determine from the bow, our next goal is the Trideen Highlands."

"That is a long trip, without the benefit of the river," Vyncent said. "We'll have to buy horses. Again. I am going to miss Mikel's money."

"Maybe not. My uncle's farm isn't too far away," Camille reminded them. "If we reach that, we could recover the ones we left."

Savanah nodded at the suggestion. "No matter what, it will take at least a month. And we have no idea how our newest member will handle on the trip. I doubt he can walk far or ride a horse."

Camille glanced back at Hali, who appeared to be examining the rigging again, the spear gripped in his webbed hands. "What about a ship like this? Could one at least get us closer?"

"It would have to be going around the continent, and I have no idea how many hundreds of leagues that would be." Savanah turned, leaning her elbows on the railing. "I recall there was a trip that transported goods between Adradena and Tromont, but I doubt anything goes beyond that. We don't have the funds to charter for that distance, anyway."

"It couldn't hurt to ask, though."

"No." Savanah's gaze went to Hali, too, as he walked about the deck. Despite his lack of experience out of water, he seemed to move about quite easily. She wondered if perhaps the hafu might have originated on land, then moved to the water, rather than the way their mythology suggested.

The trio watched as he approached a set of barrels sitting by the quarter-deck wall. When he hefted the spear and aimed it at the casks, though, Savanah shouted a hasty order. "Don't!"

Too late. From the motion of the hafu's arms, they could see the artifact had been invoked. Rather than smash through the barrels and the wooden slats behind it, the force knocked Hali backward, and he stumbled to the floor.

The women ran forward to aid him while Vyncent laughed. Savanah held back an angry comment toward him as she and Camille checked Hali over, then helped him up. "That was a stupid thing to do," she told the hafu.

"I am the relic's master," he replied curtly as he pulled his arms from their grasps. "It is my prerogative to use it as I see fit."

"Not like a fool," Camille snapped. "The spear's power could have seriously damaged the deck, along with the steering mechanism and helmsman above it. So, unless you plan to pull the ship to Adradena yourself, I suggest you wait until we are back on land before exercising your 'prerogative' again."

Hali stared at her, mouth drawn tight, as if he didn't know how to react to her rebuke. He blinked twice, then looked at the barrels. The blast hadn't even moved them. "Why did it not work?"

Savanah had wondered the same. "Perhaps it only works on living creatures."

He appeared to consider the notion. "Then stand there and I will — "

"No, no!" Camille grabbed the end of the spear as he began lowering it toward her and Savanah. "This isn't a plaything, and you are *definitely* not trying it on us."

"You shouldn't be using it at all," Savanah added. "It has a limited supply of arcana, and if that runs out, it will be useless against the creature."

Hali considered their words. "It is mine to use. You will not be telling me what I may or may not do."

"Sure, we will," Vyncent told him, gripping the hilt of his sword as he came up behind them. "You saw what I did to Mikel. Do you think you could stand up to my blade?"

Savanah felt her irritation with him rise again. "You don't need to threaten him."

But the blunt approach seemed to work, as the hafu's gills started trembling. Camille noticed it, too. "And it isn't *your* spear. That belongs to King Ecthelion. He wants it for the power it holds. How do you think he will feel if you return it empty?"

Hali stared at her, then his eyes went back to Vyncent, or, more precisely, the sword at the fighter's side. "I have decided that I will refrain from using the relic unless it becomes absolutely necessary for the greater good."

"See?" Vyncent said with a smile, taking his hand from the sword and resting it on the hafu's shoulder. "I knew you would see it our way."

Savanah bit back a response. Hali winced at the man's grip, but didn't protest further. Still, she didn't like them having to coerce a companion to behave. "If that's settled, I suggest we get some rest. We've still got a long trip to Adradena."

"Agreed," Camille said. "I'll take first watch. We might have locked up Mikel's followers, but I'm not going to feel safe until they are turned over to the authorities."

"Good idea. I'll take second. Vyncent, you take third. Let's keep them to two hours each."

"My place here is to look after the spear. I have no intention of standing guard over the ship."

"I didn't think you would. But listen, this isn't some casual trip. We could be traveling for months. Our experience tells us there will be danger. Lots of it. So when we give you instructions in the future, it would be in your best interest to follow. Understand?"

Hali ran a finger down the length of his nose. "I will listen," he said flatly, his displeasure clear at being all but ordered to behave. "However, I am certain your description is exaggerated. How hard could it be?"

Chapter Twenty-seven
THE MATCH AND THE FLAME

L IGHTREAVER FUMED ON her throne. After years of chasing the truth about her father's death, she'd finally captured the woman responsible, only to have her vanish from prison soon after.

Two days had passed since they discovered Nilado's cell open, the woman gone. Lightreaver had set every soldier available to track her down. Wolfsight was immense, and it had taken hours just to search the upper floors.

Jaron stood nearby, taking up his position at her side, despite the tension between her and him. Steelfang, the man leading that hunt, waited before her, his hands clasped behind his back.

"Are you certain she isn't in the castle?" Lightreaver asked.

"We have searched Wolfsight twice," the commander reported. "Every room, item of furniture large enough to conceal her, every curtain, has been examined. Nilado is not here." He paused. "But one of my men did receive word of someone fitting her description, leaving the city on a wagon with two guards."

Lightreaver slammed her palm on the throne's armrest. "They must be the ones who moved Linda. Do a head count and figure out who they were." An edge crept into Lightreaver's tone when the rest of his news sank in. "How could you let her escape? I thought your soldiers were guarding her."

"We were. But between manning the gates, running patrols through the city, and, if I may, standing watch over the throne room, our numbers are stretched to the limit. The ones we had looking over the dungeons were led to believe we had an incursion on our eastern gate."

The High Monarch sat back in her seat. She knew she should be angrier with the commander, but he was right about the limit on manpower. Besides, as long as Nilado was out of the castle and out of power, she doubted the woman could do much. "That still doesn't explain who let the voladorm merchant out."

"The Matron claimed he was a leader of a cult," Jaron offered from the side. "Perhaps we have some members within our ranks."

Steelfang frowned at the suggestion. "Should I try to rout them out?"

"No," Lightreaver told him. "We can't afford to put our defenses into further disarray. We'll just have to keep an eye on everyone. Take what guards you need from this room, too. The most dangerous character among us has left the city. All our enemies now lie beyond our gates."

All three turned their attention to the far end of the room as one of the main doors creaked open wide enough for a soldier to step inside. The female human bowed before speaking. "Forgive me, High Monarch," she said. "A man named Hamund, formerly of Talidith, requests an audience."

The ruler rose from her throne. *Does he bring more bad news, or has he changed his mind?* "Let him enter."

Hamund marched through the chamber, coming to a stop a few steps before reaching Steelfang. Lightreaver was pleased that he appeared in better condition than when they last met. He had shaved and donned a fresh outfit, but there was something else she couldn't define. "Greetings, Hamund. How is Pirro faring?"

"Well," came the reply, accompanied by a smile that suggested more than just relief at a friend's health improving. "As are the rest of my people. That is why I am here."

A pang of concern struck Lightreaver's chest. *If they are well, what more do they need? Are they planning to leave the city?* But she kept her face inviting, despite the thoughts. "What can we do for you?"

"I believe the request was what we could do for you. I have spoken with the former members of the Sovereign Guard. They all agreed to help defend Zatreus against whatever threat may come. We also have some among us with training and are willing to join as well, if they are provided the necessary weapons. As I told you before, it is not many, but hopefully we will make a difference."

Yes! Lightreaver nearly rushed forward and threw her arms around the man at his revelation. Such an action wouldn't suit a ruler, so she forced herself to sit again. "That is most generous of your people. Please convey my gratitude."

He nodded. "I will. It is our city now, too, and we wish to help preserve it."

Steelfang's expression remained far from neutral as a grin carved deep into his cheeks. "Most wise. I can accompany you back to your section and coordinate with your soldiers. If that is permissible."

"Quite permissible." Hamund turned to address Lightreaver. "And you will notify me once you hear anything about the rest of my citizens, yes?"

"Of course," Lightreaver assured him. Before she could dismiss the men, Steelfang and Hamund were heading toward the double doors, already discussing how best to deploy the new fighters.

"Not too bad of an exchange," Jaron approached and murmured to her once the others had gone. "Lose a Matron, gain an ally."

The woman nodded, not quite believing the turn of fortune herself. Her thoughts lingered on Hamund's parting words. Wherever Savanah and Leda's groups were, she hoped they were having good luck as well. Even with the extra defenses, if Olagkoa returned to their gates, they needed a way to stop it that didn't rely on numbers alone.

If Ludholm dared to attack, they would not find Zatreus defenseless. Nilado may have lit the match of war between the two kingdoms, but High Monarch Demzi Lightreaver would be the one to finish the fire.

Even if it meant burning Ludholm to the ground.

Continued in
SPAWN OF ARCANA

The Shadow Arcanist Series

Into the Undercastle
When the people of Talidith flee underground, they unleash an evil worse than the one they left behind and must contain it before it gets loose upon the world

The Monster's Army
With a psychic monstrosity loose on the continent, building an army of undead, Talidith's heroes must find a way to destroy it and rescue their friend

Racing the Dead
An otherworldly monster has unleased an undead army on the cities of Rapria, and only a group of friends can prevent it from destroying the world

About the Author

Alexander Dawnrider grew up reading copious amount of science-fiction and fantasy. Wherever he went, there was a thick paperback in his hands, or stashed in his satchel, or waiting beside his bed. He absorbed the works of Asimov, Heinlein, Tolkien, Foster, and countless others.

As he grew older, he applied his knowledge to the world around him. Each electronic appliance was really a robot ready to serve mankind. Each cat secretly knew how to walk through walls. It wasn't anything so mundane as bears or foxes inhabiting the nearby forest, but fiendish orcs and goblins. And just beyond the stars was a young urchin with his flying minidrag.

Now Alexander dwells in a lofty tower of a northern province, endeavoring to contribute to that fantastical world with his own ideas. When he isn't busy madly scribbling away on the scraps of parchment that cross his desk, you can find him enjoying a grilled-cheese sandwich and tinkering with his time machine. His companions are an assortment of gargoyles and a small dragon named Sea Glimmer.

Thank You!

Thank you for reading *Racing the Dead*. If you enjoyed this book (or even if you didn't) please visit the site where you purchased it and write a brief review. Your feedback is important to me and will help other readers decide whether to read the book too.

If you'd like to get notifications of new releases and special offers on my books, please join my mailing list by visiting www.alexanderdawnrider.com/subscribe

Connect Online

Website: www.alexanderdawnrider.com

Facebook: www.facebook.com/alexdawnrider

Twitter: twitter.com/AlexDawnrider

Instagram: www.instagram.com/alexdawnrider